Vespertine

by
Leta Blake
and
Indra Vaughn

Other Books by Leta Blake

Any Given Lifetime
The River Leith
Smoky Mountain Dreams
Angel Undone
The Difference Between
Omega Mine: Search for a Soulmate

The Home for the Holidays Series
Mr. Frosty Pants
Mr. Naughty List

The Training Season Series
Training Season
Training Complex

Heat of Love Series
Slow Heat
Alpha Heat
Slow Birth
Bitter Heat

Stay Lucky Series
Stay Lucky
Stay Sexy

'90s Coming of Age Series
Pictures of You
You Are Not Me

Co-Authored with Indra Vaughn
Vespertine
Cowboy Seeks Husband

Co-Authored with Alice Griffiths
The Wake Up Married serial
Will & Patrick's Endless Honeymoon

Gay Fairy Tales Co-Authored with Keira Andrews
Flight
Levity
Rise

Leta Blake writing as Blake Moreno
Heat for Sale

Leta Blake writing as Halsey Harlow
Bring on Forever

Audiobooks
Leta Blake at Audible

Free Read
Stalking Dreams

Discover more about the author online:
Leta Blake
letablake.com

Other Books by Indra Vaughn

The House on Hancock Hill
Patchwork Paradise

Christmas Books
Dust of Snow
The Winter Spirit

Shadow Mountain Series
Fated
Fragmented

Co-Authored with Leta Blake
Vespertine
Cowboy Seeks Husband

Short Stories
Hooked
Chasing Ghosts
Ties That Bind
Halcyon Hush

Audiobooks
Indra Vaughn at Audible

ISBN: 979-8-88841-027-1
Print Edition

Gay Romance Newsletter

Leta's newsletter will keep you up to date on her latest releases and news from the world of M/M romance. Join the mailing list today.
letablake.com

Leta Blake on Patreon

Become part of Leta Blake's Patreon community in order to access exclusive content, deleted scenes, extras, bonus stories, rewards, prizes, interviews, and more.
www.patreon.com/letablake

Acknowledgments

The authors would like to express their gratitude and appreciation for Vanessa North, Megan Erickson, Darrah Glass, Keira Andrews, and Anne-Marie for their amazing beta and editing work. Thank you for your support and enthusiasm for this project, and for catching our typos and mistakes.

Thank you to our friends and family who support us in ways big and small. We couldn't do this without you. Sending so much love out to you with all our thanks!

Chapter One

A LITTLE BELL jingled above the antiquated white and yellow bakery door as it opened.

"You know, gluttony *is* a sin, Father."

Without lifting his eyes from the chocolate-filled croissants, cherry-stuffed mini tarts, cinnamon rolls, raisin rolls, and colorful macarons, Father Jasper Hendricks said to his companion, "Everything in moderation, Andrew."

Easter had come and gone, but a white basket still held a collection of colorful little plastic eggs. The croissants appealed to Jasper this morning, and the sugar glaze on the cinnamon buns was dripping, like they were so fresh from the oven they were still hot.

"Shouldn't you be getting ready for Mass, Father?" Deacon Andrew Evans asked. Jasper kept his smile under control when he heard the hint of amusement in the old man's voice.

"That's why I have you. Besides, the Bible says you shouldn't work on an empty stomach."

"I'm pretty sure it says no such thing."

At last Jasper straightened and looked at Andrew, his right hand man in everything but…well no. In everything, really. "It should. Don't you think, Irena?" Jasper winked at the woman behind the counter.

"How about a cinnamon roll *and* a croissant today, Father?" She'd lived in Little Heights most of her life and yet she'd never entirely lost her Polish accent.

"The decadence," Andrew said, but Jasper paid him no mind, especially since he'd most likely end up eating half.

"Sounds wonderful." He turned to the deacon as he opened his wallet. "Anything for you?"

With a hand on his rotund stomach, Andrew said, "Oh, I couldn't possibly."

Jasper laughed and accepted the fragrant paper bag. "Come on then. Thanks to all your chit-chat, we'll be late for Mass."

Andrew sputtered as he followed Jasper outside.

Little Heights hugged the Little Bay shore and even from Main Street Jasper could smell the sea air. He breathed deeply as he listened to traffic and beyond it the exuberant call of birds welcoming summer. It'd been a brutal winter, even for Maine, but as always the town embraced summer as if the long months of ice and cold had never existed and would never come again.

Andrew cleared his throat. "So..." He eyed the paper bag. "You going to walk and eat?"

"I am." For a moment Jasper said nothing else, then he laughed under his breath and opened the bag. "And I'll break bread with you." He watched Andrew's eyes twinkle under their white, bushy eyebrows. "But only because it's Sunday."

Andrew laughed and nodded, accepting half a sticky cinnamon bun. They'd stopped walking, and Andrew lifted his face to the sky to soak up the sun. After a moment of silence, he said, "It's going to be a good summer, Father Hendricks."

Jasper's eyebrows lifted in curiosity as he bit into the still-warm bun. Cinnamon burst over his tongue. "You think so?" he asked, more to hear Andrew's reasoning than that he doubted it. As far as he was concerned, the summer couldn't get much better.

"Hmm." Andrew peered up at Jasper. "An interesting summer. But a good one."

With that cryptic statement, Andrew walked off and Jasper followed, a little bemused but not worried. Andrew had always been…not odd exactly, but certainly different.

The Sacred Heart Cathedral was built in the mid-eighteen hundreds and stood proudly in the center of Little Heights. It made Jasper think he'd gone soft over the years, but he truly considered it the heart of the town. The beautiful neo-Gothic building never failed to take his breath away, especially on a day like today when the sky seemed painted in crayon blues and cartoon sunshine. He didn't love a lot of worldly things, but this building, this house of God, felt as much part of him as his own soul.

As he always did when they climbed the steps to the back entrance, he ran his fingers along the sturdy wooden doorframe and offered a little prayer of thanks. For what, exactly, he didn't know. Maybe just the fact that a building this old would stand proudly for another day.

Andrew didn't say much as they walked the pews, making sure everything was in order. They'd worked together for eight years now, and Jasper liked to prepare for Mass in silence. He didn't need to clear his mind, really. He just enjoyed these peaceful moments in his church, with his God, alone. A selfish sentiment, maybe, but Jasper believed taking comfort where one could every once in a while wasn't necessarily sinful.

Soon the first churchgoers would enter and take their places, so they retired to the sacristy and worked companionably side by side until it was time.

Jasper took a deep, cleansing breath and let it out slowly as he closed his eyes. When he found the center of peace in his mind, he softly spoke.

"Give virtue, O Lord, unto my hands that every stain may be wiped away, that I may be enabled to serve Thee without defilement of mind or body."

Andrew stood with his head bent and eyes closed as Jasper reached for the amice, placed it on his own shoulders and fastened it.

"Place, O Lord, the helmet of salvation upon my head that I may over-

come the assaults of the devil."

He reached for the alb and began to pull it on.

"Cleanse me, O Lord, and purify my heart that being made white in the blood of the Lamb I may have the fruition of everlasting joy."

He reached for the cincture and wrapped it around his waist.

"Gird me, O Lord, with the girdle of purity and extinguish in my loins the desires of lust so that the virtue of continence and chastity may ever abide within me."

Jasper took the maniple in hand and reverently brought it to his lips, the embroidered band of silk smooth against his mouth.

"May I be worthy, O Lord, so to bear the maniple of tears and sorrow: that with joy I may receive the reward of my labor."

He wrapped the stole around his shoulders.

"Restore to me, O Lord, the stole of immortality, which I lost by the transgression of the first parent: and although unworthy, as I draw near to Thy sacred mystery, may I be found worthy of everlasting joy."

Jasper found himself sinking into a deeper peace when he finally touched his fingertips to the chasuble. Vaguely aware Andrew had already left to oversee the choir and altar servers, Jasper closed his eyes and put the long garment on over his clothes. The sleeves brushed his fingertips as it settled into place. His voice came rough and far away and he swayed a little on his feet.

"O Lord, Who hast said: 'My yoke is easy and My burden is light' make me able to bear it, that I may obtain Thy favor. Amen."

The blood in his veins warmed, and the light behind his eyelids brightened. Humbled and enlightened at once, he kept his eyes closed for a moment longer, lingering in the presence of God. He was always there, but in this moment He felt closer than usual, almost as if Jasper could reach out and touch Him. Not that he'd ever be presumptuous enough to try, but that didn't mean he couldn't allow himself to bask in the possibility for just a little longer. Secretly he'd always been of the opinion that the rituals in Catholicism held a certain pagan tone, and he loved it.

Make me strong. Give me what I need to be a better priest; a better servant. Guide me to the path You want me to take, O Lord.

A wave of goosebumps ran over his entire body, from his fingertips up his arms, over his shoulders and down his back, until the hairs on his calves rose and he shuddered lightly. Jasper opened his eyes and grinned a little.

"Showtime," he whispered.

"FIVE MINUTES UNTIL showtime."

It was hard to hear their manager's words over the rhythmic stomping feet, clapping hands, and escalating cheers of the waiting audience. Nicky sat hunched on the floor in front of a glass coffee table covered with cocaine. His bandmates, Sez and Mick, knelt on the floor too, pushing razor blades around, playing with the powder.

"Did you hear me? Five minutes? Hey, Nico, wake the fuck up!"

"He's awake," Ramona, their drummer, called back. She sat at a wide, brightly lit vanity and mirror putting final touches on her face.

"He doesn't look awake. He's just staring into space like a lunatic."

She glared. "Leave Nico the fuck alone, Harry."

The dressing room door slammed shut and Harry's ugly, oily face vanished behind it, leaving them to contemplate the nebulous roar of their adoring fans.

Nicky hated the noise.

Early on, it'd been a rush better than any other to stand backstage when the lights went down. The thrum of thousands of strangers beating out their need, their lust for Vespertine's music had sent him sailing wild and high on vindication and a fevered hope. Being Nico back then had been all he wanted to be. It was better than being Nicky. As Nico he had power. Nico could bring people to their knees. Nico could change things.

He'd sustained a fantasy that his lyrics, screamed out by Sez every show, would fly out into the night and find their way back to Maine, back to Jazz's heart. Their sharpness would tear at his ex-lover until, defeated and sorry, Jazz would show up at some random auditorium on his knees begging, needing, wanting Nicky the way the audience did. The way he had before. It'd been a heady, stupid, youthful dream. Nicky hadn't needed coke or heroin to get through a day back then.

Things change.

Over the years, the audience's call became a visceral invasion. The steady beat pulsed against his skin, rattling his guts and bone. It made him itchy, twitchy, flighty. At age thirty-four-going-on-sixty, the reality that Jazz was never going to come back to him had settled in long ago. It hurt like a soul-burn, constant and steady, and as with the screams of the crowd, he closed his eyes and huddled down deep inside himself, trying to numb it out, to drive it away.

"Showtime," Ramona said. She ran her hands over her close-cropped, fuzzy hair and double-checked herself in the mirror again, obviously pleased with her glossy red lipstick and shiny purple eyeshadow. "C'mon, boys. Snort your shit and let's go."

From his place on the floor, Nicky watched her grab her lucky sticks from her giant purple purse. Then he turned back to the glass coffee table. It was still covered with small mountains of white powder and sat out in the middle of the room presumably for the sole purpose of cutting up and snorting blow. He wished it would somehow vanish. That it would just go the fuck away.

Ramona gave them all a stern once-over. "Don't fuck it up out there, assholes."

No one replied. The coke commanded Sez and Mick's attention as they cut and snorted, then snorted again.

"Nico," Ramona said. "C'mon, you don't need to do that crap. You're high enough. Shit, you're too high already. Don't do any more."

She stood by the door and looked down at Nicky with her dark, soft eyes that always shimmered like they were somehow wetter than the average person's, somehow kinder. Or maybe that was just his fallout-triggered melancholy talking because Ramona could kick his ass with both hands tied behind her back. Ramona was stronger than any of them, and that went a hell of a lot further than most people thought. But Nicky knew.

The effect of the heroin he'd shot up in the hotel dropped off hard and fast. In the murky space he drowned in, Nicky didn't feel like Nico Blue, guitarist and chief songwriter for the still wildly popular band Vespertine. He was Nicholas Blumfeld, adopted son of Miriam and Adrian. Disconnected fuck-up. Broken boy. Always on the outside looking in.

He hadn't written a hit song in an age by industry standards. Their last two albums had been full of misshapen duds. Songs with no wings. Songs that couldn't fly. Nicky knew the truth about his music. The songs reflected their creator.

Nicky knew disgusting, ugly, hurtful things too. Like how low he'd fall and how many guys he'd pick up after the show to fuck him (three). And he absolutely, positively knew he couldn't *do* this anymore. Not tonight. Not ever.

Music had been the only thing to sustain him through the years, and now the drugs had burned it out of him.

"Jesus, Nico. Are you even in there?" Ramona snapped her fingers in his face and he opened his eyes. Mick and Sez wiped their noses free of white dust and pointedly avoided looking at each other. "You don't want Harry coming back here after you, do you?" She asked. "Get it together."

He nodded; it was the most he could manage. Ramona squatted beside him, one hand on his thigh. She studied him closely and he stared back at her. She was beautiful, in Nicky's opinion. Taller than him by at least two inches in her heels, darker than him by several dozen shades, and soberer than him by any kind of measurement. She was the only one among them who didn't regularly fortify herself with chemical helpers. Her clear-eyed control was something Nicky admired and envied. Ramona deserved good things. She was probably the only one of them who did anymore.

Ramona turned to the piles of drugs on the table and slid a razor over the top of the little ridges Sez had made, flattening them again into a smooth smudge of cocaine on the glass table. She pounded her fist beside it. "This shit is ruining us."

Nicky agreed but didn't say anything. Mick and Sez ignored her. Mick sucked up his post-coke post-nasal drip with a disgusting hocking noise. Sez shoved him, and the room twisted for Nicky as he watched them push and tug at each other. Over the last year, the energy between Mick and Sez had changed; what had once been smooth and placid was now crinkled and alight with sparks.

"Whatever's going on with them is the last thing we need," Ramona murmured, nudging Nicky's arm. "Are they fucking?"

Nicky didn't even think he could do curiosity the right way anymore. Maybe Mick and Sez were fucking. Maybe they weren't. Nicky didn't know and he really didn't care. He *should*. He was the leader of the group, the mastermind, the brains behind the music, and he should really fucking care. But he couldn't find any sort of emotion like that in the hollow where his heart had been.

Ramona clicked her teeth.

Let them bring it all down around their ears. The sooner the better. He crawled deeper into the dark place inside himself, his familiar internal cage. It would take too much effort to crawl out. Even for a line of coke. No matter how much good it would do him.

"God, Nico, you look like death," she muttered, leaning over to stroke her hand over his head. He could see his greasy, dark hair pass through her fingers on either side of his cheeks. "Seriously, pretty boy. Are you okay?"

Nicky couldn't speak. His words were wherever the music had gone.

"He shot a speedball back at the hotel," Mick muttered.

It hadn't been a speedball actually. It'd just been dope. He'd kill for a speedball now, that slow-fast that settled him into his bones so he felt almost like a real human again.

"Stupid, Nico," Ramona murmured, and it didn't sound fond at all.

Nicky's heartbeat was strong enough now. He just needed to do it. Lean over and cut a line, snort it up. He'd be fine once he did. He'd be ready to go. He just needed to *do it.*

She slid her hand over his shoulder and wrinkled her nose. "When's the last time you took a fucking shower?"

Somehow he spoke. His voice was creaky. "Last night."

"Ha. If by last night you mean Houston, maybe."

If Houston wasn't last night, then Nicky had no idea when he'd showered. Days fell into days, nights into nights. On tour it was all music, madness, and sex. Blow jobs and blow. Bending over for cocks and thrusting into throats. It was sin and misery and it was every minute of his life. It was rock-n-roll.

Nicky fucking hated it.

It wasn't him. It hadn't ever been and it never would be. He just didn't know how to make it end. He'd strapped into the rocket known as Vespertine ages ago and together they'd entered orbit. There was no way back.

Ni-co, Ni-co, Ni-co.

The pounding beat of the audience calling his name jolted through him.

"Nico?" Ramona searched his face. Sighing, she stood up and jerked the door open to call out, "Can I get some help in here?"

Then she stood back as help arrived.

"Get it the fuck together! Didn't I already tell you what time it is, shitheads?" Harry shouted. His blond hair shone green in the off-color light in the hallway leading to the stage itself. "Show-*fucking*-time!"

Sez bounced up, green eyes flashing and blond hair spiked with enough gel to put out an eye. Mick followed him up, his tight Greek-fro piled high and jiggling as he bobbed his head to the stomping beat from the audience. Both of them twitched with fresh energy. Coked up and ready. Sez pounded his chest the way he always did before a show. "Fuck yeah!" He grabbed Mick by the back of the neck and laid a kiss on him.

Mick returned Sez's kiss heartily before rearing back and punching him as they broke apart. Ramona gasped. Sez's lip bloomed red and his mouth cracked open in a wide scarlet-tinged smile as he threw his head back and laughed. "Fuck you too, bastard."

"Tonight. After. If you can keep your limp dick hard."

Sez charged out the door, arms pumping in the air, and blood running down his chin. "Showtime, pussies!" he yelled back at them.

Nicky heard the audience growing impatient, the thud of their boots and shoes on the floor speeding up until it was just a blur of vicious noise.

Ramona pointed her drumsticks at Mick. "We don't need this. We've got enough trouble in this band without throwing this in the mix."

"He started it."

She pinched the bridge of her nose before turning to Harry, inclining her head in Nicky's direction. "You leave him alone." Harry quirked an eyebrow at her. "I mean it. Just get him on stage. Don't fuck him up any more than he is now."

"No promises."

Ramona sighed and followed Mick and Sez out the door.

It was just Nicky in the dressing room then. Well, Nicky and a giant pile of coke and a tour manager who didn't have time for his shit.

"Here," Harry said, squatting down across from Nicky and picking up the white-dusted razor blade Mick had tossed haphazardly aside. "You just need a little to get through the show."

"I don't want to," Nicky said. His voice sounded small, like he was little Nicky admitting that he'd broken Mrs. Hendricks's special china Jesus that her grandmother had left her, and expecting to be loved for it, expecting to be taken into a forgiving embrace and told it was okay. That everything was gonna be okay.

Harry was not Adrian or Miriam Blumfeld.

"Come on, handsome. This'll wake you up yeah? Just a little bit to perk you up, and once you're on stage, you'll be flying. You hear that?" Harry tilted his head to the side.

Ni-co, Ni-co, Ni-co.

"I'm tired, Harry."

"Yeah. Fuck that." *Bye bye, nice Harry.* "There's five thousand people out there waiting for you. Get your ass up and get the fuck out there." He cut the three lines and tapped the table with the blade. "Tired isn't in the job description, Nico."

Nico Blue.

When had he ever thought that was a cool persona? What wouldn't he give to be back home in Little Heights again? Why couldn't he go back to being the kid who was immature for his age, awful at being human, and loved despite his damage? He wanted a magic portal to drop him back in the old fort on the island. Surely he could find Jazz still there too, and Honey with her cold, wet nose, like always. Like every summer day of his youth.

"Goddammit," Harry's voice growled but after a short silence he spoke again, his tone gentle. Yet not a scrap of real tenderness underscored his sugared words. "Come on, buddy. Just a line or two, okay? You'll feel better. A few more shows and then you'll get a rest. You can do this. I know you can. You don't want to let anyone down, do you?"

Nicky didn't. He'd let too many people down already. His mom and dad, and Jazz, of course. He'd made it almost his life's mission to let Jazz down. Because if he couldn't touch him, he had to get under his skin in some other way. Jazz had such beautiful skin. And his eyes. His eyes were—

"Here, doesn't that taste good?" Harry dipped his finger in the coke and shoved it into Nicky's mouth, rubbing the powder against his gums. Flinching away, Nicky fell backward. Harry's finger tasted of stale cigarette smoke and old sweat, but Nicky's gums went numb and he licked his lips. "Nico, look." Harry scooped some coke onto the flat of his thumbnail. He held it beneath Nicky's nose. "Sniff."

It was life burning into his nostrils. Life with a glint of hellfire.

Make me strong. Make me whole again. Make me Nico Blue.

He leaned over and took in a line on his own. Then another. Then a last one for good measure.

The room brightened, expanded, and contracted as Nicky's pupils blew wide. His heart pounded, his skin prickled, and his eyes watered as he got to his feet.

"Ready?" Harry sounded put out.

Nicky wiped at his nostrils and nodded before following him out into the hall. His breath came quickly and a dull-edged smile spread over his face like the drugs had drawn it on with crayons. He paused by the edge of the stage and closed his eyes. Facing out toward the chanting wild crowd who needed him—needed his music—his blood pulsed in his temples, in his throat, and tingled in his tongue.

"Ni-co! Ni-co! Ni-co!" the crowd chanted, catching sight of him.

He fell back and got into position to take the stage with his band-mates.

"Showtime," he whispered.

Chapter Two

JASPER LET HIMSELF drift on the beautiful hymns sung by the choir as he moved through Mass. It didn't always feel like this—as if he weren't entirely there, as if he looked on from above and was guided rather than leading Mass himself, but Andrew had been right in his prediction a few weeks earlier. Summer was in full swing now, and it was going to be a good one.

Jasper's people rose and fell like a synchronized wave and he tried not to feel pride when his words sank in and they bowed their heads. But no, it wasn't pride in himself; it was pride in them, for being here, for listening, for giving up time away from their homes to be with him in the presence of God.

A humbling gratitude overcame him as Mass ended and he watched his congregation file out of the church's large doors. When God had first called him, he'd been overwhelmed and scared, and that sentiment had lasted through college. Now his heart had mellowed and he found fulfillment in serving God, in being there for the people who needed him.

Usually he helped the altar servers and Andrew tidy up, but today he stood rooted to the spot and watched the town square from the shade of the narthex. With an odd feeling of foreboding, Jasper waited, but no one came, and eventually he turned away.

The relative darkness of the church made it difficult to see after staring into the sun for so long, and he didn't immediately make out the shape that detached itself from one of the large pillars to his right.

"Hello," Jasper said, squinting a little.

"Hi."

He blinked and his vision adjusted. Before him stood a young…girl? He couldn't quite tell, but he thought so. She was huddled into a large sweatshirt and kept her gaze down.

"Can I help you with something?" Jasper asked and she shrank in on herself. "If you just want to stay inside the church for a while, that's okay too."

"No, I…my name is Lizzie…" She glanced up at him and her shoulders drooped.

"Okay, Lizzie. I'm Father Hendricks, but you can call me Jasper. Make yourself at home. I'll be—"

"No, you don't understand. My…legal name is Stephan Benoit."

Jasper halted for a second, then recovered quickly and held out his hand. The social services file showed Stephan Benoit as a young black gay male. Not transgender. "I see. Well, *Lizzie*, it's nice to meet you. I hadn't expected to see you until tomorrow."

The almost painful looking hunch in her shoulders disappeared. She gave his hand a brief, damp shake before pulling the too-long sleeves back over her knuckles. "I just wanted to come and take a look, I guess. I've never been in a church like this before."

Jasper grinned. "Impressive, isn't it?"

She relaxed a little more and stared up at the seventy-foot-high ceiling. "It's beautiful."

"When you're settled in at the Blue Oasis Center, you can come here as often as you like."

"I'm not very religious," she admitted, her voice dropping as if she was afraid to say it.

Jasper laughed. "That's okay. This can be a place to find peace when you need it, even if you're not Catholic. Where are you staying?"

"My social worker got me a room at the Bay Heights Hotel."

"You could've moved straight into Blue Oasis if you wanted to."

"Yeah, I know. But Mr. Jones just transferred here and he had some stuff to do, so he asked me if I was okay with waiting until Monday." She bit at her lips and shifted her weight. "To be honest, I liked having the chance to be alone for a little bit."

"I totally understand," Jasper said. "Mrs. Blair at Bay Heights will take good care of you."

Lizzie said nothing and Jasper took a moment to really look at her. She had dark circles under her eyes and looked skinnier than she probably should. No noticeable bruises, but he'd learned from experience that didn't mean anything. In the years he'd been running the LGBTQ youth center, he'd seen enough to know the worst wounds were usually invisible.

"Do you play any sports, Lizzie?"

"I played soccer, but..." She grimaced and shrugged at the same time.

"You know, one of the kids who used to live at the center organizes a soccer class for kids on Sundays. He's always looking for someone to help him out. Would you like me to give him a call? It'd beat sitting in a hotel room by yourself all afternoon."

Lizzie bit her lip and he thought she was going to refuse, but she surprised him. Straightening her shoulders, she said, "Sure. Yeah, that sounds like a good idea."

"All right." Jasper smiled at her. "You can wait here in the church if you want, or I can have Lucas pick you up at the hotel."

"At the hotel, please," she said, and Jasper's heart twisted. He didn't want to draw conclusions without hearing her full story from the social worker first, but she'd obviously had a stable home at some point where she'd learned to be polite and sociable.

"I'll send him over. Mrs. Blair knows Lucas, so she can call your room when he's there, okay?"

"Okay. Thanks, um, Father Jasper. For...everything."

She turned and walked away and he watched her go. He didn't want to linger on the thought of parents showing their children the door because they didn't fit in the box they'd probably designed before the kids were even born, but it was difficult.

She's here, and she's safe. That's all that matters. Even though the road that had brought her here hadn't been an easy one.

Jasper looked down the nave of the church toward the altar and tried to find the peace he'd felt earlier. He'd take care of the remaining business here and then he'd stop by Blue Oasis before he went home. The kids would likely all be outside, and if they weren't he'd lure them out with the promise of barbecue and football.

The Blue Oasis youth group was set up in the old school building that belonged to the Catholic Church, and the huge, walled-in playground was perfect for a game on a day like this. Jasper smiled to himself and made his way down the nave toward the altar when he noticed someone sitting in the middle of the pews. He slowed his stride and his heartbeat sped up.

An interesting summer. He heard Andrew's prediction from three weeks ago echo in his mind. Jasper looked around but there was no one else left in the church. He had trouble controlling his breathing as he neared the pew with the stranger. Before Jasper could take a closer look the man rose to his feet, hands stuffed in his pockets, and disappeared into one of the old, dark wooden confessionals.

Jasper's heart thumped. The man's posture seemed familiar. The slight hunch in the shoulders and the rolling gait. They reminded him of a lanky kid who'd once been closer than a brother to him. But that kid was now Nico Blue, famous rock star who, according to gossip, could bring people to their knees with a gut-wrenching guitar riff.

At least that's what they used to say. Jasper had carefully made himself stop listening to gossip and stop looking for news on Nicky, and over the years he'd mostly managed to lose track.

Nicky's parents were Jewish, but Jasper ran into Mrs. Blumfeld every once in a while if they happened to volunteer at the soup kitchen at the same time. Last week she'd mentioned with her usual pride that Nicky was touring somewhere down South. It was impossible that the man with the shaggy dark hair was Nicky.

A familiar melancholy swelled in him, and he closed his eyes to breathe through it and let it go. Carefully, he brought himself back to the present moment before he stepped into the confessional. He settled and let the peace of the Lord fill him before he opened the sliding screen.

"Good morning," he said softly, and brought his hand to his forehead. "In the name of the Father, and of the Son, and of the Holy Spirit, amen."

Beside him the stranger shifted and Jasper waited. He caught a woody, resinous scent that brought back memories of dark, long-forgotten nights on the island. His mind hadn't played these kinds of cruel tricks on him in a long time, and his skin prickled with sweat. He tried to clear his head again.

The silence stretched on and Jasper's heart fluttered in his chest as if this was his first confession and not one of thousands. He closed his eyes, unsettled, and grasped for peace of mind so he could grant this reticent stranger absolution in God's name.

"Is this your first confession?"

There was no answer.

"I promise you don't need to be ashamed or to feel shy. Through me God hears all penance." Mainly for sins that were mundane and unimportant in the grand scheme of things. He'd learned over the years that while he could offer God's forgiveness, what people looked for was permission to forgive themselves. "But we can pray silently if you'd like. God is here with us and He is patient."

Jasper's words went unanswered and so he sought the Lord's help, praying as he waited, seeking the serenity he'd felt before he saw the man enter the confessional. He'd almost found what he was looking for when the man spoke, and Jasper's eyes flew open.

"Bless me, Father," Nicky said. "For I have sinned *so much.*"

THE SILENCE FROM the other side of the booth wasn't gratifying at all. Nicky almost wished he hadn't spoken so he could continue to sit and listen to Jazz's even breathing through the partition. He closed his eyes and swallowed the tension in his throat down before speaking again.

"Well, Father, it's been a really fucking long time since my last confession." Nicky touched the lip of the screened window between them. He could see the vague shape of Jazz through the lattice. His golden-brown hair glowed even in the shadows of the confessional, but Nicky was barely able to discern the handsome lines of Jazz's nose and chin, the length of his neck. He ached for more, wanting to see him up close, to find the differences between this untouchable man and the boy whose entire body he'd once kissed. "I'm making a new start and I thought the best way to do that would be to offload all this *sin.*"

Jazz's voice was tight and gruff as he spoke the traditional words, "May the Lord be in your heart and help you to confess your sins with true sorrow."

After Nicky had left the detox clinic, sober and on a new prescription drug regimen to help him stay that way, the only place he'd wanted to be was home. But he'd needed to do this first. The confessional was dark and intimate, a refuge from the church's stained glass windows splitting the bright sunshine into a prismatic array of colors that spilled across the pews, alternating light and shadow. Nicky knew which he belonged in.

"Should I just start?"

"If you feel ready."

"Is there a time limit on how far back I can go?"

Through the partition, Nicky could see Jazz bend his head. "There's no limit on God's grace, Nicky."

Nicky's mouth ached with his tiny, bitter smile. "Jazz."

A laugh so soft Nicky almost thought he'd imagined it drifted between them. "You'll have to forgive me."

"For admitting that you know who I am? That seems fuck-all important considering our past."

"I'm sorry to hear you're still angry."

Now *that* made him angry. He'd come prepared to make amends, but Jazz was the same smug asshole he'd been back on the day they'd broken up. "You're sorry I'm angry? What the fuck does that mean? How about you're sorry for what you *did* instead of how I'm *feeling*." Nicky's hands began to shake and he stuffed them between his knees. "So what? Am I supposed to be over it by now? We were best friends. Lovers." *You meant everything to me.*

Jazz didn't dispute this description. He sat patiently waiting, head down, as if Nicky's words washed over him like harmless summer rain. Basking in heavenly certainty, probably.

"So what should I forgive *you* for, Jazz? Maybe we should consider that. How about you letting me fall in love with you? Making me think you loved me back?" He waited and Jazz was so fucking quiet. Such a supercilious little *shit*. Nicky wanted to punch something, but everything in the confessional looked so sturdy he'd only end up breaking his knuckles.

And still Jazz said nothing. So much for the cathartic purging of nearly two decades worth of sorrow.

"Oh, I know. Maybe you'd like me to forgive you for fucking me through the mattress until I cried out for your precious God? Screwing with my head for *months* before you dropped your bombshell of priestly ambition on me?" He was on a roll now. Jazz's silence goaded him. "Or maybe I should forgive you for leaving me like you did?" Nicky laughed, but it was a disgusting sound. The wash of pain was fresh all over again, remembering their parting in the clean and sober light of day. "I was so scared."

Jazz shifted minutely, the robes rustling in the silence. "We both were."

"Not you. Not really. You can't play that card on me. You had your whole future ahead of you, all planned out while mine went up in flames. And I know you. You forget. I fucking *know* you. You destroyed me and then shut the door on the mess you made like I didn't matter, like we didn't count for anything. That's a lot to forgive you for."

Jazz was silent but Nicky could hear his labored breath and the emptiness between them stretched. Nicky flicked his finger against the screen, but Jasper still didn't speak. It was too much. He ached through and through, almost as bad as the detox pain had been back at the clinic. He needed to get a goddamn reaction out of Jazz or he'd end up doing something truly stupid when he walked out of this church.

"I remember every minute, you know? From our first kiss to our last." Nicky dropped his voice. "The first time you put your mouth on my dick. Yeah, I remember that really fucking well." A tiny superstitious part of Nicky expected to be struck down and he'd welcome it. Jazz, for all it was worth, could have been a statue sitting there. "You're not going to say anything?"

"This isn't the time nor the place for that kind of conversation, Nicky." Jazz's voice sounded strained. "I understand you're angry and if you want to talk, we can do that. But not here. It's inappropriate and disrespectful and you know it."

"Don't talk to me about respect."

Jazz sighed and brought his folded hands to his lips for a moment. "Nicky, we were just children."

"What a fan-fucking-tastic excuse!" He waited, but Jazz didn't say anything else. He lowered his voice a little, let it purr with a seductive thrill he hadn't used while sober in a long time. "I guess no one calls you Jazz now." Their time together seemed forever ago. Five forevers ago. "I bet you've forgotten all about the fort and how we used to swim there.

How I'd wait for you to finish your homework so we could explore the woods and run wild. I remember how you were obsessed with foxes. You could hang out in a tree for hours, waiting for one to show up. I guess no one calls you Fox now either. Did you forget all of that?"

"I haven't forgotten," Jasper said gently.

"But you're not Fox anymore, are you? Or Jazz. It's Father Jasper Hendricks, do-gooder and perfect, pure-of-heart, asswipe of God."

Jazz sighed and his voice was a whisper when he asked, "Do you have any sins to confess? Because if you don't, this conversation is over."

"Oh, fuck yes I do. You sure you want to hear them, *Father*? You sure you're up for it?"

There was another long moment and then Jazz began. "Let the word of God guide you." Nicky listened as Jazz recited more scripture. "Lord, You know all things; You know that I love You."

Nicky laughed with genuine amusement. "Well, I sure as shit don't know that, but what the hell. Fresh start, right?" He cleared his throat and cast his mind back to the beginning. "Heroin, that's a big one. Chasing pleasure for the sake of pleasure?" *For the sake of forgetting.* "I bet it's been a long time since you've allowed yourself to do that. What else? Pills. Coke. Cock. Mmm. In massive quantities. Do you want details, Fox? I bet you do. You always liked it when I talked dirty to you. I can give you details. Or I could just sum it up." Jazz wasn't looking at him, but Nicky let his hands drift over his torso anyway, down his legs. "Orgasms upon orgasms, rolling on a tidal wave of drugs and so many strangers' assholes and dicks that I couldn't begin to guess a number." Nicky's lips twisted. "Funny thing: they were always you, and never you, and it never meant a damn thing, but it always motherfucking hurt."

Jazz made a small sound that could have been pain but Nicky wasn't sure. And he hadn't meant to do this. He'd meant to come here and make amends, not spill his festering guts, and definitely not rip open a new rift between them.

But everything spilled out, unstoppable now. "It was you and the lack of you, and me swallowing all the cocks in the world hoping to fill the place inside that just wanted your goddamn smile; your hand in mine. Just your presence. Just to hear you breathe. It would have been enough."

Jazz's hands raised prayerfully to his lips were easily discernible through the screen. It was true. If it was Jazz's breath or nothing, he'd take his breath. If it was his hand or nothing, he'd take his hand. That was why he'd come home, wasn't it? Because of Jazz and his fucking face on *The Atlantic* magazine cover lying on the table in the detox clinic waiting room. His eyes had soothed Nicky's skittering heart and called him back to Little Heights. But this man, this *priest*, wasn't soothing at all.

"Where was I? Oh yeah. Anal sex. Mainly receiving. Miraculously, I've been told I'm still negative. I guess I didn't try hard enough to kill myself, though it seemed like I was making a good go of it at the time. You know, if the measure of despair and self-loathing is anything to go by."

"Please don't—" Jazz's voice cracked with emotion. "There's always something to live for. The Lord doesn't intend your life to always be suffering. You're strong. One of the strongest men I've ever—"

"Ha. Good one." Nicky smiled and it scared him how he couldn't hold it back. He turned his face away from the partition. "You keep messing up this anonymity thing."

"You're making it harder than it usually is."

"You're right, though. I'm not going to kill myself." He was going to stay sober and find some way to live in a world where all he could have was this: Jazz's voice, his existence, but never his touch. Never again.

He'd been denying that horrible truth with all his heart and soul for too long, writing songs about it, waiting for the boy who'd saved him from spiders as a child and from himself as a teen to realize that he wanted Nicky more than he wanted God, and the truth was this pixelated image of Jazz through the lattice of confessed sins was as close as they'd ever be.

"I'm going to make a fresh start." Nicky said again, and why? He wasn't here for Jazz's approval, damn it. He'd angled for that enough as a kid. "I'm here for a new beginning."

"You sincerely seek God's forgiveness for your transgressions?"

Jazz seemed eager to come to the culmination of the confession. Nicky considered dragging it out, confessing to specific horrors just to see if he could make Jazz break, but instead he simply said, "Yes."

"God, the Father of mercies, through the death and resurrection of His Son has reconciled the world to Himself and sent the Holy Spirit among us for the forgiveness of sins; through the ministry of the Church, may God give you pardon and peace, and I absolve you from your sins in the name of the Father, and of the Son, and of the Holy Spirit."

Nicky waited for something to happen, some sense of absolution. "What about my penance?"

Jazz laughed and it sounded so real, Nicky had to close his eyes. "If I tell you to say five Hail Marys will you do it?"

He shook his head and tried to suppress a grin. "Probably not."

"Then why don't you open a Bible some time?"

Nicky could barely contain his laughter, choking it out as he let his head fall back against the dark wood of the booth. As if that could ever wash away the stains of his life on the road, the filth of every one of his years after he'd let the owner of an L.A. bar fuck him for an introduction to the band that became Vespertine. "Sure. Why not? Any recommendations on where to start?"

"How about Jeremiah 29:11."

"Why, what does it say?"

"Look it up, Nicky. That's the whole point."

"Fine." He pressed his forehead against the divide. "So am I forgiven?"

"May the Passion of our Lord Jesus Christ, the intercession of the

Blessed Virgin Mary and of all the saints, whatever good you do and suffering you endure heal your sins, help you to grow in holiness, and reward you with eternal life. Go in peace."

"I wasn't asking God, but yeah. Peace. Right. I'll get on that." Nicky was silent a moment and then said, "I guess I'll see you around. I'm going to be staying in Little Heights for a while. And, for the record, I don't think I can forgive you."

Nicky shoved aside the curtain and stepped out into the nave. As he walked away, he wanted to hear the sound of Jazz pushing back the curtain and rushing after him. But in the silence of the church, a swollen, pregnant pause that would give birth to everything to follow, Nicky recognized the wish as the same denial he'd been living in for years, and he discarded it. It hurt like leaving his arm on the ground behind him, and he went weak-kneed with a craving for heroin to numb out the pain.

He pushed his hair out of his eyes. He walked on.

Breathe in: misguided, broken sighs

Spit out: crucifixes and stigmata lies

Lyrics and music slid into his mind and he considered pulling his phone from his pocket to sing it into the voice recorder, but what was the point? Until he could fix himself, the music was as sick as he was. If it was a song that wanted to be sung, it'd be around when he wasn't sick anymore. When he wasn't broken.

The hot sun washed over him. A fresh start.

Chapter Three

THE NOISE OF a dozen kids running wild in the schoolyard reached him before he turned the corner, and Jasper was glad. If they were outside already, chances were good he could slip in and out without having to make too much conversation. Everything felt unreal—the sun too bright, traffic too loud, and the birdsong echoing strangely off the buildings. Like he'd stepped out of the confessional and into a different world, one that grated on him like an exposed nerve.

When he pushed against the gate, he spotted Mrs. Wells and Andrew setting up the picnic tables in the shade under the large oak tree. The black steel barbecue wafted smoke as a bunch of kids played a casual game of football while others sunbathed and read on the steps. He gave Mrs. Wells—a retired school teacher who had her own apartment within the school—and Andrew a brief wave, stopped to greet some of the kids on the stairs, and then made his way into his small office. He shut the door behind him, briefly pressing his hot forehead against the cool wood and letting out a long breath.

Lucas's number was stored in the old computer, and while he waited for it to boot up, he sank into the leather chair and sighed. With his hands carefully folded in his lap, he waited to feel anything at all. Gradually, the numbness retreated and he examined his heart. He felt…strange mostly. Even after so many years, he always felt naked right after he'd taken off all the priest garb, and that vulnerability extended to his mind. That might explain the way he'd reacted to Nicky's presence.

Oh my word.

Nicky was back. Jasper looked at his hands.

He didn't even know how to feel about that. He'd sat in the confessional for a long while after Nicky's departure, praying for God's peace, knowing he needed it beneath his buzzing numbness. When he'd finally headed out to Blue Oasis, there'd been no sign of Nicky, and it occurred to him now that he hadn't even really laid eyes on him. Had he looked well? Was he actually off drugs? Jasper wanted that to be true. Needed it to be.

Hoping to fill the place inside that just wanted your goddamn smile; your hand in mine.

Jasper remembered the absolute giddy feeling of holding Nicky's hand for the first time as a teenager. The strong, firm grip of an almost-but-not-quite man's hand warming his palm. Nicky had slipped his slender, guitar-calloused fingers between Jasper's and taken his time to kiss every single fingertip. The heat of it had shot straight to his groin, yes, but to his heart too. The rightness of those kisses had wounded him, because even then his calling had been hard to ignore.

Jasper would be lying if he didn't admit he'd thought about their reunion every once in a while. Especially a decade ago when Vespertine really became famous. He'd been shocked to hear Nicky's band's name, and hadn't wanted to believe it was a message to him, but what else could it have been? He'd imagined in dramatic detail how they'd act toward one another if their paths crossed again. In some of those old fantasies they'd fallen into each other's arms, and he'd made different choices and God had guided him to a different path. In others, Nicky was patient and understanding, agreeing that their friendship was more important than a childhood romance, a puppy love that would never have sustained. In yet others, Nicky had been much like he'd been today: angry, accusing, hurtful.

Jasper had still been so young then. And when Nicky became famous, and the songs he wrote for their band didn't take much figuring out, it'd dawned on Jasper that any reunion definitely wouldn't be a happy one. So he'd stopped thinking about it. They'd been guided to their proper paths and there was no going back. He just hadn't expected…this. He leaned forward and buried his head in his slightly trembling hands.

He thinks I never loved him. Oh, Nicky.

Jasper tried to take a deep, calming breath but his chest felt tight. He glanced at the small crucifix above the door. His suffering meant nothing, but if he had wronged someone, no matter how long ago, he needed to face his actions.

He sat up again. That's what mattered. And he shouldn't lose sight of that. He was here to help, to love unconditionally the people God placed on his path. He closed his eyes and remembered the young boy Nicky had once been: the most beautiful, wicked blue eyes that always twinkled above his wide, devastating grin.

Grant me, O Lord, wisdom and courage to help Nicky find peace and strength to fight his demons. And steady me, O Lord, to do your work. Your peace is a river and Your righteousness is the waves of the sea, washing me clean of all anxiety and regret, leaving me a servant of Your grace.

Finishing his prayer just as the computer zoomed to life, Jasper's eyes snapped open. With decisive movements and no tremor in his fingers he located Lucas's number and reached for the phone.

"Hello?"

"Lucas? This is Father Hendricks. How are you?"

"Father? I…uh, I'm fine, thank you. I'm surprised to hear from you." A silence fell and Jasper didn't immediately feel compelled to fill it. "Is it because I wasn't in church this morning? Because you know I'm not… I mean, for a while I enjoyed coming to church, but lately I don't feel—"

Jasper grinned and interrupted. "No, that's not why I'm calling. You know you're always welcome, but I was wondering if you'll be teaching your soccer class this afternoon."

"Yes, at two. Why?"

"There's a young lady at the Bay Heights Hotel who could use a little distraction today. She's there all by herself until I can meet with her and the social worker tomorrow."

"Oh, sure! Yes, I can always use a hand to keep control over the little sh—"

"Lucas…"

"Cherubs! I was going to say cherubs."

Jasper snorted. "Right. So you'll pick her up?"

"Absolutely."

"Great." A little of the stress slipped off his shoulders. Lucas had always been special to Jasper. He'd been one of the first ones Jasper had pulled off the street ten years ago. Hooked on heroin and a different kind of hooking all together, he'd been the most challenging—and the most rewarding. To see him so successful and accepted in the community touched Jasper with a hint of pride that was surely something he could add to his own list of confessions.

"How's work, Lucas? I hope Mr. Blumfeld keeps you busy."

"Busy enough to keep me off drugs, if that's what you mean."

Jasper lowered his voice and added the hint of warning that had always worked on Lucas. "That's not what I meant and you know it. Do you like the job?"

"I love it," Lucas said softly. "You see some interesting sh—stuff, as a paralegal. If it weren't for you—"

"We've been over that. You should be grateful to yourself. And to God, of course, if you want."

"Yeah, yeah," Lucas said, but he laughed. "I'm actually looking some things up for a case meeting tomorrow morning, so if you don't need anything else?"

"No, of course. I'll let you go. Thanks again, Lucas."

"For you? Anything, anytime, Father."

Jasper smiled and hung up. He tilted his chair back and stared around the little office. It was an old room with faded wallpaper and furniture that could do with an overhaul, but it was functional. Jasper preferred to pour the funds in the kids' rooms since he didn't spend all that much time here anyway.

Maybe you'd like me to forgive you for fucking me through the mattress until I cried for your precious God.

Jasper rubbed at the uneven wooden surface of the desk. He'd made a decision when he was seventeen years old, one that irreparably changed his life. He'd based it on facts he'd doubted more than once since, but none of that mattered anymore. Thinking about something he did when he was young and in love with his best friend would do neither of them any good.

Two pairs of footsteps thundered down the steps along the hall and Jasper startled a little. Time to do his rounds with the kids, say hello to Mrs. Wells, and then go home.

Mrs. Wells tried to feed him and the kids wanted to rope him into playing basketball with them, but for once Jasper declined when he saw everyone was doing well. It pleased him to see that Amberlynn was interacting a little with the others. She'd been so quiet for months everyone had started to think maybe it was just her nature, but there she was, laughing with Eric and Olivia in the bright sunlight, looking carefree and happy. Mrs. Wells gave him a small smile that told him she'd seen it too.

Looking forward to some alone time, Jasper hopped on his bike and turned the corner, passing by the church so he could cycle down Main Street toward the other side of town.

The classic farmhouse he lived in was too big for just him, but Jasper loved it. It sat a little ways off the road, and stood out brightly against the summer greens with its clean white siding and dark green shutters.

He steered the bike into his drive and swung his leg over the saddle as the bike still rolled onward, neatly hopping off right before he parked it against the garage door. Taking the steps two at a time, he climbed up to his porch and unlocked the door. It opened into a small formal living room to the right and the kitchen to the left, which had a large brick-framed fireplace and warm red wooden floors.

Jasper closed the door behind him and walked underneath the thick exposed beams toward the fridge so he could grab a bottle of water. He didn't have to worry about Lizzie's accommodations; Mrs. Wells would have that all in hand and then some, but he hadn't had the chance yet to read through her entire file since he'd heard last week that Blue Oasis would get a new resident.

About to retreat to his study, Jasper turned back when he heard a tapping noise against the kitchen window. A large ginger cat sat perched between the begonias on the window ledge, and as he watched, the fat beast tapped the window again.

"Well, you're early," Jasper said when he twisted the old window lock open. "No birds to harass?"

"Meow." The cat rubbed her face against the faucet.

"Ah. Empty bird bath, huh?"

"Mrrrw."

Jasper opened the tap and let the water dribble out slowly. The cat looked at him. He held up his hand, she high-fived him, and began to drink at leisure. She'd be at it a while, so he grabbed the little red watering can he kept under the sink and went outside to refill the birdbath. The farm came with a small well he used for watering plants, and as he pumped he wondered again where the cat came from. Obviously well-cared for, she couldn't be a stray, but she never wore a collar and wasn't chipped—he'd had her checked. And yet every day she showed up at least once, and sometimes even spent the night.

By the time he'd pinched a few dead flowers from the beds hugging the side of the house, the cat was done drinking. He turned off the tap, left the window open, and retreated to his study. When she decided to follow him up, he wasn't in the least bit surprised.

An hour later, the cat had stopped purring in his lap and settled into a deep sleep, her nose whistling on every breath. He kept reading until he was done with the file, and when he slowly closed it and exhaled deeply, she woke up. She stretched, dug her little claws into his legs, and jumped off. Thoughts whirling with all he'd just read, he straightened two pens on his desk and lined up the file with the edge of the desk pad.

Foster care was never easy, not on any child. How could it be? Teens who ended up in foster homes rarely entered the system from happy families. It was even harder for a transgender girl. Jasper closed his eyes, found his balance with one hand on the desk and sank slowly to his knees where he pressed his palms together and lifted his face to heaven.

"O Lord," he murmured. "I thank You for the privileged life I've lived. I thank You for the kindness in my youth and the forgiveness and guidance You provided when I most needed it. I know I can be prideful. Help me remain humble. Let me find the way to do Your work to the best of my abilities and continue to give safe homes to people like Lizzie. I know You will not set anything on my path You and I can't handle together." Jasper paused and lowered his forehead so it rested against the tips of his praying fingers. "Give me the strength to be what Nicky needs, to show him the way out of darkness into his light."

Because he used to shine so brightly.

Jasper covered his face and whispered, "Amen."

THE ROLLING GREEN hills followed Nicky out of town. The car he'd rented at the airport was a little blue mini Cooper with white racing stripes. The turns and bumps were tighter and bigger in the small car, and with the windows rolled down, the wind tossed his overlong hair and buffeted his arms and upper body. The intense sensations comforted his jangled nerves, input canceling out craving.

He crossed the intersection where Main Street turned into the country-bound Letterhead Pike and then took the right turn onto

Androscoggin, which ran beside the river of the same name. He let his foot grow heavy on the gas pedal. The evergreens and maples flipped by him in a steady rhythm that he could almost hear—hand claps and escalating stomping feet—nature screaming for him like fans in an auditorium.

Bad blood and semen stains
Memories of you
Eating through my veins

No. He'd done what he needed to do. He'd confronted Jazz and now he was going to let it go. He was going to learn to live without him.

He snorted. He really wasn't very good at lying. Never had been. Jazz was the one who'd always been an expert at that. Which was how Jazz had ended up with a whole summer's worth of being grounded, wasn't it? Convincing little shit had insisted that the drugs were his and not Nicky's or Jimmy's. He'd done it thinking it'd keep Nicky out of trouble, but it'd just meant the beginning of the end.

He blinked, almost hearing a melancholy melody climbing to a crescendo until it subdued to the cry of a single violin. But before he could grasp it, the music was gone.

Nicky had sat in the back during Mass, observing Jazz from afar. Thirty-four looked good on him even if the priest's robes obscured a lot about his body. Nicky had been able to see that he was still lean and taller than Nicky now. Up at the altar, with the congregation rising and falling for him, he hadn't seemed like Jazz at all. He'd seemed a mystery almost, a priest with Jazz's plush mouth, dimpled chin, and long-lashed green-hazel eyes. A stranger called Jasper. Someone Nicky had as yet to know.

Nicky laughed under his breath as he lifted his foot from the gas pedal, slowing reluctantly to make the turn onto Bayview, his parents' road. He knew Jazz better than he knew anyone. No matter what named he went by. Priest or not.

The trees thinned along the banks of Little Bay and he could see the water sparkling in the summer sun. The water looked inviting and placid, and, with the back of his sweaty T-shirt sticking to the seat, he was tempted to pull over and jump in. But appearances could be deceiving. This section of the bay was unpredictable and changeable. Local lore claimed that its swift current once sucked a man in and spit him out forty miles away in the ocean.

Nicky decided against taking any stupid chances just for a thrill. That was what he was trying to move away from, wasn't it? Dr. Rodriguez, his new therapist, had spent a lot of time talking about good highs (exercise, interacting with friends) and bad highs (taking insane risks, using drugs). He figured it was progress that he remembered the discussion and was choosing to apply it now.

He pulled at his sticky shirt and cast another longing glance toward the water.

"Besides, good ol' Buckley already scored the drowning death," he murmured to himself. "If you're going to go out, at least be creative about it, jackass."

He could wait to swim in the pool when he got home. It wasn't even two miles down the road. Nicky snorted at himself. His impatience and self-sabotaging streak were truly devils on his shoulders. Where was his angel when he needed him? The top of his left foot itched and he gritted his teeth. "Fine. I'll be good. The pool will be nice. Clean. No fish."

But if he wanted fish nibbling at his legs as he swam, he could complete his experience with a dive off the dock into the cove behind his parents' house. The currents there were slow and shallow.

A few minutes later, as Nicky pulled up the drive to the blue and white Queen Anne-style house, he had his first moment of gripping doubt that coming home was the right thing to do. The place was crawling with memories. There was the basketball hoop at the wide end of the driveway where he and Jazz had played games of HORSE. Out over the glimmer of the cove, he sighted the island where their old fort still stood. Its rusted tin roof reflected the afternoon sun, glowing orange like a fire in the trees.

Nicky climbed out of the car, imagining their former selves running around the corner of his parents' home trailing a homemade kite behind them. He was relieved, though, that the small forest between his parents' and Jazz's folks' place had grown up enough that he couldn't see their barn-red clapboard. There had never been much love lost between Nicky and Jazz's mother, and he didn't need the memories of Mrs. Hendricks's cold judgment right now.

The front door burst open, and Nicky took a deep breath as his tiny mother ran out. She flew down the sidewalk with her hands outstretched and her tight salt-and-pepper curls bouncing in the summer sun. His heart lifted at the sight of her knee-length colorful summer skirt flying out behind her and her Birkenstocks flapping against the sidewalk. Her white sleeveless blouse burned his retinas in the bright sun, but he could still make out the simultaneous smears of fear and joy on her face.

"Nicky!" Miriam exclaimed.

Then she was in his arms. He lifted her up, pressing his face to her shoulder. She smelled like the rosemary hair oil she'd always used to tame her curls and he took a deep breath, tears pricking his eyes. Against his chest, he could feel the thrum of her heart. How he admired that strong, vibrant organ that had always loved him unconditionally and so much more than he'd ever deserved.

"Hey, Mom," he whispered and as he set her down on the ground, she pulled away, touching his cheeks and gazing up at him.

Miriam's dark brows lowered over her sharp black eyes, and her sloping nose pointed down to her wide, sad mouth. "Sweet baby, what have you done to yourself?"

Her rosemary scent filled him with the only sense of safety he'd ever allowed himself outside of Jazz. Nicky swallowed the lump in his throat, but it stubbornly rose again. "Mom, I need help."

He meant so many things by that but he couldn't voice them all or he'd start sobbing in the driveway while they baked in the summer sunshine.

"We'll help you, Nicky. We'll always help you."

Nicky swallowed hard and glanced out over the grass that rolled down to the cove. The old wooden steps headed past the pool and the picnic table on the left, and on down to the dock where his father's fishing boat bobbed in the drifting current across from his old rickety canoe. "Can we go inside? It's been a long day."

"Did you bring any bags?"

"No. Just the clothes on my back. Well, and my backpack." It was chock full of maintenance meds and vitamins. "But I'll get that later."

"All right. We have some of your old things in the drawers in your room." She looked him over critically. "You're so thin right now, I think they'll still fit you. Oh, Nicky. You look so…" she trailed off, her eyes tracing the sharpness of his face. He knew what he looked like: hollows for cheeks, dark rings under his eyes, and thin enough to cut paper.

"I'll be okay, Mom."

"We need to feed you."

Nicky smiled. "Yeah. I figured you'd want to fatten me up first thing."

Miriam chuckled but her laugh wasn't joyful like it'd been when he was a kid. "Of course I do." She touched his arm and then tugged his hand. "Come on in, then. I'm so glad you're here, sweetie." She slipped his arm over her shoulder and her own around his waist, authoritatively guiding him toward the house "If I'd gotten your message in time to do some shopping, I'd have made matzo ball soup, but all I have is sandwich fixings for lunch. I planned stir fry for your father tonight. Do you like stir fry now? I know you didn't as a little boy, but I think it's because I made you eat the vegetables and not just the meat."

Nicky chuckled, squeezing her as they lopsidedly navigated the front steps up to the white-trim porch. He purposely ignored the white wooden rocking chairs in which he and Jazz had played rocket ships to Mars back when they were too young to know that they'd grow up to kiss and fuck and break each other's hearts.

"You were always on me to eat my colors." He'd eaten a ton of colors over the years—pink pills, blue pills, green pot, and rainbow acid. "They fed me rabbit food in rehab, so anything you make will be amazing."

Miriam looked up at him, and her sadness twined with his own. He thought maybe he should have just given in and cried in the driveway after all because the pressure from holding it back ached and ached and *ached*.

When Nicky's eyes strayed to the curved stairs that led up to the bedrooms and the set of hidden stairs to his old attic room, Miriam said, "I got rid of all the—" Her hands fluttered. "The drug paraphernalia in your old room like you asked me to. I flushed a little bag of pot I found and threw away the rest of the things." She sighed. "I had no idea that was up there. A mother should know."

He shook his head and wrapped his arm around her shoulders again. "I didn't want you to know. You can't blame yourself."

"Well, it's gone now."

He stepped into the entryway, the scent of home flooding into him. There was no particular description for it, no particular cleanser or perfume. It was just the smell of their life here and it was as comforting as it was painful.

"Thank you, Mom."

"And I poured out your father's Manischewitz."

A sharp memory of Jazz swallowing mouthfuls of the kosher wine came to mind. His eyes had gone glassy, his cheeks flushed, and his beautiful, rich mouth had been stained red. God, how Nicky had wanted to kiss Jasper even then. But he'd never had the balls to make a move. Eventually, it'd been Jazz who'd grabbed hold of him and kissed him breathless. Over the years, there'd been plenty of time to wonder if it wouldn't have been better if maybe he hadn't.

The entryway was different. Where there had been an old family photo featuring a baleful Nicky with a mohawk and braces, there was now a large set of multi-frames with photos of magazine covers featuring Vespertine, the centerpiece being the cover of *Rolling Stone* with a very high, very numbed-out Nico Blue dominating the posed studio shot.

"When did you do that?" he asked nodding toward it. A sick feeling slinked through him. He barely remembered that day. He didn't enjoy the idea of being bombarded with the shame of it every time he walked through the foyer.

"Oh, well, that other portrait was getting a bit dated, don't you think? It seemed like we should replace it with something more recent." Miriam said, indicating the 'shoe trunk,' as they called it, standing open by the front door. "Is it all right?"

Nicky didn't know how long he would be staying, but maybe the reminder of how shitty drugs were and how fucked up they left him wouldn't be such a bad thing. "Sure, Mom. It's fine."

Miriam put her Birks inside the trunk and Nicky had to sit on the bottom step to unlace and pull off his black ass-kicking boots. The cool air caressed his sweaty toes, and he noticed his mother's eyes drawn down to his feet. He balled up his socks and tossed them into the trunk along with the shoes.

"Those are new."

"Yeah. I got this one since you last saw me too."

He held up his left hand, which was covered with black straight lines and dots from a sideways band at his wrist almost up to the nail of his middle finger. It was a masculine mehndi-inspired design he'd had done in Australia at some tiny shop in Canberra. He'd been blitzed out of his mind at the time and it was far from his favorite, but the tat was visible and pretty impressive. He hoped it would distract her from her focusing on the more important tats on his feet.

He waved his hand to draw her eyes up again. "It hurt like hell. I've got a big one on my back too." Not that he wanted to show it to her. He shouldn't have mentioned that one.

Miriam swallowed and nodded her head. She didn't like them, he could tell, but she wasn't going to say anything that might make him change his mind about staying for a while. He hated that in the past he'd given her every reason to think he would do something like that. Before he'd started on the detox doctor's new prescriptions, he'd always been incapable of seeing how much his behavior must have hurt her.

Her eyes came back once again to the tattoo on the pale skin of his right foot. "When did you get that one?"

"A few years ago."

She nodded. "It reminds me of Jazz when he was small." She smiled fondly. "The way he used to curl up on his side. Remember how he took up most of your bed? You'd be smashed up against the wall to make room for him."

The fox was a nice illustration of orange, white and black lines. Its back curled along the base of Nicky's toes and its head and paws curled up to his ankle. The sleeping fox's expression was tenderly rendered so that he seemed to smile at his dreams, and his little feet came together near the apex of Nicky's arch. A small red heart punctuated their restful pose.

Nicky swallowed and gritted his teeth. His mother had taken his homosexuality in stride, as had his father, but she'd always seemed oblivious to his devotion to Jazz as anything other than brotherly. He didn't know if he wanted her prying now. Though if he wanted her help then maybe it was time she knew the truth. But not today. He was hungry, tired, and not interested in the emotional upheaval of telling her about him and Jazz.

Her eyes shifted to his other foot, and he glanced down at the black lines of a more angular fox. That fox sat calmly on his haunches with blue angel wings sprouting from his back and his head graced by a yellow halo.

"Sometimes it feels like I've got two devils on my shoulders," Nicky said. "So I gave myself an angel on my foot. He's supposed to guide me to a better path. But he's done a piss poor job for such a smug looking little bastard, hasn't he?"

Miriam arched a brow and cleared her throat. "They're not what I would have imagined for you. But they're not bad." She smiled with a steely determination, like she was not going to let whatever was on her mind get between them today. "Let me guess: turkey and avocado with onion?"

He smiled and hopped up, clapping his hands together. "Yeah. That sounds great."

As she pulled open the fridge and the bread box in the kitchen, Nicky waited on one of the tall stools at the counter. He perused the changes in the living room since he'd last been home. A new blue sofa faced a large screen attached to the wall, and a plush rocker faced the same direction with legal files piled next to it. Closer at hand, a large throw rug with green, blue and brown accents separated the breakfast table from the rest of the room. Next to the TV, there was a framed picture of Nicky playing guitar with Vespertine at Glastonbury three years before. He got up to investigate it more closely. He barely remembered that night, either. He'd done a speedball in the trailer but then fucked it up with an extra bump, and he'd been sure his heart would explode there on stage.

"Your father likes how you've got your tongue out in that picture," his mother said, a little laughter in her voice. "You always stick your tongue out when you're playing something you need to concentrate on. It's so cute."

Nicky tilted his head. He'd needed to concentrate because he was so far gone that night that he hadn't trusted his fingers to play the music his muscles had memorized years before. He squatted down to look at the bookshelf under the picture. Murder mysteries, the Torah, the Book of Mormon, and his dad's copy of the Holy Bible. Nicky smiled, remembering how often his Jewish father had used the Christians' scripture against them in debates, pointing out the hypocrisies and contradictory passages.

Miriam set his plate down on the counter near the stool he'd abandoned.

Nicky grabbed the Bible and headed back. He took a bite from the sandwich, the taste of mustard and onion exploding on his tongue, and he murmured his pleasure around the mouthful.

Miriam stood across from him, her small fingers running over the seam in the granite counter. She good naturedly rolled her eyes toward the Bible next to his plate. "You always did seem more drawn to Christianity. I remember when you used to go to Mass with Jasper and his family."

He'd only gone because he'd loved to see Jazz's face go through the various expressions of anxiety and peace and finally to something resembling a state of ecstasy as the hymns began. He'd learned how much Jazz loved music from those trips to the church and he'd started playing him special songs written just for him shortly after that. He later realized he'd been trying to woo him. But he'd been so young and dumb in those early days that he hadn't even known.

"I don't believe in God." Nicky wasn't sure if that was true but it was closer to true than not.

Miriam shrugged. "All that matters is living a good life. If you live a good life, Nicky, you'll be a happy man." She met his eyes and said with more genuine forgiveness than he'd heard in Jazz's voice in the confessional, "It's not too late for that, sweet one."

Sweet one, sweet baby, sweetie. He'd been horrified by those nicknames most of his adolescence and enraged by them when he'd started using drugs. He wasn't sweet. He wasn't a baby. He was an angry alien that'd been dumped into a wealthy suburban dreamscape and he'd wanted to burn it all down around him and then spit in the ashes. His depression and attachment disorder had left him always feeling one step out of sync with the rest of the world, and that was one thing even Jasper couldn't fix.

"I got a phone call from a reporter this morning," Miriam said, obviously deciding his silence meant he didn't want to talk about living a good life. "He asked me if I'd heard from you and I hung up on him." She pushed a curl out of her eyes, the gray seeming less obvious in the rosy light of the kitchen. "We get calls like that pretty often. But this guy made it sound like you'd gone missing. I was worried until I heard that you were on your way here."

"I dodged the paps," Nicky murmured, flipping through the Bible with his right hand and taking another bite of the sandwich with his left. "I just want to be left alone."

Miriam leaned her hip against the counter. "Yes. That's what you need now. Privacy and time with people who love you." She paused and then asked a little tentatively, "How long do you plan to stay with us?" She held up a hand. "You're welcome for as long as you want or need to be here. Having you home is a joy for me, you know that. I just want to know what to expect."

"I'm not sure. I'd like to stay a few months, but I doubt management will allow that."

"Isn't it more important that you get well?"

Nicky shrugged. "You'd think so, but no. Not to them."

Miriam's eyes darkened. "And the paparazzi? You don't think they'll come looking for you here?"

"No. Well, they might. It's doubtful, though. Hopefully some bigger name celeb is out there fucking his life up and I'm already old news." He took another big bite, swallowed, and said, "Next time someone calls, tell them you heard I was going to rehab in Paris, and I left last week by private jet."

"All right." Miriam opened the junk cabinet and searched around in the chips and candy bags his father kept in there. "Your dad bought those nasty pork rinds you both like."

"I love how he drinks kosher wine and eats pork rinds."

Miriam smiled, fully this time, and the wrinkles around her eyes hurt his heart. "Me too. Here." She tossed the bag his way. "Eat those and help him out."

Nicky wasn't a big fan of pork rinds anymore. He'd eaten so many during his first years out of the Blumfeld household that he'd burned out on them. But he opened them anyway and ate several, enjoying their saltiness for what it was worth, especially next to the delicious, fresh sandwich.

"Well, then, what are your plans for your time here?"

A squirmy desire not to be pinned down wriggled through him. "What do you mean?"

Miriam leaned against the counter on her elbows, looking up at him meaningfully. "I just mean if you're going to get and stay sober, don't you think you should keep busy?"

She had a good point. "I noticed the steps down to the dock are looking pretty rickety. Maybe I could fix them up a little."

Miriam nodded. "That would be wonderful. Your father can't do things like that anymore. We'd planned to ask Jenny Renfroe's son Joey—he's a contractor—over to do it this summer, but if you feel up to it…?"

"Yeah. Of course. Once I get some rest, I'll get started on it. I'd like to feel useful."

"Are you going to see Jazz while you're in town?" His mother's voice sounded purposely offhand, but there was something else there. Like she was feeling him out. Had she always been this way? Or was this new? "He's doing some great things for the community."

"Of course he is." He hadn't intended it to sound so bitter.

Miriam shot him an appraising glance.

Nicky shrugged. "I saw him already."

The plate his mother grabbed from the cabinet for her own sandwich clattered on the counter. "You did?"

"I stopped by his church. He's as arrogant as ever."

"Oh, Nicky. You can't mean that. You two were like brothers. Closer even."

It was true. Once Jazz had been in him so deep he'd let himself believe they'd never be fully pulled apart.

"That was a long time ago. He's changed."

He hadn't changed. Jazz was the same old hero-complexed, do-gooding, lover-of-mankind that Nicky had always known. It was just that seeing Jazz in the flesh again made him feel like dying.

He should have gone to rehab with Mick or taken off for that Los Angeles celebrity "health spa" with Sez. But, no, he'd seen that goddamn magazine cover, and it'd been a beacon calling him home.

Remembering Jazz's face in the photograph and the sound of his voice in the confessional, he swallowed hard. Maybe he was wrong. Maybe a few Masses would do him good.

"Oh, that's nonsense and you know it." Miriam eyed him a moment. "He's running a fantastic facility for homeless LGBTQ teenagers. Blue Oasis."

Nicky's head snapped up. "Blue Oasis?"

"Yes, they're providing food, shelter, and education for homeless LGBTQ youth. Maybe you'd like to look into opportunities there? Sometimes the best medicine is helping someone else." She looked cautious again, like she was afraid she'd overstepped.

"Maybe. I'll look into that."

Blue Oasis. Nicky bet Jazz didn't even expect anyone to get the reference. Why would he? It was an old song. The first one he'd written about Jazz once they'd become lovers. It was the only love song he'd ever written that'd been full of possibility and joy. He'd penned it a few months before that summer they'd been forced apart. The dream of a blue oasis for the two of them. Forever safe. Forever in love.

There was a buzzing noise from the laundry room.

"Oh, I'll be right back, sweetie. I need to get the clothes out of the dryer before they wrinkle." She grabbed a pear and a banana from the fruit bowl and put them next to his plate. "Eat those too."

He watched her dark head disappear around the corner and when he was sure she was occupied with the laundry, he turned to the Bible and flipped it to Jeremiah 29:11.

"For I know the plans I have for you," declares the Lord, "plans to prosper you and not to harm you, plans to give you hope and a future."

He slammed the book shut and pushed it across the counter.

Chapter Four

JASPER RAN ALONG the Androscoggin River, lungs filling with the cool morning air as the sun rose over Little Bay and the Atlantic Ocean beyond it. A single kayaker cut almost soundlessly through the water, and Jasper shared a brief moment of peaceful solitude with the stranger before they went their opposite ways.

He ran under the shade of trees that had been bare not so long ago. They would glow from gold to red again in no time, but they were currently a succulent green that made it hard to believe they'd ever be anything else.

By the time he turned away from the river, the town had come alive. A few early shoppers nodded at him as he passed. It'd taken some time after Jasper had replaced his predecessor for his parishioners to get used to seeing their priest jogging through the streets three mornings a week.

Just like they were now used to the old schoolhouse being revived by a bunch of vibrant, wonderful, rejected kids desperately in need of a home.

Jasper checked his watch. Nearly eight o'clock. He'd have time for a quick shower and breakfast before he needed to meet Lizzie.

He ran all the way into his house—he'd drawn the line at stretching outside after it'd taken him an embarrassingly long time to realize the same bunch of teenage girls happened to *coincidentally* wander by whenever he returned from a run. As he tried to catch his breath in the kitchen he moved through a few sun salutations, warrior poses, and other stretches, then took the stairs to his bathroom on shaking legs.

He was about to turn the shower on when his phone rang. Bishop Murray's mildly surprised face lit up the screen and Jasper grinned as he always did when he remembered taking the snapshot.

"Thomas," Jasper said, pressing the phone to his ear. "This is unexpectedly early for you."

"I've done my time getting out of bed before dawn, Jasper. When you're almost seventy, you can sleep in every once in a while too."

"This must be a special occasion, then." Jasper's reflection smiled back at him but it slowly turned serious when silence fell and it lengthened. "Thomas? Everything all right?"

Bishop Thomas Murray had been Jasper's mentor from the very beginning. He'd been Little Heights' priest before Jasper had received his calling, so he'd been the first to advise Jasper on the path he'd taken in the end.

A deep sigh reverberated over the phone. "The archbishop called me about the article on the youth center in *The Atlantic*."

"Okay…" Jasper turned away from the mirror and switched on the shower so the water could warm. He stepped into his bedroom and closed the bathroom door behind him. "I haven't seen it yet." A copy sat waiting for him in his mail, but he hadn't looked at it. "You approved it though, didn't you? Was there a problem with it?"

"The article itself, no. But apparently the photographs that weren't published were leaked last night and other, let's say less reputable magazines and websites, have taken on the article and they're using photographs I hadn't approved."

"Oh." Jasper frowned. "What's wrong with them?"

"You didn't see any of them at the time of the shoot?"

"No. That whole photoshoot is blur. I can't really remember much about it, but I can't imagine I did anything inappropriate."

Thomas sighed. "Let's just say they drew the exact kind of attention from higher up I've been telling you to avoid."

"Attention? What kind of attention? The archbishop said yes to the whole idea of the article. He thought it would be good publicity for the Catholic Church and show how they're adjusting to the times. Standing up for the rights of all God's children, although I have my own thoughts on his motivations. I'm not going to hide—"

"No, I know that," Thomas interrupted. "And I would never ask you to. But you know you've gotten away with this much because Blue Oasis has always flown under the radar, so to speak. And now the whole country is watching. And offering opinions."

"So that's what it's about." Jasper gritted his teeth and very carefully didn't think any uncharitable thoughts. It wasn't Thomas's fault.

"Listen, maybe you and I could talk about this face-to-face sometime soon. Does Irena still make those amazing whoopie pies?"

Jasper brightened. "Does she ever. I'm free this morning. Eleven o'clock? I'll have that tea ready you like so much."

"And I'll stop by Irena's to get the pies. See you later, Jasper. The Lord be with you."

Jasper ducked his head and smiled. Over fifteen years they'd known each other now and not once had Thomas dropped the formal goodbye. "And with you," he softly said and ended the call. It wasn't good news that Blue Oasis found itself in the scrutinizing eye of the archbishop, but Jasper wasn't going to worry about that. Right now Lizzie needed him and he was going to be there for her.

The social worker who accompanied Lizzie was someone Jasper hadn't worked with before. The guy looked in his fifties, overworked and underfed. He held the door for Lizzie and then walked up to Jasper's desk to shake hands.

"Father Hendricks, it's nice to finally meet you. I'm Brendan Jones from the State of Maine Department of Health and Human Services. I hear you've met Lizzie already." He let go of Jasper's hand and gestured her forward. She was wearing a different baggy sweater with a pair of faded jeans that were ripped at the knees—and not the kind of rips meant as a fashion statement.

A small bag trailed behind her and Jasper's heart ached like it always did. These kids never came with a lot of possessions. In foster care, loving things only meant they'd be used as ammunition for bullying.

Working her hand free of her sweater, Lizzie reached to take Jasper's and smiled shyly. She had very short, curly hair and wide eyes with irises almost as brown as her skin.

"How did it go with Lucas yesterday, Lizzie?"

She ducked her head and grinned a little bashfully. "It was fun. I'm going again next Sunday. He's nice."

Oh dear. "I'm glad to hear it. Why don't you two take a seat while we go over everything. Mrs. Wells will be here in half an hour to show you around, Lizzie." And then he'd talk privately with Brendan while they were out of earshot.

Jasper signed all the necessary paperwork while Lizzie tried not to look bored. He always felt bad during this part of the process, as if the kids were a possession handed over from one pair of hands to the next. He hoped this would be her last stop.

Brendan must've been thinking along the same lines because he asked, "What happens when she turns eighteen?"

"Well, hopefully we'll be job hunting and house hunting, or applying to different colleges by then. It depends on what Lizzie wants to do." Jasper smiled at her but she looked unsure. He knew it didn't always work out that way, but Jasper had to hope. Sometimes it was all he had. "And I actually have a proposal ready to send to the archbishop. I'm hoping to expand Blue Oasis so the kids have somewhere to stay after they turn eighteen. Cheap housing in case they want to go to the community college, or at least a fixed address during the job application process."

Brendan was nodding. "That would be enormously helpful. It'd save a lot of trouble." And prevent undoing some of the work that took years to accomplish. He didn't have to say it. Jasper knew all too well.

A shadow appeared at the frosted glass door and a firm, rapid knock betrayed who it was. Jasper winked at Lizzie. Rising to his feet, he called, "Come in, Mrs. Wells." He reached the door as she stepped inside. Mrs. Wells was a good foot shorter than him and yet she always gave him that I-forgot-my-homework feeling for a minute whenever he saw her. She was heavier around the hips than shoulders, and wore her hair in a tight bun at the nape of her neck. He remembered the thick curls used to be a rich brown color, but they'd gone dark and grey over the years.

"Lizzie, this is Mrs. Wells. She's the one who's really in charge of Blue Oasis." He grinned at her. "And she used to be my teacher. Mrs. Wells lives on the premises, so she'll show you to your room, explain the rules of the house, and help you get settled."

"Do you teach the kids here, Mrs. Wells?" Brendan asked as he shook her hand.

"I've homeschooled a few, but most of them attend local schools once they get settled in. I'll do an assessment with Lizzie when she feels a little more at home. Once the new school year begins, we can decide what she'd like to do."

"I just want to go to school like normal," Lizzie said, her chin lifting for the first time since she walked in.

"That's a very good start," Mrs. Wells said, placing a hand on Lizzie's shoulder. She looked at Jasper. "Are you done here, Father Hendricks? Or do you need her a little longer?"

"No, I can always talk to her later if I need to. We're still on for Bible study this afternoon?"

Lizzie wrinkled her nose before she could stop herself. "Bible study?"

Jasper suppressed a laugh. "We still call it that, although we don't really study the Bible anymore. It's more of a group session to get everyone together, and we either talk or play games, or do something else along those lines. I try to join whenever I can, but usually it's Mrs. Wells and Andrew, the deacon, who run it."

"He calls it Bible study to keep his superiors happy," Mrs. Wells said, and Lizzie laughed.

"I'd like to see Lizzie's room too, if you don't mind," Brendan said. "I've never been here before and I have to say, Father, you're somewhat of a legend in the LGBTQ foster community. I can be right back if you need me."

"Take your time." Jasper opened the door and they all filed through. When Mrs. Wells passed by, she pushed something into his chest.

"You might want to take a look at this," she said under her breath. "And check your work e-mail when you have the chance."

"Oh." He automatically clasped his hand around the glossy pages of a trashy magazine. "I will, thank you."

When he closed the door again he lifted the magazine to look at the cover and startled to see his own face on it. He remembered the exact moment when that picture was taken. He'd felt like a complete idiot at the time with the rosary beads hanging off one hand and a scrunched up Pride flag held tight in his other fist. It'd been a spur of the moment idea of the photographer and he'd never in a million years thought they'd use it.

In itself the picture was harmless, but with the black cassock and the white strip of clerical collar, he looked provocative. It didn't help that they'd caught him with his lips parted and his eyes half-lidded. Jasper winced a little. Suddenly he didn't feel all that eager to check his work e-mail after all.

Brendan returned after fifteen minutes and he looked radiant. "You're doing great work here, Father. I have to say, it took a lot to convince Lizzie that this would be a good place for her. From what I can make out, she had to deal with quite a few Bible thumpers—excuse the phrase—in prior placements. Especially with regards to her being trans."

"I don't doubt it," Jasper said, indicating for Brendan to take a seat again. "She won't come across any of that here. All religions—or none—are welcome, and while I invite them to come to church on Sundays, it's not a requirement. We also keep a very close eye to make sure there's no sign of any bullying, but we've never had much trouble with it. I like to think it's because the kids want to be here."

"I'm sure they do."

"All right. On to the difficult part of this, then." Jasper opened Lizzie's file again. "Any signs of physical abuse?"

Brendan set a pair of half-moon spectacles on his nose and opened his own file.

"Not that we're aware. There was one incident at the very beginning. His—her first foster home, I believe. The social worker noted a black eye and bruised cheek during a checkup, but all parties involved claimed high and low she'd been hit in the face with a soccer ball. We have proof the foster mother followed up with a doctor's visit, but there was never a report made from the school about an incident. They asked for her to be transferred a month later based on 'behavioral issues.' That's usually the excuse they use." He glanced at Jasper over the rim of his glasses. "You've met Lizzie. She has as many behavioral issues as you and me."

Jasper nodded. It was always 'behavioral issues' that brought the queer kids here in the end. "Emotional abuse?"

"I think there's been plenty of that, yes. Especially, like I said, from the more religious families. If I were you, I wouldn't push any kind of real Bible study on her because she might get nervous. From what we've seen so far, she's not a flight risk, but you never know what can push some of these kids over the edge."

A little pang made itself felt in Jasper's chest. "No. We never know what can push anyone over the edge. Do you think she needs therapy?"

"Nothing beyond the usual. You still have an independent counselor who comes in and talks to these kids once a month?"

"Yes." It wasn't conventional therapy by any means but it worked for them. And Mrs. Wells and he were on top of things enough that they recognized early warning signs of anyone who might need more intensive counseling. If there had been any indication of serious abuse in Lizzie's case, Jasper would've made arrangements, but he thought it might be wise to wait and see. "They're not obliged to talk individually every time, but we strongly encourage it. We have one group therapy session a month too." Jasper grinned. "It usually ends up as a giant food fest, but I think it's a good bonding experience."

"I think it's extraordinary," Brendan said. "We'd have a lot less kids being shuffled around if everyone went at it with the dedication you do. I wish you could take more kids."

"I'm working on it."

"Well, if you don't have any more questions, I'd like to say goodbye to Lizzie and I'll contact you a week from now to see how she's doing."

"Sounds good." Jasper stood and reached for Brendan's hand. Somewhere above them a door banged, plumbing creaked and groaned, and laughter drifted down. The building brimmed with warmth and quiet happiness, and Jasper's heart swelled. "We'll take good care of her."

"I'm counting on it, Father. He's a special boy. I mean, girl." Brendan flushed.

"You're trying. That's better than most people do."

MORNING ROSE SWEETLY, like a long overdue vacation, the day after Nicky's arrival home. It was peaceful, quiet, and full of nothing much he needed to do. He lingered a long time under the blue-and-white striped comforter in his parents' guest room, staring calmly out the window at the large maple tree just outside. If he held very still, until all he heard was his heartbeat and breath, he could almost make out a song in the silver and green way the leaves rustled in the breeze up from the cove. He sighed, letting himself not-think for the first time in ages, as the sun poured white and clean across the room.

It couldn't last, though. Perfect things never did.

First, his father knocked on his door to let him know he should get up because his mother wanted them to eat breakfast with her before they headed into town to buy wood for the dock. Then the call of nature forced him into the bathroom. At that point, his brain kicked on, supplying him with the short list of imperatives to start his day: meds, vitamins, food. So he made his way downstairs and powered on his cell phone as he crossed the living room.

"Morning, Mom," he murmured as he dropped onto a stool at the counter.

"Good morning, sweetie. Did you sleep okay?" Miriam asked, already in the middle of preparing breakfast.

"Yeah," he answered as he watched the little rotating dots on his phone, hoping there weren't too many messages from people he despised. "I slept great actually."

For the first time in years, he hadn't woken in the night. He doubted it would become a regular thing, but he took it as a sign that he was right to have come home after all, despite the memories, and despite Jazz.

Miriam disappeared into the walk-in pantry and returned with the electric griddle just as his phone woke up. The bing-bing-bing announcing new texts and missed calls went on and on. Nicky didn't even want to look.

"Well, aren't you popular," Miriam said, winking at him.

"Not really. More like in demand." He scratched his thumb along his eyebrow as he reluctantly pulled up a list of the alerts. There were three texts from Ramona letting him know that Mick and Sez were supposedly doing well and asking if he was okay. He was grateful for those, but seeing all the missed calls from his management made him anxious enough to crawl back into bed. Which he'd do if his mother wasn't eyeing him while she counted out eggs.

As he thumbed in a short reply to Ramona, his phone lit up with an incoming call. The area code was Los Angeles, and the picture on the screen was T.J. Danvers'. Late-twenties and handsome in a fleshy sort of way, Danvers wasn't at the top of their management team, but he wasn't completely powerless either. He was the friendly asshole the suits at the top enlisted to deliver their threats. Nicky hated him; always had. And yet, for some reason, he found himself taking the call.

"Nico, baby, how are you doing?"

"I'm alive."

"And wasn't that a close call there for a while?" Danvers laughed like that was actually funny.

Nicky's stomach knotted. "Yeah, that's hilarious."

"Nico, my man. I've been worried about you. I just wanted to check in. See how you're doing."

"Whatever. Skip the bullshit. Why the fuck are you really calling?"

Miriam glanced over at him and concern crinkled her brow.

"What? I can't check on my boys?" Danvers chuckled and Nicky snarled. If the asshole was in the same room, he'd punch him out flat. He'd always wondered if Harry acted on Danvers' orders whenever he'd fed Nicky coke so he could perform. Though, in the end, he supposed it didn't matter if it came from Danvers or not. The suits were all the same.

Danvers went on. "You guys are important to me."

"Important to your wallet maybe."

Danvers ignored that. "So talk to me. How are you feeling?"

Rage prickling his skin, Nicky rose and moved to stand by the living room window. He gazed out at the water glittering in the mid-morning sun and tried to remember that he was safe. He was home and he was safe. For now, anyway.

"Listen, there are a fuck-ton of messages on my phone from you. I'm on medical leave, asshole, so if you're bothering me right now it better be for something fucking urgent."

His mother broke eggs into the pancake batter and tsked at him for his language.

Danvers cleared his throat, his voice going rigid with tension. "Now, obviously I don't want to put any pressure on you boys—"

"Of course you don't."

"It's just that the higher ups don't understand the delay on the next album."

Nicky's vision went dark with anger, and he rubbed his eyes. "What don't they fucking understand? We collapsed out there. I almost died." His mother gasped behind him. Fuck, he hadn't meant to say that. "Sez overdosed. Mick fried his fucking brains on the coke your team pushed into us. Your endless motherfucking tour nearly killed the whole goddamn band, got it?"

"You exaggerate—"

"No. We're getting treatment. You fucking know it takes time for full-blown addicts to get fucking sober. And we're going to take that time, you fucking asshole, so that when we get back to it we can make some goddamn music. What the fuck don't you fuckers get about that?"

"Calm down, now. Calm down." Danvers simpered. "Well, you know how they are. They expect Vespertine back in the studio on July first."

"July first? Are you fucking shitting me right now?"

Danvers went on like he'd said nothing untoward, "Sure. They're damn keen on you all working hard this summer. They're gagging for that new album. They know you've got some hits still in you, Nico. They want to push it through as a Christmas release."

"Tell them to go suck their own cocks."

"Nicholas Blumfeld..." Miriam waved her batter-covered spoon at him.

Nicky squeezed his eyes closed and pinched the bridge of his nose.

"Nico, don't get your dick in a twist, kid."

Nico glared out at the rippling water in the cove. Danvers was at least six years younger than him and he could take his 'kid' and shove it, as far as Nicky was concerned.

"I'm not saying you need to report to the studio this week, for fuck's sake. We're just trying to feel you guys out. Test the waters. Mick's facility will release him in four weeks if we put a little pressure—"

"Sure! Why not?" Nicky tore at his hair, pacing by the window. "Because why bother getting Mick fucking sober when you can get him just fucking sober enough, right?"

"Nico, we care about—"

He kept pacing because otherwise he would put a hole in the wall. "What does the goddamned 'health spa' Sez is holed up in say? How much are you going to fucking pay them so they'll send him on out into the big bad world with a month's scrip for some maintenance drug and a fucking pat on his ass?"

"I get it. You guys want a little more time. I smell what you're selling, Nico. I'll just need to see what the suits upstairs—"

"No, you think we're idiots, don't you?" Nicky pounded his fist on the wall next to the window. "We're not. Fuck this bullshit. I'm calling the bluff."

"What bluff, kid?"

"If they wanted another shitty album like they got last time, they wouldn't have insisted we all get sober in the first place."

"Sure your last two albums haven't sold as well, but Nico, you're still under contract—"

Nicky hung up. He powered the phone off and threw it across the living room onto the sofa. He wished it could have been through the window. The smash would have been fucking satisfying as hell. He never should have turned the damn thing back on in the first place.

Note to self: avoid phone.

Miriam's calm voice broke into his stormy thoughts. "I'd appreciate it if you refrained from language like that around me. You can be a foul-mouthed rock star anywhere else in the world, but here in my home you can speak like a civilized person."

Nicky snorted, rubbing a hand over his bedhead. He took a slow breath, his anger already cooling under his mother's steady, warm gaze.

"I'll try. But I can't promise anything, Mom. Especially if I'm talking to those fu—jerks." He'd already given up his worst vices. Did he really have to give up some harmless cursing too?

"Well," Miriam said with a smirk. "Everyone has to throw an f-bomb now and again, but somehow you make a whole fucking conversation of it. Fuck loses its meaning if you say it every other fucking sentence." She grinned at his surprise. "See? It's powerful when used fucking sparingly."

"I smell what you're selling," Nicky mumbled, copying Danvers' juvenile acknowledgement. He slumped down at the kitchen table and tried to keep his mind from spinning back to the phone call. He scratched at his right arm, leaving white marks over his second-largest tattoo—a floral sleeve made up of forget-me-nots, cornflowers, and violets.

"That's a pretty one," Miriam said. "How'd you choose it?"

Nicky appreciated that she was trying to accept his tattoos. He almost hated to tell her the truth. "Sez and I got into a really dumb fight. We were kind of high and really drunk..." He trailed off, feeling his throat go dry at the admission, like he was a kid she might punish with a nice long grounding. He almost wished he was because then he'd stand a chance at this sobriety gig.

She looked at him with a placid, warm expression, and he cleared his throat to go on. He knew it couldn't be easy for her to accept that he was an addict, and he was proud of her for not flinching. "Anyway, Sez said that men with flower tattoos were all flaming queers."

Miriam frowned. "Does your lead singer not accept you, Nicky?"

"Given the cock he sucked this year, I think he's fine." He cleared his throat again, heat rising in his cheeks. "Uh, I mean given the, uh, oral sex?"

Miriam shook her spoon at him again. "Enough, silly boy. On with the story."

"Well, I decided to get a flower sleeve to prove him wrong. I wanted to show him once and for all that having flower tats doesn't mean you're a fag."

She stared at him.

"I know. I don't know either. Like I said, we were high." He cracked up and shrugged. "Drugs are bad things, Mom."

"They are."

"Sez, though, he got a big sleeve of a jungle cat surrounded by skulls to prove that he was totally not a queer. But, you know what? It somehow turned out a hell of a lot gayer than my cornflowers and forget-me-nots."

"Sweetie…I don't even know what to say about that story."

Nicky chuckled. "Me either. It has a happy ending, though. Sez admitted that a dude could be tough despite a flower tattoo."

He'd actually said "tough and pretty." It was a description Nicky heard a lot about himself. Magazines especially liked to describe him as a pretty little bad boy, because, while he wasn't anywhere near as small as Miriam, he was still shorter, more lithe, and finer boned than the other guys in the band.

Miriam laughed softly, and Nicky rubbed his fingers over the scratch marks until they faded, leaving unblemished bright blue and violet behind. He carefully kept his arm rolled in, though, so his mother wouldn't see the scars and healing track marks there.

"I usually just say I got the blue flowers because of, you know—Nico Blue."

She shook her head and went back to the pancake batter. "Okay, go ahead and break your mother's heart all at once. How many tattoos do you have?"

Nicky laughed. "A lot."

She nodded and began ladling the batter onto the griddle. "Five? Twenty-five?"

"I lost count."

"Silly boy." She rolled her eyes and waved her hand at him, dismissing his comment as foolishness, and Nicky yawned and stretched. "Fifty?"

"Ten. My lucky number."

He stood and headed across the room, grabbing his father's Takamine acoustic guitar resting on the side of the sofa where he'd left it the night before. It was the instrument he'd learned on, and he was grateful to have it in his hands. His mother's piano in the fancy living room next to the dining room was also calling to him, but nothing beat the soothing portability of a guitar.

Testing the tuning, his mind went to his babies—the thirty-eight guitars back in his rental house in Santa Monica. His lease was running out this fall on the three-bedroom Spanish Colonial Revival home he'd rented for the past five years. He'd put off making any decision about whether or not to renew until after the tour. He didn't love the house, but he didn't hate it either. Its main attractions when he'd taken it had been the guarded, gated neighborhood and the private back yard. But he'd used a lot of drugs there, shot a lot of heroin, fucked a lot of guys and snorted a lot of coke. Just thinking about going back there made him feel ashamed and sick to his stomach. When he was well, he needed to figure out what to do with the house and everything in it.

But first he needed to decide how he wanted to live. His stomach tensed, and he let those thoughts slide right out of his mind along with all the residual anger from the phone call. That was all too much to deal with right now. Instead, he'd play guitar until the pancakes were done, and then he'd figure out what to do with the rest of his day.

He sat back down at the table, shoving out far enough that he could play easily. He didn't think about it, just let the fingers of his left hand press down on the strings and the fingers of his right pick out the notes that lived somewhere inside him and always had.

Miriam sighed tenderly. "I remember you were only three when you climbed up on my piano bench and started playing like you'd been born knowing how."

"You always make it sound like I plunked my tiny butt down and played a concerto."

Miriam laughed. "Oh, heavens, no. I guess I do, don't I? I'm just so proud of you, Nicky."

He swallowed and looked away from the back of her dark head and her small shoulders. *Was she really? Why?*

"But no, it wasn't a concerto. It was amazing, though. You sat there and poked at the keys again and again, like you were memorizing them." Her smile was dreamy and far away. "Then you used your fat little fingers to plunk out something that, hand to God, sounded like the kind of thing you'd hear on the radio."

"So, three or four chords over and over, basically?"

Miriam chuckled. "I honestly don't remember. But you were obsessed after that. Until Jazz's family moved in next door, and the two of you got close, that piano was your best friend. You spent hours every day with it."

Nicky smiled a little bit at hearing his mom call the local priest *Jazz* again. Apparently old habits did die hard. He changed from picking to strumming and watched as Miriam stacked the pancakes and turned off the electric griddle before pulling out plates. He should ask if he could help, but being doted on was too good to let go of yet, so he let her do the work for now. He suspected she liked doing it for him anyway.

"It looks like your dad is taking his usual ninety-minute shower," Miriam said, laying plates at each of their traditional spots. "Oh, and here. I got this out of your car this morning." She grabbed Nicky's black leather backpack from the cubby by the back door and placed it on the table in front of him. "I thought you might need it?" She nodded toward the small flesh-colored patch on his left bicep.

Nicky slid the guitar down to lean against his leg and then opened his haul of medication and vitamins. Aside from his wallet, it was all he'd had on him when he'd left the private detox facility he, Sez, and Mick had been dropped off at forty-five minutes after their last show.

It'd been a fast exit from Red Rocks. Management had arranged roadies as decoys and sent them along with Ramona back to their hotel to keep the paparazzi off their asses. Then the three of them had been hustled into a nondescript sedan and onto a chartered jet. It'd been explained to them in no uncertain terms what was expected: get sober, get sane enough to work, then make a fucking hit record, or face the consequences.

Nicky wondered what those consequences looked like. After all, he'd never been one to back away from a bad choice.

When he'd arrived at the detox clinic, he'd still been wearing the sweat-slick leather pants he'd had on for weeks. It was a blur after that, though they'd started him on the maintenance medication right away to keep the DTs from being too brutal. Then, once the three of them were stable, detoxed, and hooked up with some L.A.-based drug counselors, they'd been burped back out again into the waiting arms of their management. And Ramona. Who'd somehow been the only one to think to bring them all fresh clothes and small backpacks for the array of pill bottles they'd need to collect from the facility's private pharmacy. From there they'd gone their separate ways, with Sez going to his 'health spa,' Mick to a full-on rehab unit, and Nicky, well, he'd chosen to come home.

He should give Ramona an actual call later. He wondered what she was up to while her bandmates tried to get their shit together. Probably fending off other bands' attempts to poach her. Though he didn't know why she bothered with loyalty. She'd be better off, probably, with another group with members who were far less fucked up than them.

"So, that conversation with your management seemed tense," Miriam said eventually.

"Yep."

"Are they wanting you to go back to L.A.?" She was trying to sound nonchalant, but Nicky could read the tension in her shoulders saying what a bad idea she thought going back to L.A. would be.

"Yeah. They want us to start on the next album as soon as possible." Nicky sorted through the vitamins and medications again. Eight bottles and one box of patches.

"Are you going to go?"

Had it *sounded* like he was going to go? But he didn't say that. "No. We don't even have any songs. Usually we write more on the road while touring the prior album, but this time…" He shrugged. This time they'd all been too deep into their favorite powders and pills to accomplish anything more than the show itself and then maybe some intense, self-destructive, recreational fucking.

Miriam put the plate of pancakes into the oven to keep them warm for his father. "Do you want bacon or eggs? Or both?"

"Just eggs." Bacon reminded him of breakfast on the road. He'd eaten it every day, groggy and hungover, already jonesing for more dope. He sighed as he uncapped his antidepressant and shook the white pill into his hand. He realized with a pang that he might never want to eat bacon again. It was even possible that eating it would make him want to use.

"Fucking sucks," he breathed, reaching for the bottle of Vitamin C.

"What fucking sucks, sweetie?"

Nicky smirked at her. "You're going to give me hives saying that word, Mom."

"We'll have hives together then," she said, as she grabbed the orange juice from the fridge and placed it on the counter by the stove. "The family that curses together stays together. We can convince your father to join us. We'll curse up a storm all over town and people will say, 'Those Blumfelds are the parents of a rock star, you know. They have to curse. It's in the rock star rules."

"Okay, okay, you're not that funny." But he grinned at her, because she kind of was. Why had she annoyed him so much when he was younger? She was charming, really. "I'll put a hold on the f-bombs."

"But you never answered my question about what sucks."

Nicky lined up his pills by color, and Miriam anticipated his next need by bringing him a tall glass of cool water from the pitcher. "It's pretty self-explanatory," he said, motioning at his lineup. "Being a junkie. Needing all this stuff. Though, really, it's just this—" he touched the antidepressant and then the flat package containing his maintenance patch, "—and this that I really need, I guess. The rest is just supposed to make me feel like I'm getting healthy."

"What do they do?"

"The antidepressant is possibly temporary while I cope with everything." He didn't tell her it wasn't just about that, though. "It's not a serotonin reuptake inhibitor. It directly affects dopamine, which gives me a little more drive than other antidepressants might." And it offset the potential sexual side effects of his other prescription.

"My maintenance medication." He touched the package with his daily patches and pulled a fresh one out. "It's a new, experimental drug delivered in patch form, and it's a junkie's best friend. There was a predecessor by a similar name that worked best as a pill, but the patch is a new delivery system. It's supposed to make it all more stable. They're even looking into a subdermal possibility for the future. I wouldn't be opposed to it. So far, I'm lucky I don't seem to have any of the negative side effects."

"A maintenance drug?"

"Yeah. It, uh, keeps me from craving street drugs." As much. There were definitely psychological triggers that made him go weak with need for a needle and spoon. But the underlying physical craving was masked by the prescription drug. "And if I did give in and shoot up—"

Miriam bit her lower lip and her eyes went glossy with tears, but he tried to go on as if he wasn't saying anything he should be ashamed of. He wasn't going to lie about what he'd done and he wasn't going to let it hold him back from getting well. Not this time.

"If I did shoot up, there's a secondary agent built into this medication that would make me violently ill." He waggled his eyebrows. "So, yippee. No heroin high for me."

He scraped the prior day's patch off his left arm and folded it carefully so that the side with medication on it didn't touch the table. He fumbled the fresh packet and dropped it. It slid across the wood floor and stopped by the patio door's shoe trunk. He pushed his chair back to go retrieve it, but Miriam darted around the counter with a soapy, wet hand towel in one hand. "Here, sweetie, let me."

She grabbed the packet and knelt down beside him. She ignored his outstretched hand, using the towel to clean the area on his arm where the old patch had been, and then dried his skin with a still-dry corner. She peeled the slick paper back from the edges of the patch.

"Don't get any on your hands," Nicky murmured, turning to give her his right arm. He was supposed to switch arms every day. "It doesn't get me high at all. It just makes me feel normal. But you'd be higher than you've ever been before."

"How do you know? I had my wild days when I was young."

"*Mom*," Nicky said seriously.

"I know, sweetie," she whispered, all joking gone as she pressed the patch against his skin and rubbed the back of it until she was sure it would stick. Then she stood, kissed his forehead, and said, "Eggs coming right up. We'll go ahead and eat them even if your father is still trying to turn himself into a human prune. Nothing's worse than rubbery eggs."

Nicky positioned the guitar again and began picking the strings, the old Jann Arden song coming to him easily. He hummed the vocal melody under his breath. He didn't have a great voice, which was why Sez was even in the band, but it was serviceable, and he closed his eyes, merging emotion and melody. The sound came through clearly, though he didn't give any thought to the lyrics.

"I've always loved this song," Miriam said.

He opened his eyes again and continued on, watching as she cracked a few eggs into a clean bowl. But when he reached the chorus, still wordlessly humming, she stopped and turned to face him. "Thank you," she murmured, eyes glistening, and then she went back to scrambling the yolks and whites with determination.

Nicky puzzled for a moment over just what she was thanking him for. Then a lump rose in his throat as he finished out the last notes of "Good Mother."

V

Chapter Five

HIS FATHER'S OLD work truck rattled along Letterhead Pike, and they left the windows down to cool the cab. That morning his dad had told him that the air conditioner had broken a while back, but he'd been too distracted with work to worry about it. He usually drove his BMW and only used the truck for projects like this one. Nicky decided to have a look at the AC later. He'd learned a few things about electronics on the road in the early days of Vespertine, fixing up broken amps and shitty PA systems. Maybe it was just some faulty wiring.

"Your mother says I'm too old for projects now, but I'm only sixty-five. My father was building boats with his own hands when he was ninety-five."

"He died when he was eighty, Dad."

"Well, maybe he was only seventy-five then." Adrian winked at him. "But either way, he was older than me."

"But Grandpa did physical labor his whole life. You sit at a desk all day."

Adrian gawped at him. "Are you calling your old man fat?"

"Out of shape." Nicky glanced over at Adrian's round belly.

"Speak for yourself."

Nicky shrugged. It was true. He was weak, skinny, and definitely out of shape. Playing a show was a workout, but being a malnourished junkie overrode everything else. He hadn't really tested himself yet, but he could feel that he lacked strength and stamina. He couldn't play a show right now to save his life. Before, he'd been super-powered by coke. Now he was just...human.

The scary thing was, he had no idea what a sober life looked like. He'd been lost down the rabbit hole of the music industry for so long. How did people just...live regular lives? How did they manage the day-in and day-out? How did they create and sustain relationships that were about more than drugs and fucking? Nicky had no clue.

He had the band, at least. That was something. The band and music itself. Well, if he hadn't completely cauterized the flow of it with all the drug abuse.

"Penny for your thoughts."

Nicky smiled and rubbed a hand through his hair. In the summer humidity his dark hair bounced with waves he'd inherited from someone, somewhere—maybe the bitch who'd put him in the dumpster, or maybe the sperm donor who'd knocked her up. He'd never know.

His dad waited patiently for his answer. In the past, Nicky might have lied, but he decided to try the "talking about your problems" thing his addiction counselor had suggested. "I was thinking about my career. I got a call from Vespertine's management this morning."

"Your mother says they're pressuring you to get back to work." Adrian's hands gripped the wheel harder.

"Yeah." Birds twittered in the trees along the always-quiet street, and the breeze from the bay poured through the open windows like a cool touch over his hot neck and ghostly fingers in his hair. He shivered. "It's only going to get worse until we cave in and do what they want."

His father glanced over. "I thought you said they were the ones who insisted you guys get well in the first place."

"Yeah. They want us sober enough to make a number-one album. But they want us *high* enough that they can control us." Nicky swallowed and looked out the window at the trees flashing by and the sun glinting on the blue bay. "They give us the drugs, you know. We don't even have to buy them. They just...hand them over, or get someone on the road to do it."

Adrian frowned. "If I could turn back time, I'd have never let you go to L.A."

If Nicky could turn back time…wow, what a curious thought. In all the years since Jazz left him, he'd done plenty of numbing out, plenty of blaming and casting recriminations, but he'd never asked himself what, if given the chance, *he* might have done differently.

He took a moment to consider it now. Of all the things he'd experienced, all the places he'd been, the people he'd met and fucked and the drugs he'd done, there wasn't one he wouldn't trade in for a different, better life. Nicky thought about the albums the band had made. There were only two he was proud of. The rest were evidence.

"Not that we aren't proud of you, Nicky. You've done so much, written some beautiful songs, and your fans love you." Adrian chuckled. "The weird people who manage to find us now and again prove that."

That was the first Nicky had heard of fans harassing his parents. "What do you mean 'weird people who find you'?"

Adrian shrugged like what he described next was a fairly common event for them. "Well, we had these teenage girls show up one day claiming they'd driven all the way from Memphis, Tennessee. They asked if they could touch your pillow."

"Christ."

Adrian grinned. "Oh, use that curse word when you're with your mom. As a Jew, she can't complain about *it*, can she?" Adrian chuckled.

Nicky wasn't going to be sidetracked. "So what happened? Tell me you called the police."

"Well, no. Miriam went up to your old bedroom, brought down your pillow and held it out the front door. They screamed and burst into tears." Adrian laughed, his cheeks flushing with amusement above his beard line. "They ran off with it. Lunatics. But they were awfully cute little girls. Probably seventeen or eighteen, tops. I hope their mothers knew where they were." Adrian's tone went pensive. "I'd have gone after them to make sure they were all right, but teenagers run damn fast and they had a car." He laughed again.

"Mom shouldn't do that, Dad. They'll just come back for more."

"Well, that was three years ago and *they* never came back." Adrian's mouth twisted into a grimace. "We had a creepy guy once, though. We did call the cops on him. He'd cut your name into his chest with a razor blade." He shuddered and Nicky did too. "NICO BLUE in big bloody letters." Adrian rubbed a hand over his chest and whistled. "Looked awful."

"Holy shit, Dad." Why had his parents never told him these things before?

Adrian nodded. "Your mother nearly murdered me over that one."

"Why? It wasn't your fault."

"Because I almost passed out," he said a little sheepishly. "But I pulled it together and called Dick down at the police station and they sent a car over. We didn't press charges because the kid's father came to collect him. The man was an attorney too, very embarrassed, and he begged me to let it go." Adrian's lips sagged at the edges with a frown. "He asked that we just let the boy's scars be his punishment." He looked sideways at Nicky. "Your mom and I understood what it was like to have a kid who sometimes makes bad choices; the kind of bad choices that he'll have to live with for a long, long time. So we agreed."

Nicky swallowed hard.

Adrian shook his head musingly. "I must say that kid seemed pretty proud of himself, though. I don't think he was right in the head."

"Dad, I had no idea."

"Well, you don't call very often. Your mother wanted our phone calls with you to focus only on the positive." Adrian cleared his throat. "She's been hoping for you to come back home for a long time, you know. She won't tell you this, but I know she'd like you to stay."

Nicky worried the edge of his sleeve. "I don't think that's possible, Dad."

"Yes, I know. She's—we're both—really glad you're here with us for now, son. And I'm proud of you for admitting you need our help. Anyone's help, really, but I'm honored you trust us enough that you'd want to be here."

Nicky didn't know what to say. "You're my parents. I love you."

"Well, for a lot of years, I have to admit we weren't sure you did." Adrian swallowed hard. "I'm not trying to be passive-aggressive. I'm just stating the truth."

Nicky's eyes blurred a little and he squeezed his fist until his nails dug in. "You deserved a better kid." He'd been filth; literal trash, tossed away. Broken from the beginning. "You had no idea what you were getting into when you adopted me."

Adrian fiddled with the dead air conditioning vents. "Funny thing is, even if you'd been ours from birth, we still would've had no idea what we were getting into. No one does. It's always a crapshoot, son." Adrian looked at him from the corner of his eye. "I'd even wager that we knew better than most what we might expect. We knew your birth mother was a crack and heroin addict, that you were severely underweight and suffering from multiple infections. We knew you'd been left to die in a dumpster, and that there was a good chance, given everything you'd been through, you'd have a tough time bonding with us. And, well, that was true. For a very long time."

Nicky had written so many songs about it. Had Adrian heard them? Did he understand what Nicky had meant with his lyrics?

Curled up in safe silence
Crying for the heartbeat that fed
Vibrant crack of rushing life
In my cage of death

"I never fit in here." As he said the words, he realized that he didn't feel like that anymore. Little Heights and his parents' home was the womb he needed now. He needed to be here so he could be born again as someone new, someone not Nico Blue. He shuddered and rubbed his fingers over his eyes, a headache starting in his temples. "I felt like an alien."

"I'm so sorry about that, Nicky." Adrian sounded sad at a soul-deep level, and Nicky wanted to take it all away.

"It wasn't your fault. You and Mom tried." He squeezed Adrian's shoulder, wishing he could make him understand. "You did everything for me, but I just couldn't get to you. It was like..." he remembered more lyrics he'd written:

Pry me open, crawl inside
I'm trapped here alone
A rotting parasite

"What was it like, son?" Adrian gently prodded.

"It was like I was in a walking, talking flesh dummy and I couldn't get to you. I couldn't get to anyone."

"You got to Jasper," Adrian said softly.

Nicky stared at Adrian's profile. He sounded almost like he knew the truth about him and Jasper. It wasn't that hard to believe; Nicky had always been a bad liar, and subtlety wasn't anywhere near his middle name.

"Dad, Jazz got to *me*," Nicky whispered.

"How?" Adrian asked, and he sounded so sincere and so hurt, like he'd tried so hard to break Nicky free and it broke his heart that he'd failed.

"I don't know. A kid-sized crowbar maybe." Nicky remembered the way Jazz had shown up that first day after the Hendrickses had moved in next door. He'd been all dirty knees and elbows, his hair a paler shade of brownish-blond than it was now, and his eyes had peered right into Nicky's soul. With his first words, "Hey, my name's Jasper," he'd somehow grabbed hold of Nicky's hands and pulled him out of the cage he'd been in his whole life. He'd made him a real boy.

Fucking Jazz.

"I don't know how he did it. I wish I did." *Sometimes I wish he hadn't.*

Adrian cleared his throat. "He was a good boy, and he's grown into a good man."

Nicky snorted. "Pretty much the opposite of me then."

"Nicky, that's not what I meant."

Nicky shrugged. "I know."

"Still, you could learn a lot from a man like him."

Yes, he could learn how to suck cock and take it up the butt like a champ. Oh, wait, but Jazz had taught him those lessons and then declined to teach him about sticking around for the long haul. And when Jazz had left, that old cage had descended around Nicky again. He'd heard the iron door slam and the lock engage the night Jazz had walked away.

This—this attempt with his parents—it was the first time he'd ever been able to get out of that cage since then. It was amazing and heartbreaking to find that when he pushed, the door swung right open. Nicky knew it was the work of the new cocktail of antidepressants and maintenance meds, but a lurking fear surfaced that maybe he'd just never really fucking tried.

"I don't think he wants to teach me anything, Dad."

"Jasper has missed you in his life."

Nicky snorted. "I think you're wrong."

Adrian gazed kindly at Nicky. "He cared about you too much for too long for that to be true."

Nicky turned his head away and looked out the window. It wasn't that he was ashamed. He'd tell his father everything if he could, but despite a sad, sick part of him that still wanted retribution for the pain Jasper had caused him, he didn't want to ruin Jazz's life. And if word got around that he was a gay priest who'd once fucked someone like Nico Blue? Well, that wouldn't recommend him highly to his parishioners, would it?

No, if Nicky was going to take a pound of Jazz's flesh it was going to be one-on-one. It wouldn't involve anyone else. Though, dammit, he was supposed to be making amends. That was a step, wasn't it? One of the twelve. Not that he considered himself a devotee of that process. He believed a higher power would keep him from using again, and that higher power was his maintenance medication.

Nicky scratched his arms, conscious of the scars under his long sleeves. "How much wood are we picking up today?"

Taking the hint, Adrian said, "Thought we'd price it at Elkin's Hardware and then see how that compares with Lowes'. If it's good, we'll go ahead and order what we need. We want you to stay busy. It's important."

"Been talking to Dr. Lewis?" Nicky had been a patient of Dr. Lewis for most of his childhood. He was a nice man, and he'd tried, but attachment disorders were stubborn diagnoses and the options had been even fewer back then.

"Yes, he took my call this morning. He's not extremely well-versed on addiction issues, but he's helped some local adolescents around town get and remain sober. We discussed the importance of staying busy and having a good game plan for the future."

"As it happens, my therapist agrees," Nicky said, remembering his phone call with her the prior morning. She might be in L.A. and the phone appointments might be less personal than if they met face-to-face, but Nicky didn't mind. It felt safer saying things to her over the phone, without the pressure of looking at her face. "So I'm thinking I could try tackling the entire stairway down to the dock, and the dock itself could use some work. I'll see about fixing the truck's AC too."

"And maybe you could ask Jasper about volunteer opportunities through his church," Adrian said. "Your mother thinks helping others might do you good. Raise your spirits and change your perspective."

Nicky shrugged. "Maybe. We'll see how it goes with the dock first."

"Jasper's group—"

Nicky interrupted him. "Mind if I turn on the radio?"

Adrian motioned at the dash and Nicky pressed the knob. It was already on a local rock station and, as they turned down Androscoggin, Vespertine's first big hit single started to play. Nicky tilted his head, really listening to the cut for the first time in years.

Sez's scratchy tenor started out gentle and loving, and then, at the chorus broke into a rage.

I bleed for you

Down on my knees for you

I give you my soul

All my rock and roll

And you give me…

You give me the vespers

Adrian sang along as they passed Jasper's church. Nicky gazed at it, thinking of Jasper's hazel-green eyes and light-brown hair glowing in the light from the stained glass windows.

OVER THE YEARS, the kids had managed to make the school cafeteria a little more cozy by adding couches, slouchy chairs, rugs, bookshelves filled with just about anything but books, and sets of odd mismatched tables and stools. The kitchen sat to the right of the cafeteria, with a large counter dividing the two spaces.

Jasper boiled the kettle and prepared cups with the rooibos tea and honey Thomas liked so much. He hadn't eaten after his run and he was starving, so he peered into the large fridge. Every day at noon a bunch of retired ladies from church came over to help him get lunch ready. Mrs. Wells got the kids up in the morning and made sure they were in bed at night, but lunchtime was her well-deserved break.

Large containers with cut-up fruit filled the whole bottom shelf, and by the looks of things, Mrs. McDonald had stopped by again with a few batches of her shepherd's pie. That was lunch taken care of. On another shelf, four whole chickens were defrosting. They would be prepared by the husband and wife cooking team the church had hired to take care of dinners six days out of seven. Sundays were take-out days, and Jasper peered into one of last night's pizza boxes, but the congealed cheese didn't look too appealing, especially since he knew whoopie pies were on their way.

The kettle boiled, and on cue the large front door to the school creaked open. Gentle footsteps echoed through the empty halls, and Bishop Thomas Murray was preceded by a large white box wrapped in Jasper's favorite kind of blue ribbon.

"Father Hendricks," Thomas said, resting an age-spotted hand on Jasper's forearm. "You look younger every time I see you."

"It's all that virgin blood I bathe in," Jasper said, eyeing the box.

Thomas rolled his eyes and handed over the pies. "You better keep those jokes to yourself when you need to."

Leading the way to a small round table by the window, Jasper said over his shoulder, "I save all the inappropriate ones for you."

"I'm touched. Tea?"

"On its way."

Jasper left the whoopie pies with Thomas and went to make the tea and grab some plates. After a second's hesitation, he filled a small bowl with some fruit.

"Now it counts as lunch," Jasper said when Thomas raised a dark eyebrow at the bowl.

"Are you still running three times a week?" Thomas asked, accepting the tea.

"I am."

Thomas lifted his deep blue eyes at Jasper and smiled. "Make sure you keep it up."

Jasper sputtered a protest, but Thomas opened the box and he forgot what he was about to say. "You got the ginger pies with lemon cream!"

"If I didn't know any better, I'd say you have a problem, Jasper. Come on, sit down and eat. I need to talk to you."

Jasper sighed and sank down in the orange chair opposite Thomas. "If I'd seen that photograph I'd have told them to delete it."

To his surprise Thomas smiled. "I don't think it's that bad, really. Have you checked your e-mails yet?"

With his hand in the box, Jasper shook his head. "I've been putting it off."

"Well, don't be surprised if it's full of fan mail. We've had quite a few people express interest in coming to your church." Jasper groaned but Thomas ignored him. "The archbishop isn't thrilled, however. He particularly doesn't like the 'gay priest' in all the headlines. I talked to him and explained that none of these new articles were sanctioned and that we could try to have them taken down, but that it would probably just stir up more media interest."

"I don't like them using these pictures without permission either, obviously, but what difference does it make? Everyone in the town knows. Some people don't like it. As you recall we lost a few members of the congregation early on because of it, but we're making strides in the community. You know that I've never made a secret of it even though my orientation should be of no one's concern. I live a celibate life just like any other Catholic priest." He bristled. "And I'm not the only out gay priest in the world. As long as we don't commit sexual acts, just like heterosexual priests, we're allowed to serve. Has that changed?"

"No, that hasn't changed. But the archbishop is still of the opinion that the Church took a risk appointing you, and it's not wise to flaunt it."

"Flaunt it?" Jasper dropped his pie to the plate. "Thomas, I—"

The bishop held up his hands. "I'm on your side, Jasper. I always have been. Archbishop Ramsey is my superior and I respect him, but I've known he doesn't carry any particular fondness for you, and I've always considered it wrong of him. But *you* know the Catholic Church, and you know their stance. In fact..." Thomas put his cup of tea down and rubbed his forehead.

A sliver of worry wormed its way into Jasper's heart and he went still, waiting.

"The archbishop and I also talked about the requests you've made. He's happy with the work you do for homeless children and children who find no place within the system." For someone bearing good news, Thomas looked uncommonly grave as he folded his hands on the table, so Jasper said nothing. "He's pleased with your work and he's agreed to expand. You may hire two more people to help out Mrs. Wells and Andrew. And, yes, you can hire more if Blue Oasis continues to grow."

"I can?" Jasper sat up straight and his heart began to beat fast in excitement. "We have beds here for over fifty kids. I could fill over half of those with my waiting list alone. Social services from all over the East Coast are contacting me regarding LGBTQ children who desperately need a better place to stay. Thomas, you have no idea—"

"There is one condition." Thomas spread his hands. His palms were age-roughened and leathery, and the left hand trembled just a little. It wasn't the first time Jasper thought Thomas really was getting old. "You have to open up the youth center for children of all orientations. Not just the LGBTQ group."

The excitement inside Jasper's belly withered and died, and he stared at Thomas in disbelief. "So they can fall through the cracks of the system again. Do you know how many kids out on the streets are queer? You know how many of them have to sell their bodies to survive?" He jabbed an angry finger in the direction of the door. "These kids are rejected by their parents for who they are. I'm not saying they deserve help more than the others, but they are less likely to receive the kind of help they need in foster homes or anywhere else. Plus, they're more likely to be bullied and harassed. And now you want me to give up on them too!"

"You know that I don't. Ramsey said they would still be accepted in Blue Oasis, Jasper."

"This was supposed to be a safe place for them. Away from the fear and bullying they've known their whole lives. What do you think will happen if the majority of the kids are straight? The gay ones will feel threatened and disappear. Like they always do. Back to the streets. That was the whole point of this, Thomas. And if that's the case, I say thanks but no thanks to the condition. I'd rather help ten of them with the resources I have than none at all."

Thomas reached for his tea. "I was afraid you might say that."

"I have no choice."

"No. I can see how you'd think so." Thomas smiled. "So tell me about them. Anyone spread their wings recently?"

Jasper relaxed a little but found it impossible to let his guard down completely. "Yes. Jonathan Michaels moved out two weeks ago. He's in a small apartment off Main Street and we managed to find him a part-time job while he takes early education classes at the community college."

"Sounds promising. Does that mean you have a new addition?"

"Just today, actually. A sixteen-year-old girl called Lizzie. Very bright. I think she'll have no trouble fitting in."

"Good." Thomas's eyes twinkled. "How's Bible study going?"

Jasper snorted softly and picked up his whoopie pie. "Nothing gets past you, does it?"

"Not really. Not even those safe sex kits you have lying around in the hallway."

Jasper groaned. "Thomas..."

"Let's not talk about that now," Thomas said. He pinned Jasper with a stern look. "But we will. After tea."

"I actually have a question for you." Jasper picked at the pie but didn't eat it. Thomas inclined his head, so he continued. "Is there anything in your life, before you became a priest, you wish you'd done differently? A mistake you may have made, something that might've impacted someone else's life that you…regret?"

Thomas smiled, but his brow furrowed a little with concern. "We all make mistakes, Jasper. You know that just as well as I do. As much as we pray for guidance, we're still human, which means we're inherently flawed. We still have to make our own choices and sometimes they're the wrong ones. All you can do is deal with the aftermath as best as you can and let God show you the way."

"I realize that, it's just…something has come to my attention recently. It's…I thought it was in the past, and I've been living my life like it belonged there, but maybe—" He pushed his plate aside and wrapped his hands around his mug of tea. "What if my choices set someone on a path that pushed them into doing bad things? Destructive things."

The smile had disappeared from Thomas's face. "Are we talking about something criminal here?"

"No. At least not…not in way that it would harm anyone but this person. I just mean…there was someone in my youth. He was my best friend. In fact, he was more than that." Jasper glanced at Thomas, but all he saw was understanding. "When we were seventeen…he'd started to hang out with another kid. Someone who was into doing drugs. I was busy with school and my altar boy duties and Nicky got bored waiting for me, I guess. Then one day I felt I needed to prove I was cool too, and this kid and Nicky came to my house with a bunch of pot. We smoked it, and of course my parents came home. I convinced them it was mine because Jimmy's home situation was precarious, at best, and Nicky…" Jasper's mouth lifted in a half-smile. "I didn't want Nicky to get into trouble either. My parents grounded me for the whole summer. The next time I saw him I told him I'd be leaving for college."

"To become a celibate priest," Thomas said, nodding. "I always wondered why you seemed so torn when you used to come to me to talk about your calling. I could see God's joy in you and at the same time it was tearing you apart. I guess your friend didn't react too well. Is this the one you were always with? What was his name? Jewish boy. Blumfeld?"

"Yes, Nicholas Blumfeld. And it wasn't that he didn't react well, it just…blindsided him. I'm afraid my choices might have caused him to make some bad decisions afterward."

But had it been entirely his choice? Hadn't someone guided his thinking to some degree?

You can't understand love at your age, Jasper. I'm not saying what you're feeling isn't real, but your body is going through so many changes, and you have so much life ahead of you. I'd hate for you to throw it all away over an innocent but ultimately childish infatuation. His mother had smiled at him. *In fact when I was your age there was a boy…*

Thomas gently patted Jasper's arm. "We want the best for the people in our lives; it's only natural. But in the end they make their own choices. You following the path to your destiny can't prevent someone from finding their own. If you feel bad now about not telling this person about your choice to join the priesthood, talk to him about it. Explain your reasons. But understand that this might do no good apart from giving you closure. It would be for your peace of mind, which isn't a bad thing."

"So you're saying it's a selfish notion, to want to be rid of this guilt I'm feeling."

"Maybe, unless you genuinely regret the choice you made and you want to undo it."

Jasper laughed softly. "No, I couldn't ignore God's call any more than I could ignore going hungry. The Lord knows I tried. I just wish I'd told Nicky sooner."

"You made a mistake. That doesn't mean you're responsible for every choice he's made in the seventeen years since. Pray for him, and for yourself, and I'll pray for you both. Now eat your whoopie pie or I'll get really worried."

When Jasper walked Thomas back to the front door they passed the storage room with the unpacked boxes of safe sex kits sitting in front of it. "These," Thomas softly said, "will have to go."

"Thomas, these kids—"

"Are underage, above anything else."

"Some of them come off the streets, Thomas. They've seen and been through more than you and I combined."

Thomas was shaking his head. "You know the Church's stance on contraceptives, Father."

Jasper clenched his fists. "Even the Pope acknowledged banning condoms in this day and age is madness!"

"He said condoms should be used as a last resort. That fidelity should be paramount within a marriage, and abstinence should be practiced outside of one. The condom represents the dangerous attitude that sex has nothing to do with love and is just another drug people are using. There is no room for interpretation. They have to go."

Jasper gritted his teeth. "We set aside so many of what we consider cultural commands that are now outdated." He waved a hand at the boxes. "This is maybe the most important one of all. It's for the kids' protection. I will not get rid of them."

Thomas rose to his full height, which was still considerable. "You go too far. This is not my choice, nor is it yours. There are rules in our world and we obey them, whether we agree with them or not. Tread carefully, son. You're already on precarious ground."

Jasper wanted to yell, but he took a deep breath and let it out slowly. "At least let me hand these out. It would be a waste to throw them away."

"But you're not ordering new ones. If the archbishop finds out this is what you spend your money on he'll shut you down without blinking."

"All right." Aggrieved they were about to part ways on such rocky ground, Jasper reached for Thomas's hand. He could find other ways to provide these kids with condoms. "Thank you," he said sincerely, and Thomas's features softened.

"You only have these kids' best interests at heart." Thomas gave Jasper's hand an extra squeeze, as if to emphasize his words. "But some battles you can't fight, Jasper."

"I know."

After Thomas left, Jasper retreated back to the office. He sat staring at the blank computer screen, mind churning with a dozen different things before he pushed all but one of them from his mind. He picked up the phone and dialed.

"Blumfeld and Morgan Corporate Law, this is Lindsay. How may I help you?"

"Hello Lindsay, this is Father Hendricks. Is Mr. Blumfeld available?"

"I'm sorry, Father. He's not. Is there anything I can help you with?"

He chewed his lip. "How about Lucas? Is he around?"

"Yes, he is," Lindsay said cheerfully. "I'll put you through."

Jasper listened to a classical tune until it was interrupted by a click. "All right, all right, I'll come to church on Sunday."

Jasper laughed. "Can I have that in writing?"

"Uh, probably not. What can I do for you, Father?"

"I really need to talk to Adrian and I thought I stood a better chance with you telling me where I can get a hold of him."

"He's actually working from home today. He told me to call him if anything urgent came up. What's going on?"

Jasper thought for a second. On the one hand he knew without a doubt he could trust Lucas, but on the other hand Lucas held a special affinity with Blue Oasis and telling him it might lose the queer identity would be very upsetting to him. "I just need to go over some contractual stuff regarding the lease of the school." It wasn't a lie. "It's not particularly urgent but I'd like to get it off my plate sooner rather than later."

"Oh yeah, of course. Let me give him a call and ask if he can see you later. Maybe meet for lunch?"

The thought of more food didn't sit particularly well in that moment. "I can stop by his house if it works better for him."

"Sure thing. I'll call you right back, Father."

"I'll be here."

Lucas hung up, and Jasper stared at the phone. Going to the Blumfeld house? With Nicky home? What was he thinking?

An hour and a half later he wheeled his bike to a halt in front of what had once been a second home to him. Through the trees he caught glimpses of his own childhood house. It'd be empty at this time of the day, unless Martha was cleaning. His mom was a surgeon at General Heights and wouldn't be home until late.

He hadn't been to his parents' house in a long time and he missed it. Not living up to their expectations of adding to the medical legacy in the Hendricks family had left their relationship strained, but his belief that there was no conflict between his homosexuality and being a priest—so long as he practiced celibacy—had pushed his very conservative mother to the point that she'd stopped coming to church. Apparently seeing her son preside over Mass while still identifying as gay was too much for her to bear.

A quirky little Mini Cooper sat parked in the Blumfeld driveway, and Jasper felt his stomach do a little flop. The thought of Nicky riding in that tiny thing made him want to laugh. When they were kids, Nicky had hung on to his old red plastic foot-pedal car long after he'd outgrown it, and the image of Nicky pedaling along with his knees beside his ears crowded Jasper's mind.

He hadn't thought about his childhood in a long time, but he'd been so happy back then. Every single memory seemed filled with sunlight, despite the long, boring winters they'd had to endure. Maybe he didn't remember them that way because Nicky had been part of all those winters, and the boredom had been softened, like sepia photographs, to quiet days of companionship.

Walking up the porch felt as familiar as returning to his own home.

Jasper hesitated for a second, staring at the familiar blue siding and the reflection of himself in the glass door. He hadn't had much cause to come here recently, and the Jasper who used to stare back at him from this same reflection had been smaller, thinner, and lacking the clerical collar. As he raised his hand to ring the doorbell, he felt like two people. The Jasper who'd loved a gorgeous boy with a soulfully fragile voice and a gift to play any instrument he laid his hands on, and the one who still felt a calling so deep it reverberated in the marrow of his bones.

Feeling more like that young boy than the man he'd become, Jasper pressed the doorbell.

Mrs. Blumfeld's small shape appeared behind the glass and she smiled widely as she opened the door.

"Oh, Jazz! It's wonderful to see you." Mrs. Blumfeld reached for him and gave him a one-armed hug before quickly pulling away. "I'm sorry. Should I say Father Jazz? And is hugging you even allowed? When you're wearing the…" She gestured at her own throat, and Jasper touched his collar.

"Of course," he laughed. "And you've known me as Jazz for a lot longer than I've been a priest, so call me whatever you feel comfortable with. How have you been?"

"Fine, fine." She gestured him inside and Jasper felt the years drop away. The countless times he'd stood in that beautiful hallway, eyes for nothing but the stairs Nicky would come thundering down so they could set off on one of their adventures. It all seemed so long ago.

Like she read his mind, Mrs. Blumfeld touched his sleeve. "I sometimes forget how grown-up you boys are now." From outside came a long, loud *yeehaw* followed by an almighty splash. There was sadness in her eyes but Jasper saw a renewed glimmer of hope that had been extinguished for years. "At least one of you grew up."

"So…" He awkwardly cleared his throat. "He's really here to stay?"

"For now. We're cautiously optimistic." Her face brightened. "Go on back! You should say hi. I'm sure he won't splash you in your nice clothes." She bit her lip. "Well, fairly sure. Come on, you know the way to the pool."

Jasper tried to resist as she tugged on his arm. "I have some documents for Adrian to look over, and—"

"Ah yes, he mentioned something. Adrian's in the yard too, I think he's trimming the roses. Again. Poor things. Anyway, you can talk to him and then say hi to Nicky." Jasper said nothing and she looked up at him. "I made fresh lemonade."

Oh no. "Mrs. B…"

"And I can make fruit crisp."

His blasted sweet tooth. Giving up on resisting, he sighed and said, "Lead the way."

Mrs. Blumfeld laughed and guided him through her bright kitchen. "Take a seat. I'll go get Adrian so you can get your business over with."

He glanced outside, following her gaze through the kitchen window with its view of the pool. The sun glinted over the gently rippling water, too blue to be natural. The green rolling lawn stretched out behind it. A fisherman's boat bobbed up and down in the cove across from the canoe he and Nicky had used as kids.

As the surface of the pool broke, Jasper startled and almost gasped when a soaked but fully clothed Nicky heaved himself from the water. The dark, long-sleeved T-shirt clung to him, and Jasper could see every ripple of taut, wiry muscle and the sharp edges of rib cage and collar bone too. Jasper's blood thrummed, and he felt a strange, hot-tinged lightness wash over him.

"I know," Mrs. Blumfeld whispered. "He's too thin. But I'll make him better." She laid her hand on Jasper's forearm. "*We'll* make him better."

Nicky pushed his too-long dark hair out of his face and his eyes took the shine of the pool water and put it to shame. The water on his skin glowed in the sun. He *was* too thin, but somehow as handsome as ever. Jasper couldn't say a word, so he just nodded, and Mrs. Blumfeld left him to it.

By the time Adrian came inside, Jasper had settled himself at the kitchen island with the documents spread out in front of him. He rose to his feet.

"Adrian, good to see you." They shook hands.

"And you, Jasper. We don't see nearly enough of you these days. I keep looking around expecting one of you kids to be rooting around my kitchen eating my food." He patted his belly. "But I've got to eat it all by myself these days."

"If you want kids raiding your kitchen, I can arrange for a couple to drop by."

Adrian laughed, then nodded toward the papers. "Is that why you're here?"

Jasper hesitated. Now that the moment was here he felt a twinge of disappointment. He was going against the Order that had taken him in, that had given him hope and purpose for so long. Without the help of the Church, Blue Oasis would never have existed.

But he couldn't let them take it away from him now.

"I was wondering," he began, slowly sitting down again, "let's say in a hypothetical situation, if I had to take over the lease of the school, how would I go about that? And if that wasn't possible, could I keep Blue Oasis running without the support of the Church?"

Adrian's eyebrows rose but he said nothing for the moment. Reaching for the contracts, he leaned on the counter and leafed through them for a while, then whistled softly through his teeth.

"I'd have to look into it," he eventually said. "But I'm guessing it would mostly take time and money. Time to sort out all the legal aspects of running a youth center, but with your background that shouldn't be too much of a problem, especially since a lot of the groundwork has been done. The money however…where would you make your income? You'd depend on grants—a few of those you have in place already, but I'm guessing you'll want to hire more staff, take in more kids." Adrian bit his lip and nodded slowly. "Are they thinking about closing down?"

"They want to open it up as a shelter for all kids, not just LGBTQ ones. It'd be the end of the whole purpose of the group, Adrian. If they do that…my kids will fade away. Back to the streets. To prostitution." Jasper lowered his voice, infused it with kindness. "To drugs."

"Yes." Adrian nodded. "Yes, I see. Leave it with me. I'll read through the contracts tonight. Do some research tomorrow." He put his hand on the file. "Does Lucas know?"

"Not yet."

"Okay. Let's keep it that way for now. Come over for dinner tomorrow evening, and we'll talk about it then."

Mrs. Blumfeld burst into the kitchen before he could politely decline. "Oh what a wonderful idea!"

"I don't know—"

"Yes, you do. We miss you, Jazz. I'm sure Nicky's missed you too. It'll be the perfect opportunity to get reacquainted. In fact, why don't you go say hi now? He's outside by the pool listening to music. I left the lemonade with him."

"I—" Jasper looked to Adrian for help, but there was none. Adrian just gave a one-shouldered shrug and a comical little smile that seemed to say, *What can you do?* "All right. I'll…go say hi." Going by their last encounter he'd be saying bye straight after anyway.

Chapter Six

THE SUNLIGHT BURNED blue against Nicky's closed eyelids. Music from his parents' outdoor speaker system drifted over the backyard to where he lay stretched out across the top of the extra-long picnic table on which his parents hosted barbecues. Nicky flexed his bare toes, enjoying the wet, soggy weight of his soaked long-sleeved T-shirt and jeans baking dry in the summer sun. The pressure on his skin was just right, like he was being hugged all over, and he decided that when they'd dried, he'd jump in and do it again.

The rough wood of the table dug into his shoulder blades and the knobs of his upper spine. The discomfort was comforting, a reminder that he was sober and not numbed out on drugs or alcohol. He felt human. Real. His wet hair dripped in ticklish trickles along his scalp and down the side of his face.

He gripped the remote for the stereo unit built in by the pool tightly in one hand and held very still as the song's rhythm guitar, snare, and tom-toms grew in intensity. A racing heartbeat. Or pounding feet on pavement. It was the music of someone running for their life. Nicky knew it well. Hot breath at his neck, a knife glinting in moonlight, the sound of a window breaking, a lock failing to hold, running, running, running.

The song climaxed and in the scene behind his eyes the runner stumbled, falling in slow-motion. Instantly, the chasing demon devoured him, and the dreamer awoke, all in the short beat before the singer delivered his final poignant lines.

Nicky hit repeat, wallowing in the self-indulgent opening to the song all over again.

"Sweetie, you've got a visitor!" his mother's voice called from the direction of the kitchen door.

The formerly comfortable weight of his clothes became a terrifying restriction, and panic rose under an awful sense of being pinioned and trapped. Had Jimmy Orlean heard he was home? He shouldn't have gone with his father to the hardware store to look at wood for the steps, and he definitely shouldn't have gone into Target for clothes. Someone must have recognized him. Word had gotten out. Jimmy Orlean was bad enough. Now it was only a matter of time before the paparazzi or obsessed fans descended on him. Would his mother know better than to let one of them in?

His heart beat in time with the rising rush of the music. No, no, in all likelihood, it was just Jimmy. But then the question became how he was going to tell his old supplier and pseudo-friend to get the fuck off their property without upsetting his mother? Or, a better question was how he would pull off saying no to whatever drug Jimmy had come to offer. He swallowed dryly. God, it'd be so easy to say yes.

The maintenance medicine in his system would make him violently sick if he used heroin. But Jimmy's hottest product had always been pot, and *that* was another story altogether. He could smoke up without any risk of spending a night puking. It would be stupid, sure, but that kind of thing had never stopped Nicky before.

Panic, tight and hard, coiled in him, and he struggled to a sitting position, rubbing at the sun-blindness spotting his vision. He'd say no. He hadn't come this far to fuck it up. He'd say no. Or yes. Or maybe just a little bit of yes.

No.

Footsteps approached. Black pants and a tight black button-up shirt. A white collar. Jazz's goddamn beautiful face.

"Fuck, it's you," Nicky said, not sure if he was relieved, pissed off, or embarrassed. Could Jasper see the temptation written on his face? Would he see right through him like he had when they were kids?

Jazz glanced over his shoulder and then back toward Nicky. "I stopped by to talk with your father. Your mother insisted I say hello."

An awkward silence fell and Nicky reached for his sunglasses resting on the side of the table and slid them on. "Well, you said it."

"So I did."

Nicky expected Jazz to say goodbye then but he didn't. Death Cab's "Bixby Canyon Bridge" escalated powerfully again as Jazz fixed his gaze on the cove beyond the drop off of the hill. The cacophony grew and grew until it collapsed into feedback, and Jazz crossed one arm over his chest, clutching his bicep and leaving the other arm hanging loose. Nicky knew that particular stance so well. It was a bittersweet ache in his gut to see it again.

"So," Jazz said conversationally. "Given Vespertine's musical style, I wouldn't have pegged you as a Ben Gibbard fan."

So Jazz had heard Vespertine's songs. Satisfaction and anxiety crashed inside of him. What had he thought of them? Had any of Nicky's arrows hit home? "Oh, yeah? Why's that?"

"It's a really different sound from yours."

"Diversity makes the world go round."

"And you told me once that Jimmy Eat World was crap."

"Right. And you went off on an impassioned plea for their brilliance." Nicky snorted.

Jasper shrugged. "Death Cab For Cutie doesn't fall far from that musical tree."

"I might have exaggerated my dislike for Jimmy Eat World." Nicky pointed the remote at the stereo and shut it off. The birds filled in the silence and Jasper stood quietly, expectantly. "You seemed to like their music better than mine back then."

Jasper scoffed. "That's absurd."

"Of course it was. My music was brilliant." He shrugged and decided to poke Jazz with the sharp end of the stick too. "But the real problem I had with them was your crush on the lead singer. I was jealous. In more ways than one." Nicky watched for Jazz's reaction to his words and was gratified by the nervous bob of his Adam's apple.

"Ah. I see." Jazz shoved his hands in his pockets. His lips twisted into an amused smile. "So, can I have it in writing? You take back all the things you said about Jim Adkins not knowing how to write a decent pop-rock song?"

Nicky ran a hand through his wet hair and squeezed some excess water from the tips. "Sure. Why not?"

"Wow." Jazz's eyes sparkled. "I wish I could go back in time and play a video of this moment to you."

Nicky shook his wet hair like a dog, splattering droplets on Jazz's black shirt. "Well, if you figure out how, be sure to add this part, too: Death Cab for Cutie and Jimmy Eat World are both the epitome of wanker bands."

Jazz blew out sigh and shot him a chastising look. His parishioners probably withered under it. "You had to kill the moment, didn't you?"

"Yep. Had to be done." Nicky slid off his sunglasses and tossed them into the grass near the edge of the pool. Jazz's lower lip went between his teeth for a second as their gaze connected. "But, you know what? Turns out Vespertine's a wanker band too." Nicky nodded his head toward the stereo. "I guess I'm in good company."

Jazz's cheeks creased with his smile. "You're the same as ever."

Nicky closed his eyes and took a deep breath of fragrant summer air. The stirring scent of his father's roses and the bright spike of his mother's mints filled him up.

A clear memory of Jasper officiating over Mass swam up behind his closed lids. Jazz in his robes, presiding over the holy sacrament. Nicky had watched from the pews before he'd worked up the nerve to stay behind for the scene he'd made in the confessional. Jazz had looked so handsome and confident up there—calm and collected, like he never tossed and turned at night possessed by doubts and fears. Like he'd never thought of Nicky and wondered if he'd made the right choice.

He probably hadn't. Jazz had always been so fucking sure of himself.

Nicky exhaled slowly. "You're the same too."

"Maybe. Although, I'm sure we've both changed over the years."

Nicky's therapist had explained to him that drug abusers were often emotionally arrested at the age they first became addicts. Which meant he probably had more in common with the teenage Jasper he used to adore than the thirty-four-year-old man in front of him. Pretty humiliating.

"Sure. I guess we have," Nicky agreed. He looked around at his childhood home. He'd had it so good here; lived such a privileged, safe life, and he'd never truly known it until he left. Adrian was right. He never should have gone to L.A.

"Of course we have. You're a rock star now and I'm a priest."

"A rock star." Nicky snorted and rolled his eyes.

"Well, aren't you?" Jazz asked softly.

"I guess."

"What a strange and amazing world we live in," Jazz mused.

"Rock star," Nicky murmured again, bitterness on his tongue. "That sounds like a lie, doesn't it? You can't exactly turn up at your high school reunion and when someone asks what you do for a living answer 'rock star.' It's fucking absurd. It's not a real thing that a person can be, Jazz. It's bullshit." He swallowed and flicked a glance to Jasper. "If I've changed at all since you knew me, I guess I got even more broken out there in your so-called strange and amazing world. And given how broken I was to start with… We both know that's saying something, man."

Jazz held his gaze for a moment and then looked away. His fingers twitched by his sides like he wanted to reach out, but otherwise he kept very still. "Oh, Nicky."

Fuck it, he wasn't going to go down this path. Apparently Jazz could still strip him down to skin, bones, and honesty with a glance, but he didn't have to offer it up so easily. "Aren't you going to ask?"

"What?"

"What makes a wanker?"

"It hadn't occurred to me, no, but all right, tell me." Jazz's smile was adorable, and there was no steeling himself against it. Nicky's stomach flipped. Jazz had grown up, but his smile was just as innocent as ever. Nicky looked away from it. His sure as hell wasn't.

"Well, speaking as a wanker myself, I can tell you the defining feature is a disgusting amount of self-involvement."

Jazz laughed, a small huff that forced Nicky's lips into a twist of self-effacing amusement.

"Wanker songs are the musical equivalent to showing up at your ex's place of business and making a scene."

"Is that so?" Jazz finally sat down on the bench and rested his folded hands on top of the picnic table a few inches away from Nicky's left thigh. The sun glinting in his eyes made them shimmer gold and green. His breath was slow, and his eyes slid over Nicky's body and then up to meet his gaze. "Is that your way of apologizing?"

Nicky's laugh was sharp. "Oh, hell no. I'm not sorry for anything I said yesterday."

Jazz raised a brow. That was another expression he probably used on his flock. Nicky remembered it from every awesome (and terrible) idea he'd ever had as a kid.

"Fine. I can admit the confessional wasn't the place for it."

Jazz pressed the pads of his fingertips between two wooden slats of the picnic table and rubbed back and forth. His fingernails were clean and short and broader than they used to be. "It wasn't appropriate. The confessional and what happens in it is sacred."

"Right. Sorry. Atheist Jew here. I can't say I forgot, but I don't really get it."

"You're still an atheist?" He sounded oddly disappointed.

"Would that have changed anything?" That was one of a dozen things Nicky had always wanted to know. "If I'd been a believer, I mean?"

Jasper looked down at the table and shook his head. "No. It wouldn't have made a difference."

What would have? He didn't know how to ask.

Jazz didn't give him a chance. "Yesterday, what were you expecting from our meeting, Nicky? Did you just want to hurt me?"

Nicky pulled the sleeve of his shirt down over his wrist and fiddled with the seam. "I wasn't expecting anything. I actually went in to make amends with you. Seems funny now after what I did, huh? I did it the way I do everything in my life: wrong."

"Not everything." Jazz flattened his hands on the picnic table and fixed Nicky with his trademark earnest gaze, the one that always, *always*, made Nicky want to get Jazz into trouble and dive into it right along with him. "You're getting clean. And you're home where people can take care of you and support you. You're on the right track."

"Well, thanks for your approval, *Father*." Nicky slid off the top of the picnic table and walked toward the pool as he tried to shake the shivery-good glow of Jazz's praise. He was not that boy anymore.

He considered jumping in again, but he was afraid Jazz would take that as his cue to leave and he wasn't ready for him to walk away just yet. Nicky slid on his dad's old ugly Crocs he'd found in the shoe trunk and started back toward the steps. He'd left the crowbar there earlier after prying up some of the worst offenders. He could pull some more rickety boards up now and take some of the hurt rising in him out on the defenseless wood.

"Nicky, wait," Jazz said, reaching out to grab Nicky's wrist as he strolled by where Jasper still sat at the table. "There's something else we should talk about. In the confessional you said a lot of things, some of them really hard for me to hear—"

Jazz's fingers were electric on his wrist and Nicky pulled away.

Jazz's cheeks flushed and his eyes went dark with emotion. "You said you thought I'd never loved you."

Nicky stared at Jazz. His throat went tight, his heart pounding hard.

"What we had was special. I did love you, Nicky. But life moved on and we're grown men now. Both of us with a defining personal history that happened in the absence of each other."

"And whose choice was that?"

"It was the way it had to be."

"As God intended," Nicky mocked.

"I wanted to make this better, but I don't think I am. I should go," Jazz said, rubbing his palms against his pants, a rare expression of defeat on his face. When they were kids, Nicky would have kissed that look away. Now it just pissed him off even more.

"Sure. Run away. You're good at that," Nicky murmured.

Jazz turned toward the house.

Nicky slung the crowbar against the first rotten wooden step he came across, the sound of the splintering wood satisfying his rage. He turned to watch Jazz's escape, calling out, "What? You're not going to fight back? You're not going to point out that I'm great at running away too?" Nicky swung the crowbar up to rest on his shoulder, staring at Jazz, who watched coolly from where he'd paused by the pool.

Jazz's chin was lifted a little, his arms were crossed, feet hip-width apart and, *God*, Nicky wanted to laugh. Priest or no priest, Jazz hadn't managed to get rid of his pride. That damn collar around his neck hadn't entirely leashed him.

"Yeah, maybe you're right. Maybe I don't know who you are anymore. Because I know you used to be passionate. You used to fight with me when I was a dick. Now you just turn away like you're untouchable." Nicky shook his head, water and sweat droplets sliding down his temples. "You're not in the confessional now, Jazz. Why don't you act like a human being and not a fucking priest?"

He turned his back on him and dug the crowbar beneath the wood of another rotten-looking step. The splinter and crack was satisfying and he ripped at it ferociously before moving on to another and ripping it out too. He felt more than heard Jazz's approach but he looked up when he'd finished with a third step. He pushed the hair out of his face and glared at Jazz.

"I'm always a priest whether I'm in the confessional or not. That's the way priesthood works. You know that. And, believe it or not, priests are human beings. We're fallible and we screw up, and, yes, sometimes we can be real wankers. I still get angry. But I'm not angry at you."

Nicky sneered. "That's supposed to make me feel better? Maybe I want you to be angry at me."

"You're making this really hard, Nicky." Jazz put his hands in his pockets and tilted his head back, exposing the length of his neck.

"Are you praying?"

"Yes."

Nicky rolled his eyes and pulled up another step. When he was finished, he threw the crowbar aside and sat down on the grass. Jazz came over and sat down next to him, close enough that Nicky could almost touch his hand. He wondered what Jazz would do if he did? If he kissed his knuckles and fingertips the way he had years ago. Or maybe he should just throttle him, roll his smug ass down the hill, and dump him in the bay.

"All right, Nicky. Let's try this again. I feel like you've got questions you want to ask me. So why don't you? Maybe we can both put at least some parts of our past behind us."

Nicky scratched at his sweaty stubble. "Sure. Why not? I'll ask you a few questions and you'll give me a few answers, and poof, suddenly everything will be all right." Nicky pressed his palms together and looked to the sky. "By the blessed power of Father Jazz."

"No, Nicky. I just thought you might want to hear it." Jazz sounded tired.

He'd had seventeen years to think about what he'd ask Jasper if he had the chance. He may as well satisfy his curiosity now. "All right," Nicky said, slinging his arms around his knees and glancing over at Jazz. "How do you make it work? The whole priest and gay thing? Does it keep you awake at night?"

Jazz's lips twitched into a small smile. "No. I had all that figured out before I went to college."

Another thing Jazz had never shared with him at the time. Unsurprising, of course, but those wounds had never healed up right anyway. "Oh, this should be good. How's that justification work out exactly?"

"You really want to have a theological discussion on the Bible's stance on homosexuality, Nicky?"

"Well, if it has anything to do with why you blindsided me with the whole 'Thanks, Nicky, making love with you was great, but I'm gonna go be a celibate priest now' I'd like to know. Sure. Why not? Hit me."

Jazz plucked a piece of grass and worked the fiber of it apart with his fingers, his eyes on the bay instead of on Nicky. "You can probably imagine what it was like, being a Catholic kid and realizing I was gay."

Nicky shrugged. It'd been something he'd considered a lot back then, actually. Jazz was always devout—he'd been an altar boy for fuck's sake. He'd wondered why Jazz had never seemed especially conflicted by their relationship. "It never seemed to bother you."

"Well, it did. I knew I was gay from a very young age." Jazz's mouth quirked on one side. "See, I met this little kid with dark brown, wavy hair and sky-blue eyes and he stole my heart."

"Nah, it was just hormones."

Jasper rolled his eyes. "You can guess how scared I was when I first felt the call. For a long time I pretended nothing was happening."

"So, some people are in the gay closet and you were, what? In the priestly closet?"

"That's right."

"When did you get the call? You never mentioned it." Nicky

plucked a piece of grass and twirled it between his fingers.

"I loved being in the church. I could feel God all around me. Then I started feeling him everywhere else too."

"What's that like?"

Jazz tilted his head back and his collar shifted, exposing the flat, dark mole that Nicky had once kissed with so much passion. "Remember Mrs. Daniels? How when we were ten she lost her husband and then that same week her house burned down?"

"And then the rich aunt passed away and left her a shitload of money, yeah I remember that."

"I thought, that's the hand of God. That is God interfering with this woman's fate."

Nicky grimaced. "So God just happened to decide that Mrs. Daniels deserved financial compensation to deal with her grief, but Joe Galgovitch, whose wife died of breast cancer and left him destitute with a two-year-old, was just shit out of luck? That's God's hand?"

"I don't know," Jasper murmured. "I'm not arrogant enough to think I actually know what God's plan is anymore, but I'm trying to explain to you what it was like for me. I felt Him everywhere." Jazz turned to look at him and smiled. "I felt Him in you, in the joy I felt when I was with you. It confused things for me."

Nicky shuddered. "That's creepy."

"What?"

"Feeling God in me? Like when your dick was up my ass, you felt God?"

Jazz chuckled, his cheeks flushing. "Only you'd go there, Nicky."

"So, what? You fucked me and thought, 'Oh, wow, this is so holy'?"

Jazz lifted his chin but the flush didn't abate. "What if I did?"

Nicky couldn't stop the laughter that bubbled up. "I think you're gonna burn in hell for that." He bumped Jazz with his shoulder and then wished he hadn't. The touch burned into the place that was insatiable, the place that wanted more, more, more.

"Maybe," Jazz agreed. "But I confessed and did a penance, so I think I'm okay." Jasper's tone poked fun at the idea that his finding their lovemaking a holy experience would send him to hell. "Besides, don't tell me you didn't feel the same way."

Nicky pushed away the temptation to make another snide remark about their relationship being nothing more than puppy love and teenage hormones. How could Jazz not see that what he was saying was completely at odds with that excuse?

"You know I'm a bad liar. So I won't even try," Nicky said. Being with Jasper had been the only time he'd ever felt like sex was something divine, something transcendent and pure. Every person he'd fucked afterward had felt like a John Waters film: compelling, bizarre, and ultimately disgusting.

They were quiet for a while, the breeze up from the bay sliding over Jazz's hair and ruffling it. He cleared his throat and Nicky waited, his heart beating faster as a horrible, awful feeling he'd tried so hard to destroy over the years flowed into his veins: hope.

Fuck. He couldn't afford that. Not now. Not when it came to Jazz.

"Anyway," Jazz went on. "I think it's part of the reason why I ended up smoking pot with you and Jimmy. I couldn't be gay and feel the calling. The prevailing wisdom around me told me it was impossible. And yet…" He held out his hands and Nicky's eyes drifted toward the collar around his neck.

"I thought you did the drugs to impress me."

Jazz laughed. "Yeah. Well, that too."

"I wasn't impressed. I never wanted you involved in any of that."

"I know," Jazz turned to him, eyes soft and expression vulnerable. "You told me that at the time, and I believed you then. I believe you now as well. I never wanted you involved in that stuff either."

Nicky ignored that. "So getting high that day wasn't just about me?"

Jazz laughed again. "Sorry, wanker, few things are."

"Thanks, asshole." Nicky snorted. He scratched his eyebrow with his thumb, looking away from Jasper's wide, sweet smile.

"Eventually, I decided I had to make peace with these conflicting feelings or I was going to lose my mind. I did my research. I read the Bible over and over, especially the passages that mention homosexuality. And you know what I found?"

"Whatever you wanted to find that made it easy for you walk away from me."

"No." Jasper tilted his face toward the sun. "No, you still don't get it. I was looking for any possible way to get out of being a priest. I didn't *want* this, Nicky. I wanted you."

"Well, you could've fucking *had* me," Nicky spit out. "So don't tell me this shit. Don't tell me you wanted me over God because that's *bullshit.* You could have motherfucking had me."

"Nicky—" Jazz reached out but didn't touch, his hand falling to the grass between them. "It could never be a competition. Do you understand? God is...God."

"What the fuck does that mean? God always wins?"

"'Thy will be done on earth as it is in heaven.' But it's not about winning."

Nicky rubbed at his eyes, his head blazing with a sudden headache.

"But what I discovered, Nicky, is that what God wants above all else, is for us to love each other. Any rule may be broken if it comes from an act of love. If you act out of love for others, *selfless* love, you can do no wrong. The Bible doesn't condemn me. It doesn't condemn you either."

"Well, fuck. I wish to hell it did."

"You don't mean that." Jasper gave him the disapproving look again.

"Sure I do. I don't believe in hell or God, Jazz. If the Bible had condemned you, then you'd have picked me, right?"

"Nicky, you can't look at it—"

His banked anger flared again. "I can! Do you see what you're saying? All of this, everything, both of our lives would have been completely fucking different if you didn't fucking *believe.*"

"We were children—"

"I know. Children driven by hormones." Nicky threw up his hands.

Jasper was silent for a few seconds, and then he said quietly, "You blame me for your addictions. I understand. Sometimes I've blamed my…well, I understand your anger toward me. But blaming God, blaming religion isn't—"

"No, it's not like that. I'm not blaming God. God doesn't exist. I'm calling you an asshole."

Jasper ducked his head with a wry little smile, and it made Nicky ache. Why wasn't he hiding behind his precious Bible and flinging quotes at Nicky about how what they used to do was all so wrong? It would make it so much easier to believe that he'd changed. Maybe, if he did, Nicky could even find a way to hate him.

Jasper touched his arm gently. The sensation was like a shock to Nicky's heart. "I'm sorry. I never wanted to hurt you."

Nicky pulled his arm away. "Yeah. You said that years ago. I don't need to hear it again."

"But it's true." Jasper rose to his feet. "I really should go."

"Yeah, I guess you should." Nicky didn't look up at him. He kept his eyes focused on the bobbing up and down of his father's boat.

"One last thing before I go. If you ever need help with anything, please come to me, because I do want to help you, Nicky, in any way I can. If you'll let me."

Jasper left and Nicky refused to watch him go.

ON TUESDAY, JASPER walked through morning Mass like a ghost. Attendance for the service was typical: ten to fifteen elderly, devout Catholics, all of whom he knew by name and voice. Most of them would stay for confession, and it would be, as usual, another dull litany of impure thoughts and overindulgence in liquor. Perhaps there might be a scintillating tale of shoplifting, but he wasn't actually supposed to find those confessions amusing so much as disappointing.

Jasper always tried to give his all to every service. It was an honor to serve God and deliver the message to His flock, one that Jasper tried to respect despite the familiarity of the ritual he could practically perform in his sleep. But despite his best effort to focus, he couldn't help being distracted.

Nicky had crossed lines the day before, which Jasper should've expected. The pointed questions had awakened inner arguments and feelings he'd considered long buried. In the end he'd given up on sleep at three in the morning and turned to yoga in an attempt to relax.

Part of him dreaded the dinner at the Blumfelds' that night. Whenever he crossed paths with Nicky, he seemed to make the situation worse despite his best intentions. But another part of him looked forward to seeing Nicky again. He'd missed him more than he'd realized, and the eternal optimist in him couldn't help but hope they might find a way to be friends. Though, to do that, he needed to stop thinking about their brief and beautiful time as lovers; he needed to stop questioning everything about that one cataclysmic summer. If his parents hadn't found the three of them smoking pot in the backyard, what would've happened?

If he were to believe Nicky, everything would've been different. But if Jasper's mother was right, their paths would've remained much the same.

It no longer mattered what might have been. Only the road ahead counted. And right now the road ahead led to the confessional.

Lord, I lay my heart and soul at Your feet. Guide me toward Your true path and help me focus on those who need me.

He didn't look too closely at who waited in the rows of pews by the confessional. He just breathed until he found peace and opened the partition to offer God's forgiveness.

Jasper lifted his hand to his forehead. "In the name of the Father, and of the Son, and of the Holy Spirit, amen."

"Forgive me, Father, for I have sinned."

Oh *no*. "Nicky," Jasper whispered desperately. "Please. Not again."

"No!" The grid that separated them made it hard to distinguish any features but Jasper saw Nicky's fingers when he pressed them to the slats. "No, I'm not here to be a jerk again. Yesterday you said you'd help me if I needed it. And I guess I need help."

Jasper was tempted to ask if this wasn't something better suited for Nicky's parents, or his therapist, given the fact that Nicky had declared himself an atheist just the day before. But maybe this was God's plan to help Nicky, and Jasper shouldn't stand in the way of that. He could do this. He could set aside his own conflicting emotions and be the guide Nicky needed. He reached for the string of rosary beads hidden in his robes.

Wasn't this exactly what he'd prayed for?

Remember, O most gracious Virgin Mary, that never was it known that anyone who fled to Thy protection, implored Thy help, or sought Thy intercession, was left unaided.

"All right." Jasper wanted to put his fingertips to Nicky's to give him courage. "I'm here for you, Nicky. I'm listening. Whatever you need."

Nicky was silent. His shadow moved away from the screen and he swore softly under his breath. "Never mind, this was a bad idea."

"No," Jasper quickly said. "Please stay and tell me how I can help you." He felt shaky, like he'd had an extra cup of coffee. *Get it together, Jasper.* "May the Lord be in your heart and help you to confess your sins with true sorrow."

Nicky shifted in his seat, and Jasper caught a glimpse of dark wavy hair and a flash of blue eyes before they lowered. "I'm scared I can't do this."

Jasper frowned. "Sobriety?"

"Yeah. I've been tempted to call a guy I know here in town."

The wooden beads bit into the flesh of his palm. "You mean Jimmy?" Jasper whispered, his blood running cold.

"Yeah. He's still around, right? He's not dead yet?"

"He's not dead."

"Oh, good. Because the last time I saw him…" Nicky blew a soft breath between his teeth.

Jasper's stomach clenched. Jimmy had been bad news for Nicky when they were seventeen, and he could be disastrous for him now. He wouldn't ever wish anyone dead, but he sure wished Jimmy at the other end of the country now.

"The last time you saw him?"

"Yeah, years ago. I was here for Christmas."

Jasper remembered that year. He'd heard rumors from the kids in Blue Oasis that Nico Blue was in town visiting his parents and he'd shared their vigilance for a glimpse of him for entirely different reasons.

"I bought a dimebag off Jimmy to hold me over until I could get out of town and get my hands on some good horse." Nicky's swallow was audible through the slats. "I paid him a lot more than the shit was worth. Jimmy looked he was about to die and that was forever ago." Nicky sounded a little breathless as he asked, "Have you seen him lately?"

Jasper hesitated. He didn't want to give Nicky information about Jimmy. The guy was paving his own path to a living hell and he wanted Nicky to stay away from him. Besides, Jasper had tried to reach out to Jimmy once and it hadn't been pretty. "I see him sometimes, from a distance. He doesn't look good."

Nicky's voice was gruff. "Yeah. It hurt to see him like that. He was my friend."

Jasper closed his eyes and remembered finding Nicky and Jimmy alone in the fort. It was a surprise to discover the pain was still there just waiting for him to poke at, like a bruise that never healed. He remembered his first reaction had been anger. The fort was supposed to be *theirs* and theirs alone. But then… *"So, hey Nicky, what do you say? Can I blow you?"*

"I know." Jasper swallowed. "I know he was your friend."

Nicky's fingers worried at the partition separating them. "Seeing him like that…it could've been me."

"No," Jasper interrupted, sitting up straighter. "No, Nicky. That never would've been you."

"Wake the fuck up, Jazz," Nicky snapped in a hot whisper. "That *is* me and if I'd stayed here I'd have been just the same as Jimmy."

Jasper reeled back a little. The rosary slipped from his damp fingers and landed in his lap. "No. I wouldn't have allowed it."

"Oh, yeah? What would you have done to stop it?"

Jasper opened his mouth to say, *anything*, but bit it back. He couldn't honestly say it was the truth, however much he wished it. By the time Nicky left for L.A., Jasper had stood firmly with his two feet planted on the road to priesthood. If he'd known Nicky was in trouble though…

"I would've come to you," he admitted quietly. "If you'd asked me to. I wouldn't have strayed from my path, but I would've put it on hold."

"You'd like to think so, I'm sure." Nicky rubbed at his face with both hands. "I'm not here to fight. I believe you." He snorted softly. "That damn hero complex of yours always could move mountains."

Nicky was silent for a while and when he spoke again the anger had bled from his voice. "The only difference between me and Jimmy Orlean is I can get my hands on quality stuff instead of making filthy meth."

"No," Jasper murmured again.

"It hurt to see him like that. We had some good times together. He was my only friend except for you."

"I know." Jasper wished he could've been the only friend Nicky had needed, but that was a childish sentiment born out of a jealousy he had no right to feel. Everyone involved that fateful summer had made mistakes, but his mother had been right to point out the path the two of them were on was an unsustainable one.

"I couldn't even stick around and be near him that way, living in a dump of a house with his teeth rotting out of his head."

"So you haven't seen him since you came home?" Jasper had to remind himself to breathe.

"No. I thought about stopping by. Does he still live off Silver Road? No, don't tell me. I don't want to know where he is."

Jasper's entwined fingers tightened in his lap until the knuckles went white. "You're really afraid that you'll go to him?"

"Yeah. I'm terrified I will. And I don't even like pot. I get paranoid and feel gross for days after smoking up."

"That's a good thing to focus on. How smoking pot wouldn't really provide you with what you're looking for." And what was Nicky looking for, Jasper wondered. What had Jimmy Orlean provided years ago? Connection. A person to be with when Nicky couldn't be with Jasper. "I'm glad you came to me."

"This has got to be the weirdest confession. Shit." Nicky laughed softly.

"Not so very weird."

"Really? Do you ever get juicy stuff? Murders? Rapes?"

"You know I can't talk about that." Jasper grinned a little. "But let me tell you the Little Heights octogenarians can be a frisky bunch." Nicky laughed, which was what he'd been aiming for. *Don't deny it*, a little voice in his head said. *You still love making him laugh as much as you always did.* He cleared his throat. "Let's stick with you and what's got you looking for an excuse to throw in the towel."

Nicky made a small, pained noise. "I hate telling you this. You must think I'm so weak. And for some reason, even though we barely know each other now," the sarcasm was ripe, and Jasper could practically hear Nicky's eye roll through the screen, "I still give a fuck what you think of me."

Jasper let a soft breath escape. "We're all weak sometimes. That's why we surround ourselves with people who give us courage. Do you have people in your life aside from your parents that you connect with? People that see the best in you?"

"No. Well, maybe one."

"Someone from your band?"

Nicky sighed. "I meant you, but now that you mention it, Ramona is brave as shit. She might have some courage to spare."

"Call her. Or come to me. There are people who want to help you; people who want to know you sober, Nicky. I know you're strong enough to resist temptation. God will help you." He had to. Seeing Nicky hollow-eyed and thin by the pool yesterday had been a shock. He'd looked nothing like the phenomenon that was Nico Blue on magazine covers. Watching him slip away further into the shadows would be…unthinkable.

Nicky snorted a little derisively. "Like I said yesterday, I don't believe in God."

Then why are you here? Jasper wanted to ask. But who was he to question the reasons why God kept bringing them together? "God will still help you."

Nicky huffed softly. "That's kinda sweet, Jazz. That you still believe your God will help a person who doesn't even believe in him."

"God is always seeking you, Nicky. If you sincerely seek Him, you'll find Him right there looking for you."

"Right. Well, I'll take a make-believe God's help if it will keep me from fucking up again."

Jasper closed his eyes. If all that stood between Nicky and his next hit was a God he didn't believe in, he didn't stand a chance. Maybe he could help Nicky understand that what his soul truly craved was human connection, not drugs. "Why were you tempted to make that call?"

A swishing sound drew Jasper's gaze toward the grid. Nicky was softly rubbing the antique wood. "The maintenance medications I'm on help a lot. I don't really crave heroin at all, but my psychologist says I lack coping skills. Since I was a kid, when I can't deal with something, I look for a way to numb it out."

Good. This is good. "What can't you deal with right now?"

"What *can* I deal with? I mean, where do I start?"

"Why don't you start with the most immediate thing? The straw that broke the camel's back and made you want to call Jimmy."

"All right. But remember you asked. I've been having, um, impure thoughts. About someone I can't have. Someone who wouldn't want me thinking about him."

Jasper went hot all over as his toes curled in his shoes. "Nicky, please don't—" he whispered between his teeth.

"But it's true! And you asked!"

Jasper wanted to kick himself "No, you're right. You're safe here. God will hear your confession. You can tell me."

"There are other things I've been having trouble dealing with; other reasons I've been tempted to find a way to numb out." Nicky's voice sounded a little thready and he trailed off.

Jasper took a calming breath. This wasn't about him. This was for Nicky. "Take your time," he softly said.

"Can we leave God out of it?"

"Nicky, this is a confessional. I'm a priest." He didn't want to rush Nicky, but there were other penitents waiting, and they could have a non-religious discussion another time. But Nicky was in crisis *now.* "And I think you're feeling safe enough to tell me this because of the divide between us. Not in spite of it."

"Yeah, you're right. Okay, I'm scared," Nicky whispered. "Scared that I'm not strong enough. That I can't return to my music without using."

"You don't need drugs to write music, Nicky. You've been writing music since you were three years old."

"I know. It's not that. It's just… Jazz, I'll cave the second I'm in the same room as a bunch of coke. It's a fucking Catch 22."

"But why would you have to be in the same room with coke? Couldn't you just choose not to go there?"

"No. I can't. It's fucked up because I can't write decent music when I'm high, but I can't be in that world without drugs being literally fucking shoved in my face. My last memory before they carted us off to rehab is of my tour manager pushing coke up my nose so I could go onstage and play."

Jasper covered his mouth and needed a second to make sure his voice would come out steady. "Why would they do that?"

"Because I'd already nodded out on heroin. If they even figure out where I am, dealers will crawl out of the woodwork and show up on my parents' front doorstep. I've taken precautions against that, but I can't stay here forever. This little vacation here can't last."

"Can't you just quit?" Jasper knew it was an appalling suggestion. Nicky had breathed music his entire life.

"You know I can't. Music is my existence. Besides, my manager called again today."

"Why?"

"We owe them another album. They'll take legal action before long. And they can. We're under contract. In some ways they own us. I'm a slave to them as much as you're a slave to your Church. And they don't really want me sober, Jazz. They really don't." Nicky's voice broke. "And I'm tired. I'm just…really fucking tired."

Jasper knew he should offer Nicky God's strength. Tell him that if he only relied on the Lord, all would be well. To place his faith in heaven and everything would fall into place. But the words turned to dust in his mouth and something twisted in Jasper's stomach. His eyes stung, and he didn't know why. How could they have done this to Nicky? His love-hungry, anger-driven, and far-too-easily led Nicky? What monster would take advantage of him like that?

"Listen to me, Nicky. Do you remember Honey?"

Nicky sounded confused. "Honey? Your dog?"

"Yes."

"Sure. Of course. Why wouldn't I? She was the best dog, man."

"She was. And you loved her even though she wasn't yours." Jasper wasn't sure where he was going with this, he just knew that it had to go somewhere, that God was in the confessional with them guiding his words and He had led Jasper's mind to Honey. "Do you remember what I told you about her?"

"You mean that time you said if I got a dog then Honey would be best friends with it, the way I was best friends with you?"

"After that."

"I told you my dad was allergic and—"

"And I said that Honey could be your dog too. And she was. She was your dog as much as mine."

Nicky was quiet for a minute, no doubt remembering how they'd held each other after Honey's death—how they'd pressed their tear-damp cheeks together, and Jasper had dared a kiss to Nicky's eyelashes. Just once. It was the last time he'd kissed Nicky until the day in the rainstorm, running through the forest, when he'd been so happy and free that he just couldn't stop himself.

"She was a great dog," Nicky murmured.

"Well, you don't believe in God, but I do. And my God can be your God. I'll share Him with you. You don't have to do anything at all to have part of Him. He's an amazing God, Nicky, and he will help you." *I'll help you.* "I believe in Him so you don't have to. You're brave and you're talented. And it's okay to be scared. Because God has you in his hand. He'll keep you safe from even your worst impulses and your worst enemies." *And I'll keep you safe too.* Jasper closed his eyes. He was in no place to make those promises. Not even to himself.

Behind the partition, Nicky sniggered. "I'm imagining God as a giant Honey now, Jazz. The God in my mind is a female Rhodesian Ridgeback and she's about to lick my face."

Jasper reluctantly laughed, his throat tight as desperation still beat against his chest. "That's as good an image as any. Because God loves you like Honey did—completely, unreservedly, unconditionally."

"You're really into God, Jazz. You know that, right?"

Jasper couldn't help laughing louder. The sound echoed back in the confessional. "After everything, even knowing where we are right now, you can't really think of me as a priest, can you?"

"I shouldn't think of priests the way I think of you."

Jasper swallowed hard. His heart leapt and he pressed his fist against it, willing it to be solid and certain, to reflect only Christ's love. "Nicky, if you don't want to go back to L.A., you'll find a way to deal with it. You'll find a way to play your music. It's part of you."

Nicky flattened his hand against the grid, and slowly, as if it belonged to someone else, Jasper's hand lifted too. "I believe in you," Jasper whispered. They didn't touch and still it felt like their palms were pressed together. "I think you can do anything you want."

"You do?"

"Yes. And Nicky?"

"Yeah?"

"You're not alone."

Chapter Seven

"THIS IS RIDICULOUS." Jasper stared at himself in the full-length mirror attached to his wardrobe. His black shirt was neatly pressed as always, the black slacks fresh and clean with the straight crease down the middle. He fisted his hair. "I can't wear this."

He opened the wardrobe and reached inside. While he still wore jeans and other casual clothes during his time off, he didn't really own a lot of smart clothes that said 'casual dinner with friends' rather than 'Father Jasper is visiting.' A few years ago, he'd bought a pair of designer jeans more because he was in a hurry than for the tag. He'd only worn them once because it turned out they were pretty tight. But he'd lost some weight recently since his running had picked up in the summer, so maybe...

Jasper took off the slacks and pulled on the jeans. They clung to his behind like a peel to an apple and he groaned inwardly. With quick jerks he yanked the shirt free, smoothed it over his hips so it hung loose, and sighed. It would have to do. Lastly, he undid the top button of the shirt and went in search of his keys as he combed his fingers through his hair.

A couple of persistent waves kept springing back over his forehead but he didn't have time to go back to the bathroom and tame them. When he was about to step out of the door he paused, his hand resting against the frame. Had he been trying to look good for Nicky? He closed his eyes.

Whom have I in heaven but You? And besides You, I desire nothing on earth. My flesh and my heart may fail, But God is the strength of my heart and my portion forever.

Jasper briefly contemplated rushing back upstairs to change back into his slacks but he really was running late, so he walked through the door and locked it behind him. He considered taking his Prius, but the bike would still be quicker—though maybe a little uncomfortable in his tight jeans—if he took all the short cuts. So he swung his leg over the bike and aimed for the Blumfeld house. When they'd been kids all he'd had to do was follow the path through the dense trees from his yard to Nicky's—a path that had formed from their footsteps alone. Jasper wondered if it was still there, or if the years had eroded it as well.

He pedaled up a gentle rise. "I'm going there to talk about the future of Blue Oasis," he said to himself. "Nothing more." Was it his damn pride again? Did he *want* Nicky to turn to him for help? He should be guiding him to seek professional help. The idea of being Nicky's sun and moon again was so tempting, it had to be sinful.

Why does his presence unsettle me so, O Lord? What is Your purpose? Why have You merged our paths again?

But Nicky never did connect easily to strangers. Maybe he couldn't find the help he needed from a therapist because he wasn't capable of trusting anyone enough to build a meaningful relationship.

It might be part of God's plan, or it might not, but if he could somehow ease past hurts with Nicky so they could both move on as friends, then he would. It was his duty.

When he found himself for the second time in as many days facing his reflection in the Blumfeld front door, Jasper had to stamp on his nerves. Mrs. B's shape filled the doorway as she rushed to open it.

"Oh, Jazz, I'm glad you're here." She took him in and gave him a little surprised once-over. "Adrian and Nicky are in the backyard about to take one of the big support beams out of the steps. I'm afraid Adrian's about to hurt his back again. Would you mind helping?"

"Of course," Jasper said, and he followed Mrs. B as she hurried through the house. "I um, was going to bring a bottle of wine, but then I thought—"

"No, it's fine," she quickly said. "I'm glad you didn't. Just your company is more than enough. Adrian!" she called from the patio. "Adrian, put that down. Jasper is here, and he'll help Nicky."

Jasper watched as Nicky straightened, facing Little Bay. It took him a second to turn around and Jasper wondered if he'd been obsessively going over their morning in the confessional too. Did he regret being so vulnerable with Jasper? Had it made any difference at all? What if he'd spent the day with Jimmy? The idea made Jasper's stomach twist.

"You sure you're up for this, Father?" Adrian yelled with a big grin on his face, oblivious to the tension that rippled from his son. "You're not too holy for menial labor these days?"

Nicky snorted and averted his face again, and Jasper smiled at Adrian. He unbuttoned his sleeves and began to roll them up. "I don't mind coming down to the level of you mere humans every once in a while."

"Good man," Adrian said, clapping Jasper on the shoulder as he handed over his heavy-duty gloves. "I'll be inside with Miriam and we'll get you boys a drink." He made a face like he'd let something slip. "Of lemonade," he added, and Jasper watched Nicky roll his eyes.

"We'll be right there," Jasper said. Mrs. Blumfeld and Adrian went inside, and he turned to Nicky. "So where are we going with this thing?"

Nicky looked at him, squinting against the sunlight behind Jasper as he pulled off one glove. "You sure you can bend over in those jeans?"

"They're fine."

"They look like they'll split down the middle."

"They're not that tight. I'll be fine." Jasper fought the urge to tug his shirt down. He'd chosen to wear the jeans, and he'd have to live with Nicky's taunting. Fit punishment for his vanity.

Nicky was wearing a white long-sleeved T-shirt that had seen better days and the front of it had gone translucent with sweat. Jasper could see the outline of his chest hair and on his left pec a vague shape underneath it. At first he thought it was a faded design on the shirt, until he realized it was the shape of a tattoo. He wondered how many more of those were hiding all over Nicky's body.

Nicky pressed the back of his hand against his mouth and wiped at the sheen of sweat there. "You know, I didn't think you'd really show up for dinner." He gestured toward the halfway broken-down stairs. "Never mind help with this."

Jasper frowned at him. He had a streak of dirt on his right cheek and his face was a little red, as if he'd been exposed to the sun for too long after not being used to it anymore. "Why wouldn't I?"

"I figured you'd be, I don't know. Uncomfortable."

Jasper kept trying to catch Nicky's gaze, but apparently interesting things were happening in the grass at his feet.

"Are *you* uncomfortable?"

A hot breath hissed between Nicky's teeth, and he whispered, "Jesus *Christ*."

Jasper's eyebrows flew up. "I'll take that as a yes then."

Nicky's head snapped up and his eyes blazed along with his cheeks. "Yes. Okay? Yes, I'm uncomfortable. I don't spill my guts like that. I don't even have feelings like that. I numb them out."

"Not anymore."

"Everything feels so overwhelming and raw. It's hard to look at you."

"What's said in the confession is between you and God, Nicky. I'm not going to bring it up in the daylight unless you want to talk about it. You shouldn't feel embarrassed. You can lean on me. I'll help you in any way I can."

"Father Jazz." Nicky huffed a laugh but it sounded strained. "Patron saint of do-gooders everywhere."

Jasper gritted his teeth. "Look, I understand you're feeling awkward right now. It wouldn't be the first time people who have confessed certain things to me suddenly cross the street when they see me coming. Or what do I know? Maybe you're angry at me still. And I'm sorry for that. I will tell you right now and I should've said it sooner: I made a mistake back then in not telling you I was thinking of joining the priesthood. I'm sorry I hurt you. I'm sorry you feel this way." Jasper smiled a little to take the sting out of his words. "But right now I'm the only thing standing between you having to pick up this beam by yourself."

The blue in Nicky's eyes was unlike any color Jasper had ever seen anywhere else. When the craze around Vespertine had first started, Jasper had followed it a little bit online, and back then he could sympathize with every fan and reporter that talked about the unreal experience of really being under the spell of Nico Blue's gaze.

Right now he wished that gaze was pointed just about anywhere but at him.

Nicky took a step closer up the hill and gently touched the back of Jasper's gloved hand to remove a big wooden splinter stuck in the material. He hadn't even touched skin, and still a shiver traveled up Jasper's spine.

"You're right," Nicky softly said. He looked down at his own fingertips, dark eyelashes fanning over his flushed cheeks. "I'm angry and I'm embarrassed. But when we were kids you were always there for me. It means a lot to know you still are. And Jazz?"

"Yeah?"

"I was really sorry to hear about your dad."

Jasper nodded. "Thanks. It's a long time ago now."

"Were you still in college?"

"Yep. Final exams."

"That must've been rough. It was a heart attack?"

"Right after he finished a surgery. He died doing what he loved best."

"Still. I'm sorry."

Jasper didn't know where to look under Nicky's steady, compassionate gaze. "So, where to with this beam?"

"There's a skip beside the house. But wait—" Nicky stopped Jasper when he'd been about to bend over to pick up his end. This time Nicky's hand lay on his skin, and he'd never been so aware of a touch. He wanted to yank his arm away but held very still.

"What?" he asked, straightening again. There was a tremor on his breath and Nicky's pupils dilated when Jasper blocked out the sun.

"The wood is pretty moldy. Your clothes will get dirty."

Jasper gently worked his arm free and grinned at Nicky, his chest expanding gratefully as it filled with air. "It's fine. I have plenty of black shirts and I don't wear these jeans very often."

"Too bad," Nicky said, tilting his head to the side so he could get a better look. "You should wear them all the time. Your church would be full."

"Nicky…" Jasper glared.

"What? Just being honest. Isn't that what your God is all about?"

Jasper couldn't help it—he laughed. "You're still such a brat. Now pick up your end, Badger."

Nicky groaned. "Fuck, I'd hoped you'd forgotten about that."

"Not a chance. Fox and Badger. Protectors of the Forest. Who could forget that?"

Nicky dropped his end of the beam twice, and by the time they were halfway across the yard, sweat was dripping down the side of his face.

"Have you been doing this all day?" Jasper asked.

"Not exactly," Nicky managed. With an almighty heave they pushed the beam into the dumpster.

"You sure you don't want that wood for burning?"

"Can't be healthy to inhale all that mold." He nodded his head in the direction of Jasper's chest. A large green swipe of dirt covered his stomach. Jasper wiped at it with his gloves but it was no good. "Besides, I'm not climbing in there to get it back out. Come on, let's go get a drink." He stretched his arms to the sky and yelled, "An alcohol-free drink!"

Jasper gave him a little shove with his shoulder. "You goofball."

Nicky grinned and pushed ahead of Jasper. His lanky shoulders rose too fast, as if he was out of breath. He looked so thin, and his hair hung in sweaty strings around his neck.

"Man, I could do with a shower," Nicky said as he pushed the patio doors open. "Mom, how long until dinner? I reek."

"Twenty minutes, so you have time to clean—Oh Jasper, your shirt! I'm so sorry. I should've given you something else to wear. Nicky, take him upstairs and give him a change of clothes so I can wash his shirt while we have dinner."

Jasper closed the patio door with a much louder bang than he intended. "Mrs. B, it's fine, I—"

Nicky looked over his shoulder with a wicked gleam in his eyes. "C'mon Jazz. You can't eat my mom's Rugelach with lichen smeared all over your front."

Jasper automatically trailed after Nicky toward the stairs. "She made Rugelach?"

Laughing, Nicky began to climb, one hand heavy on the banister. "You really haven't changed."

To Jasper's surprise, Nicky turned toward one of the spare bedrooms. Hesitating, he glanced at the next set of stairs that led up to a large attic room.

When Nicky spoke, his voice came from so close Jasper startled. "I don't sleep up there anymore," he softly said.

"Oh? Did they turn it into a man-cave for Adrian after you left?" That seemed unlike the Blumfelds.

Nicky's shoulder brushed his and Jasper had trouble keeping eye contact. "Triggers. Sense memories of using up there. I need all the help I can get to stay sober." When Jasper said nothing—had nothing to say—Nicky's eyes twinkled. "But we can go up there if you like. Take a look around. Nothing has changed. That old bean bag you loved so much is still up there. Remember that bean bag, Jazz?" Nicky bit his lip and Jasper looked down.

"Don't, Nicky."

"Okay." And easy as that, Nicky stepped away and into the bedroom. "You're taller and a little bigger than me now, but I've got some baggy shirts that'll fit you."

Jasper took a careful breath, his mind reeling in so many directions he couldn't get a grip on a single thought. Not having much choice, he went into the room. Nicky was rummaging around in a drawer until he pulled out a dark red Henley.

"Thanks," Jasper said, reaching for it. He looked around.

"You can change in here." Nicky crossed his arms and leaned against the closet. Jasper didn't move, just stood with the shirt hanging by his side, staring at Nicky. "You need help?" Nicky began to smile, a slow smile Jasper had seen a thousand times, and oh God, it didn't spell anything good. "What is it, *Father*? Am I getting to you? Does it bother you that I still want you?" Nicky leaned forward a little and that wicked, *wicked* smile sucked all the oxygen out of the room. "Does it bother you that I still jerk off thinking of you?"

Jasper clenched his jaw down hard on anything he wanted to say and with brisk movements began to strip out of his shirt. He yanked so hard two buttons sprang off and Nicky's eyebrows rose in amusement. By the time he'd pulled the Henley over his head, Nicky's grin was feral.

"Satisfied?" Jasper asked, angrier than he meant to show. Anger meant loss of control, and he felt like he couldn't risk losing any kind of control around Nicky.

"Hmm. You were a good-looking boy, but as a man? Damn. And I always liked how you looked in red." He pushed away from the closet and crowded Jasper toward the door. When there was no more room to move farther back, Nicky said, "Now, if you'll excuse me, I need to take a shower."

Not until he stood outside in the hallway did Jasper realize Nicky had avoided taking any of his own clothes off with him in the room.

The sound of water from Nicky's en suite bathroom reached his ears, and Jasper headed down the hallway toward what he knew was a half bath and stepped inside. The interior had been repainted, but Jasper recognized the oval mirror and the fixtures like it hadn't been over seventeen years since he'd washed his hands in there. He carefully dabbed water on his face and then dried it—even recognizing the scent of the detergent as part of the old Nicky's smell. A bolt of something hot and no longer familiar shot through his belly and Jasper lowered the towel. The shirt hung loose against his chest but it strained around his biceps. It felt soft and worn and he imagined it was exactly the kind of thing Nicky would sleep in.

What am I doing?

Jasper carefully hung the towel back and made his way downstairs.

He managed to convince Mrs. Blumfeld he could wash and iron the black shirt himself, and when Adrian appeared with the files, she left them to it.

"Take a seat," Adrian said, indicating the comfortable couch. "Thanks for helping outside. Miriam worries too much and my son informs me I'm out of shape."

"Anytime. It's no problem. Just let me know if you need more help with the rest of it, and I'll be here."

"You always were a good kid, Jasper. Even back when you boys got into trouble. I know what you did for Nicky, and while I'm not saying it was right—"

"It's in the past," Jasper quickly said. Adrian gave him a look that said he wasn't so sure, but didn't press.

"All right. Well," he shuffled the files and placed them on the coffee table. "I've taken a good look at this, and basically, as it stands, everything is in the hands of the Catholic Church, and you have no right to claim any of it."

"So there's nothing I can do to keep it LGBTQ-only?"

"Nothing within the Church's boundaries, no."

Jasper covered his face with his hands. He tried to breathe past the sheer disappointment that made his gut ache. He'd been afraid of this, but hadn't allowed himself to worry about it yet.

"You do have some options though," Adrian said. "You'd have to reapply for several grants, find a new location, shut down the old Blue Oasis—which according to your contract you *can* do—and start all over again."

"On my own?"

Adrian shrugged. "It'll take time, and a lot of work. The hardest part will be getting the money together and finding a new location, but since I helped you get the grants in the first place, it wouldn't be too difficult to reapply. You'd have to find other investors on the side because the Church does still pay for some of the other stuff, like the bills for the school, et cetera. But it's not undoable. Especially since you are so well known with the LGBTQ homeless community, and you're the only one running a center like this for miles around. And then there's another option."

"What's that?"

"Bad publicity. If you threaten to go public with the fact that the Church wants to get rid of the only Catholic LGBTQ youth center, they might sit up and listen. I read the article in *The Atlantic*, and I wouldn't be surprised if you have a huge amount of followers and fans out there. You could cash in on that and force their hand."

Jasper was listening but shaking his head at the same time. "I don't want to do that." *But you would*, a little voice in the back of his mind said. *You would if you had to*. "And as far as taking over alone, they'd never allow me to run a place like that outside of the Church's jurisdiction."

Adrian sank back in his chair and raised his hands. "That's between you and the Church, Jasper. You'll have to search your own conscience on that one."

Jasper exhaled hard and rubbed his eyes. When he glanced toward the kitchen he saw Nicky standing there, silent and staring.

NICKY BOUNCED THE basketball against the asphalt driveway and took a shot. It ricocheted off the rim, and he took his time collecting it from the grass. Late evening light burned through the western trees. The setting sun reflected in the bay, a flickering orange as it made its way lower in the sky. Nicky loved the summer nights, how the daylight hours extended well into the evening before darkness finally fell.

The glittering ripple of the bay was rhythmic and he could almost hear it as a piano piece—a series of overlapping notes that grew and faded and grew again. He hummed the music under his breath and tapped his finger against the ball, committing the tune to memory to try out on his mother's Baldwin piano later. He'd played some fine pianos in his time, including a Steinway worth a few luxury cars, but his mother's old upright was still his favorite.

Miriam was right. He'd learned it like a best friend as a child, and its specific tones were as natural to him as the scent of his own skin. He'd spent some time on it earlier in the day. He didn't feel ready to admit to himself that he was creating new songs. They were too raw and deformed; stunted infants born from the clarity of sobriety and doomed to be sacrificed to the hunger of Los Angeles music producers.

Still, it seemed poignant that he was composing them on his oldest love. He glanced toward the kitchen window, seeing his mother laughing and talking, undoubtedly to Jasper. He wondered what they were saying and how Jazz really saw him. He was probably a pretty pathetic human being in his eyes. Fans, platinum records, and covers of *Rolling Stone* wouldn't have impressed young Jazz, and they'd impress this superior, prideful priest even less.

As Nicky dribbled the ball on the asphalt again, he considered the difference between an old instrument and an old lover. His mother's

Baldwin was the same as ever. Maybe a little richer in tone, the wood a little more resonant. It was the same with Jasper. He was taller, filled out, and grown up in a way Nicky both admired and resented. But he was still the same old Jazz. He was still funny, and a party-pooper, and relentlessly realistic, despite his illogical belief in God and his priestly calling. He was still beautiful and admirable.

Unsurprisingly, Jazz had grown into a man who could stand in front of a crowded chapel and deliver sermons that everyone took seriously. And what had Nicky turned into? He stood up nightly in front of a crowd too. He commanded their attention and devotion and *obsession*...but their respect? That was debatable. And even if he had it, he didn't deserve it. Not the way Jasper did. Jasper deserved good things. And good was something Nicky hadn't been in a long time.

A bird called. He took another shot.

"Nothing but net," Jazz said from the darkness of the open garage. Miriam must have let him out that way to collect his bike parked on the sidewalk there. "Great shot."

Jasper emerged from the gloom and the sun glinted on the blond streaks in his hair and illuminated his lashes and golden-brown brows. He looked like someone had smeared a halo all over his face.

The top of Nicky's left foot itched.

"Leaving already?" Nicky asked, walking over to retrieve the ball from where it had stopped in the grass. He tucked it under his arm and pushed his hair out of his face.

"It's not a terribly long ride home, but I don't want to get caught out in the dark. I don't have the proper reflectors."

"Yeah. I can see that." Nicky nodded south toward the woods. "You couldn't stay at your folks' place?"

"Is there a reason I need to stay?"

Nicky grinned. "Well, you still haven't beaten me at HORSE."

Jazz shook his head, smiling softly. "Because you used to cheat."

"You can't cheat at HORSE."

"You did."

"It's called being creative."

"No, it's called cheating."

"Well, I tell you what, I won't be creative tonight. What do you say?"

Jasper put his hands in his pockets and turned his head toward his bike, eyeing it contemplatively. He sighed and pulled his right hand free and looked down at something in his fingers. "Heads or tails."

"Tails. Always."

Jazz laughed and tossed the coin, caught it in his right, and slapped it against the back of his left. "Heads."

Nicky passed him the ball. "When's the last time you played?"

"Last week. The kids at Blue Oasis like to play. Sometimes I join in." Jazz stood about five feet back from the basket and shot using only his left hand. It swished through the net and bounced Nicky's way. He grinned, turning to Nicky with a challenging twinkle. "You?"

Nicky shrugged, moving into Jazz's former position, dribbling the ball a little. He was going to lose unless he found a way to cheat despite his promise not to. "Not too long ago. The band plays sometimes when we find a hoop. Our tour manager used to keep a ball for us because we couldn't keep up with one otherwise." They sounded like irresponsible children. And, in a way, that's exactly what they were.

"It's a good bonding activity." Jasper said.

"Yeah, well, Ramona always wins. Probably because she's always sober." Nicky dribbled some more. Jazz had, of course, gone for the left-handed shot because he knew Nicky sucked at left-handed shots. Well, he could dish it out too, when it was his turn to choose. "Honestly, Ramona just wins at life. She'll be beating the skins ages after the rest of us are dead."

"Stop delaying and take the shot." Jazz smirked.

Nicky narrowed his eyes at him and then went for it. The ball bounced off the rim.

Jazz jogged after it and snatched it up. He threw it to Nicky. "That's an H."

Nicky went in for the teardrop layup that Jazz always had trouble with when they were kids, and groaned as Jazz performed the shot perfectly. For his turn, Jazz chose a behind the head bank shot that went through the hoop like a dream. "You're an asshole," Nicky said, laughing, but he gamely took the shot, missing the goal entirely.

"O," Jazz called out, jogging far into the yard to retrieve the ball and then passing it over to Nicky. Color was in his cheeks and his eyes sparkled with anticipation. "You're going to have to up your game if you're going to keep your undefeated title of Horse Master."

Nicky burst out laughing as he dribbled. "God, I was such a little shit."

Jazz's eyebrows quirked in a way that said, *You still are,* but kept quiet, and Nicky went for the laying-down-on-the-ground-with-his-eyes-closed shot. It flew wide of the basket and Jasper ran over to get it.

"Feel free to get the ball yourself," Jazz said as he took a new position where the three-point line had once been painted several asphalt applications ago.

"Why? You look good running."

Jasper took a traditional bank shot and Nicky caught the ball as it fell through the net. He made his own shot easily and said, "Now you're going easy on me."

Jazz shrugged. "It looks like you can use all the help you can get."

"Okay, I call this the f-shot." Nicky placed his feet wide apart, raised his left hand in the air with middle finger raised proudly, and took an easy shot with his right hand from just to the right of the basket.

Jazz took the ball and considered for a moment before flipping off the sky and making the basket easily too. "Something to add to my usual boring confession of vanity and a slight overindulgence in sugar. Bishop Murray will be titillated."

"Father Murray? He's bishop now?"

"Yep. Ever since I took over."

"Cool beans. I think this sin still falls under the vanity heading, though. Or pride. Whatever. You just can't stand that you're going to lose."

Jasper laughed, his gravel-honey voice rumbling around and echoing off the house and trees. "Says the guy with three letters down."

"Two! Now who's cheating?" Nicky jogged back from fetching the ball, enjoying the movement of his body. He'd been in the pool and working on the steps down to the dock, but he hadn't done any healthy exercise in a long time. He tucked the ball under his arm and tugged at his long-sleeved shirt, lifting the bottom edge to wipe sweat off his upper lip.

"It's warm for long sleeves," Jazz said conversationally, but his eyes were on Nicky's abdomen.

Nicky knew he had a sharp six-pack—more due to lack of body fat than fitness—and he considered lifting his shirt higher and giving him more of a show, but he didn't want to mess up their easy rapport.

"Yeah."

Jazz took the ball from Nicky and dribbled it a few times. "Saving your parents from the worst of the tats?"

Nicky grinned. "No, I'm pretty proud of them for the most part. Though maybe some of them are an homage to things I need to let go of." He looked over Jazz's shoulder and into the woods. He shrugged off thoughts of the fox tattoos and what they stood for: permanent adhesion to a path long eroded. "But I usually like showing them off." He scratched at his eyebrow with his thumbnail and tried to sound like he didn't care half as much as he really did. "But there are some marks on my arms. Inner elbows. You know." He shrugged. "I'm not proud of them."

Jazz looked toward the house and Nicky followed his gaze to where Miriam was framed by the kitchen window, washing something in the sink and talking over her shoulder to his father. "She could handle it, you know."

Nicky bit down on his lower lip. Damn Jazz for knowing him too well and for saying just the thing that would make his throat go tight. He looked down at the new tennis shoes he'd picked up. They were still fresh and white with a navy Nike swish. So different from anything he'd wear in his rock-n-roll life. He wondered what he'd been thinking when he bought them. He couldn't just step into a new pair of ugly-ass suburban-dad shoes and no longer be Nico Blue.

"I don't want her to see them."

"Remember when we were kids and you fell off that too-high limb on Mr. Maples's big oak tree?"

Nicky didn't really want to hear where this was going, but he touched the back of his head with his hand and rubbed the line of hairless skin that his longish flop usually covered easily. "I mainly remember you puking all over Mr. Maples's hammock later in the summer. But yeah, I still have the scar."

"You didn't want her to know then either."

Nicky sighed. "Well, I'm not going to end up in the ER at midnight with a concussion because of the scars on my arms."

"I know. I just never understood that. If it'd been me… well, I probably wouldn't have been really excited to tell *my* mom about it, but I'd probably have happily told yours. She always just wanted to love you."

"I'm not the easiest guy to love. Never have been." Nicky picked at the threads at the end of his sleeve. "What? Don't look at me like that. Take your shot or are we done with the game?"

"You're as lovable as any child of God."

"Well, doesn't that just make me feel special as fuck?"

Jazz sighed and dribbled for a few moments, his expression considering, and then he seemed to shake off whatever it was he'd planned to say next. He spun the ball on one index finger and shot a sly grin at Nicky. "A little trick I use to impress the kids."

"Sexy."

Jazz grinned, and then stopped showing off to take another easy bank shot. He said a little too casually, "Well, it comes naturally. What can I say?"

Nicky snorted and caught the ball beneath the goal. "Are priests allowed to flirt?"

Jazz's expression grew serious. "I'm sorry. I don't want to lead you on or act like there's a chance for—for anything. But I'd like to be friends. I've missed you in my life, and, if I can indulge my pride again—yet another thing to add for confession—"

"Being around me is good for racking up sins."

Jazz rolled his eyes. It was adorable and Nicky wanted to kiss him, but that wasn't going to happen and what Jazz was offering was more than he'd expected.

"You need a friend, Nicky, and I think you need a good person in your life; someone who cares about you and wants the best for you. Someone who doesn't want to load you up and send you out onstage. I did some reading up on addiction and I found this article that talked about the importance of bonding to human beings who have your best interests at heart, to build meaningful everyday relationships. If you can let go of the past, I could be that friend. I'd like to be."

"Why? I'm sure you've got plenty of friends."

"I do. But I've only got one Nicholas Blumfeld in my life and I've really missed him." Jasper swallowed. "I didn't realize how much until I saw you again."

"Say that again?"

Jazz hugged his arms around his middle. "That I've missed you?"

"My name."

"Nicholas Blumfeld?"

"Yeah." Nicky scratched his eyebrow with his thumb. "Okay, it's a deal. Just promise me, you'll never call me Nico Blue?"

"Well, that's easy. I never have. Do you prefer it? Nicholas, I mean. Do you want me to stop calling you Nicky?"

"Nah." Nicky walked closer, his heart climbing up into his throat and pounding there until he could barely speak. "So you think I still have something good to offer the world?"

"Of course you do, Nicky." Jazz's arms fell loosely to his sides. "You have a lot of beautiful gifts. And, maybe someday you can share some of those with a man who loves you."

Jazz reached for the ball in Nicky's hands. Their fingers touched as they both held on. Jazz's Adam's apple bobbed and their gaze held. Nicky cleared his throat, "Whose turn is it?"

"I don't know." Jazz's eyes fell to Nicky's mouth.

Nicky licked his lips and pushed the ball into Jazz's hands, letting go and taking a step back. "I think you won." He chuckled and scuffed his foot on the asphalt, looking at the black marks it made on the white sole of his stupid sneaker. "Guess I've finally lost the title." He looked up and smirked, his stomach knotting at the murky sadness in Jazz's greenish-gold eyes. "Congratulations to the new Horse Master."

Jazz tore his gaze away and looked toward the bay, the breeze ruffling his hair. "The sun's getting low. I should go."

"Sure."

"If you need me, you know where I am?"

"Big building. Steeple on top. I think I can find it."

Jazz laughed but it sounded dry like leaves scraping together. "Call if you want. Your folks have my number."

Nicky shrugged.

"I'd like it if you did. I want to help you, Nicky. I want to make up for—"

"No. Don't do that. I don't want to hear that. Because it can't be made up, got it?"

Jazz swallowed and nodded.

Nicky tried to pull up his big boy pants and say what needed to be said. It was hard. He was so much better at tantrums and acting like a shit. "Listen, if this friendship thing is going to work, you have to let go of the past too. I don't want to be your pity-project because you feel bad for—"

"I don't." Jazz took a deep breath and looked at his hands. "I mean, you're right."

"Add lying to your confession this week."

Jasper's mouth twitched. "I probably should."

A silence fell, filled with a chorus of cicadas trying to get their say before the sun went down. "Well, this is going to be weird."

"We can do it. We were friends for so long. We can be friends again." Jasper sounded almost desperate to convince him.

"Okay. I'm up for it. Why the fuck not?"

They clasped hands and for a second Nicky thought Jazz was going to pull him in for a hug. Panic flared. He couldn't handle that. Touching Jazz, smelling him…it would be too much.

"Bye," Jazz said as he got on his bike with an easy grace. "Hope to see you at Saint Mary's. Or Blue Oasis. You're welcome any time."

Nicky waved as Jazz pedaled off down the drive, the wind flapping his hair and clothes. Then he went back to dribbling and shooting, refusing to watch until Jazz was out of sight.

He could do this friendship thing. Probably. It couldn't hurt worse than it already did. The offer was more than he'd expected, but so much less than he'd secretly hoped for. He really was stunted, wasn't he? Stuck in a fantasy that he'd fueled for far too long with drugs and denial.

If he ever wanted to stop being Nico Blue, Nicholas Blumfeld needed to grow the fuck up.

Chapter Eight

THE SETTING SUN flickered through the trees, and Jasper squinted against it. The Blumfelds' gravel drive jarred his wrists, and he stood on his pedals as the slight slope made him freewheel down. He turned right toward town as a BMW approached from the opposite direction. Jasper moved aside to let it pass but it slowed and rolled to a stop. The window slid open soundlessly, and he looked into his mother's beautifully made-up face.

"Jasper. Did you come from the house? I didn't realize you'd be visiting." She was wearing one of her impeccable suits and her dyed blonde hair was tied neatly in a ponytail.

Jasper moved his hands over the bars, like he was revving a motorbike. "Actually, I was here visiting the Blumfelds."

Crystal Hendricks frowned. "Is everything all right? I saw Miriam last week and she seemed perfectly fine."

"No, it's all good." He considered what to say but she'd find out soon enough. People thought hairdressers got all the gossip, but hospitals were ten times worse. "Nicky's back."

Her mouth tightened. "Oh."

A light breeze lifted Jasper's hair. His shadow stretched long by his side, reminding him of the falling night. He bit down the instinctive knee-jerk reaction to defend Nicky. They were adults now, and she hadn't actually said anything bad about him. Yet.

"I have to go," Jasper said. "It's getting dark and I'd like to get home before it does. I'll come see you soon, okay? You could maybe come to Mass again some time."

Crystal smiled but it wobbled at the edges. "I don't think so, but thank you for the invitation. And yes, do stop by soon. And Jasper, don't be too quick to trust that—"

"Bye, Mom," Jasper softly said, and he pushed off on his bike, listening to the rush of asphalt under his wheels to drown out any thoughts. Inevitably they circled around to Nicky anyway and while he could recite ten Our Fathers to keep his mind away from him, it felt like a coward's way out.

I'm sure you've got plenty of friends.

Did he? Mrs. Wells and Andrew counted as friends, sure, but they weren't people he invited for dinner or a drink. He had his parishioners and he had the kids at Blue Oasis. The only true friend he could count was Thomas, a man in his seventies. Did he need Nicky as much as Nicky needed him? And could that lead anywhere but down a road full of heartache?

Am I being tempted, Father? Are you testing me? Should I turn away from him and look for the true path You have laid out for me?

His mind rebelled so hard at the thought he could barely keep his bike straight. *I can't abandon him and I don't want to believe in a God who'd expect me to.*

Jasper held his breath, half expecting to be struck down, but of course nothing happened because that wasn't God's way. His phone chirped in his pocket but Jasper ignored it. The evening continued to buzz with the song of cicadas. Fragrant heat of the day released from the earth as he passed by strips of wood and water. He was nothing but a speck in the existence of the world—nothing special at all to garner God's attention—and yet, as a kid, he'd felt God like a relentless presence.

Do I still feel that way?

He'd experienced a warm flutter in his heart while playing with

Nicky—the kind he used to associate with his calling—but now it had been at the sight of Nicky grinning and his eyes twinkling, so different from the angry, sunken-eyed man who'd stared him down at the pool. *I just want him to be well again.* And even if the sentiment stemmed from a sea of guilt, it was still a good one.

The fact that his mother wanted him to stay away from Nicky… He frowned.

Jasper turned right onto the gravel path that would take him down a short-cut home and pulled his bike to a stop in a cloud of dust. A little creek ran down the side of the path and if he stayed here too long he'd be covered in mosquito bites.

He knew he didn't have Nicky's number but he had a gut feeling… There was a message waiting for him, and he let out a shuddery breath. Was it a sign?

Safe ride home, Father Jazz.

It took a while to type out the message because Jasper's fingers shook so hard.

If you could go back in time and talk to your younger self, what would you tell him?

It took a full minute for a reply bubble to appear, and it disappeared and reappeared three times before it remained for any length of time. Jasper felt like he'd been holding his breath for far too long by the time the answer came.

I'd tell myself not to be so afraid. To try to make a connection with my mom and dad. I'd tell myself to test my self-imposed boundaries because the cage isn't real.

Jasper stared at the text as the world turned dark around him. Another text bubble popped up.

Was that too much? Were you thinking more along the lines of last week's lottery numbers? Or maybe don't do drugs?

No, Jasper replied. *Your answer was perfect.*

Well, what about you, then?

Jasper didn't reply. Instead he scrolled through his contacts and pressed call.

"Mom, when you grounded me for getting high that one time with Nicky and Jimmy, did I put up a fight?"

"Jasper? What's going on? Are you home yet?"

"Almost. Was I mad at you guys?"

"If this is something that boy is—"

"Can you please just answer the question? I…find it hard to remember that summer." It was a blur of heartache and prayer he'd tried so hard to forget.

His mother was silent for a while and when she spoke, she sounded subdued. "You were distraught for days and days. I'd never seen you so upset before. Your father and I…we often talked about lightening your punishment because you refused to talk to us. You barely ate or left your room, which was so very unlike you. In the end I made you tell me"—she breathed sharply through her nose—"what was going on. With the…being gay, and that Nicholas was your boyfriend. I…we were shocked, your father and I, but we told you we loved you the way you are."

Jasper closed his eyes. "And you told me about how everything I felt had been fueled by hormones. An infatuation, you said."

"I was right, Jasper," his mom said, sounding entirely too reasonable. "I told you I knew a boy when I was seventeen—"

"Who turned out to be a complete disaster and weren't you lucky you didn't stick with him. Yes, I remember. That wouldn't have been Nicky, Mom."

"But it would've been!" she said, suddenly fired up. "It's all over the internet what he's been up to! Drinking, drugs, sleeping with several men at the same time! I'd be surprised if he's not riddled with STDs. Is that what you wanted for your future, Jasper? Yes, I did my best to keep you away from him, and I was *right* to. He's an addict and a whore."

"Mother!"

"I'm sorry." She took a shaky breath. "I didn't mean that. But Jasper, the way he lives his life, no mother would want that for their child. And of course I had no idea you'd choose to go in the opposite direction entirely."

"You mean become a priest?"

"Yes. You were sad for a little longer after you came out to us and then one day you just started to go to church more often." Jasper knew exactly what the catalyst of that had been. "You took on more altar boy duties, you volunteered at the homeless shelter, and you stayed in your room a lot. I remember when you got the acceptance letter for Catholic University and it was like you'd turned a page. As if you'd...grown up. Just like that. In a span of minutes. We were devastated to hear about your choice. You know your father and I wanted you to become a doctor just like—"

"I know you did, but that would've never worked. And I wish you'd get over it and stop letting it prevent you from coming to church." Silence fell and Jasper heard bugs buzz all around him. He shivered.

"Are you okay, Jasper?"

He sighed softly, angling his mouth away from the phone so she wouldn't hear it. "Yeah, Mom. I'm okay. I'll see you soon."

"All right. Bye, Jasper."

He disconnected and stared at the text message thread with Nicky.

You not going to answer?

That's not exactly fair you know.

I think five Hail Marys are in order. Or actually make that five Bloody Marys.

Jazz?

He took a shaky breath. *I'd go back,* he wrote, *and tell myself to stand up to my parents the summer we were grounded.*

No reply came this time. Just the update that the message had been read. Jasper stared at his phone for a while longer, willing Nicky to say something, anything at all. But he shouldn't be looking for forgiveness.

Thinking back it seemed like such a blunder to take his mom's words to heart the way he had. He should've talked to Nicky about the things she'd told him. He shouldn't have just…given up. At the time he'd thought following his calling had been the hardest part of the whole situation, but what if it hadn't been?

When a mosquito bit his neck, he swatted at it, shoved his phone in his jeans, and took off again, only then realizing he'd left his dirty shirt behind at the Blumfelds.

When he made it home, the ginger cat was perched on his doorstep, indignantly swishing her tail.

"I know you have a real home," he told her as he hopped off his bike. "You're too well-fed not to." He rolled the bike into the garage and closed it, then went to unlock the front door for the cat even though he could enter his house from the garage. "Maybe I should buy some real cat food huh? If you're going to hang around here more. I wouldn't mind the company to be honest. Evidently, since I'm talking to you."

While he rummaged around his kitchen, looking for a forgotten tin of tuna, he noticed the light on his landline was blinking and he pressed play.

"Father Hendricks, this is Mrs. Wells. I just wanted to let you know someone entered the school today pretending to be interested in writing another article on the youth group, but as soon as he was in my office, he began to ask about you and your friendship with a certain Nico Blue. I can only guess he meant Nicholas Blumfeld. I hear he's some sort of pop star these days? Needless to say, I sent this man packing, but I thought I'd warn you in case he shows up at your home."

Oh no.

Jasper grabbed his cell phone and then glanced at the clock on his microwave. Ten thirty. He didn't want to call Mrs. Wells this late. He ignored the cat's indignant meow and went to sit in the living room. Curling his feet underneath him, he pulled up the message thread with Nicky again. There were two more messages he'd missed.

Thanks.

That means a lot.

Jasper bit his lip and pushed his blunt nail into the phone's simple black case.

You still up? he typed in the end.

The reply bubble popped up, disappeared, and reappeared.

So tempted to make an inappropriate joke right now, but I won't. See how considerate I can be?

Mind blown, Jasper typed. *Can I call you?*

Sure. You made it home okay?

Jasper didn't bother replying and called instead.

"Hey, what's up?" Nicky's voice sounded soft and velvety, like he was keeping his voice down for his sleeping parents. "You all right?"

"Yes, I'm fine. I'm home. It's just that I received a call from Blue Oasis's supervisor. Apparently someone came around earlier this evening, pretending to be interested in writing an article about the youth group, but then started asking questions about our friendship as soon as he was inside."

"Shit. Fuck." There was a rustling noise, the slide of a door, and the sounds of the night. Jasper heard dim footsteps through grass and then the steadily louder lapping of the waves. Thinking of Nicky standing by the water in the dark of the night gave him a pang of nostalgia so profound he bent forward a little.

"Do you have his name? I should've known it wouldn't take long for one of those fucking vultures to show up. But the fact that they're showing up at the school means he's got nothing to go on but rumors. Did your supervisor say anything? I'm guessing not. Oh Jesus, you don't need this crap around your kids. Fuck. Chances are he doesn't know I'm back and he'll just disappear again. How would he even know we were friends? If someone from the band blabbed about you, I swear to God…uh. Maybe not to God. If I could just—"

"Nicky," Jasper said softly. "Slow down." Instantly Nicky fell silent and Jasper listened to the familiar sounds of the bay at night for a while. He wished he was there instead of talking over the phone, all alone in his house. "We'll be fine. If he shows up again, I'll call the police. Sheriff O'Neill won't put up with any of this. I was worried about you. Do you think they'll come to your house?"

Nicky snorted softly. "Apparently my parents have become pretty good at sending paps and crazed fans packing. But yeah, I'll keep an eye out and be careful. Wear baseball caps and sunglasses."

"Because that works so well," Jasper said.

Nicky snickered. "What's this, Father Jazz? You have a little bit of a thing for gossip magazines?"

"No." Jasper laughed. "But it's not like you can avoid them if you want to visit any kind of grocery store."

"Hmm that's what they all say but I bet you know all about Kim K's latest scandal."

"I do not!" Jasper grinned and settled a little deeper in his couch. "But now that we're on the topic, who did you meet and what can you tell me about what they're really like?"

"Knock me over with a feather. I never would have seen this coming. You want to use me for my ties with the celebrity world."

"Well," Jasper said primly, "I'm sure they could all use a good confession."

Nicky laughed and the sound of it was like music underscored with the lapping of the water. Jasper forgot about his evening yoga, or that he needed to be up early, and they talked for almost an hour. When he finally went to bed he had no trouble falling asleep.

AFTER DISCONNECTING THE call with Jazz, Nicky headed back into the house and up two flights of stairs.

The attic room was virtually untouched. His old Liver Pills, Evil's Tool, and Nine Inch Nails posters all hung just where he'd left them years ago. They were a little dusty, but they weren't even all that faded, protected from sunlight by the narrow north-facing windows and the blinds that were always kept drawn now that he didn't live there anymore. He sat on the narrow, extra-long twin that he and Jazz had hauled up the steep stairs when at thirteen he'd abandoned his old "baby bedroom" for the more teenage-appropriate, angstier attic abode.

The faces of his former heroes stared down at him—all of them transgressive, all of them angry. He'd thought they were kindred spirits, men that knew all about the internal cage. He'd thought they could teach him how to cope with the hurt from all the useless people who couldn't figure out how to get inside, or pull him out. All but Jasper.

God, what a piece of shit kid he'd been. He stood up and tore the posters down. They weren't his heroes anymore. He'd even met the guys in Liver Pills. They were just as fucked up in their own ways as he was.

Slithering snake, glittering eyes
Demon whispers, pretty lies
Heart of carbon in its cage
Beating, screaming, kicking rage

Lyrics he'd written after touring as an opening act for Liver Pills years before. He hated that song. He didn't want to live the kind of life where he wrote lyrics like that anymore. He knelt and rolled up the torn posters and threw them into the dusty trash can. They stuck out awkwardly and he irritably pulled them out again and tossed the paper down the stairs. He'd take it out to the trash later.

The bean bag was in the corner and he crashed down on it, gazing up at the exposed wooden beams angling up to the peak in the roof. There were some cobwebs at the apex and he remembered his mother sitting on his bed while he stood on a chair with a long extension attached to a dust-cloth, resentfully cleaning the webs away. Then his gaze fell to his bed.

"That old bean bag you loved so much is still up there. Remember that

bean bag, Jazz?"

The view of his bed was a pretty good one. He usually slept on his left side. Jazz would have had a view of his face.

Nicky breathed in and out slowly as a hot flush crept up his skin, and his cock woke from its freakishly long slumber. He'd started to wonder if he was even capable of getting hard again. But apparently, all he needed was the fresh image of Jazz's beautiful hands spanning a basketball and the memory of his blushing confession years ago.

"Don't be mad, okay?"

Nicky slung his arm around Jazz's shoulder and nuzzled his throat. "I'll never be mad at you."

But Nicky did get mad. Not because of what Jazz had done, but because of what he hadn't done. "You could have told me! If you'd just told me, we could have had this all along!"

"I was afraid to tell you. What if you rejected me? What if you didn't want me too?"

"So you just jerked off watching me sleep instead? Jazz, you're ridiculous. And I fucking love you."

They'd kissed until their jaws ached and their mouths were red and they were two seconds away from coming in their pants.

The memories used to make him so angry. Even a few days ago he'd been furious about the way Jazz had left him. But he was too tired to be angry now, and it was useless anyway, wasn't it? As useless as drugs, as useless as trying to hurt Jazz, as useless as trying to seduce him too. It really was time to be done with his past. He touched the place on his chest just over the knot of pain he'd guarded.

Go in peace, turn away
A new horizon—

Ugh, no. Terrible. His newest worry fell on him, a slithering sick thought that pulled up from his gut. What if he had to be angry to write music? Or heartbroken? What if joy wasn't something he was capable of creating? What if all he had on offer was pain?

He rubbed his eyes and shook his head. *Fuck that.* He had more to share than misery. Jazz said he had many beautiful gifts to give, and if it took the rest of his life to find them, he'd do that.

Too bad he only had two or three weeks.

"Nicky, sweetie?" Miriam's voice called from the bottom of the stairs. "Come on down. It's late and you said you shouldn't be up there."

Nicky stood up. He'd call Ramona and see if they could figure out some way to keep the assholes in L.A. off their backs for a while longer. If he wasn't ready to go make a record, then he knew the other guys weren't either. Maybe they could offer up a Greatest Hits package in time for Christmas. Or a live album. There had to be a way.

"Nicky?" Miriam's feet sounded on the risers, brushing against the paper posters, and her voice held a note of fear.

"Yeah, I'm okay. Sorry if I woke you. I was just having a look around. Getting some short-sleeved shirts from my old things." He jerked the chest of drawers open to not make a lie of it and dug out five soft old T-shirts, annoyed to realize they were all band tour shirts. He headed toward the stairs just as she reached the top. "I don't mind destroying these while I work on the dock."

Miriam went up on her toes to hug him. She held him very tight. "I know the memories are hard to deal with."

"Sometimes."

"But you don't need drugs to cope."

Nicky's throat tightened. "Go back to bed, Mom. I just want to throw those old posters away."

Chapter Nine

THE NEXT MORNING, Nicky cut the legs off several pairs of his old jeans, which, despite having already gained a little weight since he'd gotten home, still fit loosely around the waist. He also put on one of the Liver Pills tour T-shirts and went down to breakfast. He was out of shape enough that the work on the steps was going slower than he wanted, but he'd get it finished before too long. Then, if he could come up with a reason not to go back to L.A., he'd need something else to do with his time.

Over breakfast, his mother's eyes lingered on the red track-mark scars on the inside of his elbows. Touching them with his fingertips, he said, "They should fade some over time."

She nodded and went back to her coffee, but he'd seen the slight wobble of her lips.

After working on the steps for an hour and a half, he went back in the house and took a phone call from Dr. Rodriguez, his addiction counselor, and discussed how things were going with the maintenance patches and antidepressants.

"Do you plan to come home to L.A. when you're feeling ready?"

"I don't know. I haven't decided what to do. I haven't let myself get too far down that path yet. I get anxious and then I think about using."

"Have you tried the meditation we've discussed? Or yoga?"

"No."

"Nicholas, you need to follow through on my recommendations."

"They both just seem so…" Lonely. Isolating. "I feel like I do better when I'm with people."

"I agree. Maybe you could find a yoga class to take where you could be with people. It will improve your physical health and give you a place to turn when you need to rely on new coping skills. It's key that you find a support system that can keep you buoyed up. It's important to pick who you surround yourself with wisely. Users will want you to use so they can justify their own behavior. It's also important that you choose people who can support you earnestly, without any ulterior motives of their own. Being famous is another hurdle for making a true connection, Nicholas, but if you don't take things too quickly, you'll be fine."

"I'm hanging out with my parents, mainly." Did his interactions with Jazz count? "And my best friend from when I was a kid. He's a priest."

"Perfect. He'll be a good ear for you when you're struggling."

"He offered to help me."

"That's great. Now, are you still having trouble falling asleep at night?"

After agreeing to see if there were any yoga instructors in town and to at least listen to the relaxation meditation before bed, Nicky got off the phone.

After a fast shower, he dressed to go into town, telling himself he was just going to run by the little men's boutique on Lemonhart Lane to pick up a good pair of sunglasses. The ones he'd grabbed at Target were crap and left little black smudges on his nose where the dye couldn't stand up against the acidity of his sweat.

"Sweetie, hold on," his mom said as he grabbed the keys to the truck from the catch-all bowl in the entryway. She took hold of his hands and looked him in the eye. "This morning you seemed embarrassed about your arms. I wanted to tell you that your father and I love you—tattoos, scars, whatever. We love you. We're proud of you. And we believe you are strong enough to beat this, okay?"

Nicky pushed an unruly curl off her forehead and then kissed her cheek. He wrapped his arms around her and held her close. The door to his cage stood open and he took a deep breath and stepped through it, testing his freedom again. "I want to be strong enough but sometimes I'm afraid I'm not."

She squeezed him. "You don't have to be strong all by yourself. Your father and I will be with you through this no matter what."

But not in Los Angeles. Who would he have there? It would be him, Mick, Sez, and Ramona against the world, and maybe it would be enough. But it hadn't been in the past. Of course, in the past, he'd shut them all out like he had his parents when he was a kid. He'd been Nicky-in-the-cage and they'd been outside it, occasionally rattling it, but mostly just living their life without him.

Brains of the operation
Lonely as sin
All connections broken
Beginning to end
Tie a rope
Pull me in

The air conditioning on his father's truck hadn't been hard to fix and Nicky blasted it as he drove down Main Street in the wretched heat. He wore one of the black long-sleeved shirts he'd picked up at the new Target on the outskirts of town, his blue jeans, and the ass-kicking boots he'd arrived in. He didn't turn down Lemonhart Lane; instead he headed directly for the old school he'd attended with Jasper as a child.

As he pulled into the parking lot out front, he took in the changes. The building had been stark, dignified brick when he and Jazz had been submitted to the tyranny of public education, but now the bricks were painted an optimistic white and one wall was covered with a messy but enthusiastic mural of handprints, rainbows, looping, uplifting scripture quotes, and a shiny, gold-toned cross with a bunch of colors radiating out from it. It was the gayest cross of all time. Nicky snorted. How had Jasper managed to get away with that?

No one hung around the parking lot and the streets seemed free of lurking reporters, so Nicky dashed out of the car and up the stairs.

The inside of BO—Nicky's admittedly juvenile new nickname for Blue Oasis—was slightly more dignified, with the same chipped tile he remembered from his childhood. He pushed the heavy door closed behind him and let his eyes settle in the dimness. God. The long hallway even smelled the same. He took a look around, spotting an empty office to his left and an occupied one to the right.

"Oh, Mrs. Wells, hi." Nicky sounded like he had every time he'd ever been caught without his homework in her class. She looked the same too, as if she might pull a ruler from her desk and use it on his knuckles if he was anything less than perfectly polite. She'd never done any such thing, of course, but he'd always thought she might. Maybe it was because he'd been a nightmare student, what with his habit of tuning out anything that wasn't Jazz or music, but he'd been terrified of Mrs. Wells and her pressed lips of disapproval when he'd been a kid.

"Nicholas Blumfeld. I had no idea you were in town. That explains a lot actually."

"I haven't been here long." He was surprised the rumors hadn't spread already. He supposed that was one benefit of keeping his tats covered and his profile low. "But Jasper told me about your visitor last night. I think he was just testing the waters, or he'd have come straight to my parents' house. I'm sure I can—"

"We'll deal with intruders, Nicholas. We don't need your help." She cocked her head and looked up at him appraisingly. "I hear you're a big star now."

Nicky didn't know how to reply to that. It wasn't the first time he'd heard it, but he never knew what he was supposed to say. *Yeah, I am?* Or *Gosh, no. You must be talking about someone else.* Both seemed like bullshit. "I'm in town visiting my folks," he said instead.

"I know they miss you." Oh, now that was an accusation. No doubt about it.

"I've missed them too."

Mrs. Wells lifted her eyebrows and cleared her throat, restacking some papers on her desk. "Well, how can I help you?"

"I thought I'd stop by to see Jazz—Per. Um, Jasper." She narrowed her eyes at him. "Uh, I mean the Father?" She nodded and then glared at the mehndi tattoo on his left hand. Nicky sighed and shoved his hands in his jeans pockets. "I wanted to see what he's getting up to these days. My parents are really impressed with this place and all he's done here."

Praising Jazz seemed to be just the thing because Mrs. Wells smiled (had he ever seen that before?) and nearly glowed as she agreed that Jasper was a virtual saint. "I know your parents don't share our faith, but I'm so glad to see that his good works are visible outside of our little Catholic community." She seemed to take an almost vain delight in telling him, "He's such a good person, such a devoted man of God. He's a blessing to everyone who knows him."

Nicky nodded. "I'm sure he is."

"Well, he's about to start his morning Mass but he'll be around shortly. You could wait." She nodded to a blue overstuffed chair and a coffee table covered in *Catholic Digests*. "Or I could let him know you dropped in and schedule an appointment for you to come visit later this week."

"I'll wait," Nicky said, but he had no intention of sitting in that chair under her watchful eye. "Mind if I have a look around?"

"Oh, I…well, I…" She looked flustered. "We don't usually let people just walk in off the street and move freely about the facilities. I'm sure you understand the obligation we have to keep the children safe."

"Of course. But maybe you could give me a tour? If there's anyone who knows this place as well as Jazz—the Father, I'm sure it's you."

Flattery seemed like it wasn't going to be enough to work but then the phone rang and Mrs. Wells answered. "Blue Oasis. Oh, Father. Yes, there's a man here to see you. Nicholas Blumfeld." She said this meaningfully like she was trying to tell him Satan had made his way into the walls of Blue Oasis without alerting the fallen one to her indiscretion. "Oh? Are you certain? Some of the children are..." She turned away from him and whispered loud enough for Nicky's old deaf Aunt Ellen to have heard perfectly, "Very impressionable. All right. Of course. Whatever you say, Father. I'll be happy to show him around."

After a short discussion about the original purpose of Jasper's phone call, something to do with sermon notes accidentally sent to his Blue Oasis email, she hung up and said, "Well, then, Nicholas. It seems like I'm going to be your tour guide. Follow me."

She showed him the cafeteria first, which to his pleasant surprise, looked nothing like the gray metallic coffin it used to be. A cacophony of colors screamed at him so loudly he wanted to laugh in delight. He could imagine a group of kids hanging out here, talking, joking around, and erupting into the occasional friendly food fight. He glanced at the stern Mrs. Wells with her tightly bound hair and neatly folded hands in front of her. Food fights when she was on vacation maybe.

Mrs. Wells was very thorough in her tour, taking her time and showing Nicky everything. He wasn't sure if she was dragging her feet or just that dedicated.

"As you've seen, most of the building is still the same. We converted ten of the classrooms and added baths so there was one to share for every four children. Most of the other rooms are closed but we use some for homeschooling if needed, therapy sessions and recreation too. And, of course, if we get the funding to expand the program, we could convert more space." Here she looked at Nicky significantly. *Oh, she'd decided he might become a donor!* That must be why she was giving him the long tour. He wondered if Jazz had planted that idea or if she'd come up with it for herself.

When Nicky didn't respond, she went on, "The gym is still the same, and we have one large recreation room where more of the kids hang out during downtime." She eyed him. "That's where they'll be now."

"Cool beans. Can we go say hi?"

She hesitated and he was convinced she'd say no. "Just behave yourself, please."

What did she think he was going to do? Strip down naked and start pulling syringes full of heroin out of his ass? Maybe sprinkle them all with cocaine like it was fairy dust?

"I'll keep my potty mouth under control," Nicky said, and Mrs. Wells rolled her eyes and began to climb the stairs to the second floor.

The tiles of the massive room were covered with rugs of various colors and textures. A long red plush sofa was pushed up against one wall, and a cream and black plaid couch, made of some fuzzier material, was pressed up kitty-corner, making a little gathering area around a broad wood coffee table. There were bean bags and large cushions all around, some close to the cozy little meeting area and others farther away. And on these surfaces, teenagers of all shades, genders, and sizes stretched, curled, or flopped. In a corner, there was a big, full bookcase, and against it leaned an acoustic guitar. Nicky's practiced eye thought it was an Epiphone Pro-1 Plus, not a bad starter instrument, but it was a Les Paul and Nicky preferred Fenders. Next to it was a Yamaha keyboard on a sad-looking stand, a box of egg shakers, and a tambourine.

"Children, may I have your attention," Mrs. Wells called out. Nicky noticed none of them seemed especially intimidated by her; all of them remained in their same positions, at most swiveling their heads to see her better. "Father Hendricks' friend, Nicholas, has come to pay a visit. Can we all give him a warm Blue Oasis welcome?"

"Welcome," the group mumbled, not exactly enthusiastically, but not as though they really cared either.

"Let's try that again, with some life this time, shall we?"

"Welcome!"

A boy with dark black hair and freckles on his nose wore an Evil's Tool T-shirt and was hunched over a pile of books, studying and ignoring Mrs. Wells completely. A young black girl—*boy? no, girl*—sat close to him and she nudged him with her foot.

"Jason, manners," Mrs. Wells said, and the boy looked up.

His eyes went wide. "Holy crap. You're Nico Blue."

"Jason!" Mrs. Wells scolded though she sounded almost desperately helpless, like this was only to be expected, of course.

Nicky smiled. "Nah, I just play him on TV."

"No, man. Holy craparoni! You're really him!"

Nicky shrugged. He didn't want to be Nico Blue anymore. Nico Blue was an addict and a disaster, and no one these kids should ever be looking at with eyes like that. Still, he didn't think he should lie either. He looked to Mrs. Wells, hoping she'd save him. But she just frowned at him like he (and Jasper) should have known better.

The kid hopped up and came at him like a homing device. "Wow, I can't believe it's you."

The murmurs and whispers that swept over the room when Jason had first called him Nico Blue now turned into action. The kids abandoned their corners and cushions and their couches and books to come bustle around him. Their bodies somehow moved him toward the big round ottoman set off from the rest of the furniture just enough that he knew Jazz must sit on it during his visits to the group.

Then he was sitting on it too. Mrs. Wells was still close by, but the kids had crowded her out.

Jason thrust the guitar into his face. "Dude, c'mon. I know you're Nico Blue. Will you play for us? Oh, c'mon! Play 'Stigmata Hands.'"

Nicky accepted the instrument like he didn't know how to do anything else. The guitar was pretty beat up, but when he strummed, it was perfectly tuned. Nicky stared at Jason's guileless sea-blue eyes as he finger-picked the opening notes of the requested song, his hands obedient as a fucking jukebox. The culminating lyrics of the first verse rose in his mind.

My hands bleed
From all the skin I touch
That isn't you

There was no way he was going to play that song while looking at these kids' faces. Not here in Jazz's safe place for them. It would be wrong.

"How about we play a game instead," Nicky said, forcing his fingers to play something else, anything else. They defaulted to a new melody he'd been stumbling through on the piano that morning. A twisted, broken thing with lyrics that soured his mouth to even think about. It would never see the light of day, but the melody was nice, and at least Jason wouldn't recognize it and beg for more.

"What kind of game?" Jason seemed skeptical and disappointed.

Nicky tried to infuse his voice with fun, the tone he remembered Toni, Jasper's favorite babysitter, using when she'd taken care of them as a kid. "You name a song, any song, and I'll play it for you. But here's the fun catch—it can't be a Vespertine song."

"Any song?" a girl with green eyeliner asked.

Jason scowled.

Nicky nodded. "Any song at all. If I've heard it, I can play it. I might not recognize it by name, and I might forget a few of the lyrics, but you guys can help me out, right?"

"Cool!" a voice from the edge of the small mob said.

Nicky shot a smile that direction, hoping it hit its mark.

"What if I asked for something really old?" a pimply faced boy murmured, his arms crossed, but his expression avid. "Like, you know, old-old. From before you were born."

"Like what?"

"My grandpa used to listen to 'Raindrops Keep Fallin' On My Head,'" another guy said, a muscular, football-player type. Handsome in a rugged way.

Nicky immediately plucked out the chorus of the song. He'd played it for his own grandmother when he was just five years old.

"What? So, like, you're a musical genius?" Jason said, still frowning.

Nicky laughed. "You say that like it's a curse word."

"I say it like you're a liar."

He let his fingers fall hard against the strings while his left hand held down a discordant note. Then he smiled at Jason. "Well, first, that's rude, and second, I'm a terrible liar, and I'm really rich, so I can buy my way out of most problems that come from telling the truth. So I make it a policy to never lie." He made a clicking sound with his tongue against his teeth.

"My foster mom said everyone in Vespertine's a gross addict," a small boy near the edge of the group said in a sullen, hostile tone.

"Shut up, Gus."

Nicky noticed the dark circles under Gus's eyes and the insecure way his arms were crossed over his developing chest. Another transgender kid. That had to be fucking tough. If Nicky had been in a cage in his mind, these kids were in a cage in their bodies too. It made his stomach hurt to think about it. He cleared his throat and said quietly to Gus, "Your foster mom must have cared about you. She didn't want you to grow up to make mistakes."

"She kicked me out when I told her the truth about myself."

"Well, maybe I was wrong. Maybe she was a bitch."

Everyone tittered and dark smiles broke out over the faces of everyone in the group. Nicky glanced around and was glad to see Mrs. Wells had left them to it. Huh. Maybe she didn't think he was going to fuck up these fragile little minds too much after all.

"Yeah, she was a bitch. Fuck her," Gus muttered.

"Nope. None of that. You'll get me in trouble with Father Jazz and he won't let me come back here anymore."

"Father Jazz? Do you mean Father Hendricks?"

Oops? Ah, well. "Yep. He's not big on swearing. But when we were kids…" Nicky made a face. "Well, I guess he wasn't big on it then, either. He's always been kind of uptight and perfect. Annoying."

Some of the teenagers laughed.

"You knew him when you were both kids?"

Nicky nodded. "Yep. All the way through high school. Mrs. Wells was our teacher." He leaned forward and whispered, "She hated me."

Gus shook his head. "Mrs. Wells is nice. She doesn't hate anyone."

Nicky shrugged. Maybe she'd turned over a new leaf or maybe he had just been special.

"Hey, I have a question," a tall red-headed freckled girl said from where she stood with her arms crossed and her feet planted wide. "Were you boyfriends?"

Nicky laughed, throwing his head back. "You guys are worse than the paparazzi. 'Nico Blue, Nico Blue! Are you dating the guy you bought groceries from last week?'"

They all giggled and blushed.

"So, are we going to play the game or not?" Jason asked, sullen as ever, but apparently ready to hear Nicky play anything at all.

"Superbass," someone called out.

"By Nicki Minaj?" Nicky asked with a sharp grin.

"Yeah." It was obvious the teenager who'd picked the song thought he would stump him, and he seemed disappointed that he knew the artist.

"Okay." He thought for a moment and then picked out opening notes. Everyone looked skeptical until he opened his mouth and the staccato rap lyrics came spilling out. Nicky grinned as they broke into applause. Vespertine had a roadie on the last tour who was obsessed with Nicki Minaj and Nicky'd heard the song plenty of times, apparently enough to know every last lyric and not require any help from the gobsmacked kids who gathered even closer to listen.

"Something's Gotta Give!"

"Hmm, refresh my memory. I might not have heard it."

"You know, by All Time Low." The scruffy teenager was wearing an old-skool Pretty Hate Machine tour T-shirt and sang some of the chorus in a scratchy baritone. Nicky recognized it and started strumming along, nodding his head, and he joined in when the kid began the next verse. They sang the entire song together, and Nicky hit the final vocal note with a grin on his face.

"Pink Bullets," a soft voice murmured when the clapping had died down.

"Oh, The Shins." He swallowed back a comment about wanker music because Gus wouldn't understand how much he identified with that sound lately. "All right."

A calmness descended during the quiet song, and he closed his eyes, letting memories fill his mind of young Jazz in the sunshine, playing in the woods together and rowing across the lake with supplies for their fort. The nostalgic ache infused his competent-but-not-special voice.

After playing another thirty minutes worth of songs, Nicky caught the eye of the black girl who'd been sitting beside Jason when he came in. She was wearing a hoodie, and she messed with the drawstring as her dark eyes followed his fingers on the fretboard. Her lower lip slipped between her teeth. He studied the certain angularity of her face and the prominence of her Adam's apple, which told him testosterone was already working against her true identity.

"How about you?" he asked her after the next round of clapping was over. "Do you have a song you'd like me to play?"

She shrugged anxiously. Everyone had turned to look at her and she was clearly unnerved by the attention.

"C'mon, Lizzie. Give him a good one," Jason said. "Something by Liver Pills."

She made a face at him. "As if, Jason."

"How about naming a band that you like, Lizzie?" Nicky interrupted when it looked like Jason would argue. "Any band but Vespertine."

"I don't like Vespertine."

Nicky smiled. "Okay. That should make it easier then."

Her gaze met his and she sounded almost embarrassed by her request. "Fine. Play 'With or Without You.'"

"U2. Got it."

Nicky closed his eyes again for this one, feeling Lizzie's measuring gaze bore into him with suspicious judgment. She clearly doubted he could pull this off, despite having just watched him perform many other songs.

As he picked out the notes, he tried to find the emotions he needed to bring the music to life. His fingers moved over the fretboard effortlessly and he let a movie play in his mind. Green-hazel eyes that shifted color in sunlight and golden-brown hair that fell a little too thick and definitely too long for a priest. Full, almost heart-shaped lips and golden lashes against strong cheekbones. A sunset glowed behind Jazz through Nicky's attic bedroom windows, as, with desperation in his gaze, he forced a wound into both their hearts.

Yearning became a thing with a rhythm and a heartbeat, and the song grew into the past made manifest. The sound of shifting bodies stilled and Nicky's voice trembled as he sang on. His fingers never failed, though, and the broken heart he'd never recovered from bled through his voice and hands.

Halfway through, fingertips gently grazed his shoulder and he opened his eyes to see Lizzie had moved to stand beside him. She stared at him like she was seeing a human being for the first time.

He swung to the side so he was singing directly to her and, as he came to the bridge, she joined in. Her voice was a pure, thick honey and it poured over his scratchy, vulnerable tenor and soothed it. They sang together through the end of the song with her fingers resting on his shoulder. When it was over, she smiled at him. It made his heart hurt.

Applause broke out hard and wild, and he gestured to her to take a bow. She did and the other kids whistled and slapped her on the back, telling her she'd done great.

"Wow, Lizzie! I didn't know you could sing like that!" Gus whispered shyly, and Jason looked impressed, too.

Lizzie's eyes glowed.

A noise came from across the room and Nicky looked up expecting to see Mrs. Wells's usual stern expression calling an end to their fun. Instead he found Jasper standing frozen by the doorway, his eyes heavy-lidded and his mouth softly open, his right hand pressed to his heart.

"WHEN'S THE LAST time you went on vacation?"

"Me?" Jasper gave Andrew a curious look. "Don't really know. Why? You thinking of going somewhere? I'm probably not the right person to recommend a place." He tucked his clerical shirt into his pants and made sure the sacristy was tidy.

"No, I'm not going anywhere. I just figured you must have a lot of time saved up. You could use some of it, take a break. Go somewhere new."

"Andrew?" Jasper put a hand on his hip. "What's going on?"

Rubbing at his wrinkled cheeks, Andrew sighed. "You were distracted during Mass. Just like yesterday, I'm sorry to say. And now you look like you can't get out of here fast enough." Jasper froze, but Andrew pushed on. "When you saw those two people waiting for confession I thought you were about to tell them to come back some other time."

"I didn't—"

"And it's fine," Andrew insisted, taking a step closer. "Being a priest is having a full-time job in the truest sense of the word. You haven't taken a real break in years, Jasper. Calling or not, this is still a *job*. If you're getting burned out, it's normal. But don't let it get to a point where you find it affecting your mental state and your health."

"It's not. I didn't mean for any of that to happen, but you're right. I had my mind on other things and it was wrong of me. I'll pray to God for forgiveness." *Later,* he almost said, but he bit it back just in time. *Add it to the list, along with lying and giving the sky the finger.* What was happening to him?

Andrew looked at him with sadness in his eyes. "You're missing the point, Jasper. I'm not reprimanding you. I'm worried about you."

"I'm fine. I just want to get to Blue Oasis." *And Nicky.*

The sun beat down hard on the asphalt when he left the church, and Jasper's black shirt stuck to his back before he'd even rounded the corner. An almost feverish feeling urged him to be at the school, and he couldn't deny it—while spending time with the kids at Blue Oasis was always the highlight of his day, the thought that Nicky might still be there was the true pull. And yes, Jasper wanted to help Nicky, be a friend to him, make this friendship work for both their sakes, but it didn't explain why his feet seemed to have wings as they carried him up the steps to the front door.

"Father Hendricks!"

He froze in the hallway and did his very best to not curse, even inwardly. "Mrs. Wells." He turned to the office. "What can I do for you?"

She held the door and stepped aside. "Do you have a moment?"

The faint trickle of guitar notes drifted down the hall and an ache began under his breastbone, like something had hooked him there and was drawing him inexorably toward the sound.

"Yes, of course," he said and it was almost painful to make his feet move toward her.

"Nicholas Blumfeld is still here." Her eyebrows drew down. "Or should I call him Nico Blue?"

"No." Jasper fixed her with an unapologetic look. "He doesn't go by that name, unless he's performing."

Mrs. Wells blinked. "Okay. Well, he's still here and the kids are already starting to turn toward him with the kind of hero worship that I can't indulge, Father. I know you used to be friends, but surely you understand what a bad influence a man like Nicholas can be on these impressionable young children. They're already broken and some of them are kicking drug habits themselves. Having a man like that around could be very detrimental—"

Jasper breathed deeply and evenly and his shoulders relaxed as he felt God's presence like a hand on his shoulder. "A man like what, Mrs. Wells? Someone who is repentant of his sins? Who has been through hell and is trying to make things right despite prejudice and the other demons that haunt him? Someone who truly means to make things better, for himself and for the people he may have hurt in his path? Does any of this sound familiar to you, Mrs. Wells? What do you think Jesus would do, if he was here with us? *I came not to call the righteous, but the sinners.*"

She pursed her lips. "How do you know he really is repentant? How do you know he's not secretly carrying drugs in here?"

"Because I know him. And I believe in him, and I will give him the benefit of the doubt rather than judge him harshly. Do you know what addicts need the most? To build relationships with human beings who care about them, and instead society casts them aside like modern-day lepers. The entire idea Catholicism is based on, Mrs. Wells, is to do good to those who are less fortunate. Instead religion has turned into a veneer of charity and Bible-quoting while we turn our backs on those who need us, however they may look, however they may have sinned."

"Father," Mrs. Wells said, eyes wide. "I have spent every single moment of my time over the past seven years looking after these kids. I resent what you imply. Nicholas Blumfeld was a troublemaker as a child and from what I've learned about his life since, he's only worse. He may want to change, but until I've seen that change I will stand between him and these children." Her eyes shimmered a little and Jasper felt terrible when she turned on her heels and left.

Mrs. Wells was not his enemy. She'd been an ally on his darkest days and now he'd hurt her feelings. He stepped out into the hallway but she was nowhere to be seen. The music bounced off the walls like tantalizing echoes but he turned away from it and went into the cafeteria. Mrs. Wells stood by the coffee maker, dabbing her eyes.

"I'm sorry." Jasper put a hand lightly on her shoulder but she didn't turn around. "You are absolutely right in wanting to protect the kids and they, the Church, and me, we're all lucky to have you. I was out of line. But let me vouch for Nicky. He needs our help, not our contempt."

"I've been a great help to you," Mrs. Wells said hoarsely.

"Yes, you have."

"And I've always been on your side."

"I know, Mrs. Wells."

"You hurt my feelings."

Jasper's chest felt tight. "That wasn't my intention. I'm really sorry."

She turned around and gave him a weak smile. "I know you are. Okay. I'll give Nicholas a chance. But I'll be watching him."

"Thank you." Jasper squeezed her shoulder and finally allowed himself to go where he'd wanted to be all along.

He almost turned around to grab two coffees but then a melody reached him, the sound familiar and wholly different from any performance he'd heard before. His throat went tight as he realized what he was hearing and his heart began to thud. Leaving Mrs. Wells and all thoughts of coffee behind, he followed the thread of music, hearing it get thicker and fuller as he walked. His steps echoed through the hallway, up the stairs, harder and faster until he was running.

The door to the rec room stood ajar, and there was Nicky, guitar in his hand, looking more like his old self than Jasper had seen him since he'd arrived here. He sang to Lizzie as if there was no one else in the world who mattered. The kids all stared at him in rapture, for once too caught up in the moment to remember they were gangly, awkward teenagers.

Every word Nicky sang reflected on his face. Every wounding loss, every flaying emotion passed through his eyes before it left his mouth, and Jasper could only stare.

Nicky and Lizzie's voices harmonized beautifully, reverberating in a space deep inside of Jasper, a forgotten chamber of his heart that'd been empty for years. A long extinguished yearning burned in his veins, flooding his chest and belly with a warmth that spread outward until the hairs on the back of his neck rose. A thick knot settled in his throat and a tear tracked its way toward his mouth before he even realized his eyes were wet.

The ache in his chest grew and grew, until he instinctively pressed his hand over it. If this longing spread any further he'd be utterly, completely lost. His fall would be inevitable, like the rebelling angels against God.

And I'd fall gladly, Jasper thought in the deepest, darkest corner of his mind, as the song came to an end.

Lizzie looked more alive than she had since she'd arrived in the church, small and scared. Nicky seemed more real too, more solid than Jazz knew how to deal with. There were too many feelings attached to Nicky when he looked like this: beautiful, open, vulnerable.

I'll spread my arms and fall to my demise and let it embrace me like the wings of an angel.

"Hey, it's Father Jazz!"

Jasper blinked. He wasn't sure who'd spoken but the entire group began to laugh. "So you've met our local rock star, have you?" he said, finally tearing his eyes away from Nicky's intense blue scrutiny. The kids began to talk all at once and he tried to pay attention to them instead, but he remained painfully aware of Nicky gently plucking the strings on his guitar. "Okay, okay calm down. I need to talk to my friend for a second. Mark, Angie, you go down and get lunch prep started. Gus, I think you have dishwasher duty, and it was still full when I checked this morning. The rest of you, go outside, enjoy the summer while it lasts."

"Can I take a selfie with you, Nico?" Mark asked.

Nicky glanced at Jasper, who shrugged. "Sure," Nicky answered. "If you want. Just...don't put it on any social media and tag me, okay? I'm trying to keep a low profile."

"Can I put it on our Blue Oasis page? It's private. I won't tag you, I promise."

When Nicky looked toward Jasper again, Jasper said, "No one looks at it apart from the kids, Mrs. Wells, and the odd follower from the church itself. It's pretty secure."

"Okay then."

Everyone ended up crowding around Nicky. when he lifted his eyebrows in question, Jasper joined him. He crouched down beside Nicky, their shoulders touching, while Nicky hugged his guitar. Lizzie took the picture with five different cell phones and then came over for a picture with her own.

"That's enough," Jasper said when more cell phones appeared. "Get to your chores, everyone."

"Yes, Father Jazz," at least five of them said, and Jasper rolled his eyes to the ceiling.

"How long did it take you to teach them that?" he asked Nicky.

"About three seconds."

When Jasper looked down, Nicky was grinning. The kids had all cleared out and the walls of the room closed in on them as Nicky began to hum.

"Why don't you ever sing? On stage I mean. You write all the songs, don't you?"

Nicky made a face. "Don't have the voice for it."

"I think your voice is gorgeous."

Nicky waved his hand around and then continued playing softly. "For a room this size, maybe. For an arena? Not so much. My vocals aren't strong enough."

Jasper wanted to reach out and push a thick hunk of dark, wavy hair off Nicky's forehead. "Well, you moved everyone in here. Deeply."

Nicky lifted his head and stopped playing. "Did I move you?"

Jasper bit his lip and considered what to say. "You remember how I used to sit in church as a little kid and listen to the choir practice Gregorian chants?"

Nicky laughed under his breath. "God, you were such a dork. You're right, I should've seen the priest thing coming from miles away."

Jasper felt an indulgent, fond smile slide over his lips. "Do you remember what you always said to me?"

The smile slipped slowly off Nicky's face and something heartbreakingly fragile flickered in his eyes. "That you looked like you were seeing God."

Jasper felt too big for his skin. Like he was nearing the top of a roller coaster, and any second now the apex would creep up on him and over he'd tumble. And yet, he couldn't seem to stop saying exactly what was on his mind. "Because I experienced it like that. Sitting in that church with those strong voices singing in languages I couldn't understand yet…it took me somewhere higher. And you…" He faltered. "You've got to know you affect people like that. Every kid in here was spellbound."

Nicky tilted his head. His blue eyes seemed to see straight through Jasper. "You didn't answer my question."

Jasper crossed one arm over his midriff and gripped the other arm tight to his body. "Of course you moved me. That's obvious." He laughed softly and averted his eyes. "To be honest, I haven't been moved like that in a long time."

Nicky's eyes glinted and his lips quirked into a smirk but his eyes weren't smiling along. "Well, I always had a certain effect—"

Jasper gritted his teeth. "Don't turn this into a joke."

Nicky's chin jerked up. "I'm not joking. I hear what you're saying. You like my singing, that's great. Now if only I didn't need to hate the world and everything in it to be able to write decent songs, we'd be golden."

Jasper saw the opportunity to shift the conversation and escape the helpless confessions he'd been making. Instead he slowly reached for the hand that lay motionless on top of the guitar. His fingers shook slightly.

"I'm saying I love your singing. Me, Jazz, your friend. Not the priest. I'm saying I think you have a talent beyond even your own comprehension, and I've learned over the years that talented people always judge themselves more harshly than others. You'll find your lyrics, Nicky. You might just have to look for them in a different place."

Nicky kept his palm turned down onto the guitar, but he spread his fingers and Jasper's slipped neatly in between them. The calluses from the steel strings of countless guitars felt good and right against his own soft hands. He could feel Nicky's eyes on his face, but he didn't look into them, keeping his focus on their entwined fingers. He'd opened up and made himself vulnerable in ways he'd forgotten were possible. He thought he should be scared or ashamed of what he was doing, touching Nicky's hand this way, but all he felt was a sense of peace.

"You want to go get some lunch?" Jasper tightened his hand around Nicky's and then slowly made himself let go.

"Sure." Nicky set the guitar aside and rose to his feet. He grinned and bumped Jasper's shoulder on their way out of the rec room. "I moved you."

"Don't let it go to your head."

"I think there was a tear. You giant softy."

Jasper wrapped his arm around Nicky's neck and gave him a noogie. "Learn to accept a compliment, Badger."

Chapter Ten

IT HAD RAINED for hours before the sun rose on Thursday morning. Jasper could smell the sweetness of fresh summer growth even within the walls of his church. The pews were full of people dressed in black, the silence among them so pure he could hear the wood creak in the rafters as it settled and dried under the warming sun. A young girl, maybe twelve or thirteen, slowly climbed the sand-colored marble steps toward the altar. As she passed the dark wooden casket, the piece of paper she held in her hands trembled. He was ready to take over if she faltered, even though his singing voice wasn't great. It'd been trained over the years to at least keep a decent tone.

In the first row sat a young mother with a boy by her side. She cried while the boy stared empty eyed at the casket.

Thy will be done, Jasper thought. He didn't have to understand it. God acted for his own reasons.

The girl glanced at him and he offered her a small smile and a nod. "Whenever you're ready," he whispered. She didn't cry but she looked like she might, any moment now. Slowly she turned around. Her knee-length black skirt whispered around her legs. When they'd planned the funeral he'd asked the mother if it was a good idea to do this, but the girl had insisted.

When she closed her eyes and opened her mouth and began to sing it was as if the church itself let out an audible sigh. No one spoke, but everyone lifted their head, and Jasper felt goosebumps rise all along his forearms and up his neck. The feeling she infused into the words hurt his insides and, God's will or not, why did she have to lose her father so young? Silent tears dripped from her cheeks and yet only once did her voice quiver. It never gave out. *Amazing Grace indeed.*

By the time the service was over, Jasper felt drained to the depths of his soul, especially since he'd already done the daily Mass before the funeral this morning. He loved his work—he loved belonging to God and the Church—but there was nothing that took it out of him like the funeral of someone passing away too young after a grueling fight with illness.

"There's no such thing as too young," Thomas used to tell him. "We all go when God calls us to Him. We go when it's our time."

He'd known from his years studying theology that there were certain things in Catholicism and the Bible he didn't agree with. He didn't have to, as long as he had the strength to believe.

Some days it was harder to focus on the things he did agree with.

He sighed when at last the church was empty again. At least he had Thursday afternoons off.

Andrew stepped back into the sacristy with him to help him take off the priest garb.

"You all right, Father? You look tired."

Jasper smiled at him. "Just some trouble sleeping again, Andrew. Nothing to worry about."

"Your yoga not helping anymore?" Andrew grinned. For some reason he found it hilarious that Jasper had taken up yoga a few months ago to help him deal with sleepless nights.

"I haven't done it in a couple of days, so that might be it. And I have some things on my mind."

Andrew turned serious. "Anything I can help you with?" Jasper gripped his shoulder and shook his head but Andrew held on to his hand before he could pull away. "I know you talk to God, but if you need someone who actually talks back out loud, I'm always here."

"Thanks Andrew. You're a great friend."

Andrew gave him a look and then nodded, as if he accepted Jasper wasn't going to talk to him today. "Well, enjoy your afternoon off. I'll take care of the rest of things here."

He hadn't even had the chance to take off his collar yet when his phone rang, lighting up with the Blue Oasis office number.

"Father, it's Mrs. Wells. There's been an accident at the school. Gus and the others were playing football and he got tackled to the ground. He hit his head pretty hard and I think he may have a broken collarbone. The ambulance is on its way."

"I'll be right there."

Paramedics were unloading a stretcher from the ambulance when he rounded the corner to the school entrance. He found Mrs. Wells and a bunch of kids looking pale as they milled around the playground. "Where is—" he began, and then he saw Gus lying down with a blanket draped over him, a scrunched-up hoodie underneath his head. While he wasn't bleeding anymore, there was enough dried blood sticking to his hair, temple, and cheek that Jasper's head began to spin.

Mrs. Wells appeared at his side. "I forgot. Are you all right?"

He swallowed past a wave of nausea. "Yes, I will be. Is he okay?"

"Yes, they're taking him in for X-rays and such. I should've warned you about the blood."

"It's fine." Jasper took a deep breath and slowly walked up to Gus. "Hey there." He crouched down because the world seemed to be a little unsteady under his feet. "How are you feeling?"

"Woozy." He smiled weakly. "They think I might have a concussion. But I'm okay."

"Good." Jasper carefully focused on the side of his face that wasn't covered in blood. "I don't know if they'll let me ride with you in the ambulance, but the hospital isn't far. I can take my bike and I'll be there, all right?" He patted Gus's hand, then made room for the EMTs to load him up.

"You don't have to go," Mrs. Wells said. "It's your afternoon off. I can go."

"It's no big deal. I'd like to be there for him, and someone has to stay on the premises."

She was looking at him with a slight frown on her face. "Jasper, I can call Andrew to take over for a few hours." She rarely used his first name and he blinked at her in surprise, but she wasn't done yet. "You look pale, and tired. I think you should go home and do some yard work or something. You don't get enough time away from this place."

First Andrew, now Mrs. Wells. "I feel fine. I can go with Gus. The bike ride will do me good. Hopefully it won't take too long. I'll call Andrew to pick us up if they let him come home today, but I think they'll want to keep him overnight because of the head wound."

"Yes, I think so too. And I'll go pick him up tomorrow, so you don't have to worry about that."

"What did I do to deserve you, Mrs. Wells?" Jasper grinned.

"Recited a lot of Hail Marys, I imagine." She gave him a small smile and then went to talk to the EMTs.

Jasper went to grab his bike. He'd parked it in the school hallway in case it started raining again, and as he wheeled it out, a silver truck was idling at the sidewalk. Nicky stuck his head out the window.

"Everything all right? I saw the ambulance."

"Yes, fine." Jasper wheeled his bike toward the road. "One of our kids was tackled a little hard during a game of football and needs to be checked out, but I think he'll be okay."

Nicky peered at him. "Are you all right? Oh wait." He grinned and his eyes were dancing. "Still not doing so good around blood, huh?"

Jasper laughed reluctantly and looked at the ground. "You remember."

"Kind of hard not to. I don't think I've seen projectile vomiting like that before or since. And that's saying something, considering the things I've witnessed."

Jasper lifted his head and felt a pang of sadness. He wanted to ask Nicky about the things he'd been through, to invite him to talk about it and purge himself of some of it, but the ambulance drove by, reminding him this wasn't the time.

"Listen," he said. "I have to go, but maybe—"

"Are you going to the hospital? I can drop you off, if you want."

"Oh. Well, thank you. But I don't know how long it will take and I won't have a ride back. I can go on my bike. If I take the shortcuts, I can skip the traffic lights. It's faster that way."

Nicky chewed the inside of his cheek. Jasper thought he should probably say something about the streak of dirt on Nicky's nose but it made him look endearing. More approachable. Judging by the frizz in his hair he must've been working hard all morning.

"Okay. I'm running back and forth all day to get wood and supplies to fix the steps and the dock, so call me if you need anything."

"That's...very kind of you, Nicky."

Something like anger flashed in Nicky's eyes but it was gone before Jasper could be sure of what he'd seen. "By the way, only four people—five, including you—have my number so don't give it to anyone."

"I won't," Jasper said, startled. "I wouldn't." He gripped the bike handles and swung his leg over the seat, suddenly feeling unsettled. "Thanks again. I'll see you around."

Nicky didn't say anything. He rolled up his window and drove off, leaving Jasper wondering what he'd said wrong.

He spent a lot of time waiting around the ER as Gus was wheeled from one examination to the next. At least the collar around his neck seemed to be an invitation for people to come up to him and say hi, or ask him to pray for their loved ones, so he wasn't bored. By the time the verdict was in—cracked collarbone, mild concussion, and one night in observation—Jasper's head hurt. He hadn't eaten since that morning and he felt so drained even the bike ride home seemed insurmountable. But go home he must, so he said his goodbyes to Gus, assured him Mrs.

Wells would be there to pick him up in the morning, and went in search of his bike.

When he mounted it and took off, he felt the back wheel drag, and he almost cursed out loud. A small nail was sticking out of his completely flat tire. Jasper ducked his head and stood for a moment, the setting sun stretching his shadow along the sidewalk. Without allowing himself to think too much about it, he reached for his phone.

"Jazz? Everything all right?"

"Yeah, I'm still at the hospital. I have a flat tire. I was wondering if you—"

"I'll be there."

And that was that. Nicky had hung up before Jasper could say another word, and Jasper stared at his phone in mild astonishment. He still felt hungry and tired, his head beating out a background rhythm to his thoughts, but he realized the idea of seeing Nicky soon made him happy.

"THIS IT?" NICKY pulled up the drive of a two-story white clapboard farm house, surrounded by a mostly tidy garden of herbs and rose bushes. "Nice. The Church set you up well."

"I bought it myself, actually." Jasper's cheeks flushed and he ran a thumb over the afternoon shadow that had begun to grow in on his face. "When Grandma passed, she left a little bit of money for each of her grandchildren, and it happened to be enough to put down a payment on this old place."

"Why are you so embarrassed?"

Jazz fingered the crease in his pants and laughed a little. "How do you *do* that?"

Nicky blinked at him in surprise. "Do what?"

When Jazz lifted his hands and spread them palm up, Nicky noticed the little mole on the base of Jazz's left pinkie finger. It'd always been there and Nicky had kissed it once, telling him with a whisper it meant Jasper had a guardian angel. "You always were too perceptive for your own good."

It was true. It had been yet another thing Nicky had sought to dull with drugs: knowing too much about how other people felt. Not being able to feel the right way back.

"This place…it's a bit much for a priest. I probably should have been content with the house on Garvey like the other priests before me."

"The house on Garvey is depressing. It always smelled like mothballs. I don't get how Father Murray could stand living there. They should bulldoze the place if they haven't."

"I'd forgotten you went to a Bible study with me there for a few weeks." Jazz stared at his house for a long moment as Nicky put the truck into park near the butterfly bush at the end of the driveway.

"So you're home." Nicky didn't want to kick him out, but the silence was getting awkward.

Jasper nodded slowly. "Thanks for coming to pick me up. That was very nice of you. Why don't you come in for dinner?" Jasper shoved a thick lock of hair off his forehead and turned to smile at Nicky. "I order up a mean pizza."

"From Rocco's?"

"You know it."

Nicky turned off the truck. "Perfect." Then he groaned and threw his head back against the seat. "Oh my God."

"What?" Jasper's voice was raspy.

Nicky turned his head. Jazz's gaze was on Nicky's mouth and his eyes were doing their half-hooded thing again. "I was remembering that time we ordered the Firebelly Special with extra jalapeños."

Jazz swallowed and looked away, his gaze fixing firmly out the front window like he was determined not to look back at Nicky's face. "Yes, I remember." Jasper laced his fingers together like some part of him was praying. "We ate it all and we were sick beyond belief."

Nicky was silent. The next words he spoke would make or break whether or not the invite stood. He could reach over and take hold of Jasper's jaw to turn his face and steal a kiss before Jazz would pull away. He imagined Jazz might even return the kiss before putting an end to it—and putting an end to this new attempt at a friendship.

What had Dr. Rodriguez said? He needed strong relationships with good people to help him stay on track. Jazz was the best person he knew. There was no one he'd rather be friends with in this world. He'd do the right thing.

"Yeah," Nicky said, turning his mind back to the pizza. "My asshole burned for days after that. Little did I know I'd grow to enjoy that sensation later in life."

Jazz's lips twisted as he fought to hold back his guffaw of laughter. He shook his head and closed his eyes, while his shoulders shook. "Only you, Nicky. Only you."

"Well, are you still going to invite me in?"

Jasper nodded, and went to lift his bicycle out of the back of the truck. He took it to the garage, and then led Nicky in through the front door.

The inside of Jasper's house was a gory fucking mess. Blood and guts were strewn across the entryway, and bits and pieces of dead animal flesh trailed into the living room.

"Wow, Jazz. This isn't how I pictured it, to be honest."

Jasper turned on his heel and vomited into the bushes.

"Hey now, hey," Nicky said, putting one hand around Jazz's hip and the other on his shoulder, steadying him. His entire body trembled, and for a second Nicky was afraid Jazz's knees might give out.

Jasper wiped his mouth with the back of his hand, his skin a greyish-green and a fresh sweat sheen appearing on his neck. "Lord, have mercy."

"Hey, it's okay."

"That...that *cat*."

"That's a dead cat?" Nicky looked over his shoulder back into the house. "Nah, that looks like part of a dead bunny to me."

Jazz gagged again and heaved into the bushes.

"Aw, Jazzy, shh now. It's okay."

A ginger cat walked out the front door, its tail high and a smudge of red blood on its chin. It paused by Nicky's feet, tilted its head up at Jasper and said, "*Mrrow*?"

Nicky rubbed Jasper's back some more and answered, "He doesn't like your little gift."

The cat's fur ruffled on its back and it stalked toward the herb garden to disappear into the lavender bush. Nicky rubbed Jasper's shoulder and sighed. "Want me to go in and check out the damage?"

Jasper nodded, bending over and clutching his knees. "Sure. Please. Yeah."

Nicky hated to leave him when he looked like he might pass out. "Sit down if you feel faint."

"I'm okay."

A quick pass through the house showed that a) Jasper was a total neat freak and b) all the bunny pieces were on the ground floor alone. The upstairs was slaughter-free. He stepped back out the front door and said, "Okay, well, it looks like he? She?"

"She."

"Well, she tore the rabbit up pretty damn good. Parts everywhere. The head's on the mat in the kitchen, there are guts...well, like I said, everywhere. Actually I think the bunny might've been alive when she brought it in. Probably bleeding, but alive. And then it tried to get away and I'm guessing your cat didn't like that."

"Please stop talking."

"Uh, okay. Well, she's a very thorough and brutal killer."

Jazz sat down on the walkway, ducking his head between his knees and breathing slowly.

"And your folks wanted you to be a doctor," Nicky said, laughing.

"Wow. I think you're worse now than when we were kids. Though I guess you did faint that time I got cut on that nail and bled all—"

"Shh. Not now, please."

Nicky ran his hand over Jazz's head, threading his fingers into his hair and then smoothing it down. Jasper shuddered and covered his face with his hands. "Right," Nicky said. "Okay, well, I hate to break it to you, but it has to be cleaned up. Unless you want to abandon the house and go live over on Garvey after all."

Jasper didn't laugh at the joke. "I'll have to call in a cleaning service. I can't go in there." His breath came in short gasps, like he was on the verge of a panic attack. "Or a house fire could do the trick."

"Don't be ridiculous. We can deal with a little shredded bunny. It's no big deal."

"Speak for yourself."

"All right. Come on, cover your eyes, and I'll get you upstairs."

"But the mess..."

"I'll take care of it, okay?"

"You don't need to—"

"I've seen so much worse in my life. Don't worry about it."

"Worse than *that*?"

"Yeah. Well, in its own way. Don't ask. You really don't want to know."

Jasper looked up at him, his eyes dark, worry lurking there. "I wish this was the worst thing you'd ever seen, Nicky."

Kneeling on the concrete, the gravel from the garden digging into his knees, Nicky pushed his forehead against Jasper's for a second and whispered, "Me too." Then he pulled away and stood up, hauling Jazz to his feet by his hands. "Close your eyes."

He guided Jasper past the gore and up the stairs, and rather than release him and give up their physical intimacy, he steered him down the hallway toward what he'd determined was Jazz's bedroom on first glance.

"It's the second—"

"Yeah, the one with all the *neatness* and *order*. I know."

"The guest rooms aren't a mess," Jasper said a little defensively.

"Sure, those are nice too, but there's a strong uptight vibe to your room. It screams, 'The person sleeping in here isn't having any orgasms!'"

"Nicky."

"I'm just saying." He pulled the door open. "You're safe to open your eyes now."

Jasper sat on the bed, and Nicky opened the door to the small bathroom attached to the bedroom. It had a second door that opened to the hallway. He wet a neatly folded washcloth with cold water and brought it out to Jazz, who wiped his forehead and mouth with it. "Thank you, Nicky."

"No problem." Nicky reached out and pushed the hair off Jazz's forehead. His skin was sweaty, but his eyes sought Nicky's and the vulnerability in them made Nicky's knees feel weak. "You're looking better already."

There was a clatter from downstairs and a plaintive meow drifted up the stairs. A scamper of feet and a wild thunder up the stairs was followed by the ginger cat walking into the room with a slow, dignified gait, like she hadn't just been spazzing out somewhere out of sight. She jumped up onto the top of Jazz's Bible-infested bookshelf and licked her paw, cleaning the smear of blood from her chin.

Jasper sighed and shook his head, staring at the cat from where he sat on the bed. "How are you getting in?" he murmured.

"The kitchen window was open," Nicky said. "I noticed when I found the head on the—"

Jazz lifted his hand and covered his mouth.

"Anyway, she must be able to leap up to the sill and get inside, but I can't believe she dragged that bunny with her. That was a good-sized rabbit. But look at her—she's a big lady, isn't she? What are you feeding her?"

"Rabbit apparently."

Nicky laughed. He looked around the room at the cross on the wall and the rosaries hanging next to it. Three different ones. And the stack of books on the nightstand and the perfectly lined-up stack on top of the book shelf by the cat. "Don't you want to mess it up a little?" he said, striding over and knocking the books askew. "Look, that's better, right? Like a human being lives here and not a robot."

The cat purred and lifted her paw to him. Nicky instinctively put his own hand up and she slapped it. "She gives high fives?"

"And delivers death to poor innocent bunnies. I'm considering whether or not she's an agent of Satan."

Nicky laughed. "Okay, where can I find your cleaning stuff? I can't promise there won't be blood stains, but I'll do my best. I'm pretty good at dealing with blood stains actually," he grinned and spoke without thinking it through. "Me and a razor hung out for a harrowing evening or two. I've got the hesitation marks to prove it."

Jazz's face blanched and he sat up, reaching for Nicky. Without giving it a second thought, Nicky stepped forward, letting Jazz circle his wrist with still-clammy fingers. He thought for sure Jazz would check out the marks, but he didn't.

Instead he held on and said, "Don't do that again, okay? If you ever feel that way, call me. Day or night, wherever you are. However...however long it's been since we've talked."

"Aw, it's okay, I was kidding." He wasn't, but Jazz would never need to know that.

Jasper didn't look like he believed him and he didn't look like he thought it was at all funny. Because it wasn't.

"Anyway, cleaning supplies?"

"Under the kitchen sink and in the closet next to the garage."

"Great. Wait here and I'll have it cleared up in a jiffy." Nicky looked toward the cat. "And you. You sit there and think about what you've done." She *mrrowed* at him and he pointed his finger at her. "Yeah. Exactly."

Chapter Eleven

WHEN NICKY LEFT, Jasper flopped back on the bed with his arms spread wide and a grin on his face. "You two are not adorable," he said, twisting his head to look at the cat. She licked another smear of blood off her whiskers and he groaned. "Especially you, you murderer."

As his stomach roiled, he tried to look at his room the way Nicky would see it and, okay, it was a little…excessively tidy. But he didn't spend all that much time at home, and he liked to know where things were. He closed his eyes and remembered Nicky wandering around his childhood bedroom, picking things up and deliberately putting them down in different places.

"Once a brat…" Jasper muttered. Decisive footsteps stomped around below, a rustle of plastic or the rush of water sometimes interrupting the movements. It was strange to think of someone else being in this house—Nicky especially. He was here, in Jasper's only real private space, wandering around like he belonged. It didn't take long for Nicky to start humming, and a few minutes later he was singing softly. Jasper wished he could hear it better and he closed his eyes and strained to listen.

Hesitation marks. Jasper hadn't seen them, and he honestly didn't know if he wanted to. *Oh, Nicky.* It made him heartsore to think Nicky had been in places that dark. Had seen things worse than torn-up bunnies.

As a kid, Nicky'd had somber moments, but mostly he'd been happy to tear through the woods with Jasper. Until Jimmy Orlean came along anyway. The year they'd both turned seventeen had simultaneously been the best and the worst of his life.

Jasper drifted on a blanket of memories as the hollow pounding in his head eased. Once he thought he could stand without falling over, he got rid of his sweat-stained clothes and pulled on a pair of yoga pants. They were made of hemp and recycled polyester and would probably make Nicky die with laughter, but they were comfortable so Jasper tied the strings around his waist. He grinned at the thought and got a whiff of his stale breath.

"Ugh." Jasper made his way into his little bathroom and brushed his teeth. Man, he hated vomiting. Pointing his toothbrush at his reflection and with his mouth covered in white foam, he said, "If You're trying to tell me something, Lord, please use less bloody clues next time." A blob of toothpaste dripped down his chin and fell into the sink.

"If there's any interference from God in this case, it's Him making sure I was with you when you came home."

Jasper startled a little and turned to see Nicky leaning against the doorframe, unabashedly taking in Jasper's bare chest. His face went hot when he quickly bent down to rinse his mouth.

"Yes, you're absolutely right," Jasper said, eyes on the cleaning of his toothbrush. Nicky's gaze was like an electrifying thing and it made his skin pebble. "You're a gift from God. *Or*, if I hadn't driven over that nail, I'd have been here in time to close the window and prevent the murder scene." Jasper dried his hands and moved toward the door but Nicky didn't step aside.

"*Or* maybe He put that nail in your path so you had to call me because the massacre had happened." Nicky very deliberately stared into Jasper's eyes. "Small miracles, isn't that what Catholicism is all about? Shouldn't you pray to the patron saint of the squeamish?"

"The patron saint of the squeamish? And who would that be?"

"You tell me. St. Angelus No Vomitus?"

Jasper let out a weak laugh, one of those that could quickly turn into a helpless belly laugh he couldn't control. Nicky used to have a knack for bringing those out, and then keep going until Jasper's stomach hurt so badly he'd beg Nicky to please stop. "You know, there's a patron saint for musicians," he said, and just like that all the humor drained out of the bathroom as effectively as if he'd pulled an actual plug.

"Yeah?" Nicky asked softly. "And what's he called?"

"It's a woman, actually. Saint Cecilia. Good music is part of the liturgy, and Saint Cecilia watches over the choirs, but I always liked to believe she looked after rock stars too."

Nicky looked down at Jasper's bare feet. "I must've fallen off her radar for a while, then."

"You cleaned up bunny guts for me, Nicky. I'd say she found you again." Nicky began to open his mouth as he shrugged but Jasper stilled him with a hand on his arm. "Thank you."

"No thanks needed," Nicky mumbled. He ducked his head, and Jasper gripped the back of his neck. He wanted to press their foreheads together like Nicky'd done earlier, but lacked the courage.

"Yes, they are." He squeezed a little and let go. "You're a good friend."

Nicky nodded. He kept his eyes lowered and his dark lashes dovetailed out over his cheekbones. "So." He cleared his throat and glanced up. "Pizza?"

"Sure." Jasper hesitated. "All the blood is gone?"

"It's all gone. But we can eat on the deck if the afterimage is burned on your retinas. Hell, even I'm gonna have trouble unseeing how the brains fell out when—"

"Okay, okay, please shut up." Jasper gave Nicky a little shove as he shouldered past him and Nicky laughed, shoving him back. "Let me go grab a shirt."

Nicky made a noise but didn't say anything else, and Jasper didn't turn around to check his expression.

As always, Jasper wrestled over the phone with the owner of Rocco's, who tried to give him his pizzas for free, and ended up paying half price.

Nicky was staring at him with a sort of disbelieving amusement. "Seriously? You have to fight people to let you pay them?"

"Not usually, no." Jasper glanced at Nicky and opened his fridge. "Confession business," he said, when Nicky still seemed to be waiting for an answer. "And I always overtip the delivery boy to compensate. You want a beer?"

Nicky snorted and shoved his hands in his pockets. It made his shoulders round a bit. "I really do. But no."

"Oh no." Jasper closed the fridge but held on to the handles, his knuckles turning white. He felt mortified. "I'm so sorry. I'm an idiot."

"Sometimes." Nicky grinned, but Jasper didn't quite buy it and he had to stamp down on the urge to reach out and touch him again.

"I really am sorry. You're working so hard and doing so well and here I am offering you alcohol."

"It shouldn't be a big deal to offer someone a beer, Jazz. And I could probably drink one, no problem. My therapist says it's best not to at all. And I agree." He bit his lip and then laughed softly. "You know how to drag the giant pink elephant into the room don't you?"

"I really didn't mean to," Jasper said sheepishly. "Listen, do you still like that drink, what's it called? You used to love it when we were kids. The lemonade and ice-tea mix."

"Arnold Palmer? Yeah, sure. I haven't had that in ages."

"I can do that. It's not fresh like your mom's but…" Jasper dove back into the fridge and came out with two bottles. "More lemonade than tea for you, right?"

"You remember."

"Of course I do." He reached for two large glasses and mixed their drinks while Nicky leaned against the counter, his long legs stretched out before him. His dark shorts exposed knobby knees and scrawny white calves covered in dark leg hair. The afternoon sunlight always fell through the kitchen window with abundance and it bounced off the back of Nicky's head, giving his dark hair the shine of autumn leaves. The collar of his navy long-sleeve T-shirt had slipped a little to the side and Jasper caught a glimpse of bright blue ink on his pale skin.

"What's that?"

"Hmm?" Nicky blinked like he'd been deep in thought and touched the mark through his shirt. "Oh, more tattoos."

"Looks like a pretty color." What he could see of it looked like smudges of a watercolor painting, and he stood there dying of curiosity. But he wasn't going to ask.

"Yeah. That's one of my favorites actually." Nicky rubbed the tattoo through his shirt, his fingers catching on the fabric and stretching it a little, exposing the line of his collarbone. Jasper averted his eyes.

"So how did it all begin? With the band, I mean." Jasper handed over a glass and went to lean beside Nicky. "The start of it must've been an exciting time for you. Is it true you all met in a bar?"

Nicky grimaced then quickly took a drink. "Kind of. I was jobless and homeless, living in a squat with a few other guys new to L.A."

"What? Why?" Jasper nearly fumbled his drink. "I can't imagine Miriam and Adrian allowing that."

"I wasn't in touch with them at the time. I was a shitty son back then. As soon as I turned eighteen, I took off, and for a long time, no matter how shitty things got, I didn't contact them. It was part pride and part the attachment disorder and depression. It broke their hearts."

"I'm sure it did."

"Mom thought I was dead. Dad did too. I'm surprised you didn't hear about it."

"I didn't talk to many people from Little Heights while I was away in seminary."

Nicky looked ashamed, but he cleared his throat and went on. "Anyway, the rest of the story isn't pretty either. When I was twenty-two, I heard there was a job opening at this bar, so I went on down and the owner told me he'd hire me if I'd blow him."

Jasper stared at Nicky, his eyes going dry. "Did you…did you do it?"

With a one-shoulder shrug, Nicky looked at his drink. "I said no, but on my way out, Chuckers started playing. That was Sez and Mick back when they played with a drummer named Shawn. Anyway, I tried to talk to them during a break, but they blew me off. Chuckers was a nothing band on the scene in those days. No one had heard of them, but I was mesmerized by their sound. After getting blown off by them a few more times, I found out the owner of the bar handled his own bookings. So I told the guy he could fuck me if he managed to set up an audition with them for me. A few days later I got a message to come back to his bar. Sez and Mick were there and I played for them and they saw what I had to offer them." He smirked. "Which was, basically, nearly everything that got us a contract. Shitty though that contract is. So I wouldn't call the start all that exciting, really. But it got exciting after that."

Some of the nausea from earlier began to return and Jasper's mouth felt sticky from the lemonade. He set the drink down on the counter behind him. "Did you follow through? On letting the bar owner…?"

For a long moment Nicky said nothing, until Jasper met his gaze. "Yeah. Not the first or last time I let someone fuck me in this business. Like drugs, it's part of the power plays and the deal mongering."

Goosebumps broke out all over Jasper's skin. Images of a seventeen-year-old Nicky with porcelain-fragile skin and a gorgeously freckled face rose to the surface. How he'd so beautifully lifted his head to kiss Jasper, petal-mouth opening like a flower blooming for the sun. He couldn't stand the thought of Nicky only a few years later in some dingy back room with a power hungry old man just wanting him for—"Do you regret any of it?"

"Whoa. Don't hold back with the soul searching, *Father*."

Jasper gently touched Nicky's sleeve because he couldn't stand not to. "You don't have to answer. I'm trying to understand."

Nicky blew out a breath that puffed up his cheeks. "Some of it. A lot of it, in a general sort of sense. It's not like certain traumatic events stand out and give me nightmares, but hey there's always tomorrow, right? Besides, what do you care?"

"After the glory hath He sent me unto the nations which spoiled you: for He that toucheth you toucheth the apple of His eye."

Nicky stared at him. "I don't think I've heard that one before."

"It's not a very well-known one. What I meant—"

"I think I know." Nicky held on to his glass with both hands. "The rock and roll world...it's not a good business, Jazz."

"No." Jasper grabbed another glass and poured himself some water. "No, it really isn't."

THE MONSTROUS GINGER cat stepped across the back of the sofa with supreme confidence and then leapt onto Nicky's lap.

"Hey there...?" he looked to Jasper. "What's her name?"

"I don't know. She's well fed, so she must belong to someone, but I have no idea who."

"She seems to think she belongs to you. She brought you the best present ever." Nicky tickled her chin. "Yes, you did, didn't you? Such a good kitty cat. I think she's probably living off the field mice around your house. I think you're her person." He scratched her ears and thought a moment before continuing. "Actually, I read somewhere that cats bring you kills if they think you're not taking good enough care of yourself. Aww." He rubbed the cat's ears some more. "You thought your human was starving and decided to bring him some din-dins."

Jasper looked a little green around the gills again. "Don't remind me. I don't think I can look at her the same way again. Or at least for a few days."

"What? This little murderer? She's a sweetheart. Look at her." She'd curled up in Nicky's lap and was busily cleaning her front left paw. She paused and looked up at Nicky and then over at Jazz, sniffed the air, and then went back to her cleaning. "She needs a name."

"I call her Ginger Kitty, I guess."

Nicky scoffed. "That's offensive. You can't call a cat something like that. This girl is named…Disemboweler. Dizzy for short. Or Slaughter. Yeah, that's a great name. Slaughter Kitty. It's perfect."

"I'm not naming my cat Slaughter."

Nicky whispered to the cat, "He admits you're his at least. Don't worry. We'll get a cool name for you. I promise."

The cat looked up at him solemnly and nodded. "*Mrreow*."

"Totally."

She glared at Jasper and then settled herself on Nicky's legs and closed her eyes in a half-drowse.

"Dizzy wore herself out murdering that sweet little rabbit."

"Let's not talk about it anymore."

Nicky grinned. "Sure."

"Want to listen to something?" Jasper asked, moving over to his old hi-fi stereo system—complete with a turntable—and opening the cabinet where he kept his music collection. Nicky could tell he was proud of his little setup, and he should be.

"You've got a nice system." He waved his hand toward the amplifier. "Nothing sounds as good as a tube amp. Do you listen to the vinyl through it?"

"No, I have a solid state under here to put vinyl through. It gets a little—"

"Muddy. I know."

They grinned at each other. Nicky had been the one to teach Jasper about the difference between woofers and tweeters, solid state and tube. They'd carried a battery-powered cassette deck out to the fort when they were kids, an old piece of disposable junk Jasper's grandfather had given them, and they'd listened to scavenged tapes of Boston and The Cure and Miriam's Elvis Presley.

But Nicky and his father had found an almost-bonding in the search for the perfect stereo, and they'd gone from hi-fi store to hi-fi store auditioning pieces for the system Adrian eventually put together. It hurt Nicky to think that if he'd had access to the antidepressant he was on now when he was a kid, maybe he could have been the son Adrian had deserved.

Jasper flicked through his albums and pulled out a Tom Waits oldie-but-goodie.

"No," Nicky said, dumping Dizzy onto the floor and heading over to the where Jasper stood gazing into his neatly alphabetized cabinet. "Try something from all the way over on this end." He pulled out his favorite Vespertine album.

"How did you—? You snooped."

"Of course. I wasn't going to clean up without getting the lay of the land. These vinyl albums had a limited run. I happen to know this one is pretty damn rare. You could get about $500 for it on eBay last time I looked."

Jasper pulled it out of Nicky's hands and smoothed his fingers over the cover. It was a fairly sedate one of a red dwarf star and *Angry Stars Spit Red Light* across the front. "Are you sure you want to listen to it?"

"Why not? I haven't heard it in a long time." Nicky stretched and scratched at his belly before sitting back down on the sofa. Dizzy seemed unusually forgiving for a cat and plopped down on his lap again. "When we made that record…" He trailed off and closed his eyes, letting his head loll on the back of the sofa. "I was so fucking proud of myself. I thought I'd finally made something good of my life. I was actually sober then, did you know?"

"I could tell, yes. The album is cohesive. Lyrically, musically, it's some of your best work."

"It *is* my best work. It's what I want to find my way back to if I can."

Jasper didn't say anything, and the sound of the turntable clicking on and the arm dropping with a pop onto the record vibrated through the speakers. Jazz sat on the opposite end of his comfortable sofa, and they both listened.

The silence wasn't awkward at all. It was like all the times when they were kids alone in the fort or up in one of their rooms, listening to albums and not talking—just being. Jasper got up and refilled Nicky's glass when it was empty and brought out a bowl of strawberry ice cream while Nicky flipped the record over.

"Sez was at the top of his vocal game here too," Nicky murmured as Sez's voice pierced the room, holding a high note of angst and misery until it almost hurt to hear and then letting it fall to a softer sound that tore at Nicky's heart. "You know how on 'Ease On In' he lets his voice drop and it sounds like he's beckoning you? So you actually lean in toward the speakers?"

"Only to have that guitar chord strum hit like a slap in the face?" Jasper filled in.

"Yeah." Nicky grinned and played with the ice cream. Not eating much but enjoying the soup that was forming at the bottom of the bowl. "That was his idea, actually. One of his most brilliant ones. That moment on the album blew so many critics' minds. The reviews all mention it."

"It's a painful moment."

Nicky glanced over to read Jasper's expression and found it as easy as it had been to understand as when they were children. "Yeah. It's heartbreaking."

Jazz nodded. "The whole album is, Nicky. I'm proud of you, you know. For making it; for being brave enough to write all these songs. It's astonishing that you get up on stage every night and share them with the world."

"Fuck that. I was in survival mode. I wasn't on drugs, but I was still barely aware of what I was doing. There was nothing brave about it."

Outside, the wind must've changed because the room filled with the briny scent of the ocean. A soft breeze swept into the room from the open kitchen window and Nicky inhaled the familiar smell. He was about to comment on it and turned to find Jazz with his hands clasped in his lap and his eyes glassy. Along with the change in the wind the atmosphere had shifted in the room.

When Jazz spoke his voice was fragile. "It's brave to fight as hard as you have to make a connection, Nicky."

A soft sound escaped and Nicky realized it came from him. "Yeah, well. Attachment disorders stop being anyone's excuse once you turn eighteen."

"No, don't throw that away. You worked for years trying to connect with your parents, with the world—"

"I connected with you."

Nicky could see indents where Jazz's fingers dug into his hands. "And I left you."

"You had your calling. I had mine." He gestured to the stereo as the sounds of "Peter Says No," the final song on the record, washed over him. "Sometimes the answer to what we want is no. It just is."

"And even though I hurt you," Jasper's voice sounded thick. "You didn't give up. I know you think you did, but you wrote these songs trying to connect to the world, to other people, Nicky. That's not something a lazy person does. That's what a true fighter does. You never gave up. It's not your fault that heroin came along and plugged all the holes for you, leaving you more disconnected than ever."

"Huh. I'm pretty sure it's my fault I tried heroin to begin with, but I see what you're saying." Nicky held up his hand. "I don't think we need to argue about it. I'm done with blame. I only want to get better."

Jazz stood and took the bowls into the kitchen as Sez's voice faded out on the final notes of the album. Nicky sat and listened to the needle catching at the end of the record for a full minute before Jazz came back in and put the arm back on the cradle.

Dizzy had long since crawled into the space between the armrest and Nicky's leg, and he could feel her contented rumble travel up his femur.

Jazz slid down to the floor, legs out straight and crossed at the ankle. His T-shirt and yoga pants were rumpled and despite the seriousness of their prior conversation, his expression was relaxed. His shoulders, though, seemed tight, and Nicky shifted down the sofa and shoved Jazz forward a little to settle behind him with Jazz between his legs.

Jasper tensed. "What are you doing?"

"When's the last time someone touched you?"

"Nicky—"

"I mean a massage. Just, you know, friendly touch. Your shoulders are inching up to your ears." Nicky put his hands on Jazz's shoulders. "Let me help you."

Jasper let out a soft noise as Nicky started working his fingers into tense muscles. "I'm surprised I'm so tight. I do a lot of yoga. I'm usually fairly flexible and relaxed."

"Well, you experienced a severe trauma tonight. No one should come home to that," Nicky whispered, leaning forward and letting himself smell Jasper's hair. Oh God, he wanted to push his face against Jazz's scalp and just breathe. "You still use Head & Shoulders." Heat rose up his neck as he realized what he'd said. He tried to play it off. "No dandruff for you, huh?"

"It does its job. Why? Do you use special rock star shampoo now?"

Nicky laughed. "No. I use whatever's in the hotel when I'm on tour." When he showered, anyway. He pressed against the trapezius and Jasper whimpered. "You should get massages. Human touch is important. My addiction counselor says so. I'm trying this thing where I do what she says."

"Yeah?" Jasper was breathless.

"Yeah. She thinks I need to be touched more often." Nicky chuckled. "I told her I've been touched plenty but she says it should be a touch from someone who cares about me." He slid his hand up into Jasper's hair and massaged around his temples, messing up his hair. Then he smoothed his hair back down, but it still looked ruffled and hung onto his forehead. "And she also suggested I take up yoga. Is there an instructor in town?"

"There used to be, but she moved to Alaska with her husband last year. I keep up with my practice on my own, actually."

"Cool. Maybe you could teach me?"

Jazz went stiff under his hands again and a long moment passed.

"Okay, don't worry about it." Nicky worked his fingers into the back of Jasper's neck.

"No, it's not that. I teach the kids at the center. I could show you a few things to get you started."

"I'd like that." Nicky pressed the tension down Jasper's arms, lifting them out to his side and squeezing down into his wrists and then massaging his hands. "Turn around."

Jazz hesitated for only a moment and then did as Nicky asked, turning to sit cross-legged facing him. His eyes glimmered in the low light of the end table lamps, and Nicky swallowed back his desire to take hold of his chin and press a kiss to his mouth. "Give me your hands. I'll show you something I learned in Amsterdam."

Jazz held out his hands and Nicky took the left one. "Just let your other hand relax for now."

Then he massaged his fingers into Jasper's palm, rubbing and pressing the way he'd been shown. Jazz let out soft noises occasionally, his throat working like he was keeping even louder sounds back.

Nicky switched to Jasper's other hand. They were both silent while he worked, except for Jazz's little sighs.

"When your psychologist says 'someone who cares about you', does she mean a lover?" Jasper whispered.

Nicky's stomach flipped. Was he imagining the note of jealousy in Jasper's voice? He had to be. Jasper was a priest and they were friends. That was all they could ever be. He told himself these things sternly as he prepared his answer, but he didn't believe them. Some part of him never would and he was going to have to learn to live with that. "I think she meant as a friend. Someone to hug and rub and touch with affection. They say we all need that to be healthy."

Jasper nodded.

"That's why my folks used to give me all those massages as a kid. It was supposed to release oxytocin, which would help me bond with them. But it didn't work back then. I'm trying to believe it could work now. But I have to make some friends first." He cleared his throat. "It's embarrassing. It's like I'm in some foreign country and I have to start my whole life from scratch. At least I know the language, but I have no idea how to use it to make people want to be my friend and not just use me."

Jasper looked thoughtful. "Surely you have some friends in Los Angeles. You've lived there for over sixteen years now."

"Nope. I have drug suppliers, I've got star fuckers, and I've got the band."

"You're not friends with your bandmates?"

"I care about them," he paused. Did he? Yeah. He did. They'd been through so much together. They'd traveled the world with him and lived through hell with him. They were bound to the company like he was with the same terms and conditions. They understood each other because of that. "Yeah, I care about them a lot, but we aren't friends. We're business associates and we're in this deal together, but if it came down to it, I don't think any of us would choose to hang out." He frowned. "Maybe Sez and Mick. I think they're fucking. Which is weird. And disgusting." He shuddered. "Like why? After all these years, why go there with it? I don't get it."

"Is everyone in the band gay? Is that what drew you together?"

"Ramona's straight. Sez is too."

"I thought he and Mick were…?"

"Well, Mick is bi. Maybe they're both bi? I can't blame a guy for wanting a nice hard dick up his ass, but I'm not sure why it's happening now and not twelve years ago. Neither of them have gotten better looking." Nicky rubbed his hands in his hair helplessly. "I don't ask.

Ramona thinks it will end badly."

"Ah yes, Ramona Darling. She seems like she's got her head on straight."

"She does. She's also incredibly ambitious, and if it's between achieving what she wants in life and being my bestest buddy, believe me, she'll take her career. Lately I get the impression she's biding her time. I think she'll bail on us if we keep writing and producing crap. She has other offers."

"That's a shame, Nicky. You deserve more loyalty than that."

Nicky laughed. "It's not about loyalty. She wants me sober, whatever that takes, but she isn't going to allow that to fuck up the band or her career." He sighed and rubbed a hand through his hair. "You know, she was the last one to join Vespertine."

"Yeah."

Nicky looked over at Jazz in surprise. "You really kept up with my career?"

"To a degree. It got painful after a while and then I just bought the albums. The songs were…" He looked down. "They weren't too hard to figure out."

"Because they're about you."

"I couldn't resist buying them." Jasper chuckled but it was underscored with a hint of bitterness. "You know I've always been vain and, I have to admit, some part of me wanted to see what you'd sing about me next." His throat clicked as he swallowed, shame creeping into his expression. "I never know what I want most when I see you have a new album out: for you to have moved on and found someone new to write songs about, or for you to still be writing songs for me. A truly good man, a good priest, would have wanted you to have found love and happiness, and they would have wanted it with all of their heart." Jasper cleared his throat and shook his head, his eyes gleaming in the low light. "I've never admitted that before. Maybe not even to myself. Nicky, it seems possible that I'm not a very good priest."

Chapter Twelve

JASPER FELT SO loose and relaxed; under different circumstances, he'd wonder if he'd had a beer he'd forgotten about. His head rolled to the side against the couch when Nicky stood.

"I should get going." Nicky made a face. "Mom and Dad will get worried if I stay out any longer. Oh my God, I am officially a teenager again." Jasper laughed and began to climb to his feet. Nicky said, "No, I can find my way out, you don't need to—oh shit."

"What?" Jasper froze on his knees. "What is it?"

"Looks like your kitty cat is losing half her coat. Oh man, I can't go home like this. You know how allergic my dad is to all things furry."

Jasper remembered copious amounts of sneezing, tears, and hives the one time little Nicky had brought a starving kitten home. They'd gone around every day for a week to find it a new home because his parents didn't want it either. "Come on up, I'll give you something to change into."

He climbed the steps two at a time and rummaged into his closet until he found a long-sleeved Henley and a pair of yoga pants that had always been a bit too tight on him. He held them out to Nicky, who still stood in the doorway.

"Thanks." Nicky kept his eyes on the clothes, but didn't move.

Hesitation marks.

Well, that explained why he'd been in no hurry to show Jasper what he looked like when they were in Nicky's bedroom the other day.

"I'll leave you to it." Jasper made to ease past Nicky but came to a halt when Nicky curled his fingers around his wrists.

"You can stay," Nicky whispered and Jasper knew he shouldn't, but his curiosity got the better of him.

"Are you sure? I don't need to—"

"You want to." Nicky swished his thumb along the fragile crease of Jasper's wrist once before he let go. "And that means a lot."

Nicky took a step farther into the room, turned his back on Jasper, and slowly pulled the shirt over his head.

"Oh, Nicky." Jasper covered his mouth because he was afraid of what else might come tumbling out.

"I never show this one." Nicky's voice sounded soft and breakable. "I keep my shirts on onstage, although the front occasionally gets ripped, and I make sure no one ever sees my bare back when I get fuck—"

"Stop talking." Jasper walked forward. Nothing could've held him back. Not God, not his belief, and certainly not his own lacking willpower. With a steady hand he reverently traced the sleeping fox and badger on Nicky's right shoulder blade. They were arranged in a vague heart shape and their tails entwined as they dozed peacefully, facing each other. Jasper touched their noses, trailed the lace pattern surrounding them, and followed the cornflowers that trailed off into the flower sleeve that ran down Nicky's arm. "Are there more?"

Nicky didn't move, so Jasper slowly circled him, eyes on Nicky's downcast face. When they stood toe to toe he finally let his gaze wander.

An anatomically correct heart was tattooed right over where Nicky's real heart would be. Jasper touched the words above it. "*Via et veritas et vita.*" He smiled even though he felt like crying. "I am the way and the truth and the life."

"Do you know the rest of the quote?" Nicky asked. His blue eyes shimmered in the last of the orange sunlight filling the room. It'd be dark soon and Jasper knew it would bring no relief.

"*Ego sum via et veritas et vita nemo venit ad Patrem nisi per me.* I am the way, and the truth, and the life. No man cometh to the Father, but by me." Jasper laughed hoarsely. "You're terrible."

Nicky reached out and touched Jasper's cheek with one fingertip. "I know."

And there, on the left shoulder, sat the blue tattoo that had piqued his curiosity. A bright blue fox sprang from blue stripes of paint and ran toward Nicky's heart. Its little paws landed right beside Nicky's left nipple, and Jasper saw it pebble when he traced the fox's back. "This is maybe the most beautiful tattoo I've ever seen."

"Yeah. It's my favorite. Well, some days I hated it. But I never regretted it."

Jasper nodded but couldn't say anything. On Nicky's right pec lay a little red fox curled up, fast asleep, surrounded by a circle of the same kind of lace that'd been used around the sleeping badger and fox on his back. It looked so sweet he had to touch it. Nicky's breath fanned over his fingers, and Jasper put his palm flat over the fox.

"I thought you hated me," Jasper whispered.

Nicky lay his palm over Jasper's hand. "Sometimes. But no regrets. I don't think I ever realized that. Not until now."

Jasper tugged his hand free and carried on. He let his fingers roam the tattoo on Nicky's right arm, a beautiful sleeve made up of blue cornflowers and forget-me-nots. Then he moved on to Nicky's other arm, and found resistance for the first time. "What is it?"

"That one...has the worst scarring."

"Show me."

"Jazz..."

"What did you say earlier about the importance of touch by people who care for you?" Gently unfolding Nicky's arm, Jasper rubbed his thumb over the uneven skin in Nicky's elbow crease. It felt bumpy. Jasper lowered his head and pressed a soft kiss to the scars. Scent memory triggered a bunch of images to surface, all moments like this one, where they'd been close and alone with all the time in the world for nothing but each other. Slowly he shifted his grip and trailed his hand down until he found the faint traces on Nicky's inner wrist. He kissed those too.

Nicky gripped his hand before he could let go. "What are you doing?"

Jasper shook his head. He didn't know. "Are there any more?"

Nicky hesitated, scratching his eyebrow with his thumb. He took a shuddering breath and nodded. Keeping his balance with one hand on Jasper's shoulder, Nicky toed off his sneakers and bent down to take off his socks. The tops of his slender feet each had a tattoo on them. The left one had an abstract black drawing of a fox with little blue wings and a halo, and the right had a happy sleeping fox, lying on its side with a little red heart cradled in its paws. Jasper dropped to his knees and gently stroked his palms from Nicky's ankles all the way to his toes.

"Is that it?" he whispered, and his breath caught when Nicky shoved his thumbs in his shorts and pulled them down so they pooled around his ankles. His hands shook visibly and he touched Jasper's cheek, shuddering.

"There's this one."

He looked thin and fragile in his black boxer-briefs and at first Jasper didn't see it, until he noticed a little pink heart-shaped balloon peeking out from underneath the elastic band.

Laughing hoarsely he sat on his heels. He reached out but pulled his hand back at the last second. "Show me."

Nicky pulled the boxer-briefs down enough to show a tiny elephant, smiling up at the balloon clutched in its little trunk. Its cheeks were pink and its eyes were sweetly closed.

"It's ridiculous, compared to the rest," Nicky said.

"I knew." Jasper reached out and touched the elephant's ear. "I always knew you were a gentle soul deep down, Nicky." Jasper took Nicky's hands in his. The calluses on his guitar-hardened fingertips caught Jasper's skin. He pressed his forehead to Nicky's knuckles. The rug underneath his knees was coarse.

"Is it my fault? The drugs…the hesitation marks? Did I do that to you, Nicky?"

Nicky swallowed hard and shook his head, shame shadowing his features. "I did it to myself." He pulled his hands free of Jasper's tender grasp. "Can I put some clothes on now? I'm feeling kind of vulnerable here."

"Of course you can. I'm sorry I—" Jasper let go. "Nicky, I—"

"No." Nicky tried to tug his hands free but Jasper held on. "Don't you dare say you're sorry."

"I have a confession to make," Jasper whispered. He lifted his head. Nicky looked ready to bolt. So Jasper spread his hands in supplication and held his gaze. "My mother knows."

Nicky paled. "What? She…what does she know?"

"About you and me. I told her that summer. When I was grounded. I didn't eat. I didn't sleep. I didn't string two words together for days and in the end she sat me down and made me tell her. I'm pretty sure she had her suspicions."

"So…" Nicky swallowed hard.

Their hands were clammy and the floorboards underneath Jasper's knees were hard and uncomfortable but he ignored it.

"Did she tell you that you couldn't see me anymore? Is that why…?"

"Ah, Nicky, no." Jasper shook his head sadly and blinked hard. "No, I almost wish…but no. What she did was, she told me all about teenage infatuations and puppy love and how everyone goes through something like that when they're young." Nicky made a scoffing noise but Jasper pushed on. "And when I didn't believe any of that, she told—she told me all about attachment disorders and how you couldn't possibly feel the way I felt for you."

"Jasper!"

His name reverberated through the room. When was the last time Nicky had called him that? He couldn't remember. He heard the anguish and kept talking anyway. Now or never. "She was very kind about it. She held me for ages when I cried my eyes out. You couldn't feel the way I did. It wasn't possible for you and I couldn't blame you. It had to do with your past and your adoption and how you were wired. It had nothing to do with me, and it really wasn't your fault. You were a sweet boy and maybe you believed you loved me, but as soon as we were apart for any length of time you'd move on a lot faster than I'd be able to. She explained all the signs and symptoms. She explained it to death until—"

"Until you believed her."

"I didn't at first." He choked up. When he looked at Nicky's face, it was so twisted he finally couldn't go on anymore.

"And now?" Nicky asked. Jasper didn't know who was trembling. Maybe they both were. Nicky worked his hands free and Jasper stood. "What do you believe now?" Nicky asked.

"I think you're as capable of loving someone as much as anyone else is. Maybe…maybe more."

Nicky sounded so small when he said, "But it's too late now."

Jasper picked up the Henley from the floor and tugged it over Nicky's head. Holding on to the fabric he drew Nicky a little closer. "I don't know if it would've made a difference in the end. My calling was…tenacious. I'm sorry. Maybe I shouldn't have told you this. It served no purpose apart from alleviating my own conscience. It's not fair to you."

Nicky shook his head. He stuck his arms through his sleeves and bent to pick up the yoga pants. "I need to go. I need to, what does my therapist call it? Heh, yeah…'process.'"

"Sure." Jasper tried to quell the disappointment—tried to stop it from bleeding through in his voice. "But I'll see you soon?"

Nicky gazed at him with wounded eyes.

Jasper's throat ached as he opened his bedroom door. "Why don't you come by Blue Oasis tomorrow morning?" He picked up the cat-hair-covered clothes and tossed them in his washing basket, his hands shaking. "I do a yoga session with the kids every Friday at ten. In the summer anyway. It's nothing complicated since most of them haven't done much either. I find it helps them focus." Why was he still talking? It wasn't going to fix anything.

Nicky smoothed the Henley down his chest and Jasper missed seeing the tattoos. "I'll think about it," he finally said, voice distant and a little cold. "I need to work on the dock stairs. I'm not sure I'll have time."

Jasper shuddered. "All right. I'll walk you out."

They descended the stairs in silence, and Jasper flicked on the porch lamp since the sun had set completely. The light broke through the darkness as the comfortable warmth of the night enveloped them. An owl called out somewhere in the distance, and Jasper hoped all the bunnies were safe in their hidey-holes for the night. One massacre was enough.

He smiled nervously. This day had not gone like he'd expected. But then his days with Nicky never had, had they?

He didn't want to look too closely—to find parallels in the then and now, to get hung up on what could've been—but these hours spent with Nicky had been the happiest in a long time. "Are you angry with me?" Jasper asked in the quiet of the night. "I never should have told you." He never should have touched Nicky either. But he couldn't truly regret it.

"I don't know." Nicky made a soft noise in his throat, a small growl. "I don't want to be. We've wasted enough time with resentment. I just need to go."

"Will you be okay?" Jasper couldn't help touching Nicky's arm again, feeling the solid wiry muscle under his fingertips.

"If you're asking whether I'm going to relapse tonight because of what you said, no." He smirked and a wicked gleam came to his eye. "Well, probably not." He licked his lips. "But maybe you should *make me* stay here with you tonight just to be sure. Tie me to your bed. It could be fun."

Jasper's throat clicked when he swallowed. "Nicky, don't joke about this. I care about you."

"I know."

You're only going to hurt yourself. And Nicky too. He stared into the darkness, waiting for his eyes to adjust, so he could make out Adrian's truck. *The truth is something that exists. Wishing it to be different only leads to deceiving yourself.* Jasper frowned. He couldn't remember who'd told him that.

"Don't worry, Jazz. I'm going to go home and eat Dad's pork rinds and some more ice cream. My therapist tells me emotional eating is a thing other people have some success with." He snorted. "You didn't unhinge me tonight. Well, not completely." He turned to go.

"Nicky, wait."

Nicky stopped outside the ring of light, his face half hidden in shadow, arms wrapped around himself.

"Yeah?"

Jasper tried to swallow. "Would you hate it if I hugged you?"

"No," Nicky said thickly. "Not at all." He lifted his arms and Jasper walked right into them.

NICKY DROVE INTO the night trembling all over. His heart hadn't stopped pounding since Jasper had kissed his scars and slid his soft, gentle fingers over his back and chest. He'd been aching and half-hard from the first tentative touch. Seeing Jasper on his knees in front of him had been so overwhelming that he almost hadn't registered his confession. But when he had, the words sliced into him like that long-ago razor blade, and his heart had pumped wildly for an entirely different reason.

How could Jazz have believed his mother? Mrs. Hendricks had always been a bitch, as far as Nicky was concerned. But the knowledge that Jazz had allowed himself to be convinced that Nicky was incapable of loving him—that he'd taken that lie and run with it into the arms of a made-up God—woke the feelings of betrayal Nicky had been trying so desperately to let go.

But then Jazz had asked to hug him, and their bodies had fit together like puzzle pieces. Jasper was taller than him now, broader, and Nicky had tucked against him, chin hooking on his shoulder. Jasper's arms had gripped him hard, and his breath had brushed against the nape of his neck. Nicky had wanted nothing more than to press further into him until they were as inseparable as they'd once been.

Nicky drove without seeing, following roads he'd know like the back of his hand no matter how much time had passed since he last took them. His mind churned with emotions he didn't know how to categorize or adequately allow himself to feel. His chest hurt so much that he half-wondered if he was having a heart attack, and he couldn't quite grab a full breath. A tingling, thrumming under and over his skin reminded him of snorting coke and slamming back three Redbulls. He was nauseous in the same way too. And going by his half-chub, strangely aroused. He was a fucking mess.

Maybe this was a panic attack. Could he be horny and have a panic attack too? Was that possible? Leave it to him to be too broken to even panic the right way. His mind welled with the memory of Jazz's arms around him; his scent, and how he'd tried to hide his trembling by holding Jazz tighter.

The hug had lasted a long time. When Nicky had finally pulled away, emotions roaring inside him and threatening to spill out in action or words, Jasper's face had been a wash of wild vulnerability: open mouth, flushed cheeks, and dilated eyes. Nicky'd wanted to kiss him. He'd wanted to slide his hand into Jazz's hair and taste his lips, show him with his body how much he knew of love and devotion. He'd wanted to make him praise his God with shivering cries of joyous pleasure. He'd been tempted to push him back inside the house, open him up for his cock, and fuck him until neither one of them remembered why they'd ever stopped.

Instead, he'd touched Jazz's cheek and then turned away. They hadn't said another goodbye.

His dick throbbed, and he pulled off Letterhead onto a dead-end, nameless road where he and Jazz had traded blow jobs and hand jobs more than once all those years ago. Parking on the packed-dirt shoulder, he clenched the steering wheel and forced himself to remember that Jazz was a priest. He'd sat through Mass and watched him only days before.

The memory didn't help. With his dimpled chin, lush lips, and light-brown hair dashed liberally with blond that reflected colors from the stained glass, Jasper had looked like someone's masturbatory fantasy of a priest. He'd given a good sermon too, though Nicky had been so moved by the familiar sound of Jasper's gravel-honey voice that he'd barely listened to the words. He'd been absorbed by the sweet turn of Jasper's neck when he looked to the crucifix, and the smooth line of his throat when he lifted his face to heaven calling for the Benediction.

Jasper always had such a beautiful neck. There was a small dark mole at the base of it that Nicky used to kiss, and he still remembered how Jazz's neck flushed when—

No.

As he stayed motionless with his forehead digging into the steering wheel, he slowly, purposefully turned his attention to the present. He made note of the little things like his therapist had taught him, like the stretch of Jasper's yoga pants against his thigh as he pushed hard against the brake pedal. He felt like an umbrella had been shoved down his throat and opened in his chest. Choked. Pressured. Hurt.

Swallowing against the panic and arousal, Nicky wondered what Jasper's skin would feel like under his fingers now, and what his mouth might taste like. His dick pressed against his shorts uncomfortably in the darkness of the deserted road. A heavy bass beat filled his mind, aligning to the thud of his heartbeat, and he unbuttoned his shorts as a screaming, compulsive need to blunt his arousal with orgasm gripped him.

Fill me up, need like life
C'mon, and love me

Sharp, hot knife
Why don't you? Why won't you love me
Why don't you drive me home?

Lyrics and bass together rocked him and he gave into it. He took hold of himself, thumbing the slit and smearing the precome, remembering when Jazz had pressed his tongue to the head of Nicky's leaking dick for the first time, wide-eyed and so young.

"It's good, Nicky. It's not bad, really. I promise. Here, taste me."

Nicky shuddered and closed his eyes. His phone buzzed, and he grabbed it with his left hand, still gripping his dick with his right. It was a text from Jazz.

Are you safely home?

He bit into his lower lip, jerking his cock and staring at the words, imagining Jasper back in his bedroom, lying in bed thinking of Nicky. Was his hand on his cock too? Was he hard and aching? Did he want Nicky's body against his own? Did he want his kiss and his touch? He stared at the screen of his phone like it was a window into Jasper's desires, and beat himself off hard and fast, orgasm hovering over him like an angel.

"God!" he cried out as he came, jizz spurting everywhere, and he gripped the phone so hard it popped out of his sweat-slick fingers. It fell to the floorboard as he writhed in the driver's seat, moaning and milking the peak until he collapsed back, shaking and only partially sated.

"Fuck," he whispered as the phone started to ring. His hand was covered in his own come, and his heart pounded wildly. Sweat slipped down his back, and he frantically searched for napkins to clean his hand. The phone went to voicemail just as he got the glove compartment open and grabbed a handful of Starbucks napkins his father had stashed there. The car reeked of come.

He rolled down the windows, letting the cooler night air flow through and calm him. The forest surrounding the dead-end road buzzed and creaked, and Nicky took gulping breaths of the pine-scented breeze. He sat there, cock out, and stared into the night before flipping on the interior light to wipe up the clumps and streaks of come on the steering wheel and console.

What the hell had that been? He'd woken with morning wood since going off drugs, but he hadn't experienced sharp, real arousal in months—no, years. It was dizzying, and a little terrifying.

His phone rang again as he tossed the napkins into the small trash can Adrian kept behind the passenger seat. He'd need to empty it when he got home. He fumbled on the floorboard and found the phone, answering before it went to voicemail again.

"Yeah?"

"Sorry. I wanted to make sure you made it home safely. I was worried when you didn't answer my text." Jasper sounded embarrassed.

"Almost there now. Took a little detour."

Jazz was quiet before saying, "What kind of detour?"

"The kind that has nothing to do with Jimmy Orlean or drugs or alcohol." Though his masturbation had been almost as compulsive as feeding an addiction, if he was honest. "I'm okay, Jazz." He hesitated. "What about you? Are you okay?"

"Of course. I'm fine. We simply hugged, Nicky. There's nothing in my vows against hugging a man I care about."

"Okay." But what about loving a man? Was there anything about that? Because Nicky knew, even if Jasper would never admit it, and even if it was years and years too late, that Jasper didn't just 'care for him.' He never had and he never would. Jasper had touched him reverently, like a lover, like he had when they were kids. "If you're sure."

"I'm sure. Sleep well tonight, Nicky. And don't worry about me. I'm fine. Just take care of yourself."

"I will."

Nicky sighed and he disconnected the call. Jasper always had been the better liar.

Chapter Thirteen

JASPER BREATHED CAREFULLY through his nose in mountain pose. He softened his gaze and stared out the window. The sun had begun to rise, but from his west-facing bedroom Little Bay still rested sleepily in darkness. Jasper let the beauty of the silence wash over him as he breathed in and raised his arms overhead. He let his exhale carry him forward—it'd taken a good few months but he could comfortably place his hands flat on the floor now—and paused for a moment. Breath in, rise, breath out, fold forward again.

An unfamiliar warmth began to flower in his insides.

He stretched his right leg back, let the motion pull at his groin, and worked through a few more sun salutations until his body buzzed pleasantly. Coming to rest in mountain pose, he closed his eyes and let his mind drift. As it always did these days, it went to Nicky.

Does it bother you that I still jerk off thinking of you?

Jasper flinched and struggled to keep his breathing even. *Don't think about it.*

His eyes flew open. No. Not thinking about the physical side of what they used to have had been exactly what he'd been doing all week, and it was the coward's way out. Touching Nicky last night had shaken something loose in him, and he had to deal with it.

Jasper closed the blinds and turned on the light on his bedside table. It cast the room in the same warm glow from last night when Nicky had been right here.

Piece by piece he abandoned his pajamas and underwear.

It felt strange, to crawl onto his bed naked. Apart from showering, he'd gotten used to not spending too much time without clothes on.

He sat with his legs crossed in front of him and closed his eyes. Even though it was warm in the room, he shivered lightly. For the first time in over a decade he allowed himself to think of the oppressive nights with Nicky. The hot, humid struggles of their naked bodies—too young to really know what they were doing and too far gone to be able to stop. In the darkness their island had been a cool refuge until their desire had overheated everything from their dreams to their bodies to their minds. It all came back to him so vividly it was as if it had happened yesterday.

Jasper made a small sound when his cock began to fill. It'd been so long since he allowed himself this; it cut off his breath right at the source. His hands curled into fists on his knees. Nicky had been bigger than him back then—he'd pinned Jasper easily to the ground. He'd pressed their clothed bodies together until they couldn't stand it. Until the feeling of the scraping fabric over their sweaty skin had driven them to distraction.

He remembered what it was like to undress for the first time in front of the boy he loved. And oh heavens, he'd loved him so much. Even though it'd been dark, every angle of Nicky's pure, untouched body was seared into Jasper's brain like a tattoo. He'd learned to see with his hands that night. To drink with his eyes and feel with his mouth, and he'd thirsted like he'd been cursed to never be satisfied again.

Nicky had real tattoos, and Jasper now intimately knew what they looked like, what they were, how far they reached, and how they'd changed that beautiful body. He moaned when a spurt of precome dribbled from his cock, and then he breathed.

Slow, in, hold, out.

Yes, he was tempted. And yes, he was only human. But he was in control. He didn't have to give in to the sins of the flesh. He was stronger than that now. He was a priest of God. All the strength he ever needed was there for him to tap into. All he had to do was ask.

Help me, O Lord—Jasper squeezed his eyes shut harder and pressed his fists to the tight knot in his chest—*to resist temptation.*

"Our Father, who art in heaven, hallowed be Thy name…"

As Jasper prayed, his heart calmed and his breath evened. Slowly his fists loosened and he pressed his palms together. The tightness in his chest eased, and he allowed a long breath to escape through his mouth. Once he finished the fifth prayer his erection was gone.

After the Friday morning Mass, Jasper sat in the school office and stared at his computer like it might bite him. Five hundred new emails and every subject line looked scarier than the previous one. The way the kids had been teasing him over the "sexy" pictures did not bode well for the content of those emails. His phone rang and he reached for it without looking away from the screen.

"Father Hendricks."

A low chuckle made him snap to attention. "Don't you mean Father Jazz? From what I saw at the checkout this morning—I mean there was this one picture of you with—"

"Don't you start too," Jasper groaned.

"Aw, are people hating on you 'cuz you're beautiful?"

Jasper grinned at the phone, and relief flooded through him like warm wine. After last night's revelation he'd been afraid Nicky might not want to talk to him again. "How's it going, Nicky?"

"I slept like shit, but I'm okay. You?"

"I'm fine."

"Good. Anyway, I'm running some errands before our yoga class, oh yogi master. I'm looking for a miter saw but Lowes is all out of rentals and Dad doesn't want to buy one for just one job." Jasper heard the rush of traffic in the background along with the low growl of the engine. He imagined the wind whipping through Nicky's hair and took a deep, slow breath. "I told Dad I could buy him every single fucking piece of equipment he needed, but you know what he's like."

"You want to come take a look at the school?" Jasper asked. "There's a workshop that hasn't been used in a long time but it's full of all sorts of tools. You'd be welcome to any of them, if they still function."

"You think there's a miter saw in there?"

"I have no idea what that is, but feel free to take a look."

"Sweet. I can be there in five minutes if that's all right with you."

"Sure." Jasper grinned. "I'm in the office; let yourself in." He lowered his phone and stared at the screen until it went dark. *I can't see the end of this road You've put me on, O Lord, but I'm looking forward to seeing where it leads.*

Jasper went to make coffee instead of dealing with the emails, and by the time he carried two mugs down the hall the large front door creaked open. A beam of sunlight fell through, lighting the tiles in front of him, and the heat of it made his skin prickle.

As if lit by a halo, Nicky looked larger than life. He wore track pants and a dark Henley that hung against him like he was doing the clothes a favor. His hair drifted in the mild summer breeze, locks gilded by the light behind him. *This is the rock god,* Jasper thought. The enigmatic presence that could hold an audience of tens of thousands in thrall.

Here in the old school building with its chipped tiles and slightly musty smell, there was only an audience of one. Jasper thought of the Nicky he'd seen surrounded by the delighted kids as he sang that heartbreaking song. The fragility of his voice combined with the music he could coax out of any instrument juxtaposed strikingly with the Nico Blue Jasper had seen on magazine covers. He didn't understand how those two people could inhabit one body without breaking.

The door fell shut and in the semi-darkness Jasper's eyes needed a second to adjust.

"Is that coffee?" Nicky appeared in front of him and held out his hands. "Gimme. Mom's put me on a detox diet she read about online. It's supposed to support addicts and horrifically involves no caffeine."

"Hmm, I don't know." Jasper lifted both cups out of reach. "I don't think I want to go against Mrs. B's wishes." He grinned at Nicky, who looked back with a dangerous twinkle in his eyes. Jasper's heartbeat faltered.

"Careful, Fox." Nicky took a step closer and kept his voice low. He reached out and dragged a finger down Jasper's freshly shaven cheek. "Don't start something you don't want to finish."

While his heart kick-started into a canter, Jasper kept smiling. "What? You mean drink both these coffees? I think I can handle it." *This is dangerous territory. Deep breath. You're in control.* He neatly side-stepped Nicky and went into his office, where he took a seat at his desk.

"So what do you do in here all day?" Nicky asked, taking a quick look around. With a smirk on his face he reached for the coffee and Jasper let him have it. "Write sermons?"

"Sometimes, although I mostly do that in my office at home. I handle Blue Oasis business here, answer emails, that sort of thing."

"BO business." When Jasper made a face he laughed. "That's your own fault, dude." Nicky looked around with silent curiosity for a second, then peered at Jasper's book collection. "How did you even do it, dude? A shelter full of gays run by a Catholic church? Sounds like an oxymoron to me."

"History actually shows quite a few positive initiatives toward the LGBTQ community from the Roman Catholic Church. It's background support usually because of the general opposition, but quite a few priests have done their share of progressive work in the past."

"You're not operating in the background."

"No." Jasper mulled his words carefully. "But maybe that's my calling. Maybe the reason why I'm doing what I'm doing is to bring these issues to the foreground and bring the Church into a more modern way of thinking."

Nicky stared at him, wide-eyed, and then he laughed disbelievingly. "That's…that's ambitious, Father Jazz. And more than a little bit arrogant."

Jasper lifted his shoulder. "Maybe. But it won't happen until people stand up and try." He glanced back at his inbox. "Though there are some less pleasant consequences to being so public about it."

Nicky looked like he wanted to say more, but seemed to shake it off. "What kind of consequences?"

"Emails," Jasper said, sighing. "Lots and lots of emails."

"Yeah?"

"You don't want to know."

Nicky came around the desk to see the computer, gripping Jasper's shoulder briefly. "Is it hate mail? Shit, I'm sorry, man. You don't deserve that."

"Oh, I'm used to the hate mail. That doesn't get to me, although after *The Atlantic* cover there's definitely more of it. It's the other stuff."

"Well, now I really want to see." Leaning forward, Nicky peered at the screen and began to laugh. "Click on that one."

"What? No, I—Nicky!"

Nicky grabbed the mouse and clicked on exactly the email Jasper had planned on deleting without reading. A photograph of a blonde woman wearing a bikini meant for someone half her size began to load. By the time it filled the screen, Jasper had his head in his hands and Nicky was laughing so hard he couldn't seem to stand upright anymore.

"Can you please close it?" Jasper asked. "Even if I wasn't a priest I wouldn't want to see all that."

Nicky clicked. "Check this one out."

Jasper lifted his head. "No, don't—"

A photograph of a headless, ripped male torso with a hand digging deep in a pair of underpants began to load. Jasper groaned while Nicky slapped the desk as he laughed his head off. "Look!" he gasped. "Tighty-whities! You two have something in common already!"

"Please shut up," Jasper said. He made a grab for the mouse but Nicky blocked him and pinned his wrist to the desk.

"Just one more," he said. "This is too good to pass up. I had to work very hard to get to this level of intrusive fans. You should feel honored. All you had to do was look pretty on a magazine cover to make the crazies come running. Love this subject line: 'Do priests have Daddy kinks?' But no picture—boring!"

He clicked on a random email with an attachment and opened it. This time there wasn't even a ripped stomach, just a giant…

"Whoa," Nicky breathed. "That has to be Photoshopped. I have *never* seen a dick that big in my life. And I've seen a lot of dicks." He tilted his head to the side, peering intently. "Can I reverse image search this? Maybe the guy has a Grindr."

"Uh, no." Jasper wrestled his hand free, grabbed Nicky's arm so he couldn't move out of the way, and reached for the mouse. As quickly as he could, he deleted the email. "Weren't you here to look at a saw?"

"Drill bits are more interesting."

Jasper rolled his eyes skyward but a light feeling filled his belly. He'd missed their friendship and he hadn't allowed himself to think of it in so many years, which was a shame. To deny good things that happened in life was to deny gifts from God. Nicky straightened and shoved his hands in his pockets. Jasper looked up at him. "I'm happy you're back, Badger."

Nicky's face was soft and unreadable as the silence lengthened. "Yeah, I know," he said eventually, and his sharp, bright smile poked Jasper's heart. "But you can prove it by showing me your workshop." Somehow Nicky managed to make it sound like Jasper had promised to show him *his* drill bit.

He rolled his eyes, but couldn't help laughing. No one flirted with him anymore. Probably due to the whole priest thing…but Nicky wouldn't care about that. And even though the flirtation felt slightly dangerous, it felt right too. Natural and normal, and it made his heart soar a little giddily. He bit his lip and looked back at the computer screen. Why didn't it feel wrong to let Nicky talk to him like that?

As Jasper rose, Nicky gripped his shoulder. "Hold on a second. You have an email from John Arlington."

"Who?"

Nicky looked at Jazz with wide eyes. "Who? Are you kidding me? The golden child of the business world? Self-made man? One of the richest people in the world? There was that giant so-called scandal when he came out as gay after his home state was about to approve the Religious Freedom Act and he threatened to pull all his companies from the area if they went ahead with it."

"It's probably fake." Jasper tried to step around him, but Nicky leaned in and stopped him.

"Read it."

"You just want to see more naked duck-face pictures."

Nicky gave him a skeptical look. "Yeah, their faces, that's what I want to see. And trust me, I don't need your email for that. Read it."

"Fine." Jasper bent over the desk and clicked. "Dear Father Hendricks…read the article…impressed with your work…my own background…" Jasper scanned the rest of the email in silence and straightened.

"Well? What is it?" Nicky pressed into his side so he could see.

Keeping his balance with one hand on the desk, he looked back at Nicky. The knots in the wood felt familiar under his fingers. He'd traced them often enough over the years. "He's offering financial assistance, should I ever need it." The slightly sweet mingled scent of wood and polish drifted upward. "If it's real."

"And do you need it?" Nicky asked insistently, and Jasper remembered his piercing stare from the kitchen doorway as Adrian had delivered the news about the Blue Oasis contracts over their dinner table.

"No," Jasper softly said. He glanced back at the computer. "Not as long as we're part of the Church."

"Can you think of any reason why that would ever change?"

"N—" Jasper's voice broke when Nicky's fingers inched along the wooden desk.

They didn't touch, but their skin was no more than a hair's breadth apart and it was like a tiny current fed into Jasper's pores and crackled up his veins until it burned in his lungs. Lifting his eyes quickly, Jasper glanced at Nicky. His head was bent as he stared at their almost-touching fingers. Down the neck of Nicky's Henley, Jasper could see the shape of the beautiful fox tattoo. His fingers tingled with sensory memory.

A particularly long, bouncy wave of hair brushed the tip of Nicky's slender nose. Swaying closer, Jasper could feel Nicky's heat, and he realized his smell hadn't changed that much over the years. There was a tinge of sweat that was more masculine, but the undertone of him was still the same: sweet, comforting, and *home*.

Nicky raised his face and brought his mouth close to Jasper's ear. "You're starved for it," he whispered, breath hot and wet like the touch of a tongue. "Aren't you? And you don't even know it."

They still didn't touch, but Nicky's words felt like a forbidden caress down Jasper's spine.

Nicky opened his mouth again, leaning back a little. His pure blue eyes shimmered, and he sighed. "Forget I said that. I'm here for tools and yoga."

"This way," Jasper said, his voice gruff.

Nicky didn't find the tool he needed but did locate something else that might work. It was a mystery to Jasper, who'd never learned anything more useful than how to pray.

He flinched at his own thought and focused back on Nicky. "So you'll be staying for yoga?"

"Sure, why not? Offer some comic relief for these poor kids stuck in a school with a beast of a former teacher and an uptight priest all the time."

"They've been stuck in worse places," Jasper said, letting Nicky's teasing insults slide as he led him down the hallway toward the gym.

"Yeah." Nicky took a deep breath. He searched Jasper's eyes and then looked down as a soul-deep sadness seemed to envelope him. "I remember it, you know?"

"What?"

"Being in that dumpster. I remember it was raining. I was wet and cold and afraid."

"Nicky!" Jasper pulled him to a halt in front of the gym. "You never told me that. You were only a few days old, how could you possibly—"

"I don't know. But I do. I told the social worker at some point and she said it wasn't unusual for traumatic events like that to imprint themselves on babies. She said it was true, anyway. It had been raining for hours when that homeless guy found me."

Oh, how horrific. "A...a homeless person found you?"

"Yeah. That's what she told me. I guess I was lucky he took me to the shelter. Not everyone would've." His eyes went distant. "I was a baby, but somehow I understood death. I understood my mom didn't want me and that I was going to die."

Was that even possible? Jasper didn't know, but Nicky clearly thought it was, which was all that mattered. "I'm...I'm so sorry. I never knew. Oh, Nicky." Jasper stepped into Nicky's space and hugged him again, wanting to feel him tucked against his chest the way he had been the night before. He wanted to keep him safe. Nicky made a startled noise, then gingerly hugged him back. Wherever their bodies touched, little pools of comforting warmth rippled out over Jasper's skin.

You're starved for it.

Oh, he was. He *was*.

Again Nicky was the first to break away and when Jasper turned to open the door to the old gym, he saw Lizzie standing down the hallway. His cheeks heated up. But he plastered on an inviting smile. He hadn't done anything wrong. He was comforting a friend.

"Hey Lizzie, how's it going? You joining us?"

"Uh, yeah. If that's okay. I've never done yoga before."

"Of course. Come on in. Nicky is joining us, and he's never done it either. It's not difficult, I promise."

Nicky pushed the doors to the gym open and laughed. "God, this brings back memories."

Jasper glanced around the place. It still looked like it always had, and smelled a little worse, to be honest. He aimed for the stereo, pressed play on the relaxing CD with yoga music that was still stuck in the machine from last week, and began to unroll a dozen yoga mats. Slowly the other kids began trickling in, some of them yawning and still dressed in pajamas.

"To be a teenager again," Nicky muttered under his breath and Jasper followed his gaze. Gus and Jason were getting into a wrestling match, and Jasper snorted.

"Guys, this is supposed to be relaxing and calming. No fighting."

"Party-pooper," Nicky said, loud enough so everyone heard, and Jasper groaned when they all laughed loudly.

"He's got your number, Father Jazz," Amberlynn said, laughing.

"See if I invite you again," Jasper told Nicky. "You can take a first row seat for that. All right, everyone, choose your mats and sit down with your legs folded at the ankles please."

As always, there was a scramble to reach the mats in the last row, but eventually everyone settled and Jasper turned down the music a little. He folded himself on the mat in front of the class.

"Thank you all for coming," he calmly said. "I appreciate your participation. Take a deep breath, lean into your sit-bones and straighten your back. Fold your hands in front of your chest. Now remember, this is about *you.* About whatever higher power you believe in and want to be thankful for. You don't have to pray if you don't want to; you can be in the moment and breathe. Close your eyes if you haven't already. Breathe in through your nose. Hold. And out through your nose. Keep going."

Jasper closed his eyes too and found his center of peace. It brimmed with warmth today and he imagined a bright yellow light behind his heart muscle. Slowly he made it expand until the bubble of golden light reached his skin, then broke through to envelop everyone in the room.

I'm grateful, O Lord, for this life and these kids. I'm grateful You're helping Nicky find the strength to fight his demons, to believe he's worthy of being happy. I'm grateful You've reunited us. Maybe I have been adrift too.

Goosebumps rose over Jasper's arms. He hadn't felt this alive in a long time. A sweet ache heated his blood and a warm flush burst over his cheeks. God owned his soul, but Nicky would always have his heart. Even if they could be no more than friends, God had reunited them for a reason.

"One final deep breath in," he said roughly. He could hardly contain the overwhelming sense of rightness, and he squeezed his eyelids shut tight before the feeling came spilling out. He tried to steady his voice. "Hold out through your nose. And open your eyes. Come up on all fours. We're going to start with cat-cow to loosen up a bit." Jasper rose to his feet. The kids all knew how to do this one so he took the opportunity to walk up to Nicky. "Get on all fours. Keep your shoulders over your wrists, knees at a ninety degree angle. That's right." He put his hand on Nicky's back. "Now push your spine against my hand." Nicky did as he was told. "Relax your neck. That's it. Now let your spine hollow out and bring your head up. There you go. If you're feeling tension in your shoulders, this is a great way to let go of it." Jasper let his hand trail down to Nicky's tailbone. "Keep going, and try to keep breathing."

"Easier said than done," Nicky whispered.

"Child's pose," Jasper said and everyone sank down. He tugged at Nicky's hip and led him back until his sit-bones rested on his heels. His Henley caught under his left wrist and exposed part of the blue fox on his shoulder. Jasper watched it ripple, a joyful tension shimmering in his belly at the sight. "Relax your arms and let your forehead rest on the mat. There you go. *Beautiful.*"

He made his way to his own mat and lay down in child's pose for a minute, a warm tingle starting in his solar plexus and driving down into his gut. *Happiness.* "Push up into downward-facing dog." Jasper stayed in this position for a while, patiently breathing until his muscles relaxed enough for his heels to touch the ground. He glanced at Nicky, who looked impressively uncomfortable. He stifled a small laugh.

"Like this," Jasper said, coming up beside him. "Bend your knees a little. You don't have to be able to do it with straight legs." Jasper went to stand behind Nicky and tugged gently on his hips. "What you want more than anything, is to lengthen your spine." He ran his hand along Nicky's vertebrae. His fingertips brushed over the peacefully sleeping fox and badger on Nicky's back. He wished they were alone so he could tug the shirt up and take another look. "Push into your hands, press your fingers into the mat, relax your neck, and breathe." Jasper kept one hand on Nicky's right hip and put the other on the small of his back. "Pull in your navel and tilt your sit-bones to the ceiling."

"You mean my ass? Oh crap, I can't hold this for very long," Nicky said, sounding strangled.

"Come back down into child's pose whenever you need to." Jasper kept his hands on Nicky as Nicky sank down in relief, the bones in his back moving under the shirt. He was so skinny now.

"It's harder than it looks."

Somewhere behind them one of the kids snickered.

"It takes time and practice. When you feel ready, try again, because this is an excellent pose to gently build strength again. If it's too much, go back to child's pose. You can take it easy. Don't go quite so hard."

Another snicker.

Jasper rolled his eyes, let go of Nicky, and walked them all through a few sun salutes and warrior poses. Nicky couldn't hold any position for very long, and by the time they ended with a five-minute savasana, he was covered in a faint sheen of sweat.

When Jasper dismissed the kids—most of them filing out to get their breakfasts—Nicky helped him roll up the mats.

"Can we get breakfast too? I heard you hoard pastries in this building."

"Of course. But I'm afraid you'll be disappointed. It's eggs and bacon this morning. Not a pastry to be found."

Nicky shrugged. "I'll stop by Irena's on the way home, then."

"Text me if she has fresh bearclaws. I've been craving one."

Nicky smirked and rolled a mat. "Will do."

"So, what did you think of yoga?"

Nicky flushed. "It was, um, interesting."

"You're welcome to join whenever you want."

Nicky stepped close enough that Jasper could smell his sweat. He darted a look toward the door to the gym, but they were alone. "I enjoyed it, but I think I'd enjoy private lessons more. I need a lot of help." Nicky grinned when Jasper dropped the last mat. "Especially with my 'sit-bones.' They're so damned tight."

And then he sauntered off, leaving Jasper to reroll the last mat and calm his thumping heart.

Chapter Fourteen

THE FOLLOWING FRIDAY, Nicky didn't arrive at Blue Oasis until after yoga. No matter how tight his sit-bones were and how much he'd benefit from doing another hour of yoga with Jasper and the kids, he hadn't been able to rouse himself from the peacefulness of his bed that morning. The whole week had been consumed by summer-gold bubbles of pleasant things: mornings spent in warm sunshine messing with the stairs down to the dock, afternoons spent playing music with the kids at BO, and evenings talking with his parents, Ramona, or Jasper.

He'd volunteered to work with any of the kids at BO who wanted to learn to play an instrument. So far, only two had taken him up on it. Lizzie was picking up keyboard quickly and Jason was learning guitar. They were both good students and dedicated to improving. They made the work easy. Not to mention, it'd given him plenty of opportunities to see Jazz, but more than that, he liked helping the kids a lot. His heart warmed whenever either of his students showed pleasure in the music.

Strolling in with a box of Irena's cherry tarts to be shared around, he was told by Mrs. Wells that Jasper was on the phone and that Lizzie was waiting for him. "She didn't know if you were coming or not since you didn't show up for yoga." She sounded as scolding as ever.

"Sorry. I had to deal with some important things first." Like morning wood, and fantasies of Jasper coming to him on bended knee, naked and begging. And once that was settled, he'd been very busy rolling around in his fresh, clean sheets watching the trees outside his window cast shadows on the floor. He loved that the shadows moved like music.

"Anyway, I'm here now." He handed her the box of tarts. "These are for you and anyone else who wants one."

She smiled at him after opening the box. "Well, Nicholas, that was very kind of you. Father will be pleased. He loves Irena's pastries."

Nicky didn't stick around once Mrs. Wells bit into a tart with a moan of nearly obscene pleasure. He waved and then hustled up to the dorm room on the second floor, the one he knew was Lizzie's.

"Hey girl, did you miss me?"

Lizzie was curled up with a book in her twin bed. She looked up over the spine and shrugged. "I guess."

Nicky frowned. Usually Lizzie was enthusiastic even if he was a few minutes late. "What's the matter? Are you mad I didn't come to yoga?"

"No." She sat up and put her book on the nightstand beside her bed. "I'm just upset today."

"Why?" Nicky sat gingerly on the end of her bed, not wanting to get too close in case Mrs. Wells came up and thought he was being inappropriate. "Did something happen?"

"A little. I don't know. Jason said something."

"About?"

"Nothing."

"Oh, if it's nothing, the best thing to do is to tell someone else about it."

"It's just…what if Jason's right?"

Nicky scratched at his eyebrow with his thumb, nerves burning in his gut. Was he up to this? He probably wasn't qualified. "Should I get Father Hendricks for you? He'd be able to help."

"No!" Lizzie's eyes went round.

"Oh. I see." He tilted his head. "Is this about Father Hendricks?"

She shrugged shyly. "Yeah. It's dumb."

Nicky waited, but she didn't volunteer anything more. He narrowed his eyes. "Is it that he's handsome and you have a crush on him?"

Nicky couldn't understand why more of the kids weren't trying to tempt Jazz into some compromising position, actually. He was a really sexy man with a nice body. When Nicky was the age of the BO teenagers, he'd have gone to church every Sunday with the Hendrickses if the priest looked like Jazz.

"Uh, no." She wrinkled her nose at him. "He's old."

"He's the same age as me!"

"You're old. Besides, I think *you* have a crush on him."

Nicky cleared his throat nervously. "I'm allowed to look. But this is about you, Liz. What are you upset about?"

She studied her fingernails a few long moments like the answer to whether or not he could be trusted was written on them in tiny letters. "I don't know if I believe in God," Lizzie finally whispered. "And I'm afraid to tell Father Hendricks."

"You don't have to be afraid. He knows I don't believe in God." Nicky watched her eyes widen. "And we're still friends."

She sat up straight. "You don't think he'll make me leave here if he can't convince me to believe?"

"Hell, no. He'd never kick you out for that, Liz. Did Jason say he would?"

"Maybe."

Nicky smiled warmly. "Well, that's not true. Don't worry about that anymore." He reached out and tweaked a piece of her hair, and then chucked her chin. "All right?"

"Why don't you believe in God, Nicky?"

He didn't want to explain that there was no way God existed, not with all the horrible things he'd done and seen. But life was a lot prettier if you could believe. He didn't want to discourage her. "I don't know how to explain it. I wish I did believe in God. If you don't mind talking about it, why don't you believe?"

"I've tried. I prayed for strength. Like, I'd sit there and suffer and I'd pray and I'd pray and I'd pray." She covered her mouth and a single tear detached itself from her eyelashes. He wanted to offer her comfort but he thought she needed to get through this by herself. "I mean, you think I *want* this? You think I want to walk around in this body and be wrong in my head? If He's real, then why did He make me that way? What's the point? Why didn't He make me *normal*."

He almost argued that normal was a setting on the washing machine, but he knew that wasn't what she wanted to hear. She didn't want him to convince her that she wasn't different from other girls. She wanted him to admit that she was.

"I can't answer that, Lizzie. No one can, not even Jazz." She cracked a little smile at the name and he suppressed a grin. Father Jazz. Nicky didn't care how long it took, he'd have all the kids calling him that in the end. "But you're here. You made it this far."

"Yeah. But all that praying I did? It never fixed anything. And I'm so fucking angry about it." She covered her mouth. "Don't tell Father Jazz I said that."

"I promise." He reached out and took hold of her hand. Her fingers were thin and dry. "You know what, Lizzie? Maybe things will get harder for you before they get better. I'm not going to lie to you about that." Her eyes went wide. "But eventually they will get better."

She rolled her eyes and pulled her hand out of his. "How can it get better, Nicky? I'm changing every day, turning more and more into a man. I hate it. I'm just a kid. I don't have any money. I can't afford to transition. Hormones and surgery? I'll never be able to afford them. Not before it's too late."

"It's never too late, Lizzie. I promise you that."

"If I can't transition soon, it'll be harder, maybe impossible, to ever look the way I want."

"Maybe. But medicine has come so far. There's so much that can be done now. Girl, I know how trite that sounds when you hear it, believe me, but you've got your whole life ahead of you. And when you're all grown up and you've got a career and someone who loves you…all this?" Nicky gestured around them, encompassing the school, but also her current body and her past. "It'll seem like a faraway dream."

"No it won't."

"Parts of it will. I promise. And you'll have knowledge no one else has. You'll have an affinity with people around you, people who need help in ways no one else understands. That's important, Liz. It's strong people like you who change the world."

She scoffed but smiled as she reached out to squeeze his hand. "Says the famous rock star."

"I don't change the world. I fill it with noise for a few minutes and then people forget my existence. It's you who'll make this a better place. Not me, not God. You."

"Do you think that's really true? Or are you trying to make me feel better."

He squeezed her hand and stood up, pulling her with him. "Both. Now, are you ready for your lesson?"

After working with Lizzie on her keyboard skills, Nicky left her with a girl named Amberlynn. She was a few years older and owned a big pink overnight case full of makeup and a large purple mirror. As he'd put away the keyboard and guitar, he'd listened to their wary exchange of promises: Amberlynn would show Lizzie some tricks with the makeup and, in exchange, Lizzie would teach Amberlynn how to throw a real punch. How Lizzie was going to demonstrate that—or rather, on who—Nicky wasn't sure, and he decided he probably shouldn't stick around to find out or he'd be somehow to blame.

"I think you need a punching bag," he said dropping into the chair across from Jasper's desk.

Jasper frowned at the computer screen and hit a few buttons.

"Any more dick pics I should see?"

Jazz didn't bother to answer that, instead, glancing up and smiling at Nicky before going back to his screen. "Why would we need a punching bag?"

"For them to get some aggression out. You know they're one big mass of teeming hormones." Nicky slumped down in the chair, spreading his legs wide. His jeans tugged at his knees, and he pulled up the sleeve of his light shirt to scratch at an itch in the crook of his elbow. He tugged the shirt down again to cover the scars. "Violence or sex are really the only options."

"Prayer is a good option."

Nicky slapped his forehead. "Yes, of course, how could I have forgotten how prayer staved off all the sex we had?"

"Nicky," Jasper hissed, rising quickly to shut the door to his office. "Mrs. Wells is sitting out there. What if she'd heard you?"

"She's got earbuds in," Nicky said, reaching out and slapping Jasper's hip as he walked back to his desk. "Probably listening to Perry Como."

Jasper gave him his serious face and Nicky swallowed back a laugh. "No, she's probably taken them out and is intently listening to everything you say."

"Well, I hope she got good and scandalized then."

Jasper leaned back in his desk, smiling and shaking his head. "This is bringing back awful memories for me."

"What? Of me getting you in trouble?"

"That. And all the rambling conversations with you that went to all kinds of strange places but never came back to the cupcake."

"Oh, yeah. The cupcake." Nicky grinned, remembering a marijuana-tinged conversation that had started out with him declaring he'd eaten a cupcake at Irena's and ended with him babbling about triathletes and the Olympics. "Years later I still have no idea what I was going to say about that damn cupcake."

Jasper's computer binged, announcing a new message. He paused, tapped on his keyboard again and then pushed it away, focusing entirely on Nicky. "Well, today the cupcake is a punching bag. Something about violence and sex just waiting to break out amongst the children."

"Oh, yes, the *children*." Nicky laughed and leaned forward, putting his elbows on Jasper's desk. "They're teenagers, and any second now they'll be punching each other in the caféteria or screwing on Mrs. Wells's desk. I'm telling you. You can't contain it, so you should provide for it. Like with the sex kits. You need a violence kit."

Jasper sighed and templed his hands on his desk. "I've been running this place for years, Nicky, and we've never had a fight break out."

Nicky narrowed his eyes.

Jasper smiled and ducked his head, conceding, "Well, lately."

"You lie very often, for a priest."

"I never did until you came around." Jasper cleared his throat, eyes darting down and back up again. "Well, I never did very much."

Nicky grinned. "I'm such a good influence, as always."

"You never lie."

"True." He shrugged and dropped back into his seat. "But don't feel ashamed, Jasper. I have a lot worse sins to my name. You're still pure as the driven snow in comparison. Don't despair."

"You're ridiculous." Jasper laughed and leaned back in his chair too. "I'm almost done here. I still need to work on my sermon, but I could do that later at home. What are your plans for today?"

Nicky shifted in the seat and scratched his eyebrow with his thumb. "Well, that's why I'm here, actually."

"Oh? I thought you were here for the kids' music lessons." Jasper smiled.

"Yeah. Well, I'm going to throw this out there, and you don't have to say yes." He cleared his throat and his cheeks heated. He clenched the arms of the chair. "I need a babysitter."

"For?"

"For me. My parents have had their Fourth of July trip to Chebeague Island planned forever. Mom mentioned yesterday that they were going to cancel it now that I'm home, but I told them not to be ridiculous. I could handle myself."

"But they don't trust you?"

"They don't, no, but they pretend like they do. They left this morning." Nicky smiled despite his tight throat. "Mom looked like she wanted to claw her way through the car door to get to me, and Dad looked like someone had a gun to his head as he drove away."

"I see." Jasper stood and walked around his desk, leaning against it in front of Nicky. His brow creased. "But do you think they'd have left if you were really still in such a place of temptation?"

Nicky looked down at his fingers, twisting them in a knot in his hand. He wished he had a guitar to fiddle with, a way to not look at Jasper during this next part. "I told them I wasn't tempted at all. And I wasn't." He looked up at Jasper, a trickle of shame sliding down his back. "Jasper, you have to believe me. I didn't go looking for Jimmy, I swear, but I saw him yesterday morning at the coffee shop."

Jazz worried his lip. "And?"

Nicky looked down at the floor, his fingers shaking when he brushed them into his hair. "He's aged terribly. I've put my body through hell and I somehow look better than him."

"Because he…" Jasper trailed off.

Nicky met Jasper's gaze. "Because he does meth. I know."

"Did you—"

"No." Nicky cleared his throat and then let out a long breath. "But ever since Mom and Dad hit the end of the driveway I keep thinking about googling how meth and my maintenance medication mix and, well, I don't think I should do that."

"Oh, Nicky."

"It's weird. When they were home, I didn't even think about it. Then I was alone and suddenly the idea popped up in my head and I can't shake it."

"Well, I'm glad you came here." Jasper's voice was scratchy. "After everything, I'm glad you trust me with this."

Nicky stared at Jasper's earnest face. "So, Father Jazz, would you be willing to babysit me for a few nights? It would take a load off my parents' minds. And mine too."

Jasper leaned forward, putting a hand on Nicky's shoulder and then pulling him up for a hug. Jasper's body fit against his perfectly, and Nicky's pulse thudded in his ears nearly obscuring Jasper's gruff, "Of course. I always want to help you, Nicky."

"HEY BEAUTIFUL," RAMONA sang. Her voice through the tinny iPhone speakers still held that hint of gravel that so many men seemed to love. "I suppose I should give you the heads-up."

Nicky fell back against his soft bed and held his phone above him so she could see him on the FaceTime screen. "About what?"

"The paps are desperate to find you."

"Why? Can't they harass Kanye or Bieber or some Kardashian?"

"Nope, sorry." She shook her head and grinned. "They're all being very boring. You, however, are being exciting and mysterious. They want to know where you are and why, and what you're addicted to and how you got that way and when you started using, and if you're fucking anyone in particular and *so much more.*"

"I'm not that interesting and most of that is common knowledge."

"The fucking part isn't."

Nicky shrugged, and Ramona rolled her eyes. FaceTime was so awesome and so strange. He never knew if he should look at the screen or at the camera. "There's nothing to tell. I haven't dated anyone seriously in years."

"Ever."

"No, years."

She looked thoughtful. "All right, years. But as long as I've known you, there's been no one."

Nicky shrugged. "And how is that interesting enough for the paps to be trying to find me?"

"It's because you're the fairest of us all. And you give the impression of having a lot going on inside your head, but you won't share it." Ramona opened a drawer of the desk her iPad was resting on, and she fished around inside, finally pulling out an orange lip balm. "It makes them crazy. You're so aloof. So dreamy."

"You're the one with the gorgeous tits. Why don't they want to know who you're getting naked with?" Nicky turned onto his side and propped the phone on the pillow opposite.

"Because I scare them. You, though? You're filthy and gay. They're dying to know if you're sticking it in any pretty boy bums, you know."

"I don't stick it." He remembered his fantasy about Jazz the other night. "Much."

Ramona chuckled, delighted. "You should throw them that bone. They'd live off it for days. 'Nico Blue Bottom Boy! Press at Noon!' At least until some celebrity mama takes her brand new baby on a walk in a baby Prada outfit, and then they'll forget you again. For a day or so."

"They always come back." Tree limbs shifted outside the window, casting peaceful shadows around the room. "The assholes harass my mom, did you know?"

"Sure. They harass all our moms. Mine hangs up on them. Mick's cries. And Sez's mother is apparently making good money selling tidbits of gossip about his childhood whenever she needs money for a vacation or a new car."

"Fucking hell. What a bitch."

"Well, that's what Sez says, but I haven't met the woman, so I'm reserving judgment."

Nicky laughed. "Yeah, I hear all that reserved judgment in your voice. You and Jazz should have a liar's anonymous meeting."

Ramona's eyes darted away from where she was organizing her travel make-up bag. She shoved it aside and leaned in toward him through the screen. "Excuse me, did you say Jazz? As in *the* Jazz? You've seen him?"

"Yeah." Nicky sat up and shifted the phone so she could still see him. Then he picked at the sole of his cheap tennis shoe. They were already coming apart from the wear and tear of working on the dock and the stairs. Which wasn't really going too well. He'd overestimated both his skills and his physical condition, and underestimated the complexity of such a project. He'd managed to tear up a lot of stuff, and actually repair very little.

"Jazz? The same guy that ninety-nine percent of our songs are about? The one who destroyed you, wrecked you, ruined your life?"

Nicky's smile went sour at that description. "I've never told you about what happened between us. You only know the music."

"The music is loud, pretty boy. But feel free to explain yourself. I'm listening. And I swear on my soul not to spill the beans to TMZ."

Nicky scrubbed at his face and considered. What did he have to lose? Making friends with his bandmates was something on his sobriety to-do list anyway. And Ramona had always cared about him.

"Where do you want me to start?"

She pondered. "His name. So, really, his parents named him Jazz? Did they hate him or something?"

"His name's Jasper. I'm the one who started calling him Jazz. His mother hated it." He wasn't sure he could ever forgive Crystal Hendricks for what she'd told Jazz to drive him away, even if he did forgive Jazz for believing it.

"I bet she did."

"What do you mean by that?"

"Oh, it's just the way you say it. '*Jazz*,' like you're in awe of everything about him and you're going to fall to your knees and worship him…with your mouth." She waved a hand in front of her face. "The way you feel about him? It's all over you when you say his name. Like glitter or something. You can't ever get that shit off. Glitter is the herpes of the craft world. Don't get herpes from this Jazz guy, Nico."

"Nicky. And we're friends."

"Yeah. Right."

He blew out a breath, frustrated. "He's a priest, for fuck's sake."

Ramona slapped her hands down on the desk and the iPad fell over, giving him a view of her braless breasts in a loose yellow cotton sleeveless T-shirt. Then her face appeared again. "Holy freaking shit balls. Are you seriously fucking a priest?"

"What do you not understand about 'we're friends'? Friends don't fuck."

"Uh-huh. Why don't you start at the beginning, because if that is how you look when you talk about your friends, you must hate the fuck out of me and Mick and Sez, because you *never* look like that when you talk about us."

"The beginning of what?"

"The beginning of why you've written a hundred thousand love songs about a guy who is married to Jesus."

"I don't think priests marry Jesus, do they? That's nuns right?"

"How would I know? My mom was Southern Baptist, and talking about marrying Jesus in that bunch was a big enough sin to burn in hell." Ramona looked thoughtful. "Do you think Jesus was good in bed? He was probably pretty patient and self-controlled, don't you think? And he was a carpenter's son. He knew how to work with his hands."

"We've never had a conversation like this before."

"Because you were always higher than heaven. And before you got hooked, you were always weird and distant."

"I like feeling this way. Sometimes I'm afraid the medication will stop working and I'll wake up tomorrow back in that same old cage."

"Ah man, Nico, that could break a girl's heart. Have some faith."

"Can you do me a favor?"

"Maybe. No promises."

"Can you call me Nicky?"

"Nicky, huh?" Ramona looked at him through the screen like she was weighing the name. "Sure. Why not?"

"Thanks."

"Give me the dirt. I want to know. Then I'll sell it to *People* and pay the assholes in charge enough to get us the fuck out of our crappy contract."

"Sorry. No *People*."

"Cross my heart. Needle in eye. All the rest."

"We were best friends as kids, but I think I loved him from the moment we met." They'd been so young together, but his heart had recognized Jazz from the beginning. "Then as teenagers, we fell in love. We were each other's firsts. First kiss, first…loves."

"First loves don't last."

"I guess not. Because he threw me over for Jesus."

"He dumped you to become a priest?"

"Yeah. And stupid me, I'd been so blind that I never saw it coming."

Ramona listened attentively and when the story was over she asked, "So what's the plan?"

"What do you mean?"

"Are you going to try to break him and Jesus up, or are you going the 'let's be tortured friends' route?"

"I don't have a plan."

"Well, this will be a mess." Ramona smiled, not unkindly. "But let me warn you. I've got offers from Liver Pills and Burning Machine to play on their next tours. If you go off the deep end with this thing and get back into drugs, I'm going to take one of them up on it."

Nicky stared at her through the screen of his phone.

"This isn't a threat, Nico, er, Nicky. It's a life lesson. Always have a plan."

"Sounded like a threat."

Ramona shrugged. "If it helps keep you sober, I'm okay with you interpreting it that way. For a few reasons. One, I need a functioning leader of this band if we're going to make music that doesn't suck and survive this industry. Two, I like sober Nicky. He's like a real human being with a sense of humor and emotions and a history. It's cool."

"Thanks?"

"You bet. And now for the fun part of this phone call. What's *our* plan? Vespertine's plan. You know as well as I do that one of you three chuckleheads will go off the deep end again if we go on another extended tour like that. We've got to get better contracts. I think we should have attorneys look at the ones we signed and see if there's a loophole we overlooked. Something we can hold over their heads to get better terms for tours at least, if nothing else."

Nicky's dad had looked at his contract ages ago, but he wasn't an entertainment lawyer and he didn't know half of what Nicky had faced on the road. If they could prove the big guys had violated their side of the deal, maybe they could find a way free.

"How much will it cost?"

"Does it matter?"

Nicky laughed. "Fuck no. Let's do it."

THAT EVENING, NICKY loaded the last of the dinner dishes into the dishwasher, dumped more soap than necessary into the little divot, and closed the lid. "Fuck that, Danvers."

Jasper had turned up on his doorstep with an overnight bag, takeout Chinese, and a shy expression a few minutes before six. Now he sat at the kitchen table, fidgeting with his phone and pretending not to listen, but Nicky saw him flinch at the curse words.

"Listen, I don't give a fuck what you tell me about Mick's situation, or Sez's, because what I'm telling you is *I* write the songs for Vespertine and nothing, abso-fucking-lutely nothing, will be recorded until I'm on board."

"There are other songwriters, Nico," Danvers said. "If you don't show up to record by the first of the month, we'll get someone to take your place. Vespertine is more than Nico Blue."

"Then you'll need a new drummer too, because Ramona won't work for a shit songwriter."

"She's worked for you the last few albums."

Nicky laughed at the direct hit Danvers had dared. "Touché."

"I'm just delivering the news, Nico. You'll have to go over my head to get a different answer. And you go ahead and try."

Nicky snorted. "Big talk."

"Backed up by big money."

White rage pulsed in him, and Nicky hung up, throwing the phone onto the counter, not sure if he was relieved or disappointed that it didn't break. "Every time I turn that thing on, it's crap news."

"What's the problem?" Jasper's fingers twitched like he wanted to reach out to him.

Nicky leaned his elbows on the kitchen counter and ran a hand through his hair. "They're saying that if I'm not ready to make a new album soon, they're going to kick me out of the band."

"Can they do that?"

Nicky snorted. "They own us. They can do whatever the fuck they want."

"And if the others don't agree to this?"

"Then we're on our own."

Jasper cleared his throat and offered tentatively. "Would that be so bad?"

Nicky stood up straight and stretched, his back cracking a little. He sighed. "Well, it's not like I could even become an indie artist. We signed shit contracts when we were younger. They own my future songs until I've made six albums with them. Same for the others."

"How did Adrian let you sign something like that?"

Nicky walked around to the table. "Because Adrian wasn't consulted. Like I told you before, I was young and angry and pretty fucking egotistical. I thought I knew best." He laughed, pulling out the seat beside Jazz and sitting. "I thought I'd have ten albums out in less than ten years, maybe more. I was cranking out music then. It was coming out of me like I was sweating out a sickness."

"Music has always been part of you like that."

Nicky sighed and put his head down in his hands. "Not right now." He rubbed his fingers through his hair anxiously. "Can I tell you something?"

"What?"

He chewed on his bottom lip. "Everything I write since I've been on these meds? It comes out...deformed or something. Like broken pieces of song." He looked up at Jasper, and his horror must have shown clearly because Jasper's face fell into a tender mix of sadness and reassurance.

"It's going to be okay."

"Jazz, get real." He crossed his arms over his chest. "What if I can't write high and I can't write on these meds? What if I can't be the person I am now and make music?"

Jasper leaned close, carefully uncrossing Nicky's arms from where he squeezed himself tightly. "No, that's not how it's going to be. You're learning."

"I haven't had to learn a damn thing about music since I was a little kid, Jasper. It's just been there for me. Always."

"Well." Jasper seemed to carefully weigh his words. "Maybe when a gift comes so easily to someone it isn't always appreciated. Maybe it's God's way—" He took in Nicky's expression and laughed under his breath. "Okay fine. Maybe when a talent like that is taken for granted for so long without nurturing it, the well runs dry. And now you'll have to find new ways to replenish it. I don't know if I'm explaining this right. What happens when you play now?"

"It starts out okay, but then it twists up." Nicky let Jazz rub his thumbs soothingly against the skin of his soft, inner arms, even brushing against the scars. He didn't want to explain that the new music was sometimes pretty good, but then the lyrics came out like everything he didn't want to be anymore. "I still play, though. I have to play. But lately I only want to play other people's songs, like when I'm with Lizzie and Jason, because I can't stand to play the old Vespertine stuff anymore, and everything new is missing something. Maybe an arm. Or leg. It's not whole."

"People with disabilities are still whole, Nicky. They're just whole differently."

"Goddammit, Jasper, don't be PC right now."

Jazz ducked his head and an adorably thick flop of hair fell into his eyes. "I'm sorry."

"You don't believe me."

Jasper gripped his arms solidly. "I do. I think you need to be patient with yourself. You're still healing. It makes sense that your music would be healing too."

"Tell that to the goddamn, motherfucking, piece of shit assholes in Los Angeles."

Jasper grinned. "Hand me the phone next time and I will."

Nicky laughed softly. "Yeah. Maybe I'll let you if you're around."

Jazz's long golden eyelashes framed his eyes, brows low with worry, and his plush mouth was open. A tingle went up Nicky's back and his cock stirred. If Nicky leaned forward… "Let's go down to the dock. I need some fresh air."

Jasper cleared his throat. "You can never go wrong with fresh air," he agreed.

JASPER STARTLED AWAKE at four thirty in the morning, a whole hour before his alarm was supposed to go off. Although he slept under only a light duvet, his cotton pajamas stuck to his skin and his hair clung to his temple. Throwing the covers back, he shoved his hair out of the way and touched his forehead. While it was damp, he didn't feel particularly feverish. With no other intention than getting a glass of water, Jasper swung his legs over the side of the bed. It was a lot higher than his own bed and it took him a moment to find the light switch for the small bedside lamp.

At first he thought the white and blue stripes on his pajama pants had darkened with sweat, but then he realized that wasn't it at all.

"Oh!" Jasper scrambled off the Blumfelds' spare bed. The images of his dream came flooding back and his spent cock gave a weak twitch. "Oh no."

Moving jerkily, he yanked off his shirt, then the pants and his underwear. The smell of semen hit him like a visceral punch and Jasper groped for the nightstand when his knees almost gave out. He lunged for the bathroom attached to his bedroom and nearly hyperventilated when he flicked the light switch on.

The cold of the shower was welcome and he didn't bother adjusting the temperature. A penance he deserved. Fingers shaking, he grabbed the loofah he'd brought with him and scrubbed his skin as he felt his face flush hot.

"Be merciful to me, O God, because of Your constant love." The skin on his arms turned red under the assault. "Because of Your great mercy wipe away my sins." He rubbed at his thighs. "Wash away all my evil and make me clean from my sin. I recognize my faults." He poured too much body wash on the loofah and the shower stall filled with the scent of sandalwood and citrus.

Jasper couldn't allow himself to think or linger on the things he'd dreamed about. The sweaty-hot touch of skin on skin was seared into his mind, and he wiped at his groin with trembling fingers, letting the water and soap wash away the strings of semen that clung to his pubic hair.

"I am always conscious of my sins." His teeth began to chatter in the onslaught of cold water. He tilted his face and let the needle-like stream punish him. "I have sinned against You—only against You—and done what You consider evil. So You are right in judging me; You are justified in condemning me. I have been evil from the day I was born; from the time I was conceived, I have been sinful." *Mea culpa, mea culpa, mea maxima culpa. Sancta Maria, Mater Dei, ora pro nobis peccatoribus, nunc et in hora mortis nostrae. Amen.*

With a loud gasp he turned off the water and stood, breathing hard as he leaned against the wall. His face felt hot and flushed compared to the rest of his body. Inside him an emptiness crawled up his belly. He watched his fingers tremble against the tiles. They were pale and numb with cold.

Everything had seemed so easy a week ago.

Streams of soap ran down his body, and as he looked down he laughed hoarsely. "You're ridiculous," he said to himself. "You had a wet dream, so what?" Shivering harder he turned the water back on but let it run hot this time. It'd been a while since something like this had happened, but it wasn't the first time. Having Nicky near brought back old memories his tired mind tried to process in his sleep. He had nothing to feel guilty about.

And yet that was the one feeling he couldn't shake. Along with the darn erection, apparently.

He was drying his hair when he stepped back into the Blumfelds' guest bedroom and froze when he heard a noise by the door. Nicky knocked, hard, like it wasn't the first time.

"Jazz, what the hell is going on? Are you all right? If you don't answer right this second, I'm coming in."

"No!" Jasper dropped the towel for his hair and clutched the one around his waist. To his mortification the tent in the towel hadn't abated a bit.

"Are you sick? Why are you taking a shower at four in the morning?"

Jasper tried to control his breathing, to apply every single meditation and yoga practice geared toward relaxation, and still his erection *wouldn't go down.*

He leaned his forehead against the door. "No, I'm fine, seriously."

Silence followed and Jasper only knew Nicky was still there from the shadow that fell underneath the door, along with the hallway light.

"I don't want to talk about it," Jasper added helplessly.

"You do realize," Nicky said after a while, "that makes me want to come in even more, right?" Nicky's voice was still worried but a little wheedling when he added, "I've spilled a lot of my dark and sinful past to you, Jazz. You can talk to me too, you know."

Jasper exhaled a shuddery breath. Nicky was right. A friendship could never function if it remained one-sided. But *of all the things.*

"Jazz? You okay?"

"Yes. No. I'm…I don't know."

He heard the rustle of fabric and he wondered what Nicky was wearing. Just boxer shorts? Or did he cover up his tattoos even when alone in bed? Jasper closed his eyes and breathed.

"Come on," Nicky said softly. "Talk to me, Jazz."

"Nicky, it's…" He covered his eyes. "We're friends, right? I can talk to you about this? I don't know who else—"

"Of course you can. What's going on? You're freaking me out, man."

"I'm having—ever since you showed up—I'm having trouble sleeping."

A gentle swishy noise filled the silence and Jasper imagined Nicky rubbing at the door between them. When Nicky spoke his voice sounded different, more intimate. "I think that's totally normal, Jazz. It's like we were talking about earlier tonight. Being around me makes you think of things you haven't had to think about in a long time. What we did back then, it's not…I could never say it was wrong from my point of view, but I understand if you're having trouble dealing with it. I'd like to help you. Even if it means keeping my distance. I'm…I don't want to hurt you."

"I know that, it's not…that's not the issue. I never felt what we did was wrong, Nicky. Not then and not now. But it's like something woke up and it won't go back to sleep."

"Oh." Nicky fell silent for a moment. "Oh!" He laughed softly and Jasper cringed, shoulders rounding as he hid his face in the cup of his hands.

"Don't laugh at me."

"I'm not. I'm not. I'm sorry. So what are we talking about here? Are you getting, you know, boners? That won't go down?"

Jasper appreciated Nicky trying to keep the amusement out of his voice, but he could imagine all too easily how wide Nicky's grin would be. "That," he whispered. "And I woke up half an hour ago, and I'd…" He trailed off.

"Shit, man. Are you having wet dreams? About me?" Nicky's grin was so smug that Jasper could hear it through the door. "I'm *not* laughing, I promise. Because that's not funny." He let out a strangled laugh. "I'm not laughing. Okay listen, hold on. There's this article I remember reading. I mean it could be a drug-infused hallucination but lemme look."

Jasper listened to Nicky walk away, and his shoulders relaxed a little. He glanced down. His cock had abated a little, but not enough. He made a frustrated noise and pressed the towel down hard into his groin. Not that it helped. Quick footsteps approached, and part of Jasper wanted to throw open the door and just get it over with.

"Found it on my phone! See? I knew I'd read it. Okay, you listening?"

"Apprehensively," Jasper said, and Nicky laughed.

"No, man, this is super-important and it will change your life. So, it says that men, especially as they get older, should orgasm one to three times a week as a preventative measure toward avoiding prostate cancer. So there you go. You and your hand should get seriously reacquainted, because otherwise you might die, and I'm sure that's not what God intended."

Jasper laughed even though he tried not to. "I don't think that's how that works, Nicky." He sighed and softly said, "Why is this happening to me?"

Nicky was quiet for a minute. He moved around a little, the fabric of whatever he was wearing shifting against the door. "You horny right now, Jazz?"

Pure hot want zinged up Jasper's spine, and he pressed his fingertips to the door until they went white. "Don't, Nicky."

Again, silence but for Nicky's breath. "You are, aren't you? I bet you've been standing there talking to me with a boner that won't go down. How long?"

"I'm not talking about this."

"Just tell me. How long have you been hard?"

"The cold shower didn't help."

"Shit, man. This won't take you any time at all. Just do it, okay? Why are you standing there suffering? For what? Just get it over with. You heard what the article said. You can do it in the name of medical necessity."

Jasper laughed again but his eyes stung. "I don't think I can."

"You want me to come in?" Nicky whispered. His voice trembled a little and Jasper swallowed hard.

"I'm not…It'd be too much. I can't."

"Okay. I understand. I'm gonna go, and you do what you need to do. But let me tell you, talking to you has given me the biggest fucking hard-on. And I'm going to go back to my room, stick my hands down my pants, and think of you."

Jasper's heart beat so loudly in his ears it took him a while to figure out Nicky had gone.

Chapter Fifteen

"GIRD ME, O Lord, with the girdle of purity and extinguish in my loins the desires of lust so that the virtue of continence and chastity may ever abide within me."

Jasper closed his eyes and exhaled slowly. He fingered the sash he was supposed to wrap around his waist. From the sacristy he could hear the gentle buzz of people waiting for Mass to begin. He was wasting time, but he felt unbalanced and unsure of himself. He tried not to think about what had happened, but the sleepless night weighed heavily on him. Knowing Nicky was sitting in a pew right now didn't help. While he didn't have any issues being by himself for a while, he'd suggested tagging along to Mass with Jasper that morning. At least he hadn't brought up their middle of the night chat.

Am I failing, Lord? Am I failing You? Am I failing myself?

"Everything all right?" Andrew asked.

Jasper opened his eyes and nodded.

"You sure? You don't look so good."

"Still trouble sleeping." Jasper wrapped the cincture around his waist and finished the rest of the ritual. It usually felt soothing to go through the motions, but this time it made him antsy.

"You know, maybe you should go see someone." Andrew waited with his hand on the doorknob. His white bushy eyebrows were drawn down in concern.

"Hmm? Like who?"

"A doctor. For your sleeplessness? Get some sleeping pills, even if it's only temporarily."

Jasper shook his head.

"I don't want to mess with those. There's a lot on my mind lately. I'll be fine once things settle down."

"If you're sure." Andrew didn't look convinced, but he let Jasper pass him by and walk toward the altar.

The church was fuller than usual on this Fourth of July. Maybe Little Heights felt particularly pious on this gorgeous summer day, but Jasper suspected it had more to do with his recent exposure to a bit of fame than anything else. Or perhaps it was the free picnic he was hosting in the schoolyard and cafeteria afterwards.

He murmured his usual greeting to the parish and closed his eyes. "Life doesn't always turn out the way we expect," he began. He had no idea where the words came from, but when he opened his eyes they fell unerringly on Nicky. That blue gaze could guide him home like a beacon if he ever got lost. Jasper didn't look away from him. "In fact, life rarely turns out how we expect, or even want. When young people get married and have children and look toward their future, they don't think in ten years they might be looking back on their marriage with a divorce attorney by their sides.

"Sometimes illness gets in the way of our dreams. And other times we can't make our deepest wishes come true, and we settle for a more ordinary, simple life."

He touched the smooth surface of the lectern to let his words settle for a second, but when he looked up, it was yet again Nicky who drew his gaze.

"A lot rests on the shoulders of children. They have to build their futures from the ground up and decide who and what they want to turn into, all while they're still learning to *be*. And sometimes children have no support at home and rely on the kindness of others to make it, while others have loving families and still can't find their feet.

"Life is hard. It descends on you whether you're ready or not. This is when we can turn to God—" He faltered when Nicky frowned a little, but pushed on regardless. "In our hardest times He is our guide, our savior. He will listen when we need Him. But what God wants most of all is for us to love each other. To be there for each other, regardless of gender, skin color, or even sexuality."

He'd never talked about this in his sermons, but maybe it was time.

"We all know what everyone thinks the bible says about homosexuality. The quotes that are generally brought up have been used and abused by all those who think they must make a point against God's love. Against the truth.

"I'm only human. I make mistakes. Big ones, small ones, daily ones—just like everyone else. I don't pretend to know Him better than any of you do. But here's what I do know: God's truth is about His love, and the love we should feel for one another. We can't have it both ways. We can't hate a fraction of His people and still pretend we stand for God's will. The ultimate truth is that we should care for one another wholeheartedly, even those who we think are difficult to love." Jasper's fingers trembled a little. "It's never too late to turn a corner. It's never too late to right a wrong. God is there for those who see the error of their ways.

"So no, we don't always walk the path of life we set out to follow, but as long as we open our hearts to the people we find along the way, without judgment, without condemnation, God will always wait for us at the end of the road."

Nicky smiled at him and then looked up to the stained glass window behind the nave. The light danced on his features. He looked almost angelic, the way he had when they were young. Jasper's nerves quieted. God had brought him home for a reason. This was the road God wanted him to travel and He would be there at the end of it.

His adrenaline rush crashed as soon as Mass was over, and Jasper groaned inwardly when he saw the row of people waiting in their pews.

Andrew threw him a worried glance, but Jasper discreetly waved him off and made his way to the confessional.

He tried to be attentive and understanding, offering advice and prayer for the people who came and went, but when the same accountant with the office on Main Street came to confess his extramarital indiscretions with his boss *again*, Jasper felt like screaming.

After telling him rather tersely to reconsider the choices in his life, because while God might forgive the repentant, it wasn't a free pass to keep sinning, Jasper rested his head in his hands for a moment. No one else stepped into the confessional and he sighed in relief, taking a moment to sit and consider his own sins.

I rushed through Mass, he thought. *Apart from the message I imparted at the beginning, I didn't give You my full attention, O Lord. I am afraid of the path You have laid ahead of me. Please give me guidance. Help me find the solution for Blue Oasis. I don't want to abandon the children that need You most. Help me find the right way to love Nicky. Just...help me.*

"OKAY, SO, LIKE, this is a really important question," Jason said, leaning over the cafeteria table to steal the cherry from the top of Lizzie's Fourth of July sundae, a festive-looking thing made from stacked layers of blueberries, vanilla ice cream and strawberries. "It's like the ultimate personality test."

"Uh-huh." Lizzie shook her head in amusement.

"Okay, so, listen, both of you, okay? If you had to choose, would you rather be a member of The Beatles or The Rolling Stones?"

Nicky shoveled some ice cream in his mouth to keep from answering first, letting Lizzie field the question.

"The Beatles, I guess," she said, but then she frowned. "I don't know. They're both too famous. I want to be, like, intermediately famous."

"Halfway famous," Jason said, nodding. "Beatles means you're a snob, by the way."

Lizzie laughed. "I could have told you that."

Jason turned to Nicky. "What about you?"

Nicky swallowed his ice cream and shrugged. "I agree with Lizzie. Neither one. Too much fame."

"But you're almost as famous as them now!"

Nicky laughed. "Thank fu—uh, goodness that's not true."

"You don't like being famous?" Lizzie asked, peering at him with soft eyes. They reminded him of Ramona's.

"Hate it."

"C'mon, you don't like the crowds screaming your name? Everyone singing along to your songs?" Jason asked.

"You don't like the money?" she added.

Nicky considered. "Yeah, I like those things. But, to be honest, if I could go back in time and make one, big change in my life…" His eyes automatically sought Jazz's back where he stood talking to a middle-aged woman with red hair and a scar on her cheek. He couldn't help but admire Jasper's broad shoulders beneath the tight black cotton, and his hair clumping up thickly in the humidity of the afternoon. "I'd give it all up." He cleared his throat and took another bite of his sundae.

Jason and Lizzie exchanged looks, but Nicky ignored it. He couldn't stop thinking about Jasper's little sermon. It'd been so off the cuff, even Jazz had seemed startled by it. He remembered how Jasper's fingers and voice had trembled as the words had tumbled out. And yet he'd gone on with it like he didn't have a choice, like something was speaking through him. Like the way Nicky used to feel about music.

It tickled at the back of Nicky's mind. Maybe there was a higher power of some sort. He wasn't ready to concede to the idea of a God who cared about what they did on a day-to-day basis, but maybe there was a power each person carried within. Their bone-deep truth. The reality of who they were.

"What do you say, Nicky?" Lizzie asked like it wasn't the first time.

"Huh?" Nicky shook out of his reverie and turned his attention back to the kids.

"Want to go play some music with me and Jason? We could hide out in the gym. No one will be in there and the acoustics are kind of cool."

"Unless you want to get more to eat?" Jason said. "You're skinny and you didn't eat anything real, just junk."

Nicky was nearly done with his ice cream but he didn't feel especially hungry. Not if it meant he had to talk to the people from Jasper's church anyway. "I ate before I came. Let's go."

He followed them out of the cafeteria, feeling Mrs. Wells's gaze on his back, but he ignored it. If she hadn't figured out that he wasn't going to hurt these kids by now, then fuck her.

An hour later, Jason was making good progress learning the finger-picking part to "Here Comes the Sun," and Lizzie was feeling her way through the keyboard accompaniment, while Nicky made up new lyrics—silly ones about nosy churchies who brought potato salad to the Fourth of July potluck.

The door to the gym opened and Jasper leaned against the jamb. "Don't let me interrupt," he said, smiling, arms crossed over his chest. "But we can hear you guys all the way outside, you know. Maybe some less *offensive* lyrics would be possible, Nicky?"

Nicky couldn't help the smile that cut across his face, or the laugh that pushed up from his belly, and apparently neither could the kids.

"They do donate money to our cause," Jasper added, trying to look stern, but his eyes glittered with amusement.

"Of course. I'll come up with suitable suck-up lyrics ASAP."

Jasper rolled his eyes and laughed softly. "Actually, clean-up started and nearly everyone's gone now. Lizzie and Jason, why don't you guys go help out? Once everything's put away, we can get out of here," he said to Nicky.

Jason and Lizzie exchanged another glance, but they headed out of the gym without being asked twice, both of them whispering and jostling each other as they went. Jason took the guitar with him, which left the keyboard to take down off the stand and back up to the rec room.

"So, did you have fun?" Jasper asked, as Nicky hefted the keyboard under one arm and lifted the collapsed stand into the other.

"Sure," he passed the stand to Jasper who took it willingly. "I've had worse Saturdays."

Jasper followed Nicky out of the room, and Nicky could feel his questions burning into the back of him like Superman's heat vision. The rec room was empty, and Nicky set up the keyboard and stand again with Jasper waiting next to him, a furrow in his brow and his lower lip between his teeth.

"You say things like that a lot."

"Like what?"

"That you've seen worse, or done worse, or had worse. It makes me…" Jasper stared at him.

"It makes you what?"

"Tell me about what you've been through, Nicky. The things you've seen. I want to know. You shouldn't be carrying it all by yourself. I want to help."

Nicky stood up from adjusting the height of the keyboard stand and shoved the hair off his forehead. He let out a long breath. "Let go of the savior complex, Jazz. It's fine. Besides, there's too much."

Jasper stared at him and then finally nodded. "Okay. But when something comes up, tell me. I can handle the truth about your past. There's nothing you did or saw that could change how I feel, or the respect I have for you."

Nicky swallowed, relief rushing under his skin when Lizzie and Jason, along with Amberlynn and Gus, came bursting through the door to the rec room, chattering, shoving, and laughing. Jasper snapped back into authority-figure mode, and Nicky edged his way toward the stairs as

Jazz scolded and guided the kids toward a calmer deportment.

"I need to talk to Mrs. Wells, and then we can go," Jasper said, as they headed back downstairs.

Nicky waited outside in an empty corner of the courtyard. He tilted his head back, letting the late afternoon sun wash him clean. The steeple stabbed into the sky, piercing the edge of the sun. The humid air was hot, but it felt good on his skin. Real and pure. Piano chords, like shafts of light, filled his mind. He could almost make out a song in them, and lyrics that didn't hurt shifted somewhere under his skin.

Jasper's hand on his shoulder pulled him out of the silent meditation. "Do you want to get take-out? Or can I cook for you tonight?"

A weird sensation settled over Nicky, a breathless certainty that in some alternate universe where different choices had been made that question had been asked and answered many times.

"Whatever you want," Nicky said, shoving his hands in his pockets, as Jasper's fingers burned into his shoulders.

"I should stop by and check that Dizzy has food. And get my bike. I fixed the tire."

"All right. I'm sure my mom's got something in the fridge we can heat up. She stocked it before she left. Worried I'd starve, I guess."

"That sounds good to me if it works for you."

Nicky nodded, hearing the sweet sound of the kids singing some religious song, led undoubtedly by Mrs. Wells, and his heart gave a hard thump. "It sounds great."

When they got to Nicky's house, they changed into shorts and T-shirts and stuck their feet into the pool before heading back inside to start a late lunch. Nicky hadn't had much at the picnic besides ice cream.

The afternoon had such a warm, domestic feel that swung Nicky between a sense of perfect rightness, and a terrifying knowledge that it wouldn't last. When Jazz put Nicky's plate of re-heated meatloaf down in front of him, he was tempted to slap his ass and say, "Thanks, wife" to break the sweetness of the day and point out the dangerous line they were treading.

He'd been an idiot to ask Jasper to babysit him. He'd have been safer on his own.

"This is good," Jasper murmured over his food. "Your mom's ingredients always taste so fresh."

Nicky smiled and lifted his water glass. "To Meryl Reed's butcher shop. May they always prevail over the giant grocery store's meat department."

Jasper drank to that and a silence settled over the table that wasn't awful and wasn't good either. It was a silence of expectation. Something had to be said. Something had to happen. And it needed to come any second now or Nicky was going to blurt out something stupid.

Jasper wiped his mouth and smiled at him. "You're good with the kids, Nicky. It's clear that Lizzie idolizes you."

"She's fun to teach. I'm glad to help her learn to play keyboard. She says she wants to start guitar too." He stopped short of saying, "If I'm not here when she's ready for that, I'll pay for her lessons." That conversation could happen when the time came.

"Yes, she's very invested in learning. Music can be so healing. I'm glad you're giving this gift to her."

Nicky shrugged and pushed hair out of his face, heat prickling his neck.

"And Jason, too. He's been a tough nut to crack, but you've got him in the palm of your hand."

"They're good kids and they like music. We have that in common. It makes it easy. They're the ones doing all the work. For me, it's fun."

Jasper tilted his head, considering. "So you like teaching them?"

"Sure. They're so into it. It reminds me that music can be enjoyable. It doesn't have to be about figuring out the shit in my head, and it doesn't have to be a lifeline to sanity, or the chains that make me a slave to corporate assholes." Nicky's lips twisted. "It can be about making a connection to another person." He smiled. "How cool is that?"

Jasper grinned in response. "Yeah. Pretty cool. How would you feel about working with kids like them on a regular basis? I think you have so much to offer and you obviously enjoy it. Do you think you'd be interested?"

Nicky didn't mention how little time he probably had left in Little Heights. That fact was as inescapable as the feelings that pulsed between them like a separate living heart. "Do you mean when I'm out in Los Angeles?"

Jasper swallowed and looked away. "Of course. There have to be opportunities there for you to help disadvantaged kids who want to learn music. If you're up for it, it sounds like a good idea." He cleared his throat. "How's it going with your parents' stairs?"

"Well, I should probably own up to the fact that I don't know what the fuck I'm doing out there and hire Joey Renfroe."

"The contractor?"

"Yeah. His mom is friends with my mom."

"He's a good choice. It was an ambitious project and I'm sure you could figure it out given the time, but maybe hiring Joey would be the best if you want to make sure it's done before you have to go."

Nicky nodded. "Yeah."

Jasper took another bite and looked thoughtfully at his plate. He sounded a little too nonchalant when he asked, "Have you heard from your management again?"

"No, but Ramona and I talked today. Mick is making noise about leaving the rehab facility early. She's trying to talk him into staying."

"What happens if he leaves?"

"Well, it'd suck for him, obviously, because I don't think he's ready, but it would suck for the rest of us too, because the suits would use it to try and get us all back in the studio." He shrugged. "It sucks all around."

Jasper sighed and seemed to agree.

Nicky didn't want to talk about going back to Los Angeles or making a new album or the likelihood that his bandmates would stay clean. He'd had something else on his mind since his conversation with Lizzie about God and her rage that she didn't feel like she fit inside her body. He'd placed a few phone calls, asked a few questions, and talked to his accountant. He knew what he wanted to do.

"Jazz, I want to pay for Lizzie to transition. And Gus too, if he wants. Any of the current kids who are interested in physically transitioning. I'll fund their hormones and whatever surgeries they want to have."

Jasper almost choked on his water. He took a moment, wiping his mouth and then putting his napkin aside with a careful movement. Then he reached out and took hold of Nicky's hand. His fingers were cool and smooth against Nicky's palm. "That is one of the sweetest, kindest things I've ever heard you say, Nicky. You have such a wonderful heart. But the medical costs involved are obscene and you can't possibly—"

"I've got a lot of money and I can totally afford this. That is, if you figure out what needs to happen on your end to allow for it. Do you have to consult the case workers or something?"

"You're serious?"

"I'm serious." Nicky stood with his plate and carried it into the kitchen. "Find out what needs to happen. I'll have my accountant call and we'll set up, I don't know, a little trust or something for Blue Oasis kids. I'll have him put money in it every year and we'll see what it can fund." Nicky grinned as he rinsed his plate and put it in the dishwasher. "It's a tax write-off too. Charitable deduction. Win-win."

Jasper came up behind him, put his dish on the counter, and pulled Nicky around to face him. "I need to know that you're not going to back out. This is a huge responsibility, Nicky. It's not the sort of thing you can start and then forget about later. These kids will depend—"

Nicky's heart clenched. "I'm not going to forget. I care about those kids. I haven't cared about enough people in my life to let the few I have slide out of my mind."

Jasper's expression went guilty and soft. "I'm sorry. I didn't mean it like that. I admire that you want to help them and I absolutely want them to be helped. So, yes, I accept your proposal. We'll figure out how to get this done." Jasper smiled, his eyes crinkling at the edges, and his lips standing out rosy against his gleaming white teeth. "Thank you, Nicky. I don't know how to thank you enough."

Nicky could think of plenty of ways.

He shrugged and pulled Jasper into a hug. "Just try to get Lizzie on hormones soon. It's what she wants and that's all the thanks I need."

Chapter Sixteen

"REMEMBER WHEN WE used to swim across to the island?"

Jasper smirked and lifted his feet out of the bay. The droplets falling down glittered in the afternoon sunlight and he dipped his feet down again, watching their distorted, pale shape through the clear water. "I beat you every time."

"Lies," Nicky said. He was lying back on the dock with his feet propped up on the edge. He'd found a long piece of grass somewhere, and he chewed it as he basked in the sun, arms tucked under his head, eyes closed. With every inhale, his stomach became more concave, contrasting the sharp rise of his ribcage, and his T-shirt slid up to reveal a small sliver of his happy trail. He looked as peaceful as the sleeping fox on his foot. "I beat you at least half the time."

"Nope. I think you won once, and that's because I got cramp in my leg halfway there and you left me to die."

"You were fine."

"Fish food, I think you called me."

"We were literally ten feet away from the island. You could stand. You were being a fucking baby because I beat you."

"Fish food, Nicky." Jasper leaned forward quietly, dipped his finger in the water, poised it over Nicky's face, and then waited.

When the droplet fell, Nicky flinched and opened his eyes. "You little shit." He laughed and leaned up on one elbow so he could give Jasper a good shove. It didn't do much more than unbalance him, and he grinned.

"We could always have a rematch."

Nicky squinted at him. "Right now?

Jasper shrugged. It was less than two hundred yards away but he still worried about Nicky not being strong enough. "If you're up for it."

Nicky stared across the water. From where they were sitting they could see the roof of their fort, and suddenly Jasper was dying to know what it looked like—if it was still intact and if the strongbox with comic books and other things was still there or if nature had taken over completely.

Jasper's parents owned the island. It was part of the parcel of their land. He remembered how excited he and Nicky had been when their dads had built the fort for them.

The strongbox was big and heavy. It might've survived the years. They'd nearly sunk the boat bringing that thing over to the island.

"We can always take the boat and paddle across."

An angry glint flashed in Nicky's eyes and he sat up abruptly. Tugging at his clothes with jerky movements, he took off his T-shirt and the cut-off jeans. "You going to give me an advantage and swim in your clothes, Father Jazz?"

Jasper hesitated but he knew that look really well. Nicky was going in the water whether Jasper followed or not, and he wouldn't be waiting. "What do I do with my phone and wallet?" he asked, pulling his own T-shirt over his head. He hesitated for a second, but Nicky was already down to his boxer-briefs, so Jasper tugged his shorts down too.

"We can roll them in our clothes and put them in the boat. Ready?" He handed Jasper a stack of clothes and before Jasper could do much more than grab hold, Nicky turned on his heels and dove straight into the water.

"Oh jeez." Jasper quickly stuffed his phone and wallet in the bundle of clothes, tucked them under the bench in the boat and dove after Nicky, who was already a good dozen yards ahead of him. "Nicky!"

Jasper yelled. "Wait! You cheater—" He gasped at the cold water and then set off in a strong stroke that fatigued his arms and legs in no time. He wasn't used to swimming anymore, but at least he ran and did yoga and took care of his body. Nicky was... Nicky was coming to a halt and Jasper slowed in relief. At least he was waiting. But then Nicky turned back, his hand outstretched. He tried to swim in Jasper's direction and one moment he was there and the next he wasn't.

"Nicky!" Jasper yelled. Oh please God *no*. "Nicky!" Saving his breath, Jasper redoubled his efforts and swam as fast as he could to where Nicky had disappeared. Sputtering, Nicky kicked to the surface and fought to stay there. Jasper's body burned all over but he paid it no mind until he grabbed hold of Nicky's wrist right before he went under again. "I've got you!" he yelled, wrapping an arm around Nicky's heaving chest. They were both nearly swallowed up by the water when Nicky kicked out. "Stop struggling right now!"

Instantly, Nicky went limp. "I'm sorry," he gasped.

"Shh." Jasper glanced over his shoulder as he frantically tread water. They were over the halfway point and he stood little chance of making it back to the mainland dragging Nicky along. A good part of the island's shore was shallow and he'd have better luck going that way. Without speaking he began an awkward one-armed stroke toward the island. He could always gather his strength, swim back and get the boat. All that mattered for now was getting Nicky out of the water.

"It's okay, I can stand now."

They clambered to their feet but Jasper didn't let go. "You scared the shit out of me."

"You're swearing." Nicky hugged him back.

"Yeah well, this situation calls for it." Jasper leaned away a little. The sun beat down on their heads, already drying their shoulders. "You okay? Did you swallow any water?"

"Some, but I didn't inhale any. My whole body hurts though."

"Let's dry out." Jasper kept an arm around Nicky's waist as they trudged to shore, and Nicky let him hold on.

"It all looks the same," Nicky said.

"More overgrown, but yeah. Look, the rock is still there. It used to look bigger."

Nicky gave him a wry smile and pushed his wet hair out of his face. Glittery pearls of water clung to his eyelashes, inviting the light into his irises until they looked the palest of blue. "I think it's us that grew, not the rock that shrank. You wanna…?"

"Sure." It'd been their go-to sunbathing spot when they'd come over to the island as kids. It used to be big enough for both of them to stretch out on until they were dry, so they could either swim back or play in the fort. The air was thick with the typical sandy, sunny salt smell that never failed to make Jasper feel right at home. It had ingrained itself in his bones when he was a child and he'd missed it something fierce during his college years. The ocean held its own kind of call.

It turned out they still fit on that rock, although it was a tighter squeeze. Their arms brushed together shoulder to fingertips, their skin cold and still clammy from the water where they touched.

Nicky grasped Jasper's hand. "Thanks," he whispered.

Jasper let their fingers tangle a little longer. "Of course. What happened anyway? Did you tire out?"

Nicky let go of his hand. "I did. It was like…I had this burst of energy when I hit the cold water and then my strength disappeared. My arms and legs went so heavy I couldn't move them anymore."

"Your strength'll come back to you. If you want you can always start running with me."

Nicky snorted and twisted on his side, head resting in his palm. He blocked the sun when Jasper looked up at him. It felt intimate. Like there was no one else in the world. The island had always been that way for them. Here they'd never had to hide anything from anyone. They'd bared their hearts and their souls, and eventually their bodies to each other.

"I doubt I can make it a mile right now," Nicky said.

"That's okay. We'll work our way up to it. Although I have to say"—Jasper stretched his legs and groaned as his whole body quivered—"I'm not used to swimming anymore either. Everything's going to be pretty sore tomorrow. I'll go get the boat in a while. Just let me rest for a few minutes."

"We may as well stick around the island and explore. That's what we're here for, right?"

"Sure." Jasper smiled up at Nicky. The waves lapped lazily at the shoreline and the hum of the town was almost inaudible from here. Cicadas sang their chorus to the heat of the day. It felt peaceful and cozy and Jasper didn't look away when Nicky kept holding his gaze.

"Your belly's going red," Nicky whispered. He stared into Jasper's eyes and smirked a little. He still had such an expressive mouth. As a boy, it had given Jasper so many wet dreams. And it was making him tingle now. "And I fucking knew you'd still be wearing tighty-whities."

Jasper ran his hand over his navel, through the faint hairs trailing down. He had a soft, flat stomach—nothing like Nicky's sharply ridged abs cradled by two prominent hipbones. Although his underwear was drying it was still pretty see-through and he felt his cheeks stain red. The dark thatch of hair was really noticeable, as was the slightly flushed head and outline of his cock. He had to fight the urge to cup his genitals and hide them from view.

"My belly doesn't see much sun these days." A flash-hot feeling began to fill his stomach and he tried to breathe past it. "You're getting a bit of color again too. You were pale that first day I saw you by the pool. You look so much better now."

Jasper reached out and pushed Nicky's drying curls away from his face. Every time Nicky shifted a little, Jasper got a faceful of sunshine and had to readjust his eyes. "I don't think I've ever known anyone more beautiful than you," Jasper whispered.

Nicky grew very still. The sun burned over his head, turning the wayward curls into dark gold. The rock under Jasper's shoulders was hot, his skin dry, and deep inside his chest a warm comfort bloomed, a feeling of such safety and pure perfection it made the hairs on his arms stand on end. How could anyone not believe in God when moments like these existed? The bright light made his eyes moist. *Love*, he thought. *Still. Always*. He blinked. "You could do with a haircut though."

"I could do with a lot of things." Nicky's face hid in shadows and his eyes were dark pools of unspoken thoughts. Jasper knew what they were. He felt them deep in his veins. He should back off, jump in the much-needed cold water, swim away to the boat and bring them to the mainland and sanity. But his body didn't seem to want to move and the voice inside him remained silent.

Strike me down, O Lord, but there's nowhere I'd rather be.

"Jazz?" Nicky's eyes searched his face.

"Yeah." Jasper tugged gently on Nicky's hair, lifted his shoulders off the rock, and placed a soft kiss on Nicky's lips, like a benediction.

Nicky jerked back and sat up straight. "What the hell, Jazz? This is a bad idea. I'm not going to be on the other end of your guilt trip tomorrow when you regret this."

His heart pounding, Jasper sat up too. "I know. You're right, I don't know what came over me. I feel like...I wouldn't regret much, right at this moment."

The heat of the rock had bled into Nicky's hands and they felt hot against Jasper's shoulders when Nicky gripped them. "It's not 'right this minute' I'm worried about, but I'll tell you something. You do that again and I won't be letting go of you until at least one of us comes." Nicky scrambled to his feet and jumped off the rock, muttering, "*Jesus*."

Jasper followed suit. He didn't know what he'd been thinking but it had felt...right. Was he testing himself?

The thought sobered him. Doing that to Nicky was beyond unfair. Nicky was kicking an addiction. The last thing he needed was more complications. *Get a hold of yourself.* He took a deep breath and followed

Nicky toward the fort.

The rough grass-covered sand scratched the bottom of his feet uncomfortably—he'd gone soft over the years, in more ways than one—but the shade the trees offered was welcome after lying in the sun. It took a moment for his eyes to adjust to the darkness, but when they did, he laughed softly.

His brain had held onto the snapshot his mind's eye had taken of this place the first time he'd seen it. Absolutely delighted with their very own palace, Nicky and Jasper had thought themselves kings of the world. In reality the fort was nothing but a wooden square with a roof on it, a door, and a few windows. *But I can still feel the magic.* Like their happiness had permeated the sand and the rough grass and the trees, like their love and laughter had been life's blood, soaked up into the roots of the island so that coming back here would be a step back in time. Lying in wait for them, no matter when they came.

Nicky wasn't so quiet. He whooped and spread his arms wide, causing the skin and muscles on his back to ripple. It looked like the sleeping fox and badger stretched in slumber and might wake any minute. "I can't believe it's still in such a good shape!" He seemed determined to act like they hadn't just kissed, and Jasper followed suit.

"Well, our dads did work on this for ages," Jasper said, slowly walking up to him. "They had plans and everything, remember?"

"Oh yeah. I especially remember the big rusty nail your dad stood on. He had to go to the ER and everything. There was blood everyw—"

"Yes, thank you Nicky, I haven't forgotten."

Nicky looked over his shoulder and gave him a wicked grin. His eyes danced with amusement and light. *Lord, he's so beautiful.*

"The strongbox should still be there. Let's look."

The door hung a little off its hinges and seemed a lot smaller than it used to, another sign that they'd changed and grown up. *We're not who we used to be.* Jasper's chest constricted a little.

Being near Nicky and being on this island brought back parts of him that hadn't existed in so long. The slumbering magic of their childhood here awakened them. Every single inhibition was leaving him, like he was shedding layers of old skin, and while it felt freeing, it wasn't what either of them needed. Or what they could have.

Nicky disappeared into the fort and Jasper followed.

It only had one room with a solid roof and a built-in bench that had collapsed, but the rest of it had survived. Apart from a layer of dead leaves that must've blown in through the small windows and what looked like some mouse droppings, it actually looked really good.

Nicky was trying to pry open the hinged door in the floor where the strongbox sat when he suddenly hissed and stepped back.

"What is it?"

"Nothing." He stuck his finger in his mouth. Around it he mumbled, "Splinter. I might be bleeding."

"Let me see."

Nicky stared in disbelief. "Blood, Jazz. Don't make me peel you off the floor, I don't think I have the strength."

"I'll be fine," Jasper said, and he held his hand out. Reluctantly, Nicky placed his in it. "You're not bleeding, and it's a big splinter. I think I can get it out. Want me to try?"

"Sure."

Nicky winced when Jasper tried to grasp the bit of wood with his fingernails but they were too short. "Hold on." He brought Nicky's finger to his mouth and Nicky gasped, lips parting. Jasper kept looking at him as he concentrated, trying to find the edge of the splinter with his tongue. His heart hammered in his chest.

Boundaries, Jasper.

But what were boundaries in this familiar dim light where they'd been more than brothers, where they'd learned to love each other and themselves before life came along and sent them sprawling? The sunlight shimmered through the moving trees outside the windows and Jasper thought he could feel it, right there in the golden halo of their youth, the time he'd lost. But more than that, something he desperately needed to find again.

When he felt the splinter, he gently gripped it between his teeth and pulled. He released Nicky's hand.

Nicky stared at his finger like he'd never seen it before. "That…that's one way to do it," he croaked. He turned around swiftly and began to pull at the panel again. His black boxer-briefs rounded nicely against his small ass and two little dimples appeared on either side of his spine as he strained to get the door open. The hinges gave away and Nicky stepped back with a grunt. "Looks good," he said.

"Mm." Jasper plucked the splinter off his tongue and flicked it away. "I can't remember what's in it, apart from comic books."

"Oh." Nicky grew still, his shoulders rigid.

"What is it?" When Nicky didn't reply, Jasper frowned and lifted the box out of its hole. It was a lot heavier than he remembered and the lock had rusted a little so it took some doing to get it loose. He crouched down, opened the box, and pulled out two small blankets and a rolled-up sleeping bag. "I don't remember these." They smelled like earth and dust but didn't feel damp.

"That's because they weren't in there when you still came here."

Jasper looked up to where Nicky towered over him. "What do you mean?"

Nicky swallowed and averted his eyes. His throat looked long from this angle, fragile when the Adam's apple bobbed up and down. The blue fox reaching toward his heart seemed to quiver mid-stretch. "That summer we were grounded…I came here a lot. At night. I thought you'd—" He broke off and Jasper closed his eyes.

"You'd thought I'd come too," he whispered. And he had. Just once. But Nicky didn't know about that and Jasper didn't plan on telling him.

"It doesn't matter. Not anymore. What else is in there?"

Jasper could tell it did matter, and he wanted to say it mattered to him too, but he didn't think the sentiment would be a welcome one.

"Uh. I think this is a joint, actually."

Nicky's eyes went wide. "Can you...get rid of it?"

"It's fifteen years old; I'm sure it'd have as much effect as smoking hay. But yeah, I'll go toss it out. You can check what else is in there."

Jasper walked back toward the beach and tossed the spliff in the water. He tilted his face toward the sun. *Why am I here, Father? Is it to show me the mistakes of the past? Is it to rectify them? Do You want me to help Nicky? I don't know if I'm strong enough. I don't know if...* He opened his eyes and stared across the water, toward their childhood homes. Sources of love and loss. The water lapped soothingly at his overheated feet. "I don't know if I want to be."

When he returned, Nicky had draped the sleeping bag and blankets out over low-hanging branches on the large oak tree beside the fort.

"They're not moldy or anything," he said, "but I thought I'd air them out."

"Find anything else interesting?"

"The comic books. A bunch of matches, a knife, old cigarettes." Jasper opened his mouth but Nicky beat him to it. "Don't worry, I'll be able to resist those. I never did like smoking all that much. A hammer, a screwdriver, some screws, and a small brush. Those peppermints you used to consume like your life depended on it, but I wouldn't try to eat them now. Oh, and a bunch of gay porn."

"Oh man." Jasper's face flashed hot. He'd forgotten all about that.

"It's okay," Nicky said, his mouth quirking up in a not-quite smile. "I can rescue you from the porn the way you rescued me from the weed." He gave Jasper a little wave with the rolled up magazines. "Unless you want to refresh your memory."

"N—" *No need*, he almost said. "No thanks."

Nicky laughed under his breath and tossed the magazines back in the box.

"What's that?" Jasper asked, pointing to a notebook with curling edges. "I don't remember that."

"It's nothing." Nicky didn't look up. He rubbed at his top lip with the back of his hand and kept his eyes on the strongbox. Jasper could make out an upper thigh and part of a well-muscled buttock on one of the magazines. He focused on the notebook again.

"Can I take a look?"

Nicky jumped to his feet and rubbed his palms on his thighs, seemed to realize he wasn't wearing pants to soak up the sweat, and crossed his arms instead. Jasper's eyes narrowed, but before he could chase his thoughts, Nicky said, "It's music. All right? Stuff I wrote that spring. Before we were grounded. I don't…want anyone to see it."

"Oh. Sure. Do you think…is it bad?"

Nicky looked at him and glanced away again. "No, actually. It's not bad at all."

"Okay." Jasper didn't understand where the sudden awkwardness had come from. He gestured toward the door. "Do you want to go? I mean, I could go get the boat."

Nicky's shoulders softened and he gave Jasper a half-smile. "I want to stay longer. I like it here. It's very…peaceful. Do you mind?"

"Not at all. We can put one of the blankets on the beach, if you like."

"Yeah. That sounds good."

Jasper turned toward the door and grabbed one of the blankets off the tree branch. Nicky didn't immediately follow and Jasper left him to it. He walked far enough down the beach where the sand was soft and not littered with sticks and stones, but close enough to the tree line so they had at least some dappled protection from the relentless sunshine.

By the time he spread the blanket out and lowered himself down, Nicky had joined him, the old notebook in one hand and a small cigar box in the other.

"I found these," he said, and held the box out to Jasper.

"No way." Jasper took the box, and Nicky lay on the blanket, belly down. Jasper joined him, careful to keep some distance between their skin.

The box smelled of old tobacco and dried wood and the photographs inside had yellowed a little around the edges. The one on top was of him and Nicky when they were five years old, riding bikes with training wheels down the Blumfeld driveway. He laughed.

"Why on earth is this in here?"

Nicky looked up, and his eyes crinkled at the corners as he squinted at Jasper. "My mom's sentimental," he said, and went back to what he was doing. Jasper glanced over and realized Nicky was reading through the lyrics in the notebook. It was scribbled full to the brim. Page after page of unsung songs. About them, about their love, their beginning, and maybe their end. His heart contracted with a deep, yearning ache. He tore his eyes away and went back to the box.

In the next photograph they were older, hanging off each other in their disheveled school uniforms—shirts untucked and ties crooked—on the football field behind the school. Jasper remembered that moment. Their school team had won the game, and while they didn't particularly care about sports, it'd been a great day.

There were a few more of them in uniform, one with the whole junior year class where they looked well-polished, hair neatly combed and shirts still nicely ironed. He was standing beside Nicky, who, he was pretty sure, was hiding contraband candy in his pockets like he always did back then. Jasper bit his lip to hide the smile when he remembered Nicky's kisses used to taste like Twizzlers.

The smile broke when he saw the next photograph. It was grainy because the sun had been setting. Most of the day's light had left, but it had been hot and bright, and they'd been goofing around with a disposable camera on the beach. After taking stupid pictures all day long, they'd wrestled over the last one. Nicky had ended up accidentally taking a picture of their feet tangled in the warm sand. It was dumb, but Jasper had wanted to keep it. Looking at it had always made him feel like he had that evening. Happy. Free. In love. He flipped the photograph over to put it on the pile by his side.

Our Blue Oasis, it read on the back, written in Nicky's loopy handwriting, *Fox & Badger*. Jasper blinked and swallowed hard. He traced the words with his fingertips. Maybe he hadn't been the only one who liked to think back to that evening and feel the belly-deep comfort of it.

When he lifted the last photograph, he found an unopened little tub of Vaseline at the bottom of the box. Jasper laughed and his voice sounded a little hoarse. It wasn't until he looked up at Nicky and realized the shadows had lengthened that a lot of time had passed.

And Nicky was asleep.

His dark lashes fanned over the tired circles as his eyes flickered in dreams. The bruised skin was less pronounced than it had been though, and Jasper felt relief as he let his eyes roam.

Nicky's hair was a fluffy mess after air-drying in the sun. Freckles had begun to pop up on his shoulders and Jasper wondered if he should even be lying in the sun with those tattoos exposed. The muscles and bones of his back were visible under his skin. Jasper wanted to touch him so badly it was like an itch he couldn't reach.

Being careful that Nicky wouldn't wake, Jasper stroked a lock of hair away from where it brushed Nicky's nose. He traced the angular cheekbones and the sharp line of Nicky's jaw—the face Jasper used to know better than his own mirror image.

The *what ifs* drifted to the surface from a long-dormant place in his mind. Time was cruel in a way, because no matter what anyone wished, there was no way of knowing if turning back the clock would lead somewhere different, or if that place would be a better one.

A little puff of air parted Nicky's lips, and Jasper wiped away a few grains of sand sticking to his cheek. "I always loved you," he whispered. "I can't even pretend I loved God more, back then. Every minute I spend with you now I wonder if my calling wasn't a coward's path. If I shouldn't have grabbed on to your hands and taken that dive with you. My doubts…" Jasper closed his eyes and shook his head. Was his faith really only this strong? Did he only hold fast as long as no real temptation lay before him? "What am I even saying?"

You can love God and love Nicky at the same time.

He didn't know where the thought came from but he sighed softly. It was too late now. They'd made their choices years ago. Hadn't they?

Jasper opened his eyes, and Nicky was looking at him, eyes wide open. They reflected the deep and cloudless sky, and in them Jasper saw so much raw emotion it made him ache inside. Nicky's mouth opened but no sound came out and Jasper couldn't stand how helpless he looked. How vulnerable.

Jasper's bottom lip trembled and he pressed his mouth closed hard to make it stop. His eyes burned with longing and in his chest his heartbeat echoed like a warning drum. He couldn't think beyond one thing, one instinct so strong he'd have less trouble suppressing the urge to breathe.

"Nicky..."

Nicky half lifted, shaking his head, but Jasper pushed against his shoulder and rolled him over, stared into those beautiful eyes that widened with trepidation.

He lowered himself down on top of Nicky, let himself feel every single bone, every single angle and curve against his own, and then kept staring as he kissed him.

The carefully constructed walls he'd built over years and years of abstinence came crashing down.

NICKY DROWSED IN the late sun, moving between near wakefulness and a dream of playing an acoustic Vespertine show in the small fort to a massive crowd of roughhousing children. The kids in the dream shimmied up trees, sang along, and rolled around on the forest floor. Ramona's drum-kit was child-sized and Nicky crouched on the floor of the fort, using his guitar as a desk to write new lyrics on strips of paper. Somehow he was playing music at the same time, and so long as he kept feeding Sez new lyrics to sing, the guitar seemed to play itself. Mick wasn't playing at all and no one cared. He danced on the stage with an out-of-control happiness that made Nicky laugh as he pushed new lyrics into Sez's hands.

A teenaged Jazz burst out of a clot of wrestling boys and climbed on stage while Nicky was scribbling the next lines. "Nicky?" But Nicky couldn't look up. He had to keep writing the new lyrics or the guitar would stop playing and Sez wouldn't have anything to sing. But Jazz distracted him by sliding the tips of his fingers over his face, until Nicky looked up into his warm hazel-gaze. "I always loved you. I can't even pretend I loved God more."

Nicky's heart clenched and he dropped the new lyrics onto the floor of the fort, opening his eyes to the golden evening sun and the sparkle-snap of light on the waves in the cove. Jasper's eyes were closed and his lower lip trembled as he whispered, "What am I even saying?"

Nicky came fully awake, eyes going wide. A struggle filled him, a lurch of joy, a horrible hope that forced a heart-thump of panic into his throat.

"Nicky…"

Jasper leaned toward him, and Nicky half-lifted, shaking his head. Jasper's hand fell hot and insistent on his shoulder, pushing him onto his back. The cloudless sky filled his view as his body pulsed with adrenaline, roaring in his veins, clarifying and intensifying every thought and sensation. Jasper's body fell on his, and Nicky tensed, frozen between fight and flight.

No. We can't do this. Fuck.

The words stayed locked in his mind, a desperate, angry certainty filling him. This was going to happen and it was going to break him. Fuck Jasper and his beautiful face, and his earnest fucking want, and fuck the way doing this now was going destroy them when Jasper turned away again. The hard push of Jasper's erection and soft touch of his lips unlocked Nicky from his shock, and in a turmoil of lust and rage, he returned Jasper's kiss ferociously.

He'd heard Jasper talking while Jasper thought he was asleep, and now the words echoed in his mind.

"I always loved you. I can't even pretend I loved God more."

"I told you if you tried this again, I wouldn't fucking stop," Nicky hissed against Jasper's lips. He lifted his legs and wrapped them around Jasper's waist, grinding up against his hard cock shoving down to meet him.

"I know, Nicky." Jasper whispered, kissing him again before burying his face in Nicky's neck, mouthing desperately like he was starving for the taste of Nicky's skin. "*Oh.* I don't want you to stop."

"I mean it, Jasper."

Jazz nuzzled his hair and sucked his earlobe, then said brokenly, "So do I."

Nicky slid his legs higher, and Jasper groaned and shuddered, digging his cock down against Nicky's with hard, helpless thrusts. Screaming, heartbreaking adrenaline coursed through Nicky, and he pushed his hands down Jasper's sun-warm back, pressing angry, rough kisses against his shoulders.

Jasper gripped Nicky's face, holding him with shaking fingers as he kissed his mouth again. Nicky grunted, nipping at Jasper's mouth as he dragged his fingers over Jasper's skin. He dug his heels into Jasper's upper thighs as they thrust against each other. Nicky wanted to bite him, wanted to pound his fists on his back and scream, because his soul was ripping open and he was going to die here on this island when Jasper pulled away.

"Nicky," Jasper whispered, easing back and searching his eyes, lips red and trembling. His face was soft, shocked, and open, and something inside Nicky's heart, a sharp seed of hope, hurt so much that he couldn't hold back a sob. Then they were kissing again, and Nicky's anger and fear bled into need.

He groaned and gripped, shoving his hands down into Jasper's tighty-whities to grab his ass, forcing Jasper down against him harder. Jasper's eyes slipped closed and he threw his head back, riding against Nicky desperately, the ridge of his cock nearly painful against Nicky's own. Fuck it. He'd never been one to turn away from a bad idea. He pried Jasper's ass cheeks apart to press his fingers into Jasper's crack.

Jazz's eyes flew open and he stared down at Nicky with a wild, urgent gaze.

Nicky stroked over his hole, rutting up hard. He stared challengingly at Jasper. If they were going to do this, if they were going to break Nicky here on this beach, then he was going to do it fucking right. Leave nothing untouched, nothing sacred. He pushed against Jasper's hole.

"Yes," Jasper whimpered. He spread his legs a little and gasped, bent forward and kissed Nicky again. Jasper's mouth was hot and slick. He vibrated with urgent, sharp need as he gave himself over to his desire. Nicky drove his tongue deep as he pushed the tip of his dry finger in, barely breaching him, and then pulling out again.

Nicky gripped the back of Jasper's hair, tugging him up and angling his head for an even deeper kiss. Jasper shoved his hands under Nicky's shoulders, pulling him tight and using his weight to keep them flush from hip to shoulder as he ground against him with unleashed lust.

"You want this, Jazz?" Nicky whispered, the words pushing past the sharp lump in his throat. "You want me?"

"Nicky…" Jasper moaned and rubbed his face all over Nicky's, stubble scraping stubble, and their hot breath mingling.

"Prove it," Nicky muttered. "Prove you want me."

Jasper made a weird noise, worry and helpless lust combined, and he kissed Nicky softly, but it didn't last. Their noses smashed and their teeth clacked as their mouths and bodies came together with harsh, uncontrolled movements. Their lovemaking was more struggle than sweetness, and Nicky surrendered to it, waiting to shatter.

The blanket beneath them bunched against his back as they rutted and kissed, hands touching skin with hungry, gripping fingers, like they could devour one another through their palms.

"Jasper," Nicky whispered, but he didn't know what he was going to say. Maybe he was giving some kind of warning, but they were too far gone now, and he forgot everything when Jasper lifted up to slide his hand between them, cupping Nicky's dick and whimpering into his mouth.

"Oh, Nicky," he moaned. He slid his other hand up to Nicky's neck, and then glided the back of his knuckles over Nicky's cheek, dragging over the stubble.

"What?" Nicky asked. *Not yet. Don't let him pull away yet!*

Jasper stared down at him and Nicky's stomach clenched. He nearly hauled Jasper back to the kiss, unwilling to face the pain yet, but Jasper smiled softly. "I meant what I said earlier. I've never seen anyone more beautiful than you."

Nicky wanted to stay angry. He wanted to stay afraid and hurt, but he couldn't look up at Jasper haloed by the sunlight, beautiful and vulnerable, and he couldn't look into Jasper's awe-filled hazel eyes and want to do anything but love him.

"Me too," he whispered. "No one as beautiful as you."

Tears filled his eyes and clogged his throat, the resistance in him dissolving away: ice giving into the brilliant, consuming sun. Jasper slowed their kiss and rolled so that Nicky was on top.

"Let me look at you," Jasper murmured, rubbing his hands up Nicky's chest, lingering on the fox and badger tattoo, before whimpering and dragging Nicky down against him again. "I can't…oh, I can't…Nicky, I'm sorry."

"I know—" *Don't say it. Please don't say it.*

"I'm sorry. Nicky, I'm going to come."

A cool relief flooded him, blessed reprieve from inevitable pain, and Nicky lifted up to ease the friction between them, trying to prevent them from both going off like the horny virgins they'd once been together. He hadn't gotten to taste Jasper or see his cock. He wasn't going to let this end yet. Fuck no, he was going to earn his future misery.

Jasper gripped his ass and tried to drag him down again, their underwear bunching and rubbing between them. Sand prickled and scratched as they moved, kicked up by their reckless rutting. Nicky kissed Jasper and held his hips away, murmuring against his mouth. "Shh, Jazz, hold on, okay? I've got you."

But Jasper shook his head, insistent and hungry, distracting Nicky with his tongue, tangling his fingers in Nicky's hair to hold him in place. Breath and slick skin and lips moved together, the sound of the waves lapping at the shore echoing the movement of their bodies. A thumping, slapping sound that was layered over with moans and whimpers.

"Fuck," Nicky moaned and pulled away, kissing Jasper's collar bone, on the verge of coming too. "Want to see you."

Jasper grunted in confusion, until Nicky arched up and began to push his own underwear down, freeing his cock.

"Oh, uh, yeah," Jasper grated out. "Nicky, wow. It's still so...pretty." Jasper frantically lifted his hips to shove his underwear down too. Jasper's cock throbbed above his thatch of dark golden-brown hair and leaked wetly onto his belly.

"Damn, Jazz," Nicky said thickly. "You grew there too."

Jasper's thick, fat-headed dick bobbed with his laugh. "I didn't notice."

Nicky bit his lip, wanting to lick the slick, glossy precome up and then take Jasper's length down his throat, but something held him back. He waited for Jasper to take the lead. A trembling set up in his stomach, echoed in his hands and lips. He felt swallowed by an unbearable tenderness for Jasper. He needed Jasper to reach for him first, to make this more than a quick clutch and come between them.

Jasper's hands wandered up his chest, touching the fox and the heart tattoo. He stroked down over Nicky's abs to brush over his happy trail and then hesitated.

"It's okay," Nicky murmured. "It doesn't bite."

Nicky shuddered when Jasper's soft palm closed around him, tentative at first, and then with a breathtaking surety.

"See?"

Jasper stared at Nicky's cock in his hand for a moment, and then his face crumpled. He didn't let go, but he reached up for Nicky, pulling him down into a kiss and sobbing a little against his mouth.

"You're so beautiful, so perfect." Tears slipped out of his eyes. "I've missed you so much."

"Oh, Jazz," Nicky whispered, heart hurting and his own tears threatening. He tucked his knees against Jasper's side and humped into Jasper's fist. "I've missed you too," he whispered against the side of his mouth, licking his way in again.

The need in Jasper's eyes drove him on in the burning heat of the slowly setting sun. They were breath and sensation, wild joy and fear, tangled together and moving toward orgasm fast.

Jasper broke the kiss, his hands gripping Nicky's face. "I…I'm going to—" His eyes shone with tenderness as he whimpered, "Nicky." His body jackknifed from the force of his orgasm, and Nicky held on to keep from being thrown off. Jasper's cry filled the air, echoing in the cove and ringing in Nicky's ears as hot, violent spurts of come slicked their stomachs.

"Oh my God, Jazz," Nicky murmured. "Holy fuck."

Jasper shook, his body quaking through aftershocks with his eyes crunched closed.

Nicky gripped Jasper's biceps and thrust down against him, climax rising up from his skin like goosebumps and tearing through him hard and fast, almost painful as his come pumped out, smearing with Jasper's on their bellies.

He pressed fevered, trembling kisses to Jasper's mouth and eyelids.

"Fuck, Jazz," he muttered, shuddering as his cock pulsed again. He didn't know what to say—couldn't say anything more than Jasper's name, touching his face and staring down into his eyes as they trembled together.

Jazz pulled him down again, lifting his legs to wrap around Nicky's waist, holding him tight. "Stay with me," Jasper whispered. "Don't let it be over yet."

Nicky collapsed against Jasper's chest, listening to Jasper's heartbeat while the waves lapped gently on the shore.

Chapter Seventeen

NICKY ALWAYS HATED the part when the orgasms were over and things got awkward. He cleared his throat and collapsed on his back, staring up at the orange and pink sky. The sun was going down fast. They'd need to head back soon or risk being caught on the island overnight.

"Nicky?" Jasper's voice was quiet. "Was I too rough? Did I hurt you?"

Not yet.

"I'm fine." He rubbed at his eyes and then scratched his eyebrow with his thumb. "You?"

"Some bruises, maybe. This beach isn't as soft as I remember."

Nicky lay limply, his brain scrambling for some kind of purchase, but he couldn't get a grip on anything. What had they done? And what happened now? He rolled his head toward Jasper, trying to gauge what he could expect next. Jazz had never been one for dramatics unless blood was involved, so he doubted there would be gnashing of teeth, wailing, or rending of clothes, but a softly admitted *this was a mistake* had to be on its way. After all, sins didn't get much bigger than a priest having sex. Gay sex.

But Jasper only gazed up into the sky with an amazed, stunned expression, which, as Nicky watched, softened into an irrepressibly genuine smile. He turned his head toward Nicky, reaching out with one hand to slide over Nicky's hip and stomach. "Hey, that was…you…"

Jasper didn't seem to know what to say, and he laughed softly. "Yeah."

Nicky shivered under a breeze off the water. He wanted to numb out the feelings rushing under his skin. They were taking him over. He wasn't sure he could breathe, actually, though the in-and-out of his breath disputed that.

"Was that good for you?" Jasper asked quietly, looking at Nicky out of the corner of his eye, a bashful expression falling over his features.

Nicky stared at him, not sure what to say. He wanted to say *I don't know* because he had no idea how the word "good" could describe what happened between them. It was either motherfucking holy, or it was horrific, or both.

Jasper's expression faltered. "I'm not very practiced."

Nicky blinked at him and pressed his heels into the blanket before standing up and saying, "It was good."

They put on their underwear in silence. As Nicky pulled up his boxer-briefs, Jasper glanced over and gently asked, "Are you okay?"

"Yeah. I don't know." He brushed sand off his skin. "I should ask you that."

Jasper considered the question and then said, "I'm okay. But you seem upset."

"Fuck, what were you thinking, Jasper?" Nicky threw his arms out to the side, exposing his scars to the dying sunlight. "I'm a fucking junkie. You're a priest. And this can't ever work."

Jasper blew out gently. He put his hands on Nicky's arms. "To be honest, Nicky, I don't want to think about any of that right now. I feel too good."

"It's just endorphins."

It's just hormones. Puppy love. It can't last. We'll grow out of it. **Bullshit.**

"Maybe." Jasper shrugged. "And maybe it's something else." He touched Nicky's cheek and slid his fingers against his stubble. "I haven't felt this way in a long time. Being with you…it's like carbonation in my veins. It feels good. Like laughter." He smiled again and it made Nicky feel weirdly like puking. "I'd forgotten how good we are together. How good this is with you."

"And whose fault is that? Who's the one who walked away?" His skin itched. He was hyper aware of his spent dick. He was scared out of his mind.

"Nicky…" Jasper tried to pull Nicky close, but he jerked away.

"Stop. Answer my questions. We were going to be friends. We were going to be okay. We were going to flirt and laugh, and I was going to go back to L.A. and sweat you out of my system. But it was going to be okay, because I could still call you, or see you when I visited home, but what the fuck, Jazz? What the fuck happens now? Are you going to do a few Hail Marys and act like nothing happened?"

Nicky paced, raking his hands in his hair and scratching at his arms, anxiety descending on him like a storm obliterating the residual after-bliss.

"Honestly Nicky? I don't know. I don't know what happens now. I didn't mean to upset you." Jasper looked stricken.

He whirled on him. "You realize I heard you? When you thought I was asleep, saying that you have regrets, or doubts, or whatever?"

"I did…or do."

Nicky blinked. "You said you loved me more than you loved God. How could you have loved me so much and then fucking left me?"

"We've talked about this before," Jazz said soothingly, his hands out like he was trying to gentle a wild horse. "Nicky, it's okay. It's going to be okay."

"Don't be the priest right now. Be Jazz or be nothing at all." Nicky wanted to get away. He wanted to get in his car and drive to Jimmy Orleans and see what he could do to erase this panic filling him up inside. "I don't want any fucking priest stuff. Not when I'm covered in your jizz."

Jasper grabbed him, forcing him into a hug, tucking his head over Nicky's shoulder and holding him tight. "I'm scared too."

"You don't seem fucking scared."

"I was happy," Jasper whispered. "I felt like something beautiful happened. But I'm really sorry if I made you do something…I'm sorry if this wasn't what you wanted. I needed to touch you and make love to you, because nothing seemed more right in that moment." He pulled away and looked into Nicky's eyes, his face earnest and vulnerable. "I'm sorry this wasn't—"

"And what happens when you freak out and hate me for what we did? Where does that leave me? The same place I've always been." *Alone.*

Jasper looked at him like he knew that on the inside Nicky was still the same boy he'd left. That he hadn't grown at all. "I could never hate you. I love you, Nicky. I always have. I can't tell you that I'm not scared, but—"

"Don't say things like that when they don't mean anything at all. You're a priest."

"I know."

Air left Nicky like a punctured balloon. He slumped against Jasper and let him kiss his head, his shoulders, and his cheek.

Jasper tugged him down to the blanket again. Against his better judgment, Nicky allowed Jasper to pull him between his spread legs. Nicky leaned back against Jasper's torso, his thighs bracketed by Jasper's thighs. He stared across the cove to their houses, the red and blue clapboards looking wholesome and appropriately patriotic in the lowering Fourth of July light.

"What do you need right now?" Jasper asked.

"If you can wait to freak out or say what we did was wrong, that'd be great." Nicky covered his face with a shaking hand. "Fuck. I need a minute."

"You can have as long as you need."

They sat that way a long time, Jasper running his hands up and down Nicky's arms, touching his scars, rubbing over the hesitation marks on his left wrist, and then twining their fingers together. Nicky's anxiety came in waves, peaking and receding, as he considered every realistically possible outcome.

Finally, Jasper broke the silence. "Talk to me. What has you so worried right now?" he swallowed, his Adam's apple bobbing against the side of Nicky's head. "I can't promise that I can give you a satisfactory answer, but I want to try."

"How could you have left me back then, Jazz? If you loved me so much how could you stand to leave me?"

"I wasn't the same afterward, Nicky. It broke my heart."

Nicky remembered what Jasper had confessed the other night and it burned in him like a red star, pain and anger in the core of his heart. "How could you believe your mother after everything we'd done together—everything we'd been to each other? I'll never fucking understand that, Jazz."

"It wasn't just what my mother said." Jasper whispered softly. "I thought I had proof that you didn't feel the same way that I felt about you."

"What proof?"

Jasper's throat clicked and then he sighed. "I never imagined that when we finally had this conversation we'd be wearing nothing but our underwear."

"We can take them off again if it helps," Nicky snapped, his skin feeling too tight over his entire body.

"I think I'll probably be able to explain better if we're not completely naked."

"Why? All this skin against skin doesn't seem a problem for you."

"Are you always this angry after sex now?"

"Would it make you feel better if I said yes?"

"No," Jasper whispered. "It wouldn't." He rubbed Nicky's arms again. "Earlier when you said that you came out here to wait for me that summer we were apart, you said you expected that I'd come one night too. And I did. I came out here looking for you and I found you, Nicky."

"What? What the fuck are you talking about?" Nicky turned to face Jasper, moving from between his legs so he could see him better. "I was here so many nights and I never saw you. You never came."

"I did! I came out one night and you were here with Jimmy."

Nicky shook his head. "Yeah? So? I was lonely."

Jasper cleared his throat. "He asked if he could blow you."

Nicky scoffed. "He asked me that all the time."

"You didn't say no."

"I sure as hell didn't say yes! Did you even stick around to see what happened?" Nicky was up again, walking because he had to move. His muscles burned, and his throat was tight. His hands needed something—a guitar, a piano, a fucking needle—or he was going to end up pulling his hair out. He turned to Jazz and pointed a finger at him where he sat. "Are you fucking telling me right now that you left me because you heard Jimmy Orlean offer to blow me and you never asked me about it? And you decided that meant I didn't fucking love you? And you heard my goddamn albums over the years, Jasper! You knew what those lyrics meant and who they were for and you still thought your mother was right and that I'd let Jimmy Or-fucking-lean put his mouth on my dick? Instead of you?"

Jasper swallowed and nodded, the setting sunlight glinting off his lashes, hair, and brows. He still looked like a halo was smeared all over him. It wasn't fair. He was a smug, self-righteous, asshole who'd made choices based on bullshit and ruined their fucking lives for it.

Nicky had to get off the island. He started toward the water and Jasper grabbed his arm. "Where are you going?"

"Home."

"You barely made it over."

"I'm fucking pissed enough now that I'm sure I'll get there on pure rage alone."

"Nicky, I'm sorry. I was wrong. I should have talked to you and told you what was happening with me. I was convinced that I knew what I needed to do. I thought what I saw and heard was a confirmation that I was supposed to follow the calling. And Nicky, this life hasn't been all bad for me."

"Well, it's been all bad for me."

"That's not true."

"Isn't it? I'm a goddamn junkie and a whore and I'm not even a fucking decent musician anymore. What good has come out of my life after that choice you made on both our behalves, Jazz?" He got closer, up in Jasper's face. "Tell me, because I want to fucking know."

"You made some fantastic albums and you traveled the world multiple times over."

Nicky snorted and shook his head. "I'd give that all up. I'd give every last bit of it up for you, but you never felt the same. So who isn't able to love, Jasper? Maybe your mom had the wrong boy."

Jasper reached out and grabbed Nicky by the back of the neck. "Maybe she did, but she was always wrong about me. And she couldn't have been more wrong about you. Or our love."

Nicky stared at Jasper. The breeze lifting and falling in his hair, the sun sparkling green lights in his eyes and shimmering gold underneath. His lips were red and swollen from their kissing, and Nicky reached up and gripped the back of his neck too.

"You are such a dick." He jerked Jasper close, pressing their mouths together. Jasper melted against him, wrapping his arms tightly around Nicky. They stumbled down to the blankets and held each other.

"Can you forgive me?" Jasper murmured against Nicky's sweaty neck.

"For thinking I let Jimmy Orlean suck me off? Maybe. But for believing your mom? That's going to be a work in progress."

"That's fair. But can I at least point out that I was a kid? A confused, gay, Catholic kid?"

Nicky sighed and shifted to a sitting position. "I guess. I'll give you that." Dirt and grime covered them both where the blanket had shifted.

"Are you okay?"

"I think both of us are probably not really okay, Jazz." Nicky raked his hands through his hair, the whirling dervish of anxiety vibrating in his heart again, making him quiver.

"You weren't kidding about always being angry after sex, were you?"

Nicky smirked. "I don't want to be angry. I'm really fucking overwhelmed right now. I'm not used to feeling all these *feelings*. It's too much." He laughed and tried to lighten the moment. "Besides, I think I'm getting hungry. Lunch seems like forever ago."

Jasper sat up and looked around. "The sun is going down. It must be nearly eight thirty or nine by now."

A cold certainty settled in Nicky's gut. It was only a matter of time before Jasper came to his senses. He was high on sex and his first orgasm in God only knew how long, and he would realize that this had been a big, ugly mistake.

"Fireworks will start soon," Jasper said. "We need to head back."

"Yeah."

"I'll swim over for the boat and come back for you."

"I can make it," Nicky murmured. He was exhausted, emotionally and physically, but there was a strange burning in his muscles that he knew would feel better if he moved. "We'll go together, and I'll take it easy. I'll be fine."

Jasper seemed skeptical, but when Nicky stood up and dusted off his ass, folding the blanket up and heading back toward the fort, Jasper picked up the box of photos and trudged after him.

Once Nicky had secured it all in the strongbox again, Jasper touched his arm. "Okay, we swim back together. But if you drown, I'll never forgive you."

Nicky kissed Jasper's lips gently and smiled. "Well, maybe we'd be even then."

NICKY'S LIPS WERE blue by the time Jasper dragged him up to the shore.

"You okay?"

Nicky nodded and wrapped his arms around himself, skin white and covered with goosebumps. "Yeah, just cold." They pulled themselves up by the tall grass since the dock stairs were completely gone.

Jasper gently touched Nicky's hand. "Are you still angry?"

Nicky laughed. "No. I'm too tired and hungry to be angry, I guess. And, you're right. It was a long time ago. There's no going back, and being pissed won't change it."

"When did you decide that?"

"About halfway over when I got tired and you made me float on my back until I got my wind again. There's something about staring up into the night sky while floating in the middle of a cove and hoping no one's bringing their boat in to dock in the dark that gives you some perspective."

"What perspective is that?"

Nicky was panting hard. "Well, being run over by a speed boat with my priest ex-boyfriend isn't exactly how I want to go out, but it does sound like a great cover for a gossip rag, huh? But mostly I wouldn't have wanted you to die thinking I was angry with you. Because I'm not. Angry with you." He stared at Jasper, his eyes dark and unfathomable in the darkening night. "What about you?"

"I'm not too cold yet, but I will be. Come on."

Nicky grabbed Jasper's bicep. His fingers were like ice. "That's not what I'm asking."

Jasper covered Nicky's hand and tried to rub some warmth into it. "I know that." He brushed Nicky's wet hair back from his face. "I'm not angry with you either."

"You're not about to flip your shit about it all?"

"I'm fine, I promise. Come on, before you get pneumonia."

"I'm not that fragile," Nicky grumbled, but he pushed ahead of Jasper anyway. They made a little detour to grab their clothes, phones, and wallets, and then aimed for the dark house. The night was thick and rich with the sound of cicadas and Jasper wanted to imprint their song onto his brain.

Nicky's black boxer-briefs clung to his ass like paint and Jasper's face heated despite the cold. He should be feeling all sorts of things right now, but there was nothing in his heart but overwhelming gratitude and a deep-seated contentment that made his limbs heavy.

Nicky laughed. "Stop staring at my ass, Father Jazz, and let's get inside."

With a guilty jerk, Jasper lifted his head and met Nicky's eyes. He was grinning, but the apprehension that had crept into his gaze after they'd had, *oh God, sex,* wasn't entirely gone.

"Sorry," Jasper said with a wink to make sure Nicky knew he wasn't sorry at all. "Anything we can raid in the fridge? I'm starving."

He watched as Nicky scratched at his arms, shaking with cold as they reached the back porch. Jasper had noticed him doing that before and he wondered if it was a side effect of the drugs he used to be addicted to, or the ones he was on now.

"You've seen my mom's fridge. There'll be lasagna at least." His lithe muscles moved under his skin as he bent to retrieve the key so stealthily hidden under the mat, and unlocked the back door.

"Hmm, yum." Jasper crowded Nicky into the house, walked him all the way to the counter where he pressed against Nicky and kissed the back of his neck. It was like a dam had broken. Everything about Nicky aroused him. The freckles on his shoulders, his hipbones making a handle for Jasper's hands, and the bend of his neck. While he knew there would be music to be faced tomorrow morning, for now all the doors to the future had been momentarily closed and locked with the key thrown away.

"Fuck," Nicky moaned roughly. He arched his back and rubbed his ass against Jasper's front, and then turned around. "Making up for lost time?"

"Hmm." Jasper grasped Nicky around the waist and lifted him on top of the counter, then pulled him into a kiss. Their mingled taste was brine and summer and wind, and it lifted Jasper's heart until he soared.

Nicky squirmed in his arms, pressing their chests together, and gripping Jasper's hair, trying to take control, like he always had.

"Oven?" Jasper mumbled against Nicky's mouth.

Nicky blinked at him and pulled back a little, his mouth shiny and his cheeks flushed. Jasper nearly laughed at his wet bird's nest hair but figured his own wouldn't be much better with the way Nicky had been tugging at it.

"How hot should the oven be for the lasagna?"

"Oh, uh. Food. Right."

Jasper felt a tingling burst of pride and affection that he'd distracted Nicky so thoroughly with a kiss. Nicky moved to jump off the counter but Jasper held him there.

"Stay. I'll do it."

"Uh. Four hundred."

Jasper punched the button and the oven came on. In the freezer drawer underneath the fridge he found a tinfoil square of cheesy goodness. "I haven't had this in years. How long?"

Nicky frowned at him like he was a little crazy. "I don't know? Since we were seventeen, I guess?"

Jasper laughed as he pushed the lasagna into the oven. "No, I mean how long does it need to go in for?"

Nicky rolled his eyes and he jumped down. His teeth clattered. "It's a good thing you're pretty, Jazz. Forty-five minutes." He reached past Jasper and set the timer.

"Just enough time for a shower," Jasper said, and he took Nicky's hand and dragged him upstairs. When he glanced back, Nicky was looking at *his* ass, and he felt his cheeks heat with sudden, giddy awareness. He was walking through the Blumfeld house in nothing but his underwear. It was like he'd slipped back in time. A beautiful wormhole that led back to a place where he could touch and be touched, where love was everything that mattered in the universe.

"We should talk," Nicky whispered when they stopped in the hallway for a kiss. Jasper held him close and nodded against the sweet curve of his slender neck. He licked the salt off Nicky's collarbone.

"We should," he softly said. "During dinner."

"We can't pretend this is okay."

"No one's pretending, Nicky. But for now…I want it to be you and me. Can't the world wait? Please?"

Nicky closed his eyes and hung his head. He absently traced the outline of Jasper's nipple, and Jasper bit his lip. "Yeah, I guess we can be miserable later," Nicky said.

Jasper laughed. "So fatalistic."

"I know, it's charming."

The only light in the hallway was a stark beam from the moon but Jasper saw everything with the clarity of an overexposed photograph. Nicky was right, he should be panicking, but he wasn't. He felt utterly calm and…right. He rubbed Nicky's shoulders and noticed an unusual heat rise from his skin.

"Are you sunburned?" Jasper whispered.

Nicky gave a one-shouldered shrug. "Maybe a bit. Mom's got aloe around here somewhere." He lifted his head. "What about you?" His teeth glinted white in the dusky hallway. "You must be burned too, wearing nothing but robes all year 'round."

"Me?" Jasper grinned and stepped closer until he could smell the silt and sweet sweat on Nicky's skin. "I'm hot all over."

A startled laugh burst out of Nicky's mouth. "Damn right you are."

Slowly Jasper tugged Nicky's wet underwear down. It got stuck on his hardening penis, and Jasper carefully worked him loose. "Join me?" he asked, then stepped into the guest bathroom and out of his underpants. Behind him Nicky made a soft noise, and then Jasper had the water running full blast.

Chapter Eighteen

"YOU *ARE* SUNBURNED," Nicky said, touching Jasper's stomach softly.

Out of the corner of his eye, Jasper could see their bodies in the mirror outlined by the sharp bathroom light. He was a little taller than Nicky, but softer, and his shoulders and chest glowed pink with the burn he could feel setting into his skin.

Next to him, Nicky was a tight wire of bone, muscle, and flesh, still too thin, but heart-stoppingly beautiful. He touched Nicky's rosy nose, sweeping his fingers over his cheeks. "So are you."

Nicky trailed his hand south, but Jasper turned away, his cock going hard instantly like he hadn't already come that day, and climbed into the spacious shower. When Nicky didn't follow, he reached out and took hold of his hands, drawing him into the warmth and seclusion under the fall of the warm water.

Nicky leaned against the wall, his head falling back and his eyes dropping shut. Jasper let the water rinse away the worst of the dirt and sand as he admired Nicky's body. His nipples were peaked, light brown nubs against his chest, and his defined abs trailed down to sharp oblique. Next to the elephant and balloons tattoo, his cock was flushed but not hard, with a mushroom-shaped head that made Jasper's mouth fill with saliva.

"Getting an eyeful?" Nicky asked.

Jasper's skin prickled as the heat rushed to his face. "You're beautiful."

Nicky lips quirked into a half-smile. "You're fucking hot."

They were surrounded by steam in no time, and when Nicky opened his eyes, meeting Jasper's gaze with a sultry-blue, flirtatious stare, Jasper pulled Nicky against him, wet pubic hair scratching against Jasper's hardening cock.

"It's like we never stopped doing this," Jasper whispered. The intimacy came to him so easily now, despite his earlier hesitation. It felt shivery-good, like he was caught in a dream with no consequences, only sweetness, humming arousal, and exhausted bliss.

"Just like getting on a bike."

Jasper laughed and ran his hands over Nicky's body, over the canvas of scars and art, then tweaked one of Nicky's nipples.

"*Hnn.*" Nicky curved away, then pressed closer to Jasper. He flashed his eyes up under dark lashes.

"Oh, you still like that, do you? What about this?" He closed his mouth around Nicky's left earlobe and sucked. Nicky went half-limp in his arms, squirming against Jasper. Wet skin slid across wet skin.

"Ah, fuck, not fair," Nicky gasped. He reached between them and grasped Jasper's balls firmly, and Jasper couldn't stop the keening noise that came out of his mouth. "I have a good memory too, Father Jazz." Nicky grinned as if the tables had been turned. "And I remember that you used to fucking love it when I—" he put his mouth to Jasper's ear "—licked your sweet little hole."

"Nicky!" Jasper's knees nearly buckled, and Nicky used the moment to push Jasper under the hot spray.

"Don't worry, we'll get it nice and clean first."

Jasper's toes curled against the slippery tiles. "You can't talk like that." He gasped and sputtered around a mouthful of water. Nicky shivered when the hot water hit him, and his cheeks began to turn pink as he looked down meaningfully.

"I can't? You don't seem to mind so much." Nicky gripped Jasper's hard cock, and Jasper's knees went weak all over again. "Or maybe you want me to just do it, not talk about it. See if you still like it?"

"I think I'll fall," he whispered as his belly gave a squirmy lurch.

Nicky looked up at him. His eyes softened, the teasing glint disappeared, and he smiled tenderly. "I won't let you fall, baby."

Jasper's heart thumped. He wanted to hang on to those words with so much more than they meant in this moment, but now was not the time.

"Nicky..." He fingered the dark, wet strands that clung to Nicky's cheeks and pushed them aside. "C'mere." With a little tug, he drew Nicky nearer and kissed him slowly, gently, like they hadn't allowed themselves so far. On the island, they'd battled each other and had taken their pleasure almost violently. But now Jasper wanted to love him.

Nicky had other ideas, apparently. He broke free, his face twisting for a second, but the expression was gone so fast Jasper couldn't be sure he'd seen it. Water poured between them, and Jasper felt every place their bodies touched. Nicky's wet fingers gripped his shoulders, strong and firm, as he pushed lightly.

"Turn around, Father Jazz. Let me show you what I've learned over the years."

Jasper closed his eyes for a second. The image filled his mind, of him leaning against the wall, Nicky behind him on his knees and—*oh God.* He opened his eyes. His cheeks burned. "I don't want to know what you've learned over the years. I just want you." He turned around and pressed his hands on top of each other against the cold tiles, his heart beating wildly with fear and excitement.

"Yeah?" Nicky rubbed Jasper's flanks, his belly—as if he knew exactly where Jasper felt hot and trembly—and tugged lightly on Jasper's treasure trail, then moved to Jasper's hips and over his buttocks. "No one has touched you but me?" he whispered.

"You know no one has."

"That is..." Nicky let out a little laugh. "So sweet, Jazz." He ran his finger between Jasper's cheeks. Jasper tried to bite down on a moan but his legs were shaking already. "Oh yeah. *So* sweet." He pushed his thigh between Jasper's knees, and Jasper's body flushed hot all over. "Spread a little bit and hand me the soap."

"Nicky," Jasper whispered. He took his hands down and began to turn but Nicky held him there. "This is embarrassing."

"Only because you're thinking too much." Nicky kissed his shoulders and neck, and rubbed Jasper's chest. "It's just you and me here. Like you said. You don't need to hide."

A hard lump rose in Jasper's throat and he swallowed it down as he leaned his forehead against his hands. "Okay. You and me."

"The way it's always been." Nicky reached for the soap himself but stayed pressed against Jasper. "That's my good little fox."

The scent of a woodsy body wash filled the shower, and Nicky used the loofah to wash his chest, back, shoulders, and arms. It should've been calming but Jasper couldn't forget what Nicky was up to. He let out a distressed sound and hid his face against his bicep when Nicky sank down on his knees.

"Shh, you're okay." Nicky washed his calves, thighs, his feet one by one, and then finally pressed between Jasper's cheeks and soaped up his hole.

Jasper shivered with anticipation at Nicky's slippery touch. His blood ran hot, feverish, and his breathing came in shallow, nervous bursts. Part of him wanted to stop and hide; he didn't want to be so exposed to Nicky, but at the same time—

"Detach the shower head. I don't want a mouthful of bubbles."

Jasper's knees locked. "I don't think—"

"Good," Nicky said as he ran his hands over the back of Jasper's thighs. "We agreed not to do that. Shower head."

Jasper leaned back and looked up. The shower head was huge and screwed into the wall, but in the middle of it sat a smaller shower head that could come off. With trembling fingers he worked it loose, and he closed his eyes as he handed it back. In his own head his breathing sounded labored and loud. He made a startled noise when the hot water sprayed him, and then he bit his lip and pressed his forehead against his hands again.

He felt raw and vulnerable as Nicky took his time. He rinsed Jasper's legs, feet, and back, then went back to spreading Jasper's buttocks and rinsed him there.

"Your hole looks really fucking delicious, Jazz," Nicky whispered. "And it also looks really fucking clean." Nicky rinsed it one more time, and then rose up behind Jasper, fingers between his crack to gently massage his rim.

"Nicky," Jasper whispered. His voice shook and he had to force himself to stand still, to not turn away. When he looked down he noticed his cock had flagged a little, maybe because all his blood had rushed to his face.

"Can you put the shower head back now?"

Jasper took the attachment in shaking hands and reached up, but it wouldn't click back in. "I c-can't."

Nicky crouched behind him again, sliding his free hand down Jasper's sides as he went. "Just hang on to it, then. So you don't get cold."

Jasper hugged the shower head to his chest and tried to relax as Nicky placed soft, gentle kisses on his buttocks and then spread open his crack. Nicky kissed his tailbone and trailed down.

Jasper cried out when Nicky's tongue touched his hole. His legs and buttocks went rigid and tight, but Nicky dug in his fingers, fought the clench of Jasper's muscles, and pried his cheeks apart. Jasper trembled all over and couldn't find a way to breathe through it for a frightening minute. Then Nicky pushed his tongue against Jasper's rim and stayed there, waiting, until Jasper finally let go, one muscle at a time.

Fighting to get his breathing under control, Jasper pressed the shower head to his chest and concentrated on the water running down over his abs, balls, and legs. Nicky's tongue was insistent and warm, his breath huffed hot against his skin, and Jasper at last went pliant, leaning his forehead against the tiles, no longer caring they were cold.

"That's it, baby," Nicky whispered. He licked Jasper, tickling him and pressing around the rim with his tongue until everything disappeared from Jasper's mind. There was nothing but liquid heat, blissful freedom from thought, and the most intense pleasure he'd ever experienced. A warmth spread over his chest to his throat, fanning out to his arms and cheeks until his entire upper body tingled. Nicky grew more aggressive, pushing until his tongue forced Jasper's hole to open.

"Nicky!" He let the shower head fall and pushed against the wall, spreading his legs wider.

"Yes, that's it. Let me in," Nicky murmured, pulling back to kiss the apple of Jasper's right buttock. He gripped his butt cheeks and parted them, diving back in.

"Ah!" Jasper's hands slid down with a squeak as Nicky speared him with his tongue. He massaged Jasper's glutes, rubbed his thighs, and then fondled his balls. Pleasure spooled out from Jasper's hole and groin, making his cock rise rigidly against his stomach. His nipples ached, and he groaned. Beautiful, it felt so beautiful—so *good*, so right.

"Can you still come from this?" Nicky asked. He sounded out of breath.

"I don't know. Feels like it."

"Oh, fuck." Nicky rolled his forehead against the small of Jasper's back. "That is so hot. I want to try it—" Nicky broke off. He said nothing for a second, and Jasper looked over his shoulder as Nicky pressed a small kiss to the divot beside Jasper's spine. "I want to—" He shook his head and sucked a finger into his mouth with intent.

Jasper moaned, tensing in anticipation as he let his head fall forward again. He looked down at his own cock where it stood thick and erect and dripping with water.

Nicky's finger wasn't terribly slick as it pushed against his rim, and a spike of resistance shot through him. But then Nicky licked alongside the sharp intrusion, and Jasper let him in.

"You're so hot, baby."

He felt weak from his belly to his knees, and when Nicky rubbed inside him the right way, he moaned and his cock jumped.

"Oh, I felt that." Nicky pressed his cheek to Jasper's glute and rubbed his prostate again. "Oh, yeah. You're so fucking hot. Can you take another finger?"

Jasper made a noise that could've been a yes, or a no, he didn't know himself. Nicky pulled out, leaving Jasper a quivering mess. His hands skidded on the wall, and he was about to beg for something, anything, when Nicky's hand on his hip steadied him and he whispered, "Here come two fingers, baby. Open up for me."

As Nicky pressed spit-slick fingers against his hole, the tension started to build so hard Jasper began to shake.

"Easy," Nicky said. "I can't get inside if you tighten up. Don't worry, Jazz, I'll get you there. Just relax."

"I can't," Jasper cried and Nicky gently pulled out again.

"Okay, shh." He grabbed the shower head from the floor and rinsed their bodies as he rose to his feet. Reaching above Jasper's head, Nicky put the attachment back in place. Jasper stood shaking in the spray, his sunburn and anus stinging.

Nicky kissed his shoulder again and whispered, "I'm sorry. We probably should have had lube for that." He slid his hand around to grip Jasper's dick and tugged it lightly. "Turn around, Jazz."

Jasper didn't have time to look at Nicky before he was kissed breathless. Gripping Jasper's cock, Nicky jerked him hard but slow. Jasper's hips helplessly moved with him, and Nicky groaned into his mouth as he reached around to press his finger against Jasper's hole.

"I want inside you, Jazz," Nicky hissed against his lips. "I want to make love to you until you fall apart under me. I want to make you come. You want my finger again?"

Jasper couldn't speak. Scared to death, he nodded and stared into

Nicky's searching eyes.

"I'll give you what you want, Jazz," Nicky said softly. "But when I said I wanted inside you, I meant my cock. I want to fuck you until you come on my dick."

Jasper groaned against Nicky's open mouth and his thighs began to tremble again. He jerked once as his insides coiled up tight and he dug his fingers into Nicky's shoulders while he came all over their bellies.

"Shit," Nicky said, breathless, still stroking his finger in Jasper's hole. He looked between them, sliding his other hand over the mess as the water washed it away. "I should be calling you Father Jizz."

"Don't," Jasper laughed hoarsely, then moaned as Nicky milked him and pressed his finger deep one more time before gently easing out.

"That was so hot," Nicky whispered.

The water rained down on them, the only sound along with the bathroom fan as they gently kissed.

Slowly, Jasper came down from his high. He rubbed Nicky's arms as he caught his breath, but when he reached between them, Nicky stepped away.

With a small frown, Jasper looked down. "You...you're not hard," he whispered.

Nicky took Jasper's hand and kissed his knuckles. "No, I know. It's fine." He laughed softly when he read the worry on Jasper's face. "This was for you. Besides, I came once already and exercised more than I have in years. I'm wrecked, baby." He kissed Jasper on the mouth once and the teasing tone fell away. "You wrecked me."

Jasper pulled Nicky close and held him as the water began to turn lukewarm. "Likewise."

Nicky looked pale when they finally stepped out of the shower, and Jasper wrapped his towel around his own hips before taking Nicky's from his hands.

"You sure you're okay?" Jasper asked gently.

"Actually, I don't know. I feel a little dizzy and weird. I was feeling okay in the shower. I don't know what this means, I can't—" He took a shuddery breath.

"Okay," Jasper said. The water had been pretty hot so maybe Nicky's blood pressure had dropped. He pressed the towel to Nicky's arms and soaked up the water. "It's okay. Let me look after you now. Lift your arms."

In silence, Jasper dried Nicky, taking care not to miss anything. When Nicky's hair and torso were done, Jasper sank to his knees and dried Nicky's high-arched, bony feet. A gentle touch to his hair made him go still and look up.

"I like you on your knees for me," Nicky whispered. His eyes were tired but ardent in his pale face.

The burst of heat on Jasper's cheeks was so violent it made him sway. "I-I like being on my knees for you," he admitted and looked down in a hurry. He rubbed Nicky's calves, knees, and inner thighs. He hesitated, but Nicky spread his legs like it was nothing.

Jasper wasn't ashamed of his body, but he had trained himself not to think about it for so long. Everything about Nicky being naked right in front of him was making him shivery and weak. He dabbed the towel on Nicky's groin, over his balls and along his penis. Nicky turned around, and Jasper dried his ass and a few forgotten droplets in the small of his back. Which was when he noticed Nicky was trembling, but not like he was cold—like he was hurting.

"Nicky?"

"It's okay,'" Nicky said. "I'm fine. I think I really overdid it. Everything kind of hurts and I'm tired."

"Maybe your blood pressure's a bit low and it's been hours since we ate. With the swimming and the sun and the—" Jasper felt a little lightheaded too. "And the sex, it's only normal that you'd be feeling bad. The lasagna will be ready by now. Let's go eat." He rose to his feet, dried himself haphazardly, and hung their towels away. Nicky gave Jasper a pair of boxer-briefs and smirked when Jasper wrestled himself into them.

"Tight?"

"A little."

Nicky grinned.

Their clothes were where they'd left them in the kitchen and Jasper only pulled on his shorts since he'd warmed up again. Nicky put on his old, soft Candy-O tour T-shirt and some track pants, and then disappeared into the living room to come back with a thick cardigan that must've belonged to his dad.

"Sexy," Jasper said.

"Oh, so one afternoon of fucking and you're an expert now?" Nicky's voice was a snarl, not a tease at all.

Jasper froze with his hands stuck halfway in a pair of oven gloves. "I didn't mean anything by it. I'm…did I do something wrong?" Nicky wouldn't look at him. The tremors seemed to be getting a lot worse and he had his head buried in his hands. "Nicky?"

"I'm sorry. I don't know why I said that. I feel really off. I think I'm just hungry."

Jasper tried to smile but it didn't feel real. "Yeah," he said. "Take a seat. Your blood sugar must be really low. We'll get you fed." He pushed away the unreasonable hurt in his chest and took the lasagna out of the oven.

While it cooled, he filled tall glasses with water—then refilled Nicky's when he drained it in one go—took out plates and cutlery, and almost suggested a bottle of wine. He hunted around the kitchen until he found Mrs. B's spatulas and filled two plates with fragrant pasta and cheese. Sliding the plate across the breakfast bar toward Nicky, he took a seat beside him, smiling with happy anticipation.

"I don't know what it is about your mom's cooking," Jasper said around his first mouthful, "but it's the absolute best."

Nicky stabbed at his plate but didn't eat anything. Jasper put down his fork. "What's going on? You're not okay, are you?" Nicky yawned so hard his jaw cracked, and Jasper reached out to still his nervously twitching hand. "Talk to me, please."

"I don't know. I feel crappy. I'm hungry but my stomach is all knotted up." Nicky shook all over and he cursed softly. "Like sick to my stomach. Like I might be getting the flu. I hope I didn't make you sick. I—fuck—" Nicky shivered so violently his fork fell from his hand and clattered to the plate.

"Nicky! What's wrong?"

Nicky's teeth began to clatter again, like they had when they'd stepped out of the water. "Shit!" He bent forward and pushed away from the counter, chair screeching over the tiles. Clutching at his stomach, he gasped for breath, and Jasper's heart hammered in his chest. He jumped to his feet and groped for his phone as he put a protective arm around Nicky's shoulder.

"Lie down on the floor, I'm calling 911. Maybe this is some belated reaction to nearly drowning. I saw a YouTube video about it. Dry drowning or something—"

"No, don't call 911. I'm fine." Nicky struggled out of the cardigan, and Jasper wondered if he had a fever. His brow was damp and hot. "Shit." Nicky clutched his upper arm.

"Does your left arm hurt? Oh my God, are you having a heart attack?"

"No. It's not that." Nicky moaned and shivered. "Don't call anyone."

"What is it? Nicky, *please*!" Jasper begged, more scared than he ever remembered being.

"My patch is gone. For my maintenance meds. It must've come off in the water."

"What does that mean?"

Nicky reached for his glass of water, and Jasper helped him steady it as he drank and then set it on the counter.

Nicky stumbled into the living room and Jasper followed him, grabbing his arm when he nearly fell over on his way to the couch.

"I need a new one. I'm..." Nicky looked at Jasper and then quickly away again. Jasper couldn't figure out if the flush on his cheeks was fever or embarrassment. "I'm going into withdrawal," he whispered.

Jasper helped him settle down on the couch. "Okay." He nodded, some of the urgency leaving his body as he calmed. No heart attack. No dry drowning. "Okay, that's better but still...not good. Who do I call? Do you need a doctor? Do you have new patches?"

"Yeah. I don't need a doctor. I have to ride this out. Maybe—" he glanced at Jasper with red-rimmed eyes and then closed them. "Maybe you should go home now."

"What? No!" Jasper pushed Nicky's hair off his forehead. It was damp again with sweat, and Nicky grabbed his hand and held it between both of his. He might say he didn't want Jasper here, but Jasper didn't believe for a minute he really wanted to go through this alone. "I'm not leaving you. We're in this together. Tell me where the patches are and I'll help you." Nicky bit his lip and moisture gathered in in the corners of his eyes. He still wouldn't look at Jasper, but the grip on his hands was like iron. "Is it really so hard to accept my help, Nicky?" Jasper asked him softly.

"No. Yes. I don't know, fuck. It's not that. It's embarrassing."

Jasper took a careful breath. "Let me get you the patch first."

"They're in my bathroom cabinet. Be careful you don't touch the sticky side."

"Okay. Just don't move." Jasper leaned over and kissed Nicky's forehead. Nicky reached out for his arm as his eyes flew open in a panic, and Jasper bent back down to kiss him softly on the mouth. "I'll be right back, I promise."

He found the patches and brought the whole box down, determined to read the instructions in case they offered any information on what to do if a patch came off early.

Nicky was still where he left him, but he'd curled up in a ball, shivering and looking miserable.

"Oh, Nicky." Jasper knelt beside him and stroked his hair out of his face. "I'm so sorry."

"It's n-n-not your f-fault."

"That doesn't mean I can't feel for you going through this. Where do I put it?"

Nicky held out his arm. "But seriously, don't you fucking touch—"

"Shh. I know." Jasper peeled back the protective layer on the patch and pressed it to Nicky's arm, holding his hand over it so it could warm and the glue would definitely stick. "How long until you feel better?"

"I don't know." Nicky grimaced. "Shit, I'd forgotten how fucking awful this feels."

Jasper stroked his hair. "Was it always like this?"

Nicky opened his eyes and looked at him. "Worse," he whispered, then laughed a little desolately. "So much worse."

Jasper nodded and felt his heart crack. Nicky closed his eyes again and didn't say anything else, so Jasper tried to read the instructions for the patch, but there was nothing useful. He pulled out his phone and googled withdrawal symptoms. When it seemed like Nicky had fallen into a restless sleep, Jasper went into the kitchen, grabbed some fresh water, wet a towel, and then lifted a throw off the back of the couch. He covered Nicky, then kneeled on the floor again and waited.

"I want a hit so bad," Nicky suddenly said, and Jasper jolted, his stomach turning to ice. "I know it will make everything better."

"Not in the long run."

"Do you think I fucking care about the long run right now?"

Jasper ignored him. "Do you think you can sit up?"

Nicky eyed him suspiciously. "Why?"

"I have ice water and I don't want you to drown." He held up the glass and Nicky's eyes zeroed in on it. He sat up slowly, and Jasper helped him drink. "Now stand up."

"What? No." Nicky tried to lie down again but Jasper grabbed his arm—the one without the patch—and helped him up.

"Just walk with me a little." He put his shoulder under Nicky's arm and despite struggling briefly, Nicky melted into him and let himself be led around the house.

"You still smell so good," he mumbled and buried his face in Jasper's neck. "I think that was the last thing I forgot about you. How you smelled. I forgot your voice first, and I cried for days when I realized I couldn't remember it. And then I forgot the color of your eyes, although that god damn picture in *The Atlantic* was proof enough I hadn't forgotten at all." He made Jasper stop. "I grieved for you. Like you were dead."

Jasper looked him steadily in the eye. "I grieved for you too." He went to stand behind Nicky when he began to shiver again. "Breathe with me," he whispered in Nicky's ear. Gently encircling Nicky's wrists, he brought their arms up. "In." He held their arms high and paused. "And out." He lowered them down.

"What are you doing?"

"I read it helps to do gentle exercise. So we're doing some yoga. In." He lifted their arms again, and Nicky laughed softly.

"You can't help yourself can you? Saint Jazz."

Jasper shook Nicky's arms once and he obeyed by breathing in deeply. They lowered their arms. "Keep doing it." Jasper went to stand beside him and guided him through a few half sun salutes. "And no," he said when they were done. "When I'm with you I can't help myself at all."

IT DIDN'T TAKE too long for the effects of the new patch to begin to offset the worst of the pain and discomfort of the detox. That was one of the great things about it. Rapid, consistent delivery. One of the shitty things was, apparently, if he didn't realize the patch had come off, he went into withdrawal a lot faster than he'd have expected.

Nicky collapsed to the floor and rolled onto his back, gazing up at

Jasper, who was bent over with his ass in the air. "That's called down dog?" He rubbed his arms, feeling the sweat from his last chill drying on his skin. He might need another shower. "Is it a sex reference?"

"What?"

"Like doggy style?"

Jasper came down to his knees and cocked his head. "You're feeling better." He sat cross-legged with a soft smile on his face.

"Yeah. Thanks." Nicky pushed hair out of his eyes and smiled a little shyly. "For helping me out and for not leaving me."

"As if I would leave you."

Nicky broke into a delirious laugh. His limbs were heavy and in addition to the actual distance he had swum, the detox tremors had left him worn through, aching, and on the edge of passing out. "It's too easy," he said, almost choking on his laughter. "Oh God, Jazz, don't say things like that. I'm so tired I could die from laughing, I swear."

Jasper picked at a thread in Miriam's new rug. Then, apparently realizing what he was doing, he folded his hands in his lap. "Fine, should I say I was happy to help instead?"

"That's certainly less hilariously ironic."

Jazz's lips turned up at the edges and he came closer, running his hand over the sleeve of the cardigan Nicky still had on despite sweating. He'd been both cold and hot for a while right before the medication had kicked in. "Let's get some food in you and then we should hit the hay."

Nicky followed Jasper up from the floor, his muscles still cramping slightly. His stomach burned and he felt simultaneously famished and nauseated. Fucking delightful. "I don't think I can eat that lasagna," he said, running a hand through his damp hair. "Maybe a piece of bread or something."

Jasper gently took hold of Nicky's arm, leading him to a seat at the kitchen bar. "You sit there. I'll zap the lasagna in the microwave for me, and get some dry toast for you." His eyes landed on a small bunch of ripe bananas and he ripped one off, handing it to Nicky. "Eat that.

Potassium is good for muscle cramps."

"Yes, Father Jazz," Nicky murmured, a snicker of a laugh escaping as he watched Jasper grab the bread from his mother's bread box and start four pieces of toast. The banana tasted bland and sweet enough to settle him, and he took a few bites before resting his head on his arms, too tired to sit up fully.

Jasper ruffled his hair. "Rest."

He heard the beeping sound of Jasper punching numbers into the microwave, and soon the cheesy smell of lasagna filled the room. His stomach clenched a little in rebellion, but he ignored it. Jasper deserved a big, fat piece of Miriam's lasagna. After tonight, it might be another seventeen years before he had it again. If ever.

The morose thought accompanied a heavy sensation on his heart. Nicky sighed, and sat up enough to take another bite of banana. It was the same oppressive, suffocating feeling he had when falling out from heroin or coke, but this time it was from a different kind of short-term high altogether.

The sound of the toast popping brought him fully upright, and he took it from Jazz on one of his mother's small plates.

"Try to eat them all. You could probably use some protein. Maybe eggs?"

Nicky grimaced. "I'm fine. I'll be fine."

Jasper sat on the stool next to him with the steaming lasagna. He'd put the big pan of it back in the fridge while Nicky'd rested with his head on the counter. "Mmm, it's still so good."

"Yeah," Nicky said, a tingle thrilling in his taint at the thick pleasure in Jazz's voice. "I know. Mom's an amazing cook."

"So much better than my mom."

Nicky laughed. "Well, your mom has mine beat in the 'how to operate a microwave' game. Mine still has to ask my dad how long to pop the popcorn."

"Sometimes I wish my mother didn't live up to the stereotype."

Nicky took a bite of toast and sipped the water Jasper had placed near him. "What do you mean?"

"Driven, ambitious, proud, but with little to no time to raise a child, can't cook, hires out the cleaning, is distant. A little cold." Jasper shrugged. "I worked my hind end off to please her, but I was always going to let her down in the end."

"Yeah." Nicky took a bite of banana and chewed it in the silence. "But she saves lives. She's a hero to a lot of people. I know if I needed heart surgery, she's the first person I'd want to crack me open. Well, maybe not *me*, because she might actually fucking leave me there to die. But, you know, if I was another person, she'd be the one."

Jasper laughed quietly. "She didn't really hate you."

Nicky scoffed.

"Well, she didn't hate you *that much*." He grinned. "Not enough to let her Hippocratic Oath slide and ruin her reputation."

"What about your dad, though?" Nicky asked. "He wasn't around much either. No reason to dump all the cold, distant, become-a-doctor-or-else stuff on your mom."

"True. I was quite a lonely kid." Jasper knocked his shoulder against Nicky. "Until I met you."

"Me too."

Jasper touched Nicky's cheek with the back of his fingers. "Eat more. You're still shaking."

He managed to squeeze down two pieces of toast and the entire banana. Then he rested against the counter, his head pillowed on the crook of his arm, while Jasper finished his dinner.

"When do you think the patch came off?" Jasper asked. "I don't remember seeing it on you at the island."

"Maybe on the way over when you had to haul me up. Or hell, maybe earlier in the day somehow. I don't know." He closed his eyes, and Jasper's fingers found their way to his stubbled cheek again, brushing with tenderness that made Nicky's chest ache. "But they'd warned me withdrawal was harsh with this medication. Still, I wasn't expecting it to be like that."

"You said it'd been worse."

"Yeah. But it doesn't usually come on so hard like that. I still feel like a horse kicked me."

"Maybe the exercise pushed it out of your system faster."

"Could be. I have a high metabolism too, which is why this drug is ideal for me. Stable, consistent delivery, and I don't have to remember to pop pills multiple times during the day."

"I know some of the kids at Blue Oasis have kicked habits, but I've never seen one of them go into withdrawal. They're always fully detoxed before they're brought to me." He looked at Nicky with sad eyes. "I really hate that you have to go through this."

"I don't have to 'go through it,' though. So long as the patch stays on my arm." Nicky sat up and smiled reassuringly. "It's okay, Jazz. It's better than the alternative."

Jasper looked down, picking at his lasagna. "How long do you need to stay on the patch?"

"Until I decide I want to be in excruciating pain and agony, I guess." Nicky frowned. "Forever, in other words. Why?"

Jasper looked up sharply. "Wait, you can't come off this medication ever?"

"Don't get moralistic on me now, Father Jazz."

"I don't know what you mean. I'm trying to understand."

Nicky sized him up. The confusion in his eyes was sincere. "I can come off it. If I want. But I don't want."

"Okay," Jasper said, obviously still not entirely getting it. "But this drug—"

"Medication."

"You're addicted to it. If you come off it, you go into withdrawals. I don't understand why you wouldn't prefer to be clean."

"Ah. That's the word." Nicky snorted. "Do you think someone with diabetes should get clean of their insulin pump? Or that a person suffering from schizophrenia should get clean of their antipsychotics? Or any other sick person with a chronic disease and a chemical that alleviates it? Tons of medications and treatments have fucking unpleasant side effects, you know. Some even have withdrawal symptoms associated with coming off them. But people take them anyway because it keeps them alive."

Jasper gazed at him, thinking it through. "Okay…yeah. That makes sense."

"Some people think addiction is different. That all it takes is being strong enough to resist temptation, but they don't take into account that our brains are fucking different, man. They aren't the same as a non-addict. Whether the drugs did it or we came out of the womb this way—and you know about my birth mother—I don't know and I don't care. In NA they talk about a higher power and turning to it to keep from being tempted. They mean something more like your God, but for me, the only higher power I believe in is this drug. If anything's going to save my life in the long run, it'll be staying on this."

Jasper finished eating and wiped his mouth with a napkin before turning to Nicky. "Do doctors think it's okay to stay on this medication for so long?"

"They don't know. This one's still a little experimental, but its relatives in the drug family are safe to stay on for decades. Assuming this one doesn't backfire and somehow cause me to go into spontaneous cardiac arrest or stroke out, I don't think it will be any different."

Jasper swallowed, his Adam's apple bobbing nervously. "I understand that this is a sensitive subject for you, and I'd never think less of you for choosing to safeguard your sobriety in whatever way possible, so please don't think I'm questioning your judgement. I just want to understand better."

"But—? I hear the 'but' coming, Jazz."

"No 'but,' only concern. After seeing the way you were hurting tonight, I can't help but wish there was some way for you to not need the maintenance medication at all. Are you sure you couldn't be sober without it?"

"Is it worth me maybe dying to find out?"

"No, never."

"My thoughts exactly." Nicky took another drink of his water and watched Jasper twist on his chair.

"But, what if something went wrong in L.A., or while you're out on the road touring? If your patch came off out there without you noticing, who would help you? Who would make sure you didn't shoot up like you were craving earlier?"

Nicky rubbed his eyes and yawned again. He shook his head and shrugged. "Maybe Ramona. Maybe not. Maybe no one."

Jasper's eyes went wide, his cheeks flushing. "That's not an acceptable answer. It's too great a risk!"

"Are you going to come out on the road with me to babysit?" Nicky's lips went up tightly at the edges. "Didn't think so. Listen, I don't want to go back to using. This drug is the best way I know to do that."

"But having a support system is key. Everyone knows that, and you've told me that there's no one out there you can lean on."

Nicky sighed. "I guess that means I'll have to lean on myself. And there's FaceTime and Skype, and my mom and dad have a phone. I've got a therapist that I could see in person instead of doing phone sessions. Ramona and I are getting closer. It'll be okay."

Jasper didn't look entirely confident in that assessment.

"Besides, I'm not leaving yet. I'll be stronger by the time I get out there again."

Jasper's fingers moved against the counter, stroking it as if he could find a solution in Braille there.

"You can't control everything, Jasper. Not even you." He smiled and cut a flippant grin at him. "Besides, I think that's the purview of your

God."

Jasper looked down. "I want what's best for you, so you'll be safe."

"I like that you want me to be safe." He wanted to ask whether he could count on Jasper's friendship when he went back to L.A., whether he might be on the other end of a FaceTime chat, or a phone call. But he didn't want to burst the bubble of just-the-two-of-them with the pinprick of future consequences yet.

Jasper stood to take their plates to rinse in the sink, ripping off a third of the leftover toast on Nicky's plate and handing it to him. "Just have a few more bites or you'll wake up hungry in the night."

Nicky watched Jasper bend over to put their plates in the dishwasher. "Oh, I'm sure I'll wake up hungry."

Jazz looked at him over his shoulder, clearly trying to gauge if that had been innuendo or not. "We could bring a snack upstairs to keep by the bed in case."

Nicky cocked his head, ogling Jasper's butt. "Your ass looks tasty enough for me. Grab the whipped cream from the fridge. I bet they'd go good together."

Jasper flushed and stood up, snapping the dishwasher shut and pushing buttons on the front to start it. Then he leaned back against the counter and shook his head. "What am I going to do with you?"

Nicky dropped his lashes and gave a coy smile. "Well, you've exercised me, bathed me, and fed me. I guess you should put me to bed."

Jasper rolled his eyes, but came around the counter reaching for Nicky's hand. "C'mon. I'll tuck you in."

"You better do more than that," Nicky whispered.

Jasper stroked his thumb over the back of Nicky's wrist, then pulled Nicky up from the stool. Nicky followed obediently up the stairs to his room. They both relieved themselves in the en suite bathroom, and Nicky brushed his teeth while Jasper went to the guest room to get ready for bed. Nicky took another fast shower, washing away the sweat and easing the sore muscles from his earlier muscle spasms. When he stepped out, Jasper was waiting with a towel, wearing pajama pants and a white tank shirt.

"Full service, I like it," Nicky said as Jasper wrapped the towel around his shoulders.

"I think you can dry yourself," Jasper murmured. He leaned back against the wall and watched as Nicky rubbed the towel over himself, lingering over his dick, which seemed cautiously interested in being observed. He was too tired to get fully hard, but it tingled nicely as it filled halfway with a sweet rush of blood.

Jasper passed him a T-shirt and some boxers, but Nicky tossed them aside. He took hold of Jasper's hand and led him into the darkness of the bedroom. Nicky climbed beneath the soft, fresh-smelling sheets that Miriam had put on the bed before she'd left.

Jasper stood by the bed, looking down at him with uncertain eyes. "Well, goodnight."

Nicky lifted the covers. "Stay."

Jasper swallowed in the dark stillness of the room.

"I want it to be just you and me," Nicky said softly, evoking the words like a summons that neither one of them wanted to deny.

"Yes, all right," Jasper agreed, lying down next to Nicky and letting the covers fall over him. "You and me for tonight."

Nicky nodded and scooted close, drawing Jasper near. He didn't know the last time he'd cuddled with anyone. Unless being passed out next to some groupie with their body parts still touching counted, it hadn't been since he and Jazz had last made love at seventeen. And it was kind of annoying that Jazz's pajamas were preventing him from feeling his skin.

"Really, Jazz?" he asked, plucking at the soft T-shirt. "Really?

"What?"

"This isn't an overnight retreat for the clergy. Take your clothes off."

"Oh." Jasper giggled a little and it made Nicky's heart clench. "Right, of course. I can do that."

"Well, you don't *have* to do that if you don't want to. I won't fucking kick you out of the bed or anything. But I'd like to touch you."

Jasper sat up and pulled his shirt off and wriggled out of his pajama bottoms and underwear. He sat with them in his hands like he didn't know what to do with them. Nicky grabbed them and tossed them across the dark room. Then he leaned across Jasper and turned out the lamp on the table, throwing them into complete darkness.

Pressed against each other in the quiet of the empty house, unable to see in the dark, they kissed. Their bodies slid together easily, and Nicky pressed his hand to Jasper's chest, feeling his heartbeat as Jasper tenderly touched and stroked Nicky's body. Neither of their cocks grew hard as they cuddled. They were too tired to do much more than lie twined together, brushing lips and kissing. They whispered to each other, sweet nonsensical words of tenderness, and tasted each other's mouths again and again.

Eventually, drifting in a beautiful, sweet place where only he and Jasper existed, Nicky fell asleep.

V

Chapter Nineteen

JASPER PEELED OPEN his sticky eyelids and was momentarily disoriented. *God, why was he so hot?* He licked his lips in an attempt to generate some moisture in his mouth as he stretched his stiff legs.

He was curled protectively around a sleeping Nicky, and a dizzying lurch of longing and intangible loss made him clutch the thin sheet covering them both. No matter how hard he wanted to grasp these last twenty-four hours, he knew time was slipping through his fingers like sand from a broken hourglass. And waking up next to Nicky after all these years was…unbelievable. A warmth spread through him, slowly at first, then faster and faster, like a piece of paper catching fire. It was doused as fast as if someone had thrown a bucket of water on the flames.

Was this it? Would it be no more than a moment's reprieve in their adult lives, a shard of blissful happiness already turning into nothing more than a memory?

His heart rejected the idea, too painful to even contemplate.

Nicky's chest rose and fell under his palm, and Jasper drew him gently nearer. He closed his eyes and buried his face into Nicky's hair. He'd found himself in Nicky when he was a teenage boy. And he'd rediscovered himself in him now. How could he let this go? *But how can I not? I made vows. I pledged my life to the Lord.* He should have been horrified by what he'd done, yet…he wasn't.

"I can hear you thinking from here," Nicky mumbled.

Jasper smiled and allowed himself another whiff of Nicky's fragrant hair before he lifted his head and said, "I'm sorry I woke you."

"It's fine. We should get out of bed anyway. My parents will be home soon."

"What?" Jasper sat up so fast Nicky bounced onto his back. The dark circles of his nipples nearly distracted Jasper, but he groped around for his phone before remembering it was still downstairs. "What time is it?"

"I don't know." Nicky stretched luxuriously, hands skimming the headboard before he let them drop down and gently stroked Jasper's naked back. "About ten or something. Don't worry they won't be here for another hour or—"

"Ten?" Jasper scrambled out from under the sheet. "Oh no. Oh no, no, no."

"What?" Nicky sat up and yawned. "What is it? What are you—"

"It's Sunday, Nicky. *Sunday.*" Nicky gave him a confused look. "Sunday Mass?"

"Oh." Nicky bit his lip but it didn't do much to hide the smile, and Jasper took some time out of his underwear hunt to scowl at him. "Well, you're screwed."

"It's not funny, Nicky."

"It's a little bit funny." Nicky sniggered.

"What the heck did you do with my underwear? I can't—how can it be ten o'clock and still be so dark in here?"

"Blackout curtains, my friend. When I'm on tour, I do most of my sleeping during the day, so mom installed them in this room too in case I stopped by for a visit."

"I really wish I could swear up a blue streak right now." Jasper yanked open the curtains and flinched at the bright sunlight that spilled through. Yep. Definitely not eight in the morning anymore. Behind him Nicky whistled.

"Go for it, baby. Swearing's the least of your sins right now." Nicky flopped back down on the bed. He let his hand trail over his chest. "I think your underwear is under the sideboard by the door."

Jasper hurried over and bent down. "What? I don't—"

Behind him Nicky laughed. "Just bend over a little more and you'll see th—"

"Nicky!" Jasper tried not to laugh, but he couldn't help it. He jumped onto the bed and mercilessly tickled Nicky until he was laughing so hard he had tears running down his face.

"Okay, I surrender, fuck. Isn't there some sort of commandment preventing priests from torturing innocent people?"

"Innocent?" Jasper dropped down and framed Nicky's head with his forearms. "You are many things, Nicholas Blumfeld." He kissed the end of Nicky's nose. "Many, beautiful, clever, talented things. But innocent isn't one of them." He groaned when Nicky pushed his hips up, feeling the bulge of his morning erection through the thin sheet. "I really can't, Nicky."

"Hmm, why not? Mass is over by now." Nicky ran his hands over Jasper's bare shoulders, down his flanks, and over the swell of his ass. They kissed languidly, sweetly, and it didn't taste like goodbye at all.

"Because," Jasper murmured. "All my parishioners might be out there. Maybe they're starting a search and rescue. They'll be here any minute."

Nicky's eyes widened comically and he shoved Jasper off him. "Yes, you're absolutely right, you should get out of here right the fuck now."

Laughing, Jasper rolled onto his back, and in a swift, giddy move, onto his feet at the other end of the bed. "Oh, so now you're kicking me out."

"Uh, yeah." Nicky swung his legs out of bed too, and walked over to where Jasper finally managed to locate his underwear underneath the bedside table. "Doesn't mean I don't want you to come back as soon as it's dark." He trailed his finger down Jasper's spine, and Jasper shivered. "My illicit lover."

Jasper stilled. He turned, caught Nicky's hand, and pressed a kiss to the center of his palm. "Come to my house tonight?" he whispered.

He didn't say, *we need to talk*. He didn't have to. It was in Nicky's eyes. It had been there since the moment they'd kissed for the first time on the island, and Jasper understood the foreshadowing of pain Nicky had seen. And he'd tossed it aside and taken the leap anyway.

Nicky nodded. Jasper closed his eyes and pressed Nicky's palm to his mouth again.

"I love you," Jasper whispered.

Nicky offered him a small, sad smile. "I know."

After a whirlwind of finding his clothes all over the house, getting dressed, and stopping time to kiss Nicky into sweet oblivion, Jasper found himself standing on Nicky's doorstep.

"I feel like a kid," Jasper said. "Having to do something I don't want to do. It's been a long time since that happened."

Nicky tugged at a loose thread on Jasper's sleeve. "You trying to tell me you don't want to go, Father Jazz?"

Jasper grinned, cupped the back of Nicky's head, and kissed him lightly. "I don't want to go, Badger."

"As soon as you're at the end of that driveway, everything will be different."

Jasper lost himself in Nicky's eyes. "I hope not."

Nicky forced a smile. "I'll see you tonight."

"I'll be waiting."

As soon as his bike tires hit the gravel, Jasper's heart lurched uncomfortably in his chest. It'd been a long time since he'd lost control over any aspect of his life, and sweet Lord, had he lost control this weekend.

He wanted to look behind him, but he'd heard the door click into its lock and knew Nicky had gone inside. Lifting his face to the sky, he inhaled deeply, letting the scent of summer and silt wash over him as he freewheeled down the hill. He felt no regret, but he didn't know how long that would last. A screech of tires brought him back to the present, and he yanked at his handlebar to avoid the BMW that came flying around the corner.

Oh no.

He squeezed his brakes. The car stopped and the window lowered. "Jasper." His mother's mouth pinched together. She looked tired and a little more disheveled than usual. They must've called her in for surgery in the small hours of the morning. "I guess I don't need to ask if you've been at the house looking for me."

A flash of anger boiled in Jasper's gut and he pressed it down. "No, Mom, I was with Nicky. His parents are out of town and I stayed the weekend."

She ground her teeth together and leaned out of the car. With a quick glance left and right, she whispered harshly, "I don't need to remind you that you're a man of the cloth, do I? You look…you look…" She shook her head hard and fast.

"What, Mom?" Jasper asked. Why wasn't he freaking out? Why could he not care less whether she knew or not? What was wrong with him? "What do I look like?"

"You look like you had a good time."

"I did. And I'm sure Nicky did too. We swam to the island and then—"

"That's not what I mean, and you know it. That boy has never been anything but trouble and he never cared what kind of damage he inflicted upon any—"

"See, but that's where you're wrong." Jasper lifted the right pedal with the tip of his toe and set his foot on it. "Nicky cares a lot." The resentment he'd trained himself out of for years flared hot and bright, and this once he couldn't—didn't want to—fight it. "He cares a whole lot more than you ever did."

His mom gasped and stared at him. "All I ever wanted was what's best for you."

"And did you ever consider that the best for me through your eyes wasn't the best at all?" Jasper asked her mildly.

"What difference does it make?" Her cheeks stained red, and sadness crept into Jasper's heart. "You did what you wanted to anyway."

"Did I? Or did I do the only thing I thought I could, under the circumstances?" He shook his head. "I don't want to fight with you. Everyone makes mistakes. But just once I'd wish you could stand beside me instead of in front of me, wielding judgement like one of your scalpels." He pushed down with his foot and the wind rushed in his face again as he sped up. He didn't look back to see the car pull away from the curb behind him.

I'm too old to seek approval from my mother.

But what about God's approval? a small voice asked him. *When did you stop caring about that?*

When he came home, he plugged in his phone and winced when it beeped and then kept beeping. Message after message, missed call after missed call. He didn't bother listening to his voicemail. Instead he called Andrew.

"Father!" He sounded out of breath. "Where are you? Are you all right?"

"Yes, I'm fine, Andrew. I'm sorry about this morning. Did you do Mass?"

"I didn't have much choice." A brief silence. "Are you sure you're okay? I was worried you'd been hit by a car or something. I've been driving around and I've called the hospital..."

Jasper closed his eyes and sighed inwardly. "I'm really sorry I worried you."

"What happened?"

"I spent the night with a friend. I forgot to set my alarm."

"That's it?" Andrew laughed. "Okay, well, when I suggested you'd take some time off, I kind of thought you'd let me know first. But I'm glad you did. If you want me to take over this evening's Mass too, I can—"

Tempting, but it felt too much like an easy escape. He needed to face what was coming, and sooner rather than later. Mass might help him sort his thoughts out, and his feelings. "No, it's fine. I'll be there. Thank you, Andrew. And I really am sorry."

"I'm glad you're all right, Father. Don't worry about it."

That evening, the empty church smelled vaguely of incense and polished wood. Jasper sat in a back pew, tucked away to the side where the last of the dying sunlight didn't reach him. It cast beautiful patterns through the ornate stained glass windows, turning the marble floor to a rippling sea of oranges and reds. On most days he loved the way the light played with the beautiful interior of the church, but tonight he wanted to stay in the shadows.

He sat with his elbows on his knees, leaning forward. As he looked down he noticed his hands were still. When he turned his attention within himself he realized he felt steadier than he had in a long time.

Jasper closed his eyes. "Forgive me, Father," he whispered, "for I have sinned."

The guilt didn't come.

"I have wronged you. I have broken my vow. I must seek penance."

But what good would atonement do, if he didn't feel repentant? How could he find absolution if he felt no remorse for what he'd done?

Maybe you've done nothing wrong.

Jasper blinked his eyes open, but the church was empty. He wasn't vain enough to assume the voice he heard was the actual voice of God, especially since it seemed so ready to submit to his deepest, darkest desires.

But when he thought about Nicky's mouth on his, and the breath they'd shared, and the touch that had made him feel so loved—so alive—it didn't make him think of darkness. It made him think of light and freedom and everything that he strove for others to find in life.

Before Nicky came back, life had been a series of motions and habits that were good, but maybe not what he should've been striving for.

He lifted his face to the cross above the altar. Jesus Christ, Son of

God, looked down upon him. Blood dripped down His cheek from the thorned crown. His head was down but his gaze rested steadily on Jasper's.

You are King. You are God. Are these the sins You died for? Or am I rising from my slumber to live the life I am meant to live? Show me the way, O Lord, for I have been misguided. I have prayed to help Nicky find his way while it is I who am lost. It is I who needs to find a path true to You and to myself.

He could sit there and tell himself what had happened with Nicky had been nothing but a moment of weakness, of temptation. That would be easier in the long run. But he knew, deep down, that all he had felt and done was born from a strength he'd lacked when he was a teenage boy. That made everything a lot more complicated.

THE DAY WAS surprisingly busy and, like when he'd been a teenager, Nicky's parents didn't seem to get any "I got laid" vibes off him. For the first forty-five minutes after his parents got home, Miriam told him all about their trip. As she lovingly described the lobster soup and the time she'd spent reading romances by the water while his father fished, he half-listened and half-panicked that Jasper was, at that very moment, deciding everything had been a mistake.

The rest of the morning was taken up with calling Elkin Hardware about the unfinished dock-steps project, and then standing there while Joey Renfroe talked to Adrian about rebar and supports. Once they'd shaken hands on hiring Joey and Elkin Hardware for the job, Nicky was freed from the responsibility of finishing a project he was in no way qualified to have even begun.

Somehow, in the distraction of checking his phone and seeing that Jazz still hadn't texted, Nicky agreed to go fishing with Adrian. After donning long sleeves to protect his tats, slathering on sunscreen, and slapping on a weird, musty-smelling hat his mother used in the garden, they went out into the cove and beyond. They spent three hours catching tautog and a few nice herrings.

When they got back, Adrian cleaned the fish and Miriam put some in the freezer before cooking up one of the bigger togs for an early dinner. Nicky picked at it. His stomach still felt off, but he didn't think it was from having gone into withdrawal the day before. He thought it was because for a few hours in the middle of the night, he'd had the most perfect feeling that everything was going to be all right. Now that feeling was gone.

After dinner, Miriam set about cleaning the house and Adrian went into his office to do some work, leaving Nicky with nothing to distract his mind. The piano called to him, and so did his father's guitar, but he couldn't let himself make music right now. It scared him what might come out. He had a feeling if anyone heard the music stirring up inside him, they'd know exactly what he and Jazz had done.

So Nicky sat by the swimming pool with his feet in the water, cradling his phone in his other hand. He listened to the birds chirp. He could feel the heat waves lifting from the earth around him, humid and buzzing with its own sort of sound. The rustle in the trees and the roar of an unseen lawn mower echoed around the cove, culminating in a pulsing rhythm in his mind.

Your skin tastes of ocean and sin
Your lips sink me like ships
In a wave that holds on so strong
It's impossible to sail on

He sighed and looked down at his phone again. There were still no messages from Jasper. There were, however, dozens from Danvers and a few from Harry, and one from Ramona.

Call me. Important.

He looked toward the house and could see his mother vacuuming through the back windows. He selected Ramona's name, and it barely rang once before she answered.

"Let me tell you, pretty boy, you've been pissing some people off," she answered.

"What did I do now?"

"Oh, you know, not answering your phone, not returning messages from management, pretending they don't exist. Anything else you've done that might make people angry?"

"Sure. Plenty of things." He remembered Jasper's eyes as he'd come all over them both in the shower the night before. "But nothing that's any of management's business."

"You realize that pushing their buttons isn't going to change anything?"

"I know."

"Well, here's the scoop. They've busted Sez and Mick out, and now they want you to come home. Vacation time is up, pretty boy. It's showtime."

Nicky ducked his head, the sun pouring onto his back and breaking in shards over the blue pool water. "No."

"I'll let Danvers explain to you why no isn't an answer they'll accept, but I think you already know why."

A bird cried overhead. "But I'm not ready."

"When will any of us ever be ready? It's the sort of thing you just gotta do, Nicky. Leap off the diving board and hope you remember how to fucking swim."

"Things here are complicated."

Ramona was silent for a moment, and then she let out a soft hoot. "Oh, tell me you did not actually sleep with your priest?" She laughed, and Nicky could imagine her dark head thrown back and beautiful lips stretched wide over white teeth. "Never mind, I know you did. Only you, Nicky. Only you are hot enough to seduce a motherfucking priest."

"Well, actually, statistically—"

"Statistically? Did you research this?"

"I'm saying that other people have been known to seduce a priest. Not that I seduced him. No one seduced anyone. It was—" *a mistake* "—a spontaneous explosion of emotion." He raked a hand through his hair. "I love him."

She was quiet a moment. "Oh, Nicky."

"I can't leave him after this." He closed his eyes. "I have to make sure he's all right."

"Are *you* all right?"

"Probably not. But if I stay here, then..." He'd be a distraction for Jasper; a temptation, a constant reminder of what they'd done, and a persistent invitation to do those things again. And while most of him wanted exactly that, a very quiet, sane part of him said that if he did that, Jasper would become a man Nicky didn't recognize. As for himself, he'd never be truly free, truly sober.

"Then what?"

Nicky shook his head hard, though she couldn't see him. "I shouldn't stay here."

"Flip-flops are for feet, Nicky."

"If I stay here, I'm going to hope for something and want something that I doubt I can ever fucking have. And if I did have it—if he gave in now and let himself love me again, it would ruin the best parts of him. But if I leave..."

She made a frustrated noise. "Then you'll never know if it could have been more."

"No, if I leave, then we'll know for sure. Both of us. Either he'll go back to his life like it never happened, or he won't. And I either go on without him or I don't."

"And if he goes back to his life like it never happened?"

"Then I fall apart in the loving arms of my dysfunctional-as-fuck band and double up appointments with my new therapist, all while management holds a gun to my head. I'd make a motherfucking heartbreaking album out of it." As for what happened after that, he couldn't say for sure, but he didn't want to die. He could have this connection with Ramona, the relationship with his parents, and maybe he could learn to love someone else. He was discovering how to live a real life, and it was like being on the moon. But one day, if he stayed sober, maybe he'd earn his moon-feet.

"Excuse me, Egomaniac? *We'd* make a motherfucking heartbreaking album out of it. There are four of us, you know."

Nicky laughed softly. "I know." He kicked his feet to splash the water again, and then looked back toward the house. His mother was still vacuuming, and his heart ached when he thought about telling her he was leaving. She'd be so scared for him. "I don't want to come out there."

"Of course you don't. But it's like I told you the other day when I heard back from those attorneys I hired. Our contracts are ironclad. So it's not like you have a real choice in the matter. They've got your nads all tied up in so much legal red tape that you're stuck doing what they want unless you want to castrate yourself."

"Colorful language, Ramona Darling."

"Fuck you, Nico Blue. I can be a poet too."

"New song title: *Cock & Ball Torture*. Featuring lyrics by Ramona Darling."

Her laugh was husky and fond. "I love you sober, Nicky."

He scratched his eyebrow with his thumb, watching the sun shatter across the ripples in the pool. "Thanks. I like me sober too."

DIZZY LEAPT OUT of a lavender bush to meet him in the front garden. She rubbed against him and purred like he was her long-lost best friend.

"You're adorable," he whispered, balancing his small box of whoopie pies from Irena's as he knelt down to scritch at her ears. "I wish I'd gotten to know you better, you sweet, fat, murderer."

The front door opened like Jazz had been waiting for him. He wore his black priestly shirt and pants and looked deliciously fuckable. Thank God he'd taken off his collar because that was one fetish Nicky didn't need. Jazz smiled serenely when he saw them coming.

"She left a dead vole for me to find on the back mat. I had to get rid of it. I suppose she still thinks I'm starving, but I don't understand why. I think it's obvious I have enough meat on my bones. How can I convince her that you're the one in need of a good meal?"

"Dizzy, I'd eat your voles, sweetheart. Jasper's a meanie and throws them away." He grinned up at him. "I'm surprised you didn't pass out."

"I am too. There wasn't any blood, which helped."

Nicky stood up while Dizzy continued to wind between his legs. "Hi," he said shyly, offering up the box. "I brought whoopie pies. I figured you still liked them."

"Well, those should help fatten me up. I do still love them. Oh, and Irena's cinnamon rolls, and the fudge that she makes in wintertime too. It makes the bitter cold and driving snow seem momentarily worth it."

Nicky's throat was tight. Jasper's eyes had grown dreamy talking about the goodies from the sweet shop, and he was going to miss that expression already. He'd never be able to look at a whoopie pie, or cinnamon roll, or fudge again without wishing Jazz was there to look blissed-out over it.

"Come here," Jasper said, coming back to himself with a tender glance at Nicky. He held out his hand. "Come inside."

Chapter Twenty

JASPER TOOK THE box and left it on the kitchen counter before suggesting they sit in the living room.

On the sofa, Nicky turned to face him. "Father Jazz, I do believe evil and chaos has been introduced into this house." He pointed at an untidy stack of books on the coffee table.

Jasper grinned. "I knocked them like that when I heard your car pull up. I thought it would make you feel more comfortable."

Nicky couldn't help himself. He grasped Jasper by the back of the neck and pulled him forward, kissing him with the rising wave of affection he couldn't begin to hold back. Jasper didn't push him away, instead bringing his hands up to Nicky's face to hold him steady.

Breathlessly, Nicky finally broke the kiss, his cock hard against the zipper of his jeans and his heart thundering madly. "I'm sorry. I didn't mean to do that."

Jasper's lips shone in the early evening light spilling in from the west-facing windows. A bird called nearby, and the sound of their breathing filled the small space between them. Jasper looked from Nicky's mouth to his eyes, and then leaned forward to kiss him again.

The couch was a surface that seemed impossible to resist, and Nicky went backwards as Jasper pushed him down and climbed on top of him. Then it was hands under clothes, shirts shoved aside, mouths against necks, and hearts hammering hard together as they made out like teenagers on Jasper's sofa.

Yanking down on the collar of Jasper's black shirt, Nicky exposed the dark, flat mole he'd always loved. He pressed a kiss to it and then sucked hard at Jazz's collarbone, bringing up a red mark with sharp satisfaction. That bruise was big enough to last a few days. It was a temporary mark, but it pleased him that it would be there even after he'd gone.

Jasper groaned and pushed their groins together until Nicky gripped his ass in both hands and flipped them over. Their legs and arms knocked together, and Jasper's head bumped the arm of the sofa.

"Mrrow," Dizzy said, jumping from the floor to the cabinet that held the stereo components, and then leaping over to the bookshelf and doing a crazy, hopping monkey climb to the top, where she hid herself behind a large, green vase.

Jasper panted beneath him and they both broke into laughter. "C'mere," Jasper murmured, pulling Nicky back to his mouth. "You taste so good."

"Better than whoopie pies?"

"The best thing I've ever tasted."

They kissed until Jasper was writhing beneath him, and they were both on the edge of coming in their pants like the teenagers they'd once been. Then Nicky scooted down, opening Jasper's slacks and pushing his legs apart, hunching between them and drawing out his cock.

"Ah, it's been…oh, wow, Nicky," Jasper whispered, letting his head fall back, mouth open, staring at the ceiling. "It's been a long time."

Nicky could feel the want, the need, and the sheer anxiety pouring off him. "We don't have to do anything else. We can hold each other. Or…we could tal—"

"No. I'm okay. Will you….I shouldn't be saying this. I realize that this puts you in an awkward—"

"What do you want, Jasper? Just tell me what you want right now."

Jasper's breath pulled in fast and tight. "I would love it if you would please put your mouth on me."

"Oh, baby. I can do that. I can absolutely do that." Nicky worked to get Jasper's pants and underwear off, leaving him with his shirt shoved up, revealing his stomach and cock, which Nicky took in his hand.

Jasper couldn't seem to choose between watching and not watching. He closed his eyes and held his breath, and when Nicky let go of his cock to stroke his palms soothingly down Jasper's thighs, he quivered.

"Shh. It's okay. Are you sure you want me to?"

"Please don't ask me to say it again, Nicky," Jasper whispered. He threw his arm over his eyes. It was so endearing, so sweet and vulnerable, it made Nicky's belly ache in a good way.

He didn't drag it out any longer, taking Jasper's thickness into his hand and pumping gently, admiring the pearl of precome that squeezed out. Jasper gasped, and Nicky leaned forward, licking the tip and following the vein down the side.

He took pity on Jasper before his small sounds of urgency grew louder. Nicky was good at this. He knew he was. He didn't even know how many dicks he'd had in his mouth, but the only dick that had ever mattered was this one, and he was going to make it so good. So very good for Jasper.

Opening his mouth wide, he took in almost all of his length in a slow, seductive push down to Jasper's quivering belly. Pubic hair crinkled against his lips, and the scent of Jasper's musk filled Nicky's nose. He closed his eyes, a warm, tenderness swelling hard inside him as Jasper's thudding, soft-skinned thickness filled his mouth, pressed against his tongue, and slipped down into his throat.

"Oh, Nicky, sweet Nicky," Jasper moaned, threading his fingers into Nicky's hair and holding on. He held very still, letting Nicky move up and down, sucking and pressing his lips firmly around Jasper's shaft. "I'm not going to last."

Nicky didn't care. Jasper could come right away and so long as it was good for him, then Nicky wanted him to have it. He wanted him to have every beautiful thing in the world without waiting. And he wanted to be there to give it to him. Jasper's thighs shook, and his breaths were puffs of air in the quiet of the room, little gasps of disbelief that made Nicky harder than any loudly moaning porn star ever could.

"Nicky, slow down, I'm going to—oh! Ohh!" he tugged Nicky's hair hard and curled up, his breath holding and then releasing in cries of pleasure as Nicky swallowed the bitter taste of his come.

Afterward, Nicky kissed Jasper's softening cock, loving the sticky press of it against his lips. He buried his face in Jasper's pubic hair to breathe in his scent, imprinting it in his memory. Jasper released his hair slowly, and then patted it down again, smoothing it from the wildness he'd clawed it into. "Oh. I didn't…I didn't yank your hair too hard, did I?"

"Uh, no. That was hot as fuck." Nicky wanted to laugh when Jasper ducked his head and a flush rose across his cheekbones, but he held it back.

Jasper stroked Nicky's hair, the back of his neck, and shoulders. He chewed on his lip like he was chewing over thoughts, and Nicky waited.

"Can I…? Let me do you now."

Nicky pressed his face in the place between Jasper's leg and groin, rubbing his cheek against Jasper's cock, making him hiss from the scratch of his stubble. "No, it's okay. I'm okay."

Jasper pulled at his shoulders and started to sit up until Nicky climbed up to lay on top of him, his jeans-covered cock pressing against Jasper's naked hip. Vulnerable, with a tightness in his chest and throat that threatened tears, Nicky wrapped his arms around Jasper, shaking his head. "I don't need to come. I want you to hold me."

Jasper murmured in his ear, some nonsense sounds and another fervent "I love you," before Nicky allowed more kissing. Eventually, he let Jasper open up his fly and push his jeans and boxer-briefs down so that his cock dragged against Jasper's naked skin. Their hips moved together, and Jasper reached down between them, adding his grip for Nicky to thrust into, and it wasn't long before he was trembling, crying out against Jasper's shoulder, and coming on his stomach.

Jasper rubbed Nicky's back and kissed his hair. Nicky closed his eyes, wishing this wasn't going to be so hard—that he didn't have to tell Jasper he was leaving and that he didn't have to hear whatever Jasper said after that.

"Mrrow-row!" Dizzy exclaimed, startling them both. And then she spastically climbed down the bookcase, leapt to the floor, and with a funny series of pounces and leaps, scampered out of the room.

"She's a murderer and a voyeur," Nicky said, laughing softly with Jasper. "You take up with creatures of bad character, Father Jazz."

"Perhaps their character is good, but some of their behaviors have been ill-chosen."

"'Ill-chosen.'" Nicky snorted and propped himself up, looking down at the mess between them. He'd gotten some jizz on his T-shirt too. "You must sound so pompous up there in the pulpit."

"You heard me speak the other day. Do I?"

"No, you sound brilliant and pious and all the things a good priest should be."

Jasper touched the come on his stomach and lifted his fingers, looking at them. "I guess appearances can be deceiving, can't they?"

Nicky sighed and began to sit up. "Let me get something."

"Just use my underwear," Jasper said, gesturing to the floor where they'd kicked off their things.

Nicky grabbed the tighty-whities and mopped up the jizz on both their stomachs and chests. He was tempted to touch Jasper's nipples, to lean over and kiss a trail to his cock and suck the soft head into his mouth again, just to taste it before it all came to a hurting, grinding end.

"I guess we should talk," Nicky said, straightening his clothes and pushing his hair out of his face. "I have something I want to tell you."

Jasper sat up and kissed him again. He reached for his pants and pulled them on without underwear. "Let's clean up and eat dinner first. Have those whoopie pies you brought and pretend for a little longer that we don't have to talk about anything at all."

Nicky studied his face, and then kissed his mouth softly, reaching up to press his thumb into the dimple of Jasper's chin. "I love you."

Jasper's eyes went warm with joy and he kissed Nicky again. "I know."

Nicky laughed and stood up. "All right. We can pretend for a few more hours, but then we have to be grown-ups."

Jasper nodded, smiling down at where he sat rumpled on the sofa. "I know that too. It doesn't make it any easier, though. I feel like I'm about to be grounded for the summer again."

Nicky put his finger on Jasper's lip. "Shh. We're not talking about it yet, remember? What did you pick up for dinner?"

Jasper hauled himself off the sofa, flashing Nicky his gorgeous smile as he tucked his black shirt into his pants. They deserved one more evening of being just them, Nicky decided. Just Nicky and Jazz.

NICKY HAD A little blob of vanilla cream on his cheek, but Jasper wasn't in any hurry to let him know. He was imagining licking it off later, when they were sprawled out on the couch again. If it was winter he'd stoke the fire and lay Nicky out on a rug and be a stereotype until they could stereotype no more.

"Stop it," Nicky said from across the kitchen table.

Jasper blinked and lifted his chin from his palm. "Huh?"

"That come hither look you've got going on. You're not doing my resolve to adult my way through this any good. I want to drag you upstairs and fuck you senseless." Jasper gasped a little as his insides clenched with fear and excitement. "Oh, Jesus, no, not helping," Nicky groaned. "Seriously, stop looking at me like that."

"Sorry." Jasper took a deep breath, sat up straight, and clasped his hands in his lap. With a start he realized this was the closest he'd come to private prayer in days. He reached for the coffee decanter between them and filled up their mugs. "Okay, I'm listening."

Nicky raked his fingers through his hair and looked down at his plate. There was half a whoopie pie left and he dragged his finger through the cream before putting it into his mouth. Jasper tried not to stare, but then Nicky looked him into the eye, determined. Strong. Afraid.

"I have to go back," he said.

Jasper nodded and waited, but Nicky said nothing else. "Yes, I know eventually you'd have to and we'll—"

"No." Nicky reached across and grabbed Jasper's hands so hard his nails dug into his flesh. "Jasper, I have to go back tomorrow."

Jasper's ears began to ring. He opened his mouth but no sound came out. Nicky's grip eased, and he soothed the sting of his nails with his thumb. "Tomorrow?" Jasper managed. "I don't understand. Why?"

"The big assholes got tired of waiting. We get into the studio to make that album or we get sued until they own the blood in our veins. We have no choice."

"But—" *You're not well enough*, Jasper wanted to say, but honestly he didn't know if that was the truth. Nicky was a lot stronger than he'd given him credit for. The addiction wasn't some weakness, some lack of willpower that could only be cured by staying away from the drugs. It was an illness and Nicky was being treated for it. *And yet*. "What—what about the others? Are they okay with going back already?"

"Ramona is, but she never had a problem to begin with. Sez and Mick…" Nicky dropped their eye contact and tried to let go, but Jasper turned his hands palm up and thread their fingers together. "I have no clue. I haven't talked to them since I left. I'm guessing Sez could possibly be okay, but Mick…" Nicky shrugged. "Management won't care if we're okay or not. They want an album."

He had to ask. "What about you? Will you be okay?"

"If you'd asked me that two weeks ago I'd have said no. But I think…I think yeah, maybe I'll be okay."

"Ramona will be a good friend to you?"

Nicky snorted. "Oh yeah, she'll kick my ass if I try to use again."

"But who will be there for you when you feel the need to use? Who will you talk to?"

A burst of naked fear flashed behind Nicky's eyes and then it was gone. "Will you?" he asked softly. "I mean I know that this…" He waved a hand between them and his face twisted. "This was never going to last. But it would mean a lot if I could call you every once in a while."

"Every day," Jasper said, holding tight to Nicky's hands. "I want to hear from you every day. Even if it's just a text. Or a one minute call. I want to know you're okay." Jasper's voice broke on the last word and he pulled a hand away and covered his mouth. Nicky stood so fast his chair tipped over, and then he was there, clutching Jasper's shoulders, holding him close. Jasper clung to his waist and buried his face in Nicky's T-shirt. "I thought we'd have more time," he whispered.

"Me too. But Jazz, you have to know this was never going to be a forever thing. It's a…an interlude. And now we've got to go back to our real lives. It was good while we had it and I still want to be friends. I'll be fine if we can be friends."

Jasper sharply lifted his head and looked at Nicky. He was lying. "Take me upstairs," he whispered. "What you said earlier. I want that. I want you to do that."

Nicky went very still. He cupped the back of Jasper's neck and stared into his eyes for a long time. Dozens of emotions flickered over his face, none lingering long enough to decipher, until at last there was something that looked very much like acceptance and desperation. Jasper thought his own face pretty much reflected the same.

"Then let me hear you say it, baby," Nicky said. His voice had gone low and thick, husky with a hint of tears.

Jasper swallowed, still trapped in Nicky's gaze, caught in the palms of his hands. *Nowhere I'd rather be.* With a shaky voice he whispered, "I want you to fuck me, Nicky."

They didn't say anything on their trek upstairs. Nicky left the lights off in the bedroom. They stood on either side of the bed and looked at each other. Nicky didn't say anything but Jasper heard his questions anyway. He nodded. *Yes, I'm sure.*

Nicky stripped off his T-shirt and jeans, eased his boxers down, and tossed his socks aside. There was no artifice to it, no seduction—just a clinical getting naked so they could get to the fucking. Jasper shivered, and Nicky knee-walked across the mattress and gently kissed him.

"Now I can concentrate on you," he whispered. "How do you want to do this?" Jasper opened his mouth but again his voice failed him. He shrugged helplessly and Nicky smiled softly. "Okay baby, I got you."

He slipped his fingertips over the buttons of Jasper's shirt and undid them. There should've been something unholy about being undressed from his priestly outfit like this, but all it felt was right. Obediently, Jasper held out his arms and let Nicky strip him naked, piece by piece. He couldn't stop trembling, no matter how kindly Nicky soothed him and kissed him and caressed him. The last of the setting sun filled the room and a hidden part of him wanted the curtains closed to the world. But there was no one out there who could see, and he liked the look of the sweet fading light on Nicky's skin.

"Get on the bed," Nicky said, when Jasper was finally naked. "I think on your front will be easier for you."

Jasper nodded and obeyed. He lowered himself down onto his pillow and made a shivery, helpless moan when Nicky grabbed the other pillow and put it under Jasper's hips.

"Do you have lube or anything like that? Do you want a condom?"

"I don't have either," Jasper managed. The skin on his back jumped when Nicky caressed his spine.

"I was tested at the clinic and came out negative for everything, but we still shouldn't do it without one. And we definitely shouldn't do this without real lube, Jazz."

"I want it to be just you, Nicky. Just you and me. The tests say you're fine. And how about suntan lotion? Olive oil? I have both of those. Or I do have some Vaseline."

Nicky hummed and stroked Jasper's flanks and hips. "That'd work, but it requires some extra clean-up. You okay with that?"

Jasper hid his face into the pillow and nodded. He was doing this. He was really going to do this.

"Are you sure about the condom? I might have one in my wallet, but..."

"I'm sure," Jasper said, and his voice came out a little sharper than he meant, but Nicky soothed his sides.

"All right. Where's the Vaseline, baby? I'll go grab it."

"In the bathroom. Medicine cabinet."

Nicky lowered himself down and covered Jasper's body with his. "You going to freak out while I'm gone?"

Yes. "No."

Nicky laughed softly against the back of Jasper's neck as if he knew exactly what he'd been thinking. "I'll be right back." He stroked Jasper's spine all the way down to his ass and let his finger slip between his buttocks.

Jasper closed his eyes and tried to remember his *pranayama* breathing from yoga. It helped to calm his mind, but his body still shook by the time Nicky came back. He looked glorious in the sunset, like the rock god he was.

Jasper shifted a little so he could stretch out an arm and reach for him. "Nicky..."

"I'm here. I got the condom, too. I'd feel better if we use it." He kissed Jasper, soothed him with his hands, then gently pried his thighs apart and climbed back on the bed to settle between them. "Tell me if you want me to stop and I will, okay? Otherwise let me take care of you."

Nicky kissed the dimples on either side of Jasper's back, and he shuddered out a breath into the pillow. His fingers were cramping around the sheets. The tear of the condom wrapper and the click of the Vaseline lid was loud in the quiet room, and Jasper tried to control his stilted breathing as his entire universe narrowed down to the space between his legs.

This isn't the first time, he told himself. Even yesterday, Nicky—He gasped and lost his train of thought when Nicky held his buttocks apart with one hand. He'd tried to warm the Vaseline but it was still a cold shock when Nicky touched his hole.

"Breathe, baby," Nicky murmured. Jasper nodded and closed his eyes. They were dry and itchy and he squeezed them until red fireworks danced behind his eyelids. He breathed slow and deep, reaching for that trancelike state he sometimes found in yoga, and managed to take the first of Nicky's fingers without too much of a fight. "Yeah, there you go, look at you." Nicky let go of Jasper's cheeks and rubbed his lower back gently. "How's that? Good?"

Jasper nodded. Nicky stayed away from Jasper's prostate, and Jasper breathed a little easier. He didn't think he could take that electrifying shock of pleasure yet. With a slow, easy pace, Nicky pushed in and out of him, no tricks, no aim to please, only a soft glide to open him up.

"Ready for another one?"

"Yeah," Jasper whispered. He kept breathing and felt the sting, heard Nicky shush him and tried to relax. He lost himself for a little bit to the care Nicky was taking, to the sounds of the night drifting through the window, and the rhythm of his own breathing. Maybe Nicky said something—maybe he imagined it—but he knew when Nicky sat back on his heels and sheathed his cock. He tried not to breathe harder, but didn't quite manage it.

This was going to happen. He was going to do this. His heartbeat kicked up a notch like it did when he reached the halfway point of the hill on his run. It rang hollow in his chest. He tried to breathe through. No one had been with him like this since he was seventeen years old. He was falling in love with Nicky all over again, and if he did this, if he went this far, there'd be no going back. *Oh God.*

But he wanted it. Nicky was leaving. Maybe not coming back for a long time—if ever. He had to…he… Jasper looked over his shoulder and saw Nicky poised above him, hair wild and a soft sheen of sweat sparkling like diamonds on his skin. The sunburn had faded to a mellow tan and he looked so good Jasper's heart couldn't contain it. Nicky had a hand on his cock—and it was glorious and hard, and oh so frightening. He lifted up and leaned on Jasper's back.

"Can you lift your hips a bit, baby? Maybe get on all fours for now." Shaking, Jasper did what he was told. First he let his head hang between his arms, but he had to see. He had to see Nicky. "Oh yeah, holy fuck." Nicky bit his lip and his eyes burned like coals as he stared at Jasper's hole. "That's the sweetest sight I've ever seen."

The blunt pressure of Nicky's cock forced an undignified sound out of Jasper's throat, and Nicky immediately stopped.

"You okay?"

"Yes."

"All right, relax. I won't hurt you."

Jasper tried. He really did. He closed his eyes, dropped to his elbows, and rested his forehead against the pillow. But when Nicky pushed against his rim and made it part he couldn't—he couldn't let go. He wanted to, so badly he could taste the need; the ache. He wanted to feel the discomfort tomorrow when Nicky was gone, along with the pain of missing him.

He tried to wipe his mind of all thought. He willed his body to relax. His arms gave out, and so did his knees. Jasper sank into the mattress and Nicky slipped deeper.

"Jazz," Nicky groaned. "Fuck, you feel so…Jasper?" Nicky stilled and lifted Jasper's hair off his forehead. With one finger he traced the salty path of a single tear. "Oh, no baby. No, not like this." He took such great care to remove his cock from Jasper's body, Jasper was afraid he'd really start crying. "Hey. Hey, it's okay. I love that you want to do this for me, but I don't need it. All I need is you, right here, with me tonight. Jasper, look at me, please."

He opened his eyes and saw Nicky there, his face bright like a shining star, and Jasper reached for him. They lay tangled like that for a long time, with Nicky gently stroking Jasper's sweaty back.

Chapter Twenty-One

"WHEN'S YOUR FLIGHT?" Jasper asked, smoothing his hands over Nicky's chest like he was cleaning off lint or cat hair that wasn't there.

"Four-thirty." Standing in Jasper's room, he took hold of Jasper's hands and twined their fingers together. "Hey, it's a clean shirt. You just pulled it out of your drawer. It's fine."

"I know. I need to touch you."

Nicky pulled Jasper into a hug and rested his head against Jasper's shoulder. "Me too."

"Does your mom know yet?"

Nicky shook his head. "Figured I'd do it like ripping off a Band-Aid. Fast. No time to try to talk me out of it."

Jasper moved back to see Nicky's face but didn't let go of him. "She's not going to like that."

"Good thing she's had a lot of practice at not liking what I do." Nicky touched Jasper's chin, thumbing the dimple. "I was serious the other night when I said I wanted to fund Lizzie's transition, and Gus's too, but especially Lizzie's."

"I know you meant it. It's very expensive—"

"We talked that out already. Make it happen. Have my father draw up papers, get whatever permission from whatever judge, and get that girl on hormone therapy for fuck's sake. I'll pay the bill."

"Thank you. I wish you were going to tell her yourself."

Nicky shook his head and looked away. "Don't tell her it was me. Just let her know that someone out there gave enough fucks to make sure she gets the care she deserves, all right?"

"I'm going to let you do this, of course, but you can't fund the transition of every child that comes through Blue Oasis."

"I can try."

Jasper kissed his knuckles. "You're a good man, Nicky."

Dizzy leapt onto a window sill nearby, and Nicky broke free from Jasper's grasp.

"This isn't goodbye," Jasper insisted.

"No. Not unless you want it to be. And you can change your mind later. We've both got shit we need to do right now to figure out where we fit. If we fit."

"We'll always fit."

"My romantic little fox." He stood on his toes to kiss Jasper's nose, and then rubbed his lips against the stubble by his chin. "I hope you're right, but if it turns out your puzzle doesn't need a recovering junkie rocker in it, I'll understand." *No. Please, God, if you exist, let him want me always as a friend.*

Jasper huffed. "What if you get out to L.A. and realize that a priest who can't tell you what he wants right this second doesn't fit into your puzzle? It's not all up to me."

"No, it's not. I get to choose too." He smiled. "I'll always choose you."

"Not over your music."

"Over making albums, over touring, over Los Angeles, over being famous or rich." He looked into his eyes. "But I won't ruin us by trying to make you leave the priesthood, Jazz. I fucking won't."

Jasper's eyes burned brighter. "Promise you'll call me if you get in a situation where you feel like you can't resist. Promise you won't—that you'll—that you *will* call me."

"Okay."

"Badger and Fox promise."

Nicky laughed and crossed his heart, spit in his hand, and wiped it on the front of Jasper's shirt. "I promise."

Jasper nodded. "Okay, good." He looked down at his shirt. "Whose idea was this spit-wiping promise, anyway?"

"Mine."

Jasper laughed. "Even at nine you had a crush on me, didn't you?"

"That was no crush. It was full-on love. And I wanted to put my mouth on you so badly—somewhere, anywhere. Wiping my spit on you seemed like a viable alternative."

"Marking me."

Nicky touched the place on Jasper's collar bone where, beneath his shirt, a dark red love bite bloomed. "Yeah."

"Nicky—"

"I should go. The longer we drag it out, the more it's going to suck."

"Like a Band-Aid."

"You have my number," Nicky said. "Use it."

"There's FaceTime and texts. We'll stay in touch."

"Sure."

Jasper reached and wrapped his arms around Nicky hard. "I need to know that you know how much I love you."

"I do."

"And?"

Nicky laughed against his hair. "I love you too, baby."

Then he pried himself away and forced himself to walk to his car without looking back. He was afraid if he did, he'd run back to Jasper's arms and refuse to leave.

JASPER GROUND HIS teeth together so hard a headache began to flare from the back of his skull. He pressed the office phone to his ear harder when Mrs. Wells's shadow appeared in the frosted glass door. She knocked briskly and stepped inside, but he shook his head at her before she'd begun to talk. Her eyes widened a little and she paused, then mouthed, *it's urgent* before leaving. Jasper had time to notice she looked pale and grave, and he wished he was allowed to swear.

"Unacceptable," Archbishop Ramsey was saying. "He's a drug addict, for crying out loud! My assistant checked some of his music and the songs are an abomination! They are a direct attack on God." *No,* Jasper thought, *they're an attack on me.* "And you let him sing to those children. He cannot be allowed to interact with them again. They're already sinners—"

"As you said." Jasper couldn't keep quiet any longer. His heart beat too fast from the three cups of coffee he'd drunk after two sleepless nights, and it only amplified the unease and crushing guilt that crawled under the surface of his skin. "They're children."

"Their lifestyle choices will lead them down a path of sin. Much like your own would've done if you hadn't been called to God. I've expressed my doubts to Bishop Murray of having someone like you be in charge of children like that, and all I'm seeing after those pictures with that man is my doubts justified. Blue Oasis should be a shelter for all homeless children, not just the ones you feel an affinity with."

Jasper squeezed his eyes closed. He had to fight back, to stand up for himself and the kids in his care, but his brain couldn't function. He was filled with self-doubt, a sinister little voice suggesting that maybe Archbishop Ramsey was right.

He tried anyway. "Children who are gay, lesbian or trans run a far greater risk of ending up on the streets—kicked out there by their own parents. They face more bullying in foster homes and they're passed through the system a lot more often. I showed you all these figures when I proposed the opening of Blue Oasis seven years ago. These kids run a bigger risk of ending up in prostitution, or as drug addicts, or both."

"If the school was run with an iron hand a zero tolerance toward bullying, that wouldn't be a problem."

Unless it's the iron hand that does the bullying. His phone buzzed in his pocket, but he ignored it for now. "I've showed you research—"

The archbishop didn't let him finish. His voice had dropped from the loud righteous rant to a low, no-nonsense tone that scared Jasper more. "Let me set this straight, Father Hendricks. The future of Blue Oasis is hanging by a precarious thread. If you allow that Nico Blue back into the building, I will sever that thread in an instant. Do I make myself clear?"

Jasper's chest tightened like a snake had wrapped itself around him. His fingers shook against the old wooden grain of the desk, and he watched tiny dust particles dance in the beams of sunlight that fell through the slightly grimy window. He could easily tell Ramsey that Nicky was gone and probably wouldn't be back any time soon, but why should he?

Jasper closed his eyes and rubbed his chest. Nicky had to come back. He was safe here. But that wasn't Jasper's call to make.

"Crystal clear," Jasper gritted out. The connection broke. He set the phone down slowly. What could he do? Nothing was worth the safety of these kids. He'd give up everything he owned to keep this place open. The thought of Blue Oasis closing made him feel sick to his stomach.

Mrs. Wells needed him urgently but instead of going to see her, he picked up the phone again.

It only rang twice before he was met with a cheery, "Hello?"

"Thomas, it's Jasper. Can you come to the church this morning? I'd like to do a confession."

A startled silence followed. Had it really been that long since he'd confessed? Jasper was far from perfect. He was driven by pride at the worst times and he'd let himself become complacent and distracted.

"Sure," Thomas said. "But I can come to your office at Blue Oasis, if you want. You're not back at the church again until tomorrow morning, right?"

"Not this time, Thomas." Jasper squeezed his eyes closed and swallowed past the fear in his chest. "I—I need the confessional."

The silence felt charged and it made the hairs on Jasper's nape rise. *Right where Nicky caressed you and held you and kissed you.*

"Jasper?" Thomas asked gently. "Is everything all right? I heard the Archbishop was pretty angry about those leaked pictures, but—"

"Yes, I'm fine." He took a shuddery breath and thought of Nicky about to take off on an airplane right now. "Actually, no. I'm not really."

"I can be there in an hour. Will that do?"

"Yes." Jasper sighed but he didn't feel any relief. He felt torn in two directions and neither were a road he could possibly take. Where did that leave him? He said goodbye to Thomas and lifted his phone out of his pocket. Two messages from Nicky.

About to take off so no more texting.

I miss you already.

There was a new little scratch on his screen and he wondered when it had happened. When he'd tossed the phone in the boat without second thought and dove after Nicky like he had no other choice? He could've taken the boat out instead and hauled Nicky in it before returning them both home safely, integrity intact.

You didn't do anything you didn't want to do, Jasper thought. He picked up his phone.

I miss you too. Have a safe flight.

The message didn't deliver. Nicky was probably in the air. He'd send it again later. He took a moment to compose himself and then stood, feeling shaky.

Mrs. Wells's office was closed so he knocked gently and waited for her, "Enter."

A small shape sat in oversized clothes in one chair and Mrs. Wells sat beside it, holding a small, dark hand.

"Keshaun? This is Father Hendricks, although I think the kids are calling him Father Jazz these days."

The boy lifted his head and turned around. Jasper had to do everything in his power to keep his expression under control and he stepped forward to kneel beside the boy. He would do whatever it took to keep Blue Oasis LGBTQ only. Whatever it took.

"Nice to meet you Keshaun," he said, and because he couldn't ignore it, "Are you okay?"

Keshaun glanced at Mrs. Wells and nodded once.

"A foster brother found out he's gay," she said. "You're looking at the result. The social worker called me this morning and I picked him up straight from the ER."

"Well." Jasper tried to look past the black eye, the swollen cheekbone, the stitches on his forehead and the missing tooth. No doubt the ill-fitting clothes hid a whole other world of pain. "Welcome home, Keshaun. How about we show you to your room and you can get settled in for a little while. On Mondays in the summer holiday, Mrs. Wells sets up an art class for those who are interested. It starts at eleven, and then I'll be around for lunch again. Does that sound good?" Keshaun nodded. "If you don't feel up to socializing yet, I understand."

"No, I'd like to come. They're all…the others…?" Keshaun looked at Jasper with his one good eye full of hope and fear.

"Like you?" Jasper asked softly. Keshaun nodded. "Yes. Everyone here, excluding Mrs. Wells, is either gay, lesbian, transgender, or bisexual, or any combination thereof."

"Even…?"

Jasper smiled. "Even me? Yes."

"Okay." Keshaun looked down, and Jasper saw a single tear fall to the boy's knee. He looked like a ten-year-old, but Jasper guessed he was more a malnourished fourteen-year-old.

"You hungry, Keshaun? We can make a detour to the kitchen and check out the fridge." Jasper leaned in and whispered, "I have a terrible sweet tooth."

Keshaun didn't laugh, but he looked less sad when he nodded and stood.

"After you, Father," Mrs. Wells said, and she too looked a little teary-eyed. "Off to raid the fridge, and then I was thinking the room at the end of the third floor would work nicely."

Because of the kids' orientations it seemed a little silly to keep the halls separate by gender, so they were all mixed together. Boys and girls and those who identified to certain genders flocked to the same bathrooms anyway. The room Mrs. Wells was talking about would be beside Lizzie. It had a great western exposure, with an amazing view of the town and the bay beyond it. On clear days the sunsets were mind-blowing. "Yes," Jasper said. "That would work very well."

While Mrs. Wells helped Keshaun pile up a plate full of food, Jasper fingered his phone, his thumb hovering over a text to Adrian. He hesitated and put his phone away again. Not yet. He'd talk to Thomas first.

Jasper walked to the church and nodded to the people he met on the way. The sky was stark blue, not a cloud in sight, and the tall spire of the neo-Gothic building rose high and dizzying above him. Jasper fingered the wooden doorframe before he entered the church, but the usual rush of gratitude and peace didn't come.

It was cool inside, and he fought the urge to unbutton the collar of his shirt. The white strip felt suffocating, like a heavy weight around his neck. Not about to fool himself this time, he realized he was feeling the lingering longing for Nicky; the wish to be near him, to have the immediate gratification of being needed by someone else and being free to need in return.

All these years. Did I fool myself, or is this, like Nicky said, an interlude? Will this longing and pain fade like it did when we were seventeen? Or will I learn to live with it? Did it ever fade? He tilted his head and stared up into the rafters of the gorgeous nave. Here too, the sun reached him and he tried to feel God's scorn, but there was nothing.

"Father."

He jolted and turned to see Thomas standing behind him. "Thomas." He sighed in relief at the sight of his mentor.

"Are you all right? You look exhausted."

"Yes. I just…" He buried his face in his hands and shook his head. "I don't know." Thomas put his hand on Jasper's shoulder, and the weight of it comforted him. He'd been so starved of touch for so long. How could he learn to live without it again?

"You sure you need the confessional?" Thomas asked him gently.

"Yes—" Jasper began, but stopped himself. He only wanted it so he could hide behind the grid. No more hiding. "No. We can do it here."

Thomas nodded once and gently guided Jasper into one of the pews. "Tell me what's wrong. Take all the time you need."

Jasper tucked his hands between his knees. "Do you remember that old lover I told you about?"

"Yes, of course."

"I…I gave in to temptation." Jasper waited for a reaction, but none came. Thomas watched him steadily. "It was…this weekend. I know it sounds weak, but I couldn't have stopped it any more than an oncoming train. I-I love him. I think I always did." Jasper glanced at Thomas. His expression was grave, but he didn't look angry or shocked.

When he didn't go on, Thomas said, "You wouldn't be the first priest to stray from the path of virtue, Jasper. Not even the first to do it with a man. All that matters is where you want to go from here on out. Are you repentant?"

Jasper chewed the inside of his cheek. His eyes found a painting of Christ nailed to the cross. Even in his excruciating pain, he gazed lovingly upon Mother Mary. Jasper shook his head, and this time he did hear Thomas's soft inhale. "I can't regret it, Thomas. I've struggled with it, but not in the way I should have. It hurts me that I've broken my vow. It hurts me that I did it so easily. But I can't renounce my love for Nicky."

"Not at all?"

"No."

"Not even if it meant being defrocked?"

Jasper winced and closed his eyes. He hadn't expected Thomas to be so blunt about it, but there was no doubt in his mind. His voice didn't waver when he whispered, "No."

There was a long silence, and eventually he opened his eyes again to look at Thomas, who was remarkably smiling softly.

"And somewhere a rooster crowed," Thomas murmured. "The decision is yours, Jasper. You know you won't be able to keep Blue Oasis as part of the Church. You know you will never be able to love a person the way you wish to love your friend while you are part of the Church. All you can do is think if it's worth giving up what you have. Ask yourself, what do you like the most about being a priest?"

"I like reading Mass," Jasper said.

"Why?"

"I like spreading God's word, but that's not all of it. I like having the parishioners' attention. I like when they listen to me." He covered his face and laughed. "Vanity. I'll never be free of it, will I?"

"Like I said, everyone has their faults, Jasper. But what is it you love about your job? What makes it all feel worthwhile?"

"Blue Oasis. No question. Those kids need me."

Thomas gave him a quirky smile. "You mean they need the shelter. And right now you're the shelter's only hope. God calls to everyone, and some hear him loud and clear—like you. But that doesn't mean we've deciphered his whole message in one go. He keeps calling us, and sometimes he might guide us down an unexpected path." Thomas rubbed his palms over his knees. "I'm too old to be sitting on these benches." He rose to his feet and clapped Jasper on the shoulder. "God works—"

"Don't say it."

"In mysterious ways." Thomas grinned and his eyes twinkled. "Maybe this was His plan all along." He sobered a little. "You have a lot of thinking to do, Jasper. And you may need to do it fast. But don't be hasty, and know that whatever you decide, I will always respect you and support you. In me, you have a friend for life."

Jasper lifted his face and smiled. "Thank you. That means a lot." Thomas nodded and without another word, he was off.

THE SUNSET FROM the back of Ramona's beachside cottage in Malibu was mind-blowing. Nicky tried and failed to take photos that could capture the complexity of the layers of color and light. He sent one to his parents anyway with a message saying: *Maybe before long I'll get my own place on the water and you could come visit. See the sunsets for yourselves.*

He'd wanted to send the same message to Jazz, but didn't want it to seem like he was trying to tempt or lure him away from carefully considering what he really wanted. Instead, he sent a shot of the sunset with the words: *Cool, huh? Ramona's backyard.*

"Pretty boy, get your tiny ass over here and help me figure out what these knobs on this gas grill mean. I can barely deal with the ones on the stove. I mean, Jesus, do I look like a cook to you?"

Nicky snorted and headed over to help Ramona with the steaks they'd picked up at the all-organic supermarket on the way home from the airport. As they sat down to a dinner of meat and salad on her very beachy, sand-strewn back patio, they didn't talk too much, listening to the waves as the tide went out. There was a gentle white noise in the rhythm that allowed Nicky's brain to switch off, and he dwelled in a quiet place in his mind, where song lyrics and music swept by like clouds in the sky.

Finally, Ramona toyed with her bottle of Mexican Coke, and said, "Let's get this part over with. You can stay here as long as you want, so long as you're clean."

"Thanks. Being here will help with that."

"Cool. Also, don't put your shoes on my coffee table. I dumped my last lover for that shit."

"Fair enough. I'm not a big shoes-on-coffee-table perp anyway."

She grinned. "Because you had a mama that raised you right. Speaking of, how's your mother? I know you were worried about how she'd take you coming back here."

Nicky sighed, recalling the scene at the airport. "She was brave about it. It was my dad who cried actually." His phone dinged and he looked at the message. "Her ears must have been burning."

"What's she say?"

"Here." He handed her the phone.

Your dad and I would love to come visit, but it won't be for the sunsets. We love and miss you very much, sweet baby.

Ramona lifted her brow at him as she passed the phone back his way. "Aww. She loves you a lot. You better stay sober for her, dude."

"I'll stay sober for me." He cleared his throat and pushed his hair out of his eyes. "I should get a haircut. It's been since, God, maybe Miami."

"Since fucking Miami?" She laughed. "Jesus. Whatever, you look adorable. Everyone likes that moppy-haired, emo-eyed pretty boy look. Just keep rockin' it." She smoothed her hands over her own close-cropped head. "Now, we should talk music. And, a little later, after the food has digested and we've walked on the beach, we should go jam and see what we can show up with for the studio tomorrow. But for now, I need the scoop."

Nicky shook his head. "I don't know what you're talking about."

"Your priest. Tell me about all the blessings he bestowed on you." She laughed and then softened considerably. "Actually, no. Tell me how you're doing after leaving him. Really."

"I miss him. He hasn't texted and I don't fucking know why. But I can guess."

"And that makes you want to…? Shoot up? Kill yourself? Get a plane back to him?"

"None of the above. Okay, a little of the above. But mainly I want to know he's okay. I didn't mean to cause him any trouble."

"Well, what time is it there? Maybe he's already asleep and there isn't any trouble at all. You're worried for nothing."

"My mother is still awake."

"She's a mother. Mothers worry. Priests pray on their troubles and then drift into a peaceful fucking sleep. Well, probably. I don't know any priests..." Ramona trailed off, sitting back and pushing her finished plate away. She said nothing else, staring off into the lowering darkness. Finally, she put her hands on the table and pushed herself up. "Let's go on a walk. Then we'll make some music about love, okay?"

"Sounds good."

The next morning there was a message from Jasper but it wasn't very forthcoming.

Beautiful backyard. Reminds me of the sunset on the cove.

Nicky hadn't had time to reply. Their call time at the studio was early, and he'd had to head out with his head still fuzzy with sleep.

Everything at the studio was weird. Nicky couldn't remember the last time he'd seen Sez and Mick sober, and they seemed a little freaked out to be in each other's presence not-high too. If they'd been fucking before rehab, it seemed pretty clear they weren't fucking now, and neither of them seemed to know what to say to the other.

"Hey," Sez said, sitting down next to Nicky. "'Sup?"

"Wishing I had Mary Fender, but she's at my house."

Sez tilted his head, confused. "You forgot her?"

"Nah. I haven't been back there since I left it before the tour. Seems like a bad idea, you know?"

Sez shot a glance toward Mick and shrugged. "Maybe, yeah. My place is weird now, too."

"Yeah." Nicky looked over where Mick was shoving hair out of his eyes and sending wounded glances Sez's way. "I think I'm going to let the lease go. Stay with Ramona for a while and when I'm feeling good enough, find a new place. Get a fresh start."

"Yeah, man. What about Mary Fender and Princess Takamine and all the rest of your guitars?"

"Ramona said she'd take me to get what I need tonight." All he had at the moment was his father's Takamine, given to him at the airport with teary eyes and a bear hug. He'd been reluctant to bring it to the studio. It seemed dangerous somehow, like being in the place could make the guitar unclean. But it sat calmly across his knee and the fretboard soothed his fingertips.

"We won't be laying any track today, anyway," Sez said. "Just figuring shit out. Got any songs for us?"

"A few."

"Cool." He caught Mick's eye and then shook his head fast, looking away and back to Nicky. "Wanna get a beer after? I don't want go home."

Nicky glanced toward Mick, who was eyeing them jealously. "Sorry, dude. Not drinking anymore. I didn't think you were either."

Sez frowned. "Fuck, I'm not. Easy to forget, huh?"

"I guess."

"Well, how about we head down to Tats & Cat's Coffee. Coffee and new sobriety tattoos. Sounds like a good night, yeah?"

"Yeah." *Not really.* "But like I said, Ramona's taking me to get Mary Fender, and then we'll head back to her place." He didn't really want to offer, because he'd enjoyed being at Ramona's house alone. It was comfortable and quiet, and she liked to stare off into space with him, listening to the ocean waves. Sez had always been more frantic than that. Still… "You could come to her place. Hang there if you don't want to be alone."

"Oh, I wouldn't be fucking alone," Sez snarled. "*He*'ll be camped out on my front porch again, scratching at the door and begging for me to let him in. And I can't do that. I can't fuck him sober."

Nicky swallowed the harsh swell of awkwardness that came up his throat. "Oh. I, um, I…"

"Fuck it. I need to deal with him, I guess."

"Yeah, that's…yeah." Nicky pulled a stack of papers he'd photocopied from a notebook he'd filled on the plane from home. "Here. These are the lyrics. I've made some notations for melody and key."

Sez took them and stood, heading into a corner to sing softly to himself, making his own marks on the pages.

Nicky met Ramona's eye where she sat at the drum kit, and she gave him a wide-eyed well-that-was-fucked-up stare.

Management had left them mostly alone. When the sound engineers were settled in their booth, ready to sit back and record whatever proto-songs they worked out today, and once Mick had his bass tuned and ready to go, Nicky turned to them all.

"I don't know about you guys, but if we're going to be here—and really we have no choice about that—I want to make a damn hot album. The last few have sucked, and we all know why." He looked at Sez and then at Mick. "I was worried at first that my new medications would fuck me up too much to make music. Then I was scared that being *better* and almost happy would ruin it too. But I'm not going to talk myself out of doing this. Fear isn't going to stop me."

"Stop *us*," Ramona said, rolling her eyes.

"Any of us. We're going to dive off the board—" He cut his eyes at Ramona and grinned cheekily. "And hope we remember how to fucking swim."

"Stealing my inspirational speeches, huh?"

He picked up his dad's guitar, hit a chord, and said, "Sez, this is the one on top. 'Fall or Dive.' Mick, whenever you're ready come in with a bass line. Sez, feel free to experiment with the vocal melody. Ramona, count it off."

She clacked her sticks together. "One, two—a one, two, three, four!"

Chapter Twenty-Two

"HEY."

One syllable, and the weight of the world dropped off Jasper's shoulders. He sank back into his office chair like he was suddenly made of liquid. "Nicky. It's so good to hear your voice."

"Yeah, same. I'm…how are you doing?"

"Things are…a bit crazy here. How about you? What's it like being back?"

"Weird. I mean, we fell into recording and stuff pretty easily, but we keep staring at each other like deer caught in headlights because suddenly we're all these sober people with feelings and thoughts and mistakes we have to face instead of selfish drones, you know?"

"Yeah." Jasper laughed a little. "Actually, no, I don't know at all. But you're doing okay? I…I sent you a text yesterday afternoon but you were already on the plane. I don't think it came through."

Nicky made a small noise and Jasper pressed the phone tighter to his ear. He didn't want to miss anything. He wished he could see Nicky. Maybe next time they could FaceTime. "Yeah? You texted me yesterday?"

"Yes. I should've tried again before this morning. I'm sorry."

"No, it's good. It's fine. How's BO? How's Lizzie?"

"She saw through my good Samaritan tale like it was nothing. She knows it's you, Nicky. And she's ecstatic. You'll never know exactly what a difference you made to that girl. I wish you could've seen it. She's intent on thanking you in person and I'm sorta worried I should be jealous."

Nicky was silent for a breath, then he whispered, "Never."

Jasper closed his eyes and smiled. "No?"

"No." Nicky fell silent, but Jasper could tell he wanted to ask something. He didn't, though. "So yeah, things here are weird but cautiously good? I realized I didn't really know Mick and Sez at all. Or Ramona either, but I think she'll end up being a good friend. I don't know about the other two. They seem to have some fucked-up issues of their own."

Jasper frowned. "What kind of issues?"

"The 'I'm straight when I'm sober but gay for you when I'm high' kind of issues."

"Oh. Yeah, I could see how that's problematic."

Nicky snorted. "I have to say, I expected you to be more upset, I guess."

"I'm so glad to hear your voice. I can't…I don't think I can be without you in my life anymore."

"Ah, Jazz," Nicky whispered. "Don't say that when I can't be there."

"It's true though. I told Thomas. The bishop. I confessed."

"Oh my God."

He heard bedsprings squeak and he wondered where Nicky was. Still in Ramona's house? Or a hotel room? It was early in California. Jasper hoped he was with Ramona but if he wasn't…he trusted Nicky and believed in his strength.

"Oh my God, are you okay?" Nicky asked.

"Yes, it was a really enlightening talk, actually. He made me understand there is no way I can save BO—I mean Blue Oasis—as long as I work for the Church. And he also told me there is no harm in loving you, if that's how I feel. I thought about it long and hard, and I know God won't hold it against me." The Church and the parish however…

"Jazz…what are you saying?"

"I'm saying I can't be a priest and stand by and see the Church destroy these kids. And I can't—I can't not love you, Nicky. I just can't. You're in my soul."

"Jesus. Jesus, I—oh my God."

Jasper heard Nicky sniff, and his throat felt tight. "I'm sorry if I upset you," he whispered. "Are you alone? Where are you staying?"

"I'm with Ramona and I'm not upset. I'm happy, you asshole. Fuck. Shit. At this rate, I'll be writing lyrics for Celine fucking Dion." Jasper heard him take a few shuddery breaths. "I can't come back home for a while, obviously, and I know we can't make any promises, and you might change your mind—"

"I'm not going to change my mind."

"Really? Fuck, are you sure? Because I don't know if I can afford to look forward to this, to have hope, and then have it not pan out. I think I'll just pretend you're still thinking about it, okay? It's safer."

"If that's what you need to do, but I'm not changing my mind, Nicky."

"Right. Not changing your mind. Um, but you've given me something to look forward to. Like I haven't had in a long time. I love you, okay? But, uh, I gotta go now because I'm full of all these big fucking feelings, and, shit, I don't know what to do with them. Maybe run or something. I gotta get myself together. Fuck, I'm gonna cry."

"Okay, Nicky," Jasper whispered, his own eyes filling. "I love you too."

"I know." He sniffed again.

They hung up, and Jasper picked up his phone again. It rang twice and went through to Adrian's receptionist.

"This is Father Hendricks," Jasper said, and wow. He'd have to get used to not saying that anymore. The thought was surreal, but somehow not upsetting. "Is Adrian around?"

"He's not; can I take a message?"

"How about Lucas? Can I talk to him?"

"Sure, let me put you through."

Jasper waited for less than ten seconds before Lucas was saying in his ear, "Okay look, I really don't want to come to church. There, I said it."

Jasper grinned. "Are you sure about that, Lucas? You protest an awful lot whenever I talk to you. Something on your mind?"

"What? No! I was kidding!"

"Sure, whatever you say. Listen, did Adrian talk to you about Blue Oasis yet?"

"About the Church closing it down? Uh, yeah. And you wonder why I don't want to come. We better be fighting this, Father, or I'm going to the press. I'll lose my job but I don't care. Without that place, I'd have been dead by now."

"Okay, whoa, hold on. Before you set out on a crusade, let me say we're not fighting this."

"We're…not?" Lucas sounded so small, and Jasper's heart clenched.

"No, we're going to do better. I need to talk to Adrian first, and you probably should too before you do anything, but I'm going to need the information on all the grants the Church applied for over the past seven years."

"I can do that," Lucas said.

"Okay great. Then I have one more call to make." Jasper said his goodbyes and hung up. He sat with his phone in his hands for a while, stomach jittery with nerves, but they were the good kind, the excited kind. Change was coming, and while not all of it would be easy, it felt right.

He pressed Adrian's cell number and held the phone to his ear.

Showtime.

"WELL, SHIT." RAMONA said, hanging up her cell phone. "That was Danvers."

Nicky's blood pressure rocketed up at the mention of the name. He ran his hands over his fresh haircut, missing his former length. Ramona had taken shears to him the night before and he felt almost bald. "What's that fucker want?"

"Mick's done a goddamn runner."

"What?"

"He's on the lam, pretty boy. He left a note on Sez's door saying he wouldn't be at the studio today, or ever, and to hire another bassist to take his place. Danvers wants us to consider Perry Rogers, but I'm thinking maybe we should all spare some fucking concern for our current bassist and figure out where the fuck he is and if he's okay." She blew out a lungful of air and stroked her hands over her shorn head. "Remind me the next time I'm joining a goddamn band to vet everyone for a tendency to be fucking drama queens first, okay?"

"Sure." His guts churned.

He didn't really know Mick. When they'd all been high, he'd been a reckless, horny, feckless daredevil who got up on stage and played his bass like his hands were made of rhythm. But since they'd ended up back in the studio together sober, he'd been a completely different person. Quiet, shy—timid even. He could still play his instrument, but he couldn't seem to really jump off the cliff with them and do anything new. The truth was, Perry Rogers would probably be a better bassist, but Mick was in their band. He was part of them, and maybe he needed more help.

"Get Sez on the phone," Ramona said, getting her car keys. "We need to make a list of places to look. You take the Beemer and I'll take the Harley, and we'll track his ass down."

Two hours later, Ramona roared off on her bike to check some of Sez and Mick's favorite former haunts, including the houses of their dealers, none of which she wanted Nicky anywhere near. While he wasn't comfortable sending her off alone to drug dealers' houses, he didn't think he should know the addresses either.

Sez told Nicky to check out the Beverly Hills Presbyterian Church.

Apparently, Mick was originally from Los Angeles and he'd attended the church as a child. He still went there sometimes, according to Sez, when he felt depressed.

It was in a beautiful Spanish-style building that Nicky admired as he approached from the parking lot across the street. He'd explored the dark sanctuary and was headed out to the courtyard when his phone buzzed with a message from Jasper.

Lizzie saw on TMZ that you'd checked into the Beverly Hills Hotel. It's unsettling the things the paps know about you before I do. Is everything all right? I thought you were happy staying with Ramona for a while?

Nicky frowned and started to type in a message denying that he'd checked into any hotel anywhere, when it hit him. Mick. *Mick* had checked into the Beverly Hills Hotel. It was a short walk from where he was, and he hoofed it up the street toward the oh-so-familiar salmon-and-white wedding cake that had sheltered so many of the rich and famous. He'd partied in their bungalows a few times himself.

He tried Ramona's number and got nothing. He hoped she was all right. He tried Sez and it went straight to voicemail. He didn't know what had happened between him and Mick, and what it was about being sober that changed things for him, but Ramona had been hard-pressed to get the information she was looking for out of him to begin with. He supposed it was too much to hope that Sez was out looking for Mick too.

He walked past security and straight to the front desk. He heard whispers behind him. *Nico Blue, no way, really, Nico Blue? Yes, Nico Blue!* He passed all the well-dressed people. He didn't give a shit that he was in scruffy jeans and a Perfume Genius shirt he'd found in a box of clothes he'd grabbed along with Mary Fender from his place.

It'd been weird going inside again and seeing everything the way he'd left it, only covered with dust. Luckily, Ramona had been with him. She'd gone in ahead of him and cleared out his stashes of drugs, flushing them before he came in to grab what he needed. He hated to think about packing everything up. He wondered if he could have someone else fetch all of his guitars and then hire a junk crew to take the rest of it all away.

The front desk worker was brittle but polite when he let him know that Mick had checked in and then turned around and checked out again within an hour that morning. Nicky thanked him and avoided the hopeful eyes of some fans, keeping his head down as he walked out the door and headed back to where he'd parked the car.

A text came through from Ramona.

I hate to ask you to do this, but could you check your place? Sez says Mick had a key. I'll meet you there if you want.

Nicky remembered when he'd given Mick a key to his house. It was almost three years ago when Mick had been kicked out of the hotel he'd been crashing in between residences.

Yeah. Meet me there if you don't mind.

Ramona replied that she was following a lead from Twitter that someone had seen Mick hanging around outside the Roxy, but she was on her way to his place after that.

Nicky's stomach knotted up thinking about going back to his house. He would just make sure Mick wasn't there and that would be it. He drove with a sick feeling in his gut. When he arrived at his home, he pulled up to the garage and sat in the car, breathing in and out for a few minutes.

"C'mon, Nicky. It's just a house. Just an empty house. Get it over with."

He got out of the car and walked up the front path, ignoring the overgrown rosemary and mint that brushed against his ankles. Just as he started to unlock the door, it opened from the inside. He swallowed hard and his heart dropped into his shoes. His head buzzed and a surge of fear hit him hard enough that he felt weak-kneed.

"Man, you came," Mick said, relief shining through his drug-slurred words.

"We've been looking everywhere for you, dude," Nicky said, reaching out to take hold of Mick's arm.

Mick shook free. "I didn't think you'd look for me. I hoped you would. But I didn't think you cared, you know?" He leaned against the door jamb, white as a sheet and shaking like a leaf. "Surprise. You found me."

"In my house."

"Yeah, I figured why not. You weren't using it." His grin seemed to slide all over his face. "C'mon. Come inside. See what I've got for us."

Nicky swallowed thickly. He hung back. He didn't think he should go inside, actually. He was pretty sure he needed Ramona here, or his mom, or Jasper, because he had a really fucking good idea of what he was going to find inside, and he was terrified he couldn't say no to it.

"It's good stuff, man. So good. I feel so fucking much better. You will too." Mick wandered back into the darkness of the hallway where Nicky couldn't see him anymore.

The top of his left foot itched and burned, the angel fox sending up a flare of warning.

Slowly, his feet moved forward, and Nicky shut the door behind him.

JASPER PUT DOWN the phone with a click that felt understated compared to the roaring thunder in his veins. His hands were clammy, and he had to pry his fingers loose from where they'd cramped around the horn. He closed his eyes and tried to swallow but his mouth was too dry. It was done. The archbishop's condemning voice still reverberated in his head, but he pushed it aside.

Almost afraid to try, but knowing he had to, he reached within himself and searched for the core of strength that had always been there. It glowed as steadily as ever; his love for God would never change.

Thank you, he thought, feeling the gratitude in the bottom of his heart. His nerves steadied. *Thank you for giving me this second chance.*

He glanced at his phone but there were no new messages. The last text he'd received from Nicky had been a photograph.

This is what happens when a drummer lady corners you, it read, and Jasper grinned. A fresh faced Nicky was smiling at him, hair a lot shorter, but still long and choppy enough to fall around his forehead in a boyish way. He looked guileless. Happy. Jasper's heart soared.

For a moment, he sat in his office, closed his eyes, and thought about the things he'd miss. Andrew. The rituals of preparation for Mass. The calm of the church. The parishioners and the people who needed him. *Vanity*, he thought, and smiled.

He'd have to add another sin to his list soon. Jealousy over watching someone else preside over Mass. But it would fade over time, especially… He opened his eyes. Nicky. He should call him and tell him it was done. Or maybe he could surprise him. Take some time off. Blue Oasis was safe now. He had his work cut out for him with reapplying for the grants and funding. It would require a ton of paperwork before BO was in his own hands. And he'd have to work like a horse to keep it that way, but not today.

Telling people wasn't going to be easy. He'd lose the respect of many, and that stung his pride, but in the long run he knew it wouldn't matter. He rose to his feet, hesitated for a second, then moved to the small antique bookcase tucked into his office. The glass reflected him like he was looking into still water, but the white of his collar was crisp and clear. With sure, gentle fingers, he worked it loose and popped the button of his shirt.

Then he opened the door of his office and crossed the hall to Mrs. Wells's.

"Father." She smiled. "What can I do for y—" Her eyes flicked to the collar in his hands. "Everything all right?"

"Yes. Everything is fine, Mrs. Wells. Things are going to be different. But fine."

She rose to her feet, abandoning what looked like Keshaun's case file. "Different how?"

"Blue Oasis won't be affiliated with the Church anymore. The archbishop's secretary will be sending the first of the paperwork through sometime today. We'll have a meeting with lawyers present before long to sort everything out, but for now we have permission to continue as we are until the end of the year."

"But...why?"

Jasper looked down at his hands. "The easiest thing to do would be to tell you that the Church wanted to make Blue Oasis a shelter for all children, not just queer ones." Mrs. Wells gasped, but Jasper held up his hand. "Which is true, and you know as well as I do what that would've meant. I could tell you the price of keeping it open was to leave the Church quietly. The archbishop never liked me, so that part is true as well. But the real truth is, if it wasn't for Nicky—Nicholas Blumfeld—I'd have fought him. I'd have tried to stay in the Church and I'd have kept Blue Oasis open too. But I love Nicky, Mrs. Wells. And I can't be a priest and love him at the same time."

She gaped at him—there was no other word for it—and despite the racket of his nervous heart, he looked her steadily in the eye. If she condemned him, he didn't stand a chance with the rest of Little Heights.

Just as she opened her mouth to say something, they heard the pounding echo of footsteps down the hall.

"Father! Father!"

Alarmed, he stuck his head out of Mrs. Wells's office. She joined him in a hurry. Some of her grey hair had come loose from her bun, and she looked rattled, but all her attention was on the girl racing toward them.

"Ms. Benoit," Mrs. Wells began, "no running in the ha—"

"Father." Lizzie came to a halt, so out of breath the word was barely audible. Tears ran down her face.

"Lizzie, what is it?" He grabbed her shoulders when her knees almost buckled. Sobbing, she thrust her phone at him. He looked at Mrs. Wells, then at Lizzie, and then at last at the phone between them.

Breaking News: Rock God Nico Blue Feared Dead of Alleged Overdose in His Home; Music World in Mourning.

He nearly dropped the phone, but Mrs. Wells caught it. "What's going on?" she asked, but he barely heard her. A surge of cold adrenaline roared through him. He grabbed his own phone from his pocket and hit Nicky's number, but it went straight to voicemail.

Mrs. Wells was patting Lizzie's head and talking to her, but Jasper couldn't hear a word she said. His fingers shook as he sent a text. *Where are you? What's going on?* Nicky didn't respond so he tried calling again. Voicemail. He stared at the last text he'd sent asking about the rumor that Nicky had checked into the Beverly Hills Hotel. He quickly Googled Nico Blue.

Nico Blue Found Dead This Morning After Alleged Overdose. A picture of a body being wheeled from a home into an ambulance.

Has Another Rock Star Partied For The Last Time? A picture of Nicky looking skinny and bedraggled after his last concert.

Nico Blue of Vespertine Rumored Dead. A photo of Nicky's house and a BMW parked in the driveway with an ambulance beside it.

Nico Blue's fans mourn and celebs react on Twitter. Fans crying around the front of Nicky's gated neighborhood, and screencaps of condolence tweets.

Nicky's sharp smile and blue eyes crinkled in laughter flashed into Jasper's mind and speared his heart. He made a mournful noise and shoved the phone back in his pocket.

"Take…take care of Lizzie," he whispered.

"Fath—Jasper, what—" Mrs. Wells must've looked at Lizzie's phone because she gasped. "Oh no. Jasper, wait. Where are you going? You need to come and sit down. I'll call someone. I'll call Andrew, don't—"

"Take care of Lizzie," he repeated, pushing the sobbing girl into her arms, and then he was out the door.

He ran.

His bike was at the school, but he left it. He ran down the street, not caring who stared at him. He began to sweat almost immediately in the July heat, and he ripped the buttons off his shirt and pulled it out of his jeans. Desperately, panting on the side of the road, he yanked his phone from his pocket again and managed to type in *Nico Blue news* in the search engine. Again came a barrage of news sources proclaiming that he'd been found dead, but there was one with a video from a "witness." Jasper clicked play.

"I saw him just a few hours before it happened. He walked right past us on the sidewalk by the church over there and he looked determined, like he had some purpose." She started to cry. "I can't believe he's dead. It's insane."

Jasper's chest felt like it would crack open. He called again. Still voicemail. He sent another text. *Please Nicky. Please.*

Then he ran on. He reached the short cut through the woods to his parents' and the Blumfelds' houses and ripped off his shirt. The tank top underneath was soaked through, and still he ran and ran until he didn't know if the salt stinging his eyes was tears or sweat. He stopped in the Blumfeld driveway, pulled his phone out of his pocket, and dialed.

"Yeah, it's Nicky. Chances are I don't want to talk to you, so go away."

Jasper sobbed and nearly sank to his knees, exhausted, but he pushed on. Trembling, he knocked on the Blumfeld door, but no one answered.

He stayed there for fifteen minutes, knocking until his fist felt raw, alternately trying Nicky's phone, sending texts, and looking at the latest news trying to find some evidence that these reports were wrong. He tried Adrian's cell phone, but that went to voicemail too. Was Adrian at work? Did they already know? He circled the house twice to make sure they weren't in the yard, which was when he noticed the biggest of the Blumfelds' two boats was gone.

He had to find Nicky's parents, he had to—His head jerked up when he heard wheels over gravel, but it wasn't Adrian or Miriam's car, it was his mother's next door. Jasper stepped back and looked up at Nicky's childhood home. It looked as peaceful as it always did, but completely empty.

With every step weighing on him like he couldn't take another, he aimed for his mother's house.

Is this my punishment? But no, that was just more arrogance. People died and the world kept turning. All it meant was that Jasper's world would be a monochrome copy, devoid of color and music.

Oh, Nicky, why?

His mother opened the door, looking mildly put-out to be disturbed, until she saw his face.

"Oh my God, what happened?"

He held it together long enough to say, "It's Nicky. He's dead." Then he crumpled, and she caught him, and for the first time in forever, he found comfort in his mother's arms.

Sometime later—he had no idea how long—he came back to himself in the living room. Jasper sat on the immaculate leather sofa while his mother perched on the ornately-carved wooden coffee table. Sunlight spilled through the two-story windows into the living room and it was all too bright. His head hurt.

"I'm so sorry," Crystal said. She reached for Jasper's hands. "Oh my boy."

Jasper was hollow; cried out. "I don't understand. I talked to him this morning. He was…happy. I—" He glanced at his mother. "I told him I was leaving the Church." His mother's grip tightened on his fingers.

"Well, at least that's good. I never thought you were suited—"

"Mom."

She went quiet. "Yes. You're right, of course. Now is not the time. Honey…" She shifted so she could look Jasper in the eye. "This is how addicts are. Any kind of emotion, whether it's good or bad, can swing them right out of their carefully constructed balance. It's not your fault. It would've happened sooner or later."

"I don't believe you," he whispered. "He was strong. He was happy. He wouldn't…he wouldn't have risked it." His face twisted, because obviously Nicky had. A sharp pain shot through his chest and he gasped and doubled over.

"Let me get you some water."

He nodded and sat in silent disbelief until she returned. How could Nicky be gone? How was he supposed to go on now?

"Listen to me, Jasper. Nicky wouldn't have taken those drugs thinking they would kill him. He's been off them for so long, his resistance would've worn down completely. He might've taken a dose he was perfectly fine with before, thinking one last time wouldn't matter."

"But he had a patch. A maintenance medication. A new one. I can't remember. It would've made him sick, he knew that." He reached for the water and drank, surprised to find himself parched. His face throbbed like it was bruised.

"That patch wears off fast if he doesn't keep up with it. Who's to say he hadn't stopped applying it, thinking he didn't need it anymore, and then when temptation came he couldn't resist? Addiction is an illness, but it's a beast, Jasper. It will trick your brain into doing what it wants. There is no rational thinking at that point."

Jasper closed his eyes and remembered how badly Nicky had wanted a hit of just about anything to make the withdrawal of the patch go away. If it had come off, and he hadn't noticed, or didn't have a replacement ready…

"He's dead, Mom." Jasper hugged his arms around himself and hung his head. "What am I going to do?"

She gently ran her fingers through his hair, and he had a vague memory of her doing that when he was a child. She wasn't maternal, but she loved him. "Did you leave the Church for him?"

Jasper shook his head. "It was certainly a big part of the reason why

I'm doing it now, but I had to save Blue Oasis."

"Then that's what you'll do." She cupped his face. She was pretty, his mom, in a severe sort of way. Her eyes glistened wetly and some of her mascara had smudged. "You're strong and intelligent, and I'm so very proud of you. I realize I never said it, but I am. You go after what you want and you don't look back. You will mourn him, and you will help these kids, one day at a time. Then sometime in the future you'll wake up, and you'll realize thinking of him doesn't hurt so much anymore."

The idea of it not hurting seemed utterly impossible. He sighed. "The Blumfelds…they're not home. I don't know if they know."

"Why don't you go lie down for a bit? I'll keep an eye out for them."

Jasper nodded and stood. He imagined his childhood bedroom, where he'd spent so much time with Nicky, and none at all since.

"Actually I think I'm going to swim to the island."

"Jasper—" His mom began, but she stopped and nodded. "Okay. Whatever you need, honey. I'm here if you need me."

"Thanks, Mom." Jasper hugged her and then walked out of the house and onto their pristine dock. The Blumfeld house was still quiet and Jasper's heart ached at the thought of the pain that would live between those walls from now on.

You can't be dead. You can't. I don't believe it.

He took his phone out of his pocket and dialed. He tried again and again, and every time Nicky told him to go away.

Yelling, Jasper threw his phone into the water. With a splash he dove in too, and he didn't look back as he swam to their island—what once had been their refuge, and now would be the grave of their love.

Chapter Twenty-Three

NICKY'S PLANE TOUCHED down in Philadelphia. When he turned his phone back on, it binged and pinged with dozens of messages and missed call notifications. With shaking hands, he put the phone back in his pocket. He needed to get home. He needed Jazz and his mom and dad, and he needed to forget the horror of watching Mick die on his bathroom floor while he'd screamed at the 911 operator to please hurry.

In a daze, he walked through the airport looking for his next gate to catch the connecting flight back to sanity and safety. He'd given his statement to the cops before they'd wheeled Mick out of his house. As they'd snapped pictures of Mick's body, he'd told them how he and Mick had argued about the drugs. He'd told them how Mick had locked himself in the bathroom with a needle, and when Nicky had finally managed to kick the door open it'd been too late. He remembered how they'd patted him on the shoulder and told him he'd done all he could, while he'd stared at the zipped body bag the paramedics were lifting onto a stretcher.

Nicky was still surprised they hadn't arrested him, or at least insisted he be tested for drugs too, but maybe he'd been convincing enough in his shock and panic. Or maybe they didn't give a shit about celebrities and their addictions. Regardless, they'd agreed he could go home to Little Heights so long as he stayed available for future questioning.

Wearing sunglasses and a baseball cap, he kept his head down, hoping no one would recognize him with his new haircut and healthy weight gain. Philly wasn't LaGuardia or JFK, so he could at least hope the place wouldn't be full of paps. But by now the news of Mick's death would be out, and he'd lose his shit if he had a camera and voice recorder stuck in his face right now.

When he reached his next departure gate, he dropped into a corner chair, planning to fade into the background so no one would notice him. He pulled his phone out of his pocket. He supposed there really was no getting around looking at the messages. Ramona or Sez might need him. Fuck management and the label, though. Fuck them and whatever they had to say about anything.

He touched the message icon on his phone, but his attention was arrested by the news on the TV screen across from him. His throat closed off as he recognized the tragic scene they were covering now. The Spanish Colonial Revival home was his own and he understood the footage of a white-cloth-draped body bag being wheeled into an ambulance. But the words in medium letters along the bottom of the screen made no sense to him.

Nico Blue, guitarist and songwriter for Vespertine, feared dead of apparent overdose at age 34.

He looked down at himself. A weird fear gripped him. Was he dead? No, of course not. He was right here. Flesh and blood, and absolutely alive. A laugh burst through his mouth like a hiccup of shock.

"I'm not dead, fuckers."

A talking head type with a bob and a lipsticked mouth looked solemn as she discussed him in the past tense. "Despite the lack of confirmation from Blue's management or the police, fans are already grieving, leaving candles and flowers on the sidewalk by the community gates mere hours after rumors began. Lead vocalist, Seth "Sez" Cunningham, posted a cryptic confirmation of a death in the band to his Twitter and asked for privacy during this time of grief. Officials from the LAPD will make an official statement as soon as relatives of the deceased are contacted. We'll report back on this tragedy as more information comes in."

"Holy shit." He needed to call his parents. His mom and dad must be out of their minds. He needed to call Jazz. The first number he dialed was the house phone and it went to the machine. "Mom? Hey, it's me. I'm not dead. I'm totally and completely not dead. I need a better manager though, and a new agent, and whatever the fuck else, but I'm alive. So don't freak out. I'm calling Dad's phone."

His father's phone went to voicemail too, and he remembered they'd texted their plan to take the boat out that afternoon. His mother spent the time reading while his dad caught fish. They always came home sunburned and refreshed. He had no idea how good reception was out on the water, but he couldn't reach his dad. So he left another message on his dad's cell phone that he wasn't dead and sent a text for good measure.

Then he called Jasper. There was no answer. He tried calling again. Power dialing had never been his style but he needed to let Jazz know he was okay before he saw the news and thought the worst.

"Hey, it's me, Nicky. I'm not dead. I'm fine. Don't look at the news, it's not true. I'm all right. It was Mick. But I'm coming home. Okay? I'll be there in a few hours. I wish I could have gotten through to you. I'll try calling BO. But I'm fine."

Well, he wasn't entirely fine. He'd watched his bandmate die. But it was what he needed Jasper to hear, and it was the closest to the truth he could find right then.

He pulled up the messenger app to text Jazz and his stomach fell as he read through the increasingly desperate pleas that Jasper had sent.

Please, Nicky, answer me!

Please, please! Just pick up your phone.

He was nauseous and dizzy, his heart hammering so hard he felt it in his fingers, which shook outrageously as he responded.

I'm okay.

I'm okay, Jazz. I'm sorry. I was on a plane.

But there was no reply. Nicky quickly googled the number for Blue Oasis. It rang and rang, and Nicky had no idea where Mrs. Wells might be. He didn't leave anything on their answering machine, but dialed back immediately in hopes of getting through. No luck. He felt sick to his stomach.

He hung up and called his dad's office in case someone there had seen the news. He didn't want them to try to get a message to his dad unless it was that he was very much of the living. He left a message with the receptionist, who sounded very relieved and happy to hear he wasn't dead. She'd heard the news and been in a panic about finding Adrian.

For the first time in his adult life, Nicky wished the airport was swarming with paparazzi. He stood up and looked around, trying to find someone, anyone, with a professional-looking camera and a ratty face that screamed "I don't give a fuck about your privacy," but there was no one. Frantically, he tried to download and set up a new Facebook profile, but realized he had no followers. If he knew the password for his professsional page the record company ran for him, he could login and post there. But he had no idea how to post a message anyway. He should have let Lizzie and the kids show him.

He called Danvers and had to leave a message. "I am not fucking dead, you son of a fucking bitch. Fucking fix this by the time I land in Maine, or I swear to God, I will—"

"Flight 321 to Portland International Jetport will begin general boarding in five minutes. Will first class passengers, and all passengers needing additional assistance, please approach the gate with your boarding pass ready."

First class. That was him.

"Just fucking fix it, you douchebag."

He sent another text to Jasper.

I'm so sorry. I'm okay. I love you. Please let me know you're getting my messages.

He called Ramona. "Holy fuck, Ramona, they're saying I'm dead."

She sounded like she'd been crying. "What the fuck are you talking about?"

"Haven't you seen the news?"

"No. Fuck, no. I don't want to see that crap. My phones have been ringing like crazy. I had to take my landline off the hook, and I only answered my cell because it was you."

"The news is reporting that Nico Blue is feared dead of an overdose. Me, not Mick. No one's corrected it." He was shaking all over. He took off his sunglasses and baseball cap, looking for some sort of recognition in the eyes of the people around him, but everyone seemed weirded out by his eye contact. "They're trying to find Mick's parents or something before setting the record straight."

Ramona was silent for a moment and then Nicky heard the sound of an all-day news station in the background of her call. "They're saying our last album has shot to number one on the charts in the wake of your possible death. This is fucking unconscionable," Ramona said.

"I have to get on a plane now."

"It's okay. I'll take care of it. I'll call Danvers and get this shit straightened out. I'll call the local news station myself if I have to. Fuck, can anyone else in this world do anything without me?"

"I guess not."

"Get on the plane, pretty boy. Call me when you're home."

Nicky tried one last time to get through to Blue Oasis, but the machine picked up again. He texted Adrian once more, letting him know that he was boarding in Philly and would be home soon. Settling into his seat on the plane, his heart pounded and his stomach knotted up. He needed to see his parents and Jazz, but now he needed his parents and Jazz to see him too.

JASPER COUGHED UP a lungful of briny water as he dragged himself onto the sand. He'd apparently lost his tank top and shoes somewhere on the mainland, but his pants dragged him down. He coughed again, wiped the water from his eyes, and tried to struggle out of his remaining wet clothes, but they twisted wickedly and clung to him. He cried out and kicked, sending wet sand flying, making it stick to his skin as he finally freed himself. On hands and knees, he crawled up the beach, exhausted.

He should probably be worried about kneeling naked on the island in the early afternoon when anyone boating past could see him, but he didn't care. The water was calm, rippling gently, and there was no sound other than the wind in the trees. Jasper rested his hands on his thighs, tilted his head to the sky, and closed his eyes. His heart felt bruised and sore, and his throat hurt, but he couldn't stop crying.

Eventually even the worst grief ran dry, and when his voice turned hoarse, he let himself fall sideways. He hugged his knees as he watched the sun sink toward the water. Waves lapped softly at the shore, and Jasper let the motion lull him, waiting for whatever he'd feel next.

Oh, Nicky. Wicked-sharp pain in his chest made him curl up tighter. He hadn't run out of anger yet, but for now he was too tired to stir it back to life. A bone-weary loneliness settled inside him, weighing his limbs. The desolation of it made his heartbeat echo hollowly in his chest.

He thought about reaching out to God, but no. He didn't want to feel His calming presence. He didn't want to lessen this hurt. Not yet. In a twisted way it felt good, because he thought when the anger and sadness ran out, there'd be nothing else left.

Loss was part of life. He knew that. He'd seen it enough over the years, but to lose so cruelly when he'd only just found Nicky again…

His face twisted in agony. He could've had him since he was seventeen years old. If he hadn't chosen priesthood, Nicky'd still be here. Jasper still would've lost him one way or another down the line, but maybe by then whoever went first would've found peace in the memories they'd made. All he had now was an abyss of what ifs.

You could always stay a priest, a small voice whispered in his ear, but Jasper shook it off like an annoying fly. Nicky's death—*oh God*—didn't mean Jasper loved him any less.

A part of him that could function beyond the loss made him stand and stretch out. Like it was someone else making the decisions for him, he walked into the shallow water, wincing when it touched his toes. His body felt tight and hot and he was sure the sun had burned the salt into his skin as he'd lain there on the beach. He rinsed his face, arms, and legs, wanting to get used to the cold of the water before he dove in completely. As welcoming as the darkness seemed, he didn't want to take permanent residence in it.

He needed to swim across and be a responsible adult. His mom would be worried. He'd need to talk to the Blumfelds and offer them support.

But the island called him one last time. The fort could shelter him; the blankets could keep him warm. He looked behind him. *Just one night. One last time, and then I'll never be back.*

He made his way to the fort, shivering as he went, and pulled the strongbox out of its hiding place. It took nearly all his strength to drag it back to the beach. He reached for the blankets Nicky had aired out less than a week ago, and used one to dry himself. He spread the blankets out and wrapped the sleeping bag around him. He wouldn't find peace, no. But he could hold vigil this night, and remember.

He covered his face, felt the sand sticking to his palms scrape his skin, and cried desperately, the loss carving hoarse, painful breaths from his aching lungs until it dragged him under in a restless, twitching sleep.

He is fourteen and standing under Nicky's window, eyes closed, listening to the music that falls so easily from Nicky's fingers. The guitar riffs drift down toward him and touch him like raindrops after a brutally hot day. For the first time in his life Jasper thinks, **I love him**.

He is sixteen and watches Nicky in the attic room. There should be nothing attractive about a sweaty boy sleeping with his mouth open while little snuffly sounds come out of his nose, but the ache between Jasper's legs makes him squirm with embarrassment and arousal. **I want him**.

He is seventeen and they run free like wild horses, through the torrent of summer rain, the oak leaves and pine needles at once dampening and amplifying their solitude, alternately covering them in excess water and shielding them from the onslaught of the wind. Soaked to the bone, they find shelter under a gnarled, unrecognizable tree, and he grabs hold of Nicky, uses his stone-cold fingers to push Nicky's wet hair off his face.

"You're crazy." Jasper laughs. "I told you it was gonna rain."

"Yeah," Nicky gasps, completely out of breath. "So crazy."

Their first kiss tastes like cloudburst and smells like wet leaves and damp mold, and it feels like the world ends and begins all over again.

"I love you," Jasper says. "I want you."

Jasper jerked awake. Eyes gritty with salt and sand, he blinked at the rising moon. His hands closed convulsively on the cool sand beneath him as he waited for clarity to come, for the realization of which was dream and which was reality. It came, and he lay his head on his arms and sought oblivion again.

Chapter Twenty-Four

WHEN HE LANDED in Portland, Nicky's phone dinged with considerably fewer texts. At least one of his texts to Jasper was bounced back from the server, and he tried to call him again, but it went to voicemail. He left a message and tried Blue Oasis and still got no answer. He wished he had Jasper's landline. He tried calling the Hendricks's house using the number he remembered from childhood, but someone named Josiah answered cheerfully announcing he'd reached Piggies BBQ and Chips. He sent another text to Jasper before turning to the messages from other people.

Ramona was freaking out about the mix-up and management, but he couldn't cope with that right now. She knew he was alive, after all. Nicky looked down at his phone and skimmed through a few more texts from management.

Danvers: *Don't threaten me, Nico. Call me. Urgent.*

Harry: *You dead?*

Nicky opened the text thread from his father. Adrian had replied: *Son, we're so relieved you're okay and on your way home. Call as soon as you land again.*

Once he had the keys to a rented Chrysler of some variety or another and was walking through the summer night toward it, he put the call through to his dad. He was ready to drive the forty-five minutes to Little Heights with the gas pedal pressed to the floorboard. He needed to be home.

"Dad?"

"Nicky! My God, the news is horrible!"

"Are they still saying I'm dead? The record company hasn't issued a fucking correction? Or even the police for fuck's sake?"

"They issued a retraction a little while ago. How did this happen? Our message machine is full of condolences!" He huffed and Nicky could practically see him raking a hand over his head as he paced by the phone. "This is a disaster, son. Where's your management? Your agent?"

"I don't know. In need of a new job, apparently."

"Now they're saying it was your bassist, Mick." His father's voice lowered. "Is that true? I don't know what to believe anymore."

"Yeah," Nicky's throat closed off tightly, but he forced himself to go on. "He overdosed. But I'm okay, dad. I was there when it happened, but I wasn't using." His eyes burned. "I'll tell you more when I get home. Have you talked to Jazz?"

"We got in an hour ago and your mother tried to call him a few times. We figured he'd be upset. But we didn't get through on his phone or reach anyone at Blue Oasis."

"He's probably at the church." Praying for Nicky's soul. God, Jazz. Just the thought of how he'd feel if someone told him Jasper was dead made him want to collapse. He needed to find a way to get a message to him so he wouldn't be scared; so he wouldn't hurt.

"I already called there, but no one has seen him since this afternoon." Adrian paused. "Do you want us to call his mom?"

"I don't know. He doesn't go over there very often. But sure. You might as well let her know in case he does call. I'll keep trying him and Blue Oasis." His fingers tingled and his head felt a little light. He opened the car door, tossed the keys on the driver's seat, and pulled the edge of his sleeve up to make sure he hadn't lost his patch in the insanity. He sighed in relief to see it was still there.

"I'm going to start driving now. I just want to be home. And I need to find Jazz."

"I know, son. Your mom and I will look for him, okay?"

"Okay. Thanks, Dad." Nicky hung up. He was hungry but the thought of food made him feel woozy. Still, passing out driving home wouldn't do him any good, and it'd been a long time since the eggs and waffle he'd shared with Ramona that morning.

Snickers bars, peanuts, and cola mixed horribly in his stomach, but Nicky drove with determination. The trees and other cars whipped by outside his windows in the darkness, and the white and yellow lines raced beneath his car. He glanced at his phone often, but saw nothing new from his parents or anything at all from Jasper.

Finally, at the long red light just outside Little Heights, Nicky put another call through to Blue Oasis. A breathless Mrs. Wells answered, "Blue Oasis, Mrs. Wells speaking. How can I help you?"

"Hi, Mrs. Wells, this is Nicholas Blumfeld. I need to talk to the Father, please?"

Mrs. Wells gasped.

"Yeah, um, no matter what you saw on TV, I'm not dead."

She made a strangled noise and then a small sob escaped. "Well, thank the Lord above. Still, I always knew you were trouble, Nicholas Blumfeld! I knew from the moment you stepped into my classroom—but thank goodness you're safe. Lizzie and Jasper, they thought you were dead. The kids have all been a mess crying about it. They're doing better since the retraction was issued a few hours ago. But I don't know where Jasper's gone. He thinks you're dead. He's devastated. If a hair on his head comes to harm from this pain inflicted on his heart, Nicholas, I will hold you and your troublemaking ways personally responsible, but, oh, praise God that you're alive."

Nicky's mind whirred. "He's not at the church?"

"Andrew hasn't seen him since this morning. I've tried his mother's house, but she's not answering. She's at the hospital likely. She probably doesn't even know." She seemed judgmental of his mother, and Nicky didn't blame her much.

"I'm almost in Little Heights. I'll find him."

"Well, I'll let the children know I've talked with you personally. It will relieve their minds."

The light had been green for a while, but there was no one behind him. He ended the call with Mrs. Wells and drove on. He knew where Jasper had gone. It's where he would go if he thought Jasper was dead.

JASPER HAD NO idea what time it was. A huge moon hung low over the blackness of the bay, its weak light turning the world into a shadow of itself. It must've been the cold that had pulled him from his fugue state, because he felt stiff and shivery as he stretched his limbs and sat up.

He listened to the water lap at the beach and let it calm him as he closed his eyes and conjured up Nicky's face—his blue eyes, the art and scars on his body. How had it happened? Jasper knew next to nothing about drugs. Had it been a syringe? Had Nicky thought of him before he'd plunged it in his vein?

Jasper shook the thought loose and remembered Nicky singing "With or Without You" with Lizzie at Blue Oasis. His vocals might not have held up in an arena, but he'd enthralled everyone in the room that day. He'd spun a web of magic and caught them all in it, with nothing but the power of his voice and the touch of his hand on the guitar. Jasper could almost hear the hollow tap of the music, like water hitting…

His eyes snapped open.

Like water hitting the side of a boat. He froze, convinced it was a hallucination at first, but the sound was unmistakable.

Nicky didn't rise from the lake like a reincarnated King Arthur from the mists of Avalon, but as far as Jasper was concerned, he may as well have.

Under the luminance of the full moon, a small boat neared the island. At first he thought it was Adrian coming to get him, but Jasper would've known the shape of his man anywhere, even in the darkest hour of the night. He rose to his feet, not caring that the blanket slipped off his shoulders and that he should be cold, and slowly walked toward the water.

For a moment it was as if time stood still. The slapping sound of the oars slowed, the wind stopped rustling the leaves, and even the moon seemed to brighten and quiet the tides. Then all at once, Nicky was scrambling out of the boat and Jasper ran into the water, and they were in each other's arms.

"Am I dreaming?" Jasper gasped, kneading at Nicky's back, bunching up his clothes until he could feel the heat of his skin. He trembled. If this was a dream it'd be the cruelest he'd ever had. "Nicky?"

Nicky cupped his face and drew it down so they were eye to eye. "I'm here. The news was wrong; it wasn't me who died. It was...it was Mick. Jesus Christ, Jasper, you're—you're stark naked. Oh." He gave a low moan when Jasper pressed closer and buried his nose into Nicky's hair and inhaled.

He smelled like he hadn't slept in a long time, and it was so good, Jasper's knees buckled. "Nicky," Jasper said, and his voice broke. "I thought—I thought..."

"I know, I'm so sorry. Fuck, Jasper, I can't hold you up and this water is really fucking cold at night. Come on."

Jasper pulled back a little and looked at Nicky, at his beautiful face and his trembling mouth, and leaned down and kissed him, hard. Nicky made an *umph* noise, but then yielded to the pressure and let Jasper in. A rush of heat burst inside him, igniting all over, every part of him that had slowly been shutting down coming back to life. He dragged Nicky out of the water, tearing at his clothes as he went, until they fell down on the blanket with Nicky's jeans halfway down his thighs.

"Jazz," he gasped. "We should probably—oh okay, talking can wait. *Gnnn.*"

Jasper squeezed Nicky's cock too hard, but the way he bowed off the blanket must've meant he didn't mind all that much. Jasper worked him out of his clothes the rest of the way, then sat back on his heels and stared down at Nicky.

"Jazz, what—"

"On your hands and knees," Jasper whispered.

"Oh God," Nicky said in a trembly voice and went limp on the blanket. Jasper reached out but before he could flip Nicky over, Nicky scrambled up and presented himself. Jasper was mindless with adrenaline and lingering grief, anger, and heartbreak, but here Nicky was, open and exposed to Jasper and the night.

He bent down behind Nicky and draped himself over his back so he could whisper in Nicky's ear, "I'm going to fuck you now."

"Oh fuck, yes." Nicky arched his back like a slinking cat. Jasper dug around in the strongbox until his hand closed on the old, unopened tub of Vaseline. He uncapped it, found it slick enough still, and coated his fingers.

Nicky's hole tightened when Jasper pressed his fingers to it, so he eased it with his thumb, circling and pressing, circling and pressing, until Nicky made a rough noise and yielded. Jasper hooked his thumb into Nicky's ass and drew down. The muscle contracted around him, quivered, and took him deeper. Jasper pulled out, returned with two fingers, and steadily opened Nicky up. Part of him remembered that he hadn't done this in a long time, but it was buried deep. What ruled him was a burning need to be as close to Nicky as possible, and he needed it right now. Jasper pulled his fingers out, spread Vaseline on his cock, and lined himself up.

"No," Nicky suddenly groaned, and Jasper startled. "No, you're not doing me like this."

He sat up and gave Jasper a little shove as he spun around. He held onto Jasper's face and stared into his eyes until Jasper felt himself falling, chest aching and bottom lip quivering.

"I'm here," Nicky whispered. "I'm here and you're going to look at me when you fuck me." Jasper nodded and Nicky kissed the tear off Jasper's cheek.

In the deep of the night with the moon as his witness, Jasper laid Nicky down on the blanket and didn't look away as he buried his cock inside him.

"Ah, Nicky." Jasper shook all over. "You feel so good."

"Fuck." Nicky arched against him, wrapped his legs tight around Jasper's waist, and took Jasper deeper into the silky heat of him. This was going to be over way too fast.

Jasper drew out again and Nicky made a bereft noise. "What—"

"Shh." He rubbed the head of his cock over Nicky's hole, pushed in a little and pulled out again, and did it again and again until he came down a little from the crest. Nicky gripped his own thighs so hard he was leaving white finger-shaped indentations. He had his head thrown back and was biting his lip.

"How did I fucking manage to forget," he groaned, "what a fucking tease you are."

Jasper laughed and moaned when Nicky spasmed around him. He pushed a little deeper, and oh, he couldn't hold back anymore. He shoved himself all the way in, and Nicky's legs jerked. Jasper fucked him gently, cupped Nicky's tight balls, and watched as a dribble of precome spurted from Nicky's cock and onto his belly. He leaned down so he could kiss him.

"Harder now?" he whispered.

"God, yes," Nicky cried out, and then he clung onto Jasper's shoulders for the rest of the ride. It wasn't hard to remember the angle Nicky liked best, and he was loud and amazing every time Jasper stroked his sweet spot. "Ah, Jazz, it was never like this." He kissed Jasper's cheeks, the bridge of his nose, his eyelids. "Never like this with anyone else."

Jasper hooked his arms under Nicky's shoulders and used the last of his strength to give Nicky everything he had. Nicky cried out to the night and went completely rigid in Jasper's arms. He hung on to that state of ecstasy for so long that Jasper thought he wouldn't be able to keep going until Nicky went over the crest. His thighs burned, his back ached, and he was so out of breath the air hurt his lungs. Then Nicky gasped loudly, and his eyes flew open as he came in thick, ropey pulses.

"Oh, Nicky." Jasper buried himself deep and let go.

Eventually the sound of the waves on the beach brought Jasper back to himself.

"We should probably head back," Nicky murmured. His heart was still beating fast under Jasper's palm, and Jasper didn't want to move. "C'mon, Jazz. It's cold. We're caked in sand and come. I'm tired out of my mind. And you have Mass soon."

"I don't."

"What?"

Nicky stroked Jasper's hair, and Jasper smiled into Nicky's neck. "I don't have Mass because I'm not a priest anymore, effective immediately."

"What?" Nicky sat up and Jasper rolled onto his back, laughing softly. "Holy crap! That's…that's huge! Why didn't you say something?"

"We were busy, in case you hadn't noticed."

"Don't be such a smart ass. What does that mean? I know you said you were going to, but I thought you meant eventually. Not right now. Oh my God. Holy fuck. What about Blue Oasis? Is that why you had to do it?" Nicky gasped. "Did that asshole archbishop blackmail you out of the Church?"

Jasper drew Nicky down again and kissed him lightly. He was beyond wrecked too, and sticky in uncomfortable places, but he was here with Nicky. It was utterly surreal. *If this is a dream, I don't ever want to wake.*

"No, not exactly. I mean, I think I could've fought for Blue Oasis from within the Church if I really wanted to, but I don't think I'm priest material anymore, Nicky. I don't think I ever was. And then there's you."

"Me?"

"Yeah. You."

Nicky gave him a sappy smile and Jasper laughed. He carefully sat up too. "Okay, yes, ow. I think going home and showering wouldn't be a bad idea."

The first fingers of dawn trailed the horizon. It'd still be a few hours before the sun rose, but the morning hung in the air like a promise, and they piled into the boat after Nicky wrestled himself back into his clothes.

"For the record," he grumbled. "I still hate fucking on the beach as much as I used to."

Jasper clutched his blanket tighter, nuzzled Nicky's neck, and said, "Yeah, you always used to say that, and then you'd let me fuck you in the sand anyway."

"Baby." Nicky turned and softly kissed Jasper's mouth. "I will let you fuck me wherever and whenever you want."

A hot punch of want made Jasper's stomach contract. "I'll take you up on that. I have a lot of time to make up."

When they noticed that the Blumfeld house was still dark, Nicky aimed the boat toward the Hendricks's pristine and unused dock.

"They probably haven't done this in a while," Nicky mumbled and Jasper snorted. Every once in an odd while as teenagers they'd been spectacularly late and had faced both sets of parents waiting in one of the houses. Given that he was naked aside from the blanket wrapped around him, Jasper felt rather like an awkward teenager.

"I feel like we're about to be grounded again," Jasper said, and Nicky gave him a sharp look.

"Don't even joke about that."

Jasper touched Nicky's slightly greasy hair. "Don't worry. Not even God could keep me away from you this time."

Nicky averted his eyes, but Jasper caught the pleased little smile.

The lights shone in the Hendricks' windows, and Nicky led Jasper in through the back door. It was a strange, holy atmosphere they walked in on. Their parents had never been close, but now Adrian, Miriam, and Crystal sat together quietly in the Hendricks' tidy living room drinking tea and coffee, acting like maybe someone they loved had actually died.

Jasper's mom quietly rose to her feet and walked toward them. Nicky tried to let go of Jasper's hand but he didn't let him. Jasper was half expecting a hug, so when she zeroed in on Nicky instead and hugged him, everyone in the room blinked in surprise.

"Um," Nicky said. He awkwardly patted Crystal on the back. "Hi."

"Nicky." She pulled back and delicately dabbed at her cheeks. "I'm glad you're all right." Her eyes darted down to where Jasper's fingers curled between Nicky's own. She lifted her gaze. "Oh, honey, we were worried about you." She hugged Jasper too, and he shared a slightly baffled look with Miriam and Adrian, who looked on a little teary-eyed. Miriam was laughing and crying and Adrian was holding her tight.

Crystal smiled tentatively at Nicky. "I'm really glad you're okay. And thank you for bringing Jasper back safely."

Nicky put his arm around Jasper's shoulder and kissed the side of his head. "Anytime," he said, and Jasper felt some of the hurt inside him heal.

"Do you want to put some clothes on? I think some of your old stuff might still fit you. I have some clothes that belonged to your father, if you want."

"I left some of my old sweats and t-shirts upstairs," Jasper said and he reluctantly left Nicky behind to dart up the familiar stairs to his old room.

When he returned, relieved to be not-naked at least, Miriam was hugging Nicky and Adrian had his arms around them both. Miriam caught his eye, kissed Nicky's cheek and said, "Well, I think we'll leave you all to it then. Now that everyone's safe and sound, and back where they belong. We old people need our rest." Miriam walked over and hugged Jasper, and then kissed his cheek, too. Even without saying a word, Jasper understood that Adrian and Miriam knew about him and Nicky, and probably had for a long, long time. "Will you be coming with us?" she asked Nicky, but Jasper figured she already knew the answer.

"No, I don't think so. But I'll call you later."

"You can both stay and rest here, if you like," Crystal said, when they'd seen the Blumfelds out. "Jasper, your old bedroom is freshly made if..." Her eyes darted to Nicky. "If you both want to stay there."

"Thanks, Mom, but I really just want to go home. I need to feed Dizzy."

She tilted her head to the side. "Dizzy?"

"His cat," Nicky said with a grin. "She likes to kill things and bring them to Jasper because apparently he can't feed himself."

Crystal covered her mouth and laughed. "I bet that goes over well."

Jasper rolled his eyes. "Yeah, yeah, laugh it up."

"Well, I'll have to come and meet this cat soon. Take care of yourselves, okay? And call me if you need anything."

Jasper smiled at her before leaning in and kissing the top of her head. "Thanks, Mom."

"It's late. Are you sure you don't want to stay?"

"It's only a short drive, and Nicky has a car. I'll be fine."

Crystal gave him a mildly disappointed look but she let it slide. "All right then. Good night, boys."

And then Nicky and Jasper stood on the driveway, the gravel stretching out before them in the dark.

Chapter Twenty-Five

THE NIGHT WAS peaceful and calm as they pulled up the drive to Jasper's farm house. Given the kind of day they'd endured, Nicky half expected to find another shredded rabbit waiting for them. But Dizzy sat peacefully by the front door with an air of polite expectation. She followed them inside and bounded off into the living room.

Nicky turned to flip on the light in the entryway, but Jasper grabbed his hand. "Wait," he whispered, pulling Nicky close in the darkness and nuzzling his hair. "Nicky, I—I felt so helpless."

"I know. I felt helpless too." The cold wave of despair as he'd watched Mick die and the churning ice in his guts when he'd read Jasper's texts still chilled him to the bone. "Everything's so fragile in this damned world."

Fragile flame
Guttered between
One second and the next
Fire and gasoline

"So fucking fragile, Jasper."

Jasper cradled Nicky's head. "I want you alive, Nicky. For as long as I live, I want to know you're alive too."

"I promise to do my damnedest not to let death happen any fucking sooner than necessary." He smoothed his hand through Jasper's hair, hoping it made him feel better. "There's one thing we need to talk about. Something we need to deal with right fucking now."

"Yes?"

"You stink." He kissed Jasper's chin and tugged him toward the stairs. "You need a shower."

"And some tea," Jasper murmured, following close behind.

"I can make some while you get cleaned up."

Fifteen minutes later, Nicky had Jasper bundled sleepily on the sofa with a cup of tea, and wearing a blue robe with nothing underneath. He was tempted to sneak a hand up under it just because he could. Touching Jasper was grounding and exciting at once. But he needed a shower too. He was travel-filthy and the sexual collision on the beach with Jasper hadn't left him any cleaner.

"But you look and smell fine to me," Jasper murmured a little petulantly as he sipped his tea.

Nicky sniffed his pits. "Lying liar who lies."

"Maybe I don't want you to leave me."

"Maybe you could come upstairs and watch then."

Dizzy seemed to hate that idea because she hopped onto the sofa, plopped her fat butt onto Jasper's outstretched thighs, and settled in, licking a paw and purring.

"Ten minutes. That's all I'm giving you," Jasper said with a mock threat in his tone. "Then I want you back with me."

"I won't even take that long." Nicky stroked a hand over Jasper's damp hair, pushing a longer piece off his forehead, and kissed his temple. Jasper held onto his fingers as Nicky walked away, letting go only as distance broke them apart.

The excellent water pressure in Jasper's shower pelted Nicky's exhausted muscles, and he was tempted to linger but he'd promised to be fast. In Jasper's bedroom chest of drawers, he found a T-shirt and sweats. Sliding them on, he stopped to mess up the contents of all the drawers a little, even the little one on top that held neatly organized cufflinks and tie pins he figured Jasper rarely used. Then he padded down to join him again.

When he reached the sofa, Jasper was asleep. His long, gold lashes fanned on his cheeks, and his lips parted wetly. The half-full tea cup sat precariously on his chest with his fingers barely gripping the handle. Dizzy blinked up at Nicky from her place on Jasper's thighs. Carefully, he took the cup and saucer from Jasper, and tip-toed into the kitchen to put it in the sink.

When he returned to the living room, Jasper was half sitting up, rubbing his eyes. "Nicky, I had a terrible dream."

Nicky squatted beside him, feeling the sweats ride low on his hips. He smoothed his fingers through Jasper's nearly dry hair. "Let me guess, I was dead and you swam out to our island where you tried to drown your horrific sorrow by swallowing sand?"

Jasper smiled at him wryly. "No, that was all too real."

Nicky tried to move Dizzy so he could sit with Jasper's feet in his lap and got a hiss and a scamper for his effort. "I know. I'm sorry about that."

"I was going to joke that I'd dreamed I was out of tea, but I don't actually feel much like another cup."

Jasper lifted his legs, and Nicky sat on the couch under them. He rubbed Jasper's calves and stared at the speakers. Images of the day flashed in his head. He should have put some music on. Vespertine's first album again. Back when they'd all been at the top of their game.

"What happened out there?" Jasper asked softly.

Nicky shook his head. He couldn't tell Jasper about the way Mick had lain there on the bathroom floor, his breathing slowing, his life leaking out as Nicky screamed into the phone at the 911 operator. "I'm not sure. All that matters in the end is that Mick is dead."

Jasper sat up and scooted so he was nearly in Nicky's lap. It was an awkward position now that he was taller than Nicky, but it was comforting too, to have him so close. "Do you want to talk about it?"

"Not really. I was there when he died."

"Oh, Nicky." Jasper's eyes were puffy from having cried so hard.

"I'd gone looking for him. Your text about the hotel made me think he might have checked in there, and he had, but then he'd left again. Then Ramona texted to look at my house. I wasn't staying there, and he was on the list for the guard to let through."

"He was there?"

"Yeah. Well, him and his massive stash of drugs." Nicky shivered, remembering the rush of temptation that had filled him from head to toe.

"Did you…?"

Nicky shook his head and thumbed Jasper's dimple in his chin. "I don't ever want you or anyone else to feel the way I did when I kicked the bathroom door in to get to him."

"Oh, Nicky. Sweet Nicky."

"I'm not going to touch drugs again, Jasper. I know I said I planned to stay sober before, but the whole time I was trying to save Mick, I kept thinking, 'I can't do this to Jazz. I can't do this to my folks.' Hell, I couldn't even do it to Ramona. No one should ever feel that way because of something I did to myself."

"I'm so sorry you had to see that, Nicky."

"I didn't have to, but I did. I'm not sorry I was there with him when he died. He wasn't alone. Not everyone gets that much, I guess."

"He was a friend of yours," Jasper said.

"He was a stranger to me. I wish I knew him at all. If they asked me to say something about him at the funeral, I wouldn't have a clue." He thought about Mick's devotion to Sez despite the rejection. "Maybe I'd say that he was a great bassist and a loyal guy." He rubbed his eyes. "Speaking of, I should find out from Ramona when the funeral will be. I guess I should go to it."

"Tomorrow. You can call and find out everything you need to know tomorrow."

"Yeah. Tomorrow."

"We need some sleep."

Nicky laughed softly, grit and exhaustion stinging beneath his lids. "We really fucking do."

Jasper stood and held his hand down to Nicky. "Come on. Let's get some rest."

"Rest" was apparently code for "love-making," and Nicky didn't mind at all.

They lay naked in the bed under the cool top sheet, kissing and touching, pressing together and pulling apart, changing positions, and pressing together again. Jasper kissed every tattoo, licked the edges of each line, and sucked Nicky's nipples until he squirmed. He disappeared under the cover, kissing Nicky's hip bones and dipping his tongue into Nicky's belly button.

When Jasper's hot breath gusted across his dick, Nicky tossed the sheet back. "If you're going to do that, baby, I need the full fucking view."

Jasper's cheeks were flushed and his ears pink, but his eyes were hot and urgent when he looked up from between Nicky's spread legs. "It's been a long time since I had any practice at this." His voice was thready.

"You'll be great." *You'll be* **you**. "Don't stop now."

Jasper smiled up at him. "Never."

The slick heat of his tongue snaked up Nicky's sensitive length, and he took the head between his warm lips, sucking lightly. Nicky's smile tugged the corners of his mouth. "Harder, remember? It's okay to suck it harder, baby."

Jasper's eyes burned golden as he looked up under his lashes, mouth full and sliding further down. Then he pulled up on a harder suck, and Nicky groaned. "Yeah, like that. You remember how I like it."

Jazz huffed softly as he shifted angles and took Nicky in deeper, and then set up a rhythm of bobbing and sucking, his mouth hot and tender as he moved. Nicky threaded his fingers into Jasper's hair, holding on, gazing down to watch. He'd never thought he'd have this again. Even that morning when he'd woken up, he hadn't been sure this tenderness could be his. His balls tightened and his groin twinged hard, pushing a swell of precome from his dick.

"Hey, c'mere," he murmured, pulling Jasper up.

"I was getting the hang of it again."

"I noticed."

They kissed again and the taste of himself in Jasper's mouth was like comfort food and he couldn't get enough. "You're so beautiful, baby. What did I do to deserve this?" He breathed against Jasper's hair. "I've done things—"

"Shh. That's over now."

"But you don't know everything, Jasper."

"I don't need to know much. I love you and that's all that matters."

In the end, forgiveness was easy like a flowing river, like the tides in the cove. It came in and covered the worst sins and carried them away to the depths of the sea.

"Jazz, there's one thing I need you to know." Nicky clutched Jasper's ass and hauled him close, their bodies slotting together, dicks gliding next to each other.

Jasper shuddered, his hips rutting against Nicky's and his head tipping back in pleasure. He tried to focus on Nicky's face, but was apparently losing the battle to his lust.

"It's important. I need you to know."

"H'okay," Jasper gasped. "It's okay, Nicky. Whatever it is we'll deal with it."

Nicky reached between them and gripped their cocks. "Jazz?"

"Yeah?"

"It's true that I cheated at HORSE when we were kids."

Jasper laughed and whispered against Nicky's lips. "Such. A. Brat." Then he kissed him again, rolling him over and sitting up on his heels between Nicky's thighs. His cock stuck straight up against his belly, wet with precome. "I've got condoms and lube."

Nicky blinked up at him. "What?"

"I took one of the safe sex kits from Blue Oasis the other night. I wanted to make sure, if you came back, we were prepared."

"After the island, it seems like the horse already left the stable, Jasper. I trust you to fuck me. I know you're not carrying anything. Like I said the other night, if it was the other way around, me penetrating you, there'd be more to worry about." The tests kept coming back negative for all varieties of sexually transmitted diseases, but it hadn't been three months since he'd last been with a stranger. Strange, since it felt like a lifetime ago. "But if you want to use one, we should." Nicky stroked his hands up Jasper's thighs and took hold of his dick, loving the feel of it thudding in his palm. "I don't mind. Easier cleanup too."

Jasper licked his lips. "I want something different actually. Nicky, I want you inside me. I asked before, but I wasn't sure, and it was good that you slowed it down and took it another direction, but this time…I'm ready. I'm not a priest. I'm not breaking any vow. I want to feel you like that again." He bit into his full lower lip. "Please, Nicky. It's been so long."

"You don't have to beg. I'll do whatever you want." His cock pulsed and leaked on his stomach at the thought of having Jasper that way again. "Where's the stuff? Please don't tell me it's downstairs."

Jasper leaned over to the night stand drawer and pulled out a string of condoms and a fresh tube of lube.

"Holy shit, you're prepared. It's downright fucking virtuous to be this prepared, Fox."

"I'm hoping you'll take care of my remaining virtue, Badger."

Nicky's lips curled into a grin. "Oh, baby. When I'm done with you, getting 'defrocked' is gonna have a whole new meaning."

Jasper laughed helplessly. "You are so—"

Nicky cut him off with a kiss, and then distracted him with lubed fingers working around his asshole. Jasper shifted to straddle Nicky's legs, kneeling up so that Nicky's fingers slipped inside, one after another, working him open with determined, firm movements, until two went in, and then, on a hot sigh that gusted over Nicky's chest, three.

"Oh, Jazz. Look at you. Riding my fingers like a beautiful wanton angel. Christ." He slicked his other hand and took hold of Jasper's cock, jerking him as he played, seeking the gland that he knew would make Jasper's eyes roll back and his back bow. "Oh, yes. Yes, like that. Give it to me," he whispered as Jasper cried out, his cock pulsing another spurt of precome.

"Hurry up, Nicky. I won't last if you don't hurry up."

"So you want me to fuck you?"

"Yes."

"How much?"

"I thought you said I didn't have to beg? You were going to give me anything I wanted?"

"I've been taking lessons from you, Fox. Lies, lies, lies." He left two fingers hooked into Jasper as he handed up a condom. "Put this on me. Get me ready. Tell me what you want me to do with my dick that you're wrapping up like a fucking present."

Jasper's cheeks were red and his ears glowed, but as he rolled the condom on and lubed it up, he met Nicky's eye. "I want you to fuck me in the ass with your cock. And I want you to make me come so hard I lose my voice screaming for you, Nicky."

"Oh, Jesus, baby. Who taught you to talk dirty like that?"

Jasper kneeled up and Nicky took hold of his own cock, holding it steady. "You did."

Nicky bit the inside of his cheek as Jasper bore down, his asshole spasming against the head before relaxing. With a tight, mind-blowing pleasure, Jasper pulled him in. "Fuck," he hissed. "Fuck you're tight, Jazz."

"Mmngh," Jasper answered, his eyes glassy and his head tilted back. He looked almost as if he was praying.

"Fucking holy, yeah?" Nicky murmured.

Jasper smiled and looked down at him. "Yes, Nicky, being with you is always holy." He lifted and lowered his body until Nicky was buried several inches deep.

"I love you."

"I love you too." Jasper rode him shallowly, his face slack, his expression far gone.

"I want to hear you." Nicky gripped Jasper's hips and fucked up hard, pushing into him fully. Jasper grunted, his eyes rolling back and his mouth hanging open. "Yeah. Let me hear you."

He fucked him harder and harder, and Jasper groaned and grunted, squawked and cried out, his body taking everything greedily as his cock flexed between them, wet and so damn hard. When Nicky rolled them over, flipping Jasper to his back to get in deeper, to cradle Jasper's head in his hands and kiss his mouth, the swearing started, and pride swelled hot in Nicky's chest.

"Oh, *fuck* Nicky," Jasper cried. "You're gonna make me—*Nicky*!"

Each stroke in pounded Jasper's prostate, and Jasper's ass convulsed. He quivered in Nicky's arms, and his dick slapped wetly between their stomachs. "Come for me," Nicky whispered. "Come for me, Jasper. I want to feel you squeeze me."

"Nicky, oh, sweet God, it's good."

"Mmm-hmm, you're amazing." He was on the verge of coming; his body was strung tight and he could feel it pulling through him. "Are you close? I'm close."

Jasper reached between them and gripped his dick, his hand flying over it fast. "Oh God, oh, holy *fuck,* Nicky!" His voice was hoarse and his ass clamped down hard, locking Nicky in place as the first spasm of orgasm took him. Jasper held his ass hard, pulling him in tight, and fell apart under him.

Nicky didn't last any longer. Collapsing on Jasper, he shoved in deep as he could and came, burst after burst of pleasure in his head and heart and groin. "Love you," he grunted as the scent of come filled his nostrils. "Love you so fucking much."

"Love you too," Jasper said between small convulsions. "Love you too."

THE NEXT MORNING, breakfast was a bowl of honey nut cereal and eggs that Jasper fried up while wearing nothing but tightie whities. Nicky slouched around in Jasper's sweatpants and entertained all kinds of fantasies about seeing whether the eggs would burn if he pushed the tightie whities down and stuck his tongue in Jasper's favorite spot. But in the end he'd been too exhausted to try it. Maybe tomorrow. Or the next day. He didn't have to rush anything. He could have Jasper forever.

Afterward, they got dressed. "This is harder than it looks, huh?" Nicky said, leaning against the wall in his freshly washed jeans and T-shirt that smelled of Jasper's detergent. He was watching Jasper go through his closet, pulling out the black pants and shirts and putting them aside.

"We need to take you shopping for a new uniform," he said, putting his arm around Jasper's slumping shoulders. "Unless you want to take it back? Maybe this was the right uniform for you, Jasper?"

Jasper shook his head and nuzzled Nicky's neck before pulling down the tight pair of jeans he'd worn to the Blumfelds' house for dinner and a blue short-sleeved golf shirt. "I guess you're right. I'm not sure I even know what I want to wear. I'm used to wearing the same old thing nearly every day."

"We'll get you up to date in fashion. I'll hire a stylist if you want."

Jasper laughed.

"C'mon, feed the vanity a little."

Jasper kissed him, and they spent some time taking their clothes off before they put them back on again.

In the late morning, Nicky fielded some phone calls with his for-shit agent in order to issue a press statement confirming his status as alive and well. He then got Jasper to show him how to get on Twitter, where he let his fans know he was okay and apologized for the mess up and their grief. It was overwhelming to get literally hundreds of responses within minutes of making his first social media post.

@NicoBlueLives I love you. So sorry for your loss. Stay safe and sober!

@NicoBlueLives ur my favorite! I cried 4 hours! So happy ur okay!

@NicoBlueLives Dude, last time I saw you, you looked pretty dead.

@NicoBlueLives, U rock, bro!

@NicoBlueLives, so sad about Mick. Take care of yourself!

"How do you know how this all works?" Nicky asked, watching as Jasper made the privacy selections for his account.

"We have one for Blue Oasis. I usually let the kids handle it, but I needed to make sure it was safe for them to use."

@NicoBlueLives, when will the new album be out since Mick is dead?

Nicky blinked at that Twitter message, and Jasper put a hand on his shoulder. "You don't have to reply to them. You did what you needed to do by letting them hear from you and that's all you really owe them, all right?"

Nicky nodded. He wouldn't know what to say.

After dealing with the immediate issues of trying to correct the damage done from the mistakes of the day before, Nicky and Jasper decided to face the next hurdle head on. They put in a call to Nicky's parents. It was time to tell them everything. Nicky was surprised by how easily his parents accepted the news of his relationship with Jasper. "Well, of course you love each other, sweetie," was all his mother said. "You always did."

"But, Mom, that's not all of it. What I'm telling you is that we're lovers. Jasper left the priesthood."

There was a short pause. "Well, if that makes him happy, and it makes you happy, that's all I care about."

And his father added, "He's a good man. You'll be good together."

Adrian and Miriam had actually been much more worried about how he was dealing with Mick's death, suggesting he contact his therapist as soon as possible, and curious about what losing their bassist meant for Nicky's career.

"I guess I should talk to Ramona next," he said, disconnecting the call.

Jasper sat close to him on the sofa with Dizzy on his lap. Nicky reached out to pet her and she abandoned Jasper to curl up on Nicky's legs instead.

"I'm here with you, Nicky. Go ahead and call her. We can handle it together."

As it turned out, Ramona was, as usual, two steps ahead of him.

Her voice was a controlled growl through Nicky's cell phone pressed to his ear. "They actually *gave* him the shit. Can you believe it? Danvers decided that all Mick needed was a little pick-me-up in the studio to get back on game. So he had a dealer stop by Mick's place with enough coke and China White to blow him to the moon and back."

"Why'd he go to the Beverly Hills Hotel? He lives in Laguna." *Lived. Lived in Laguna.*

"You remember how paranoid coke made him? He'd get violent and kinda out of his mind. Punch people. Decide people were spying on him. Just off his fucking nut."

"Yeah." But then he'd been off his nut too, and hadn't really given a fuck what was going on with Mick.

"Apparently he told his landlord there were bugs in the walls. Surveillance type of stuff. Was convinced the FBI and the motherfucking terrorists in the Middle East were after him. He told the guy at the desk of the Beverly Hills Hotel the same thing. So he took off with his Danvers-supplied stash to hole up somewhere 'safe.' We know his next stop."

"My place."

Jasper's lashes shone in the golden light of morning slipping through the curtains. He watched Nicky intensely while he waited for him to finish the call. Nicky touched Jasper's lower lip with his thumb, and Jasper kissed the pad softly. His stomach twisted knowing that Mick would never have a moment like this, and probably never had. Had anyone ever loved Mick the way Jasper loved Nicky? He doubted it. Would it have solved anything if someone had? Would Mick have ended up on that tile floor?

Nicky refocused. "Danvers told you this himself?"

"Flat out. He's soulless." She growled again. "So I told Danvers to take a message to his fucking boss. I said, 'Tell him that I recorded our little conversation and uploaded copies to multiple cloud locations. So unless they let us out of our contracts, I'll send the file to the authorities and the news outlets.'" She laughed. "Yeah, pretty boy. From now on? We'll make our own rules. We'll design the tours. We'll decide when enough is enough. And we'll fucking crowd-fund our albums if we have to, but we are no one's fucking slaves."

Nicky didn't know what to say. He was overwhelmed by the idea of freedom from the contract that had bound him so tightly. "What did he say?"

"He screamed and cursed and I hung up on his sorry ass. Fuck him. Fuck them all, Nicky. We don't need them. We never fucking have, but especially now. We've got a huge fan base. They'll support us. All we have to do is ask."

"We're really done with them?"

"We could not be more done. Not if they know what's good for them. It's over."

Nicky sat in stunned silence. He wished Mick had lived to see this moment. Of course, his death is what had bought their freedom. How horrible. How absolutely wrong. "We have to make sure we earn this, Ramona. We have to make good music. Be good people."

She was quiet. "I hear you."

"We have to pay him back for this."

"We will. Stay clean. Make music. Do Vespertine albums with me. The real kind, like we used to do when it all started… only with less fucking miserable lyrics, maybe. That's all I want."

Nicky scratched his eyebrow with his thumb. He could agree to that, but there was one more remaining piece to the puzzle that was Vespertine. "How about Sez?"

"He checked himself back into the 'health spa.' I told him I'd come visit him on Monday and let him know what's going on. The guy's a mess, and I can't say I blame him."

Nicky remembered the bloody mouth Mick had given Sez, the kiss they'd shared, and the horrible tension at the end. "He must blame himself."

"You know it."

"What are we going to do?"

"We're going to make good records. And we'll make 'em when we're good and ready. Not this month, or next month, or even two months from now. We'll get ourselves healed up for real this time, Nicky. Then we'll head into the studio and make something worthy of what we've lost, okay?"

"Of who we've lost."

"Damn straight, pretty boy." She sniffled a little. "Listen, I need to go. I've got to practice for some drum-art thing I'm doing for a performance artist I've been seeing." She sounded a little embarrassed.

"Performance artist? Really?"

"Shut up. The guy's a fruit-loop but he's good in bed." She laughed. "He should do his next performance piece on cunnilingus, to be honest. Just line the women up in the art gallery, lay 'em out on a bed one at a time, and make them come."

"He's that good, huh?"

"I wouldn't do this dumb shit for just anyone, Nicky. But his tongue should be given a gold medal. Otherwise, he's an idiot. But, fuck it, good orgasms are hard to come by." She sighed. "I don't know why you're giving me shit, though. You're fucking a priest. Tell him hello from me."

"I may have to wash that hello before I pass something from that dirty mouth of yours over to him."

"Oh please, you've filthified him entirely by now, if I know you. And, Nicky? I know you."

"Guilty."

Jasper looked up from where he sat across the sofa, making notes in some kind of calendar. "Tell her hello," he said.

"My priest says hello."

Jasper scoffed. "I'm not a priest anymore, Nicky."

"And he says he's not a priest."

"Tell me he saved the collar, though. Please. For the love of all that is holy, promise me you'll role-play that in bed, Nico Blue."

Nicky grinned. "I solemnly pinky swear, Ramona Darling."

Hanging up the phone, Nicky moved to kneel at Jasper's feet. "Guess what?"

"I don't know." Darkness passed over his face. "You don't have to go back do you?"

"Mick's funeral is Friday and I should be there for that."

"I'll go with you."

"I'd love it if you would. It'd mean a lot. But after that, I'm free. For as long as you want me to be free, and for as long as I want to be free too. Ramona's getting us out of the contracts with the record company."

"How?"

"I'll tell you later. Just…right now, I want to know…"

Jasper touched his cheek. "What? Anything at all."

"Will you be okay with having sappy, adoring love songs written about you?"

Jasper grinned, his face like the sun. "I might need a sample in order to say for certain."

Nicky closed his eyes and sang softly.

"Running like wild horses
In the summer rain
Oak leaves, and pine trees
Shelter us again
Love shines too bright for darkness
Goodbye to uninspired songs of sin
Sweet dreams my love,
Sleep tight, settle in."

Jasper laughed. "Wow. That *is* sappy." He shrugged. "But I think I'll need to hear another five hundred just as sappy as that one before I'll have my fill."

"Are you sure?"

Jasper stood and pulled Nicky up into his arms as Dizzy scampered past chasing a shadow on the floor. "I've never been more sure of anything in my life."

Epilogue

"LIZZIE, YOU'RE A drill sergeant," Nicky said, pushing sweaty hair out of his face. "The new fort doesn't have to be built in a day."

Lizzie gazed at him seriously, her lipsticked mouth going into a flat, disapproving line. "It's already been ten days, Nicky. You and Jasper leave for your shows next week. The other kids need to stop slacking so much."

Nicky looked around at the twenty-five LGBTQ kids who'd taken over his and Jasper's island in order to build a new and improved, much larger and stronger fort for Blue Oasis retreats. In the year since Nicky first returned home, Jasper had been able to expand Blue Oasis the way he'd always wanted, and he'd done it on his own terms. Nicky was proud of him for that. And he was proud of Lizzie too. She'd come far from the shy girl he'd first met, blossoming into a lovely and confident young woman. Still, she wasn't really in charge around here, even if she liked to act like she was.

"Lucas!" Nicky called, motioning him over and seeing Lizzie's cheeks blush the way they always did when Lucas came around. "I have to get back to Blue Oasis to see Jasper. Can you take over here?"

"I've got it under control," Lizzie said, haughtily.

Nicky sighed. "Next year, when you age out, then you can be in charge. But until then, you're one of their peers, and you'll make it hard for yourself at BO if you piss the other kids off, girl."

Lizzie pushed her long hair off her neck and looked up at Lucas. "I can handle them. Can't I, Lucas?"

Lucas cleared his throat and looked flustered when she gave him her best and prettiest smile. "Sure, Lizzie. It's, uh, yeah. I'll be your backup."

She grinned. "Perfect. Go on home and shower, Nicky. Don't make Jazz wait for you."

"When did you get so bossy?" Nicky asked, wrapping his arm around her shoulders and kissing her cheek.

"Like Beyoncé says, I'm not bossy—I'm the boss."

Lucas looked away, still flushing and shifting awkwardly. Nicky didn't know what was going on there, and he didn't want to know. It wasn't physical, that he was sure of, and legally that was all that mattered, but he didn't doubt that two minutes past Lizzie's eighteenth birthday, she'd do everything in her power to change that. He just didn't know if Lucas was actually interested.

"Be good," he said seriously.

"Like you can tell us to be good." Lizzie snorted.

"Do you want to make Jasper cry?" Nicky asked. "If you like the idea of his pretty face in tears, then go right ahead and be bad."

Lizzie rolled her eyes but seemed to consider it. "He'd be pretty crying, wouldn't he? But, no. I'd feel too guilty. Fine, we'll be good. Gus! Stop lazing around! You're supposed to be helping Calista with that beam!"

"I'll deal with it," Lucas said under his breath and hurried off.

"He follows direction really well," Lizzie said admiringly. "Don't you think?"

Nicky wasn't going to answer that. "Okay, Lucas is in charge and so is Mr. Drummond," he pointed at the volunteer engineer who'd helped draw up the plans. "Don't give them back talk."

"Shoo! Leave! You're going to be late! You've got that big phone appointment with Jasper, don't you?"

Nicky rolled his eyes and stood back to look at what they'd accomplished. The fort was coming along nicely, no matter what Lizzie thought. It would be amazing when they were done. The kids would have a great time camping out here in the summers, like Nicky and Jasper had when they were younger. It was a beautiful way to carry on the tradition and honor the place that had meant so much to them.

"Be good," he said once more and turned his back on the work.

The paddle back across the cove to his parents' place was slow, and he didn't stay to say hello to his mom. He'd seen her that morning before heading out to the island. Instead, he drove home to the farmhouse, gave Dizzy a high-five hello and fed her an afternoon treat in hopes she'd leave the baby rabbits he'd spotted in the garden alone. He showered and changed, and put on a fresh patch of his maintenance medication. Then he made sure to mess up Jasper's drawers like always before pulling fresh clothes from his own.

He drove past the Androscoggin and admired the way the light flickered on the water. Music filled his mind—piano and guitar riffs, and lyrics that made his face ache with a sweet smile. He'd get it down later that night using the digital multitrack recorder and load it up to the cloud for Sez and Ramona. Additional lyrics came to mind, along with a fresh bridge.

"Yeah," he whispered. "That's what I'm talking about."

JASPER PUT DOWN the phone and tried not to smile. Nicky hung over his desk, chewing his lips, his eyes wide with anticipation. He looked so gorgeous. Over the past year, Miriam and Jasper's cooking had fattened him up a little, so the gauntness was gone, as were the dark circles under his eyes. Jasper knew Mick's death still haunted him, but he was doing so much better.

"Oh my God, will you tell me already?"

Jasper let the threatening grin break free. "It's ours," he said.

"Jesus! Jesus Christ, oh my fucking God!" He rounded the desk and climbed into Jasper's lap. He cast a quick look toward the office door, but he'd closed it and all the kids were on the island anyway. "Holy crap, Jazz, that's awesome."

"Mmm," Jasper said under the kiss. "It is. Nicky, I know I'm not a priest anymore, but would you mind your language? Especially here."

Nicky sat back and gave Jasper his best "you're shitting me" look. "Oh please. Like you weren't swearing up a storm last night when I had my tongue up your—"

"Nicky!" Jasper clasped a hand over Nicky's mouth. The kids might be gone, but Mrs. Wells was always around. Against his palm, Nicky laughed and licked him, so he let go.

"Now what?" Nicky asked.

"Well, this division of Blue Oasis stays the same. We have a contract with the Church, and they can't retract the lease on the school for the next ten years. Hopefully by then the archbishop will have kicked the bucket. I've heard his likely successor is a *lot* more open minded."

Nicky guffawed. "And you're worried about my swearing. You're ruthless."

Jasper shrugged. When it came to the kids…yeah, he was. "And now we own that half-converted warehouse that's been empty for the past five years because the construction company went bankrupt. Our philanthropist John Arlington signed the paperwork today, and we're allowed to do with the building as we please. Most of the apartments are already built. We need to add the finishing touches and then we'll have a low-rent building available for any kids who want to move on from Blue Oasis."

"You'll have to put some sort of system in place. No drugs, no alcohol, no hooking. And they need to be in college or actively searching for jobs. And once they earn over a certain wage, they need to move on and make room for the next person."

"See?" Jasper squeezed him tight. "I knew you'd be useful."

"Oh, I can be useful." He gave Jasper a lecherous look.

"I'm pretty sure I saw Mrs. Wells walk by."

With a small squeaky noise, Nicky jumped off Jasper's lap, looking far too guilty. When Jasper laughed he threw him a dirty look, but went to check the hallway anyway.

"You're a liar, Jasper Hendricks. You need to go to confession."

"I don't think I will be able to anytime soon, Nicky." He tried not to feel a stab of sadness, but it was inevitable. Immediately Nicky was by his side.

"I'm sorry," he said, grabbing hold of Jasper's hands. "I didn't mean to remind you."

Jasper waved it away. They'd talked this to death already and there was no way Nicky really thought Jasper regretted any of it. He missed it, sure. And he wished the congregation had reacted a little better than they had, but he thought it was understandable.

"Well, you know I still think it's bullshit," Nicky said, his face turning red with anger like it always did when reminded of the way certain members of the congregation had turned on Jasper. "A gay celibate priest? Oh yeah, bring it on. We're open minded, we can accept you, look how forward thinking and modern we are! But as soon as you fall in love with a man and they have to see you—"

"I know," Jasper said softly. "And it's fine. The worst of it has died out by now, and no one ever outright said anything."

"But they acted differently. It's been a year and they still try to make you feel ashamed."

Jasper gently worked his hands loose and threaded them through Nicky's hair. "And that would've been the exact same for a straight priest defrocking for a woman, Nicky. It's okay. I'm okay. And I do love you. I wouldn't want it any other way."

"It pisses me off," Nicky murmured, but the fight had gone out of him.

Jasper kissed his temple. "I know." He rubbed small circles against Nicky's neck with his thumb. "I do have some other news though."

Nicky lifted his head. "Yeah?"

"Arlington thought it might be a good idea to open a similar shelter in L.A. He's funding the whole thing, and he wants you and me out there looking for a venue and doing the start-up work. We could go out there every year to help run the place and get away from these awful winters."

"Oh my God," Nicky whispered. "Oh my fucking God. And you can always be there when I need to be in L.A. for the recordings and local gigs. Oh. My. *Fucking*. God."

"Nick—" Jasper didn't get the rest of the reprimand out before Nicky was in his lap again, kissing him breathless.

"YOU SPEND TOO much money on me," Jasper said right when the captain announced they were preparing for landing.

"Hmm?" Nicky's knee bounced up and down and Jasper put his hand on it.

"Everything you poured into BO—Blue Oasis, damn it—that whole new wardrobe you got me." He plucked at the fine cashmere of his V-neck sweater. "And keep getting me. And all this." He indicated the first class cabin. "It's too much."

Nicky shrugged but didn't say anything. His eyes were glued on the LAX landing strip they kept circling.

Jasper leaned across and pressed a kiss to Nicky's temple. "It will be okay, you know."

"Okay? It's going to be a shitshow. They know we're coming. I don't know if I'm ready for this." He began to bite his fingernails. "*Fuck*."

Jasper clasped Nicky's hands between his. "You've been writing and rehearsing non-stop for months. I've heard you get up in the middle of the night to practice." Jasper waved away Nicky's contrite look. "Don't worry about it. I will always wake up when you move away from me during the night, and I'll never be annoyed about that. My point is..." He squeezed Nicky's fingers and the plane began its stomach-lurching descent. "You've got this. You're amazing, and everyone will love you all over again."

Nicky nodded, then shook his head. "But it's the paps I'm worried about right now."

"Ah, Nicky." Jasper watched the ground soar toward them. "I can deal with the paps."

The plane hit the ground and the madness began.

"Nico Blue, over here! Over here!"

"Can you play the air guitar, Nico?"

"How's your mother, Nico?"

"Did you have a good flight, Nico?"

"Hey Father Jazz, do you still get on your knees for God, or just Nico Blue now?"

There was a lull in the yelling as everyone *ohhh-ed* and Nicky's head snapped up. Jasper tightened his grip on Nicky's arm so hard he was afraid he might leave a bruise. The flashes of the camera intensified to the point he was grateful for the bodyguards crowding them. Without them, he wouldn't be able to see where they were going.

"Don't react," Jasper said in Nicky's ear. "That's all they want. A shot of you losing your temper and it'll be spread all over the internet within seconds. Goodness knows with what kind of captions. We're almost out of here."

Nicky nodded once, tightly, but he looked like a large cat ready to pounce on its prey and for a brief second Jasper wondered if this wasn't a mistake after all.

When they finally made it out, the path to the nondescript black car was pretty clear. A guy in a suit and a cap was holding the back door open, and Jasper steered Nicky toward it. Out of the corner of his eye movement flashed, and Nicky tensed, clearly about to snap, when a bodyguard intercepted a skinny girl, maybe fourteen years old.

"It's okay," Nicky said, relaxing, and the bodyguard let her pass. "Hey lady, what's your name?"

"Emily," she said, face turning as red as her shirt. "Would you sign my phone? I have a sharpie."

"Sure thing, Emily." Nicky nudged Jasper a little so he could use his shoulder as a writing support. The girl looked up at Jasper and bit her lip.

"What is it, Emily?" Jasper asked.

She glanced around. A few yards behind her, what could only be her parents waited somewhat impatiently.

"I like girls," she whispered. "My parents don't know."

Jasper smiled, reached into his pocket for his wallet, and drew out a card. "That's perfectly okay. If you ever need someone to talk to, give this number a call."

She took the card and blinked at it before slipping it into her little green shoulder bag.

"Take care, Emily," Nicky said as he handed her phone back. The flush on her cheeks rose even higher and she ran off.

Nicky and Jasper piled into the car, and to the driver Nicky said, "Can you give us two minutes of privacy, please?"

"Of course, Mr. Blue. Just tap your window when you're ready." He shut the door.

Jasper gave Nicky a worried look. "What is it?"

Nicky put his forehead on Jasper's shoulder and rolled his head side to side. "I hate what they say about you in the press."

"I know you do. And I don't care. Also, it's not all bad."

"Yeah. But when it's bad, it's awful."

"Nicky…"

Nicky grabbed onto Jasper's sweater but didn't lift his head. "Is it worth it, Jazz?" he asked. "Because I will quit. Just say the word and you and I can become recluses on the island."

"The kids would never forgive us if we kicked them out of their fort."

Nicky laughed a little hoarsely. "They can come visit. But no one else."

"Nicky." Jasper shrugged his shoulder lightly so Nicky's head bounced and he sat up. Carefully Jasper cupped his face and stared into those wonderful sky-bright eyes. "It's worth it. It's all been worth it. I wouldn't trade this for anything. You're amazing. Your fans love you. *I* love you. That girl..." Nicky broke into a smile. "See? That's why you do it. Not for the press. Not for the paps. But for girls like that who lock themselves up in their bedrooms and dare to dream to your music. I've said it before. You move people. You move *me*."

"Okay." Nicky nodded against Jasper's palms. "Yes. But you have to promise me..."

"What?"

"Before it becomes not worth it anymore, you tell me. When you've had enough, you promise me you'll tell me before it's too late and you hate me. I can't do this without you."

"I could never hate you, Nicholas Blumfeld," Jasper said softly. "And I don't want to do any of it without you either. I promise I'll always tell you how I feel. And you have to do the same."

"I will."

Jasper drew him closer and kissed him softly. Outside madness waited, but as long as there were moments like these where he had Nicky all to himself, in these pockets of love and tenderness, it was all worth it.

"Nico! Nico! Nico!"

Jasper's eyes were wide as he stared out from the darkness of backstage, taking in the massive crowd. "They're screaming for you," he said, his voice thick with wonder.

"Yeah. They do that." Nicky grinned, trying to affect nonchalance, but his heart was pounding to the rhythm of his name. He wrapped his arm around Jasper's shoulder, trying to absorb his calm energy. "They'll scream for Ramona and Sez, too."

He didn't know if they'd scream for Perry. It was their first live set playing with him, and the new album didn't drop until next week. This was a teaser show, arranged by their new management, the first of four. Then they'd break for a couple of weeks, hit five big cities, take three weeks off, and hit five more. No more endless tours. No more years of being on the road with no reprieve. And he'd already told the band if it got too hard, if his sobriety was at stake, then they could hire Wendy Staggs, a studio guitarist Nicky trusted, to take his place for shows. He'd always be Vespertine's songwriter and guitarist, but he didn't have to tour to do that.

"We're ready, Nicky," Ramona said, stepping up close and nodding toward Sez, who was drinking from a bottle of water and shaking a little. "He's scared but he'll make it."

"You ready?" Jasper asked.

Nicky swallowed hard, and then he nodded sharply. "You're here. The songs are tight. I'm ready." He nuzzled Jasper's ear and whispered, "What if they hate the new stuff?"

"They won't, and even if they do, I love it."

Nicky snorted and kissed his temple, nuzzling at the scent of hotel shampoo. He dragged Jasper around front and center, gazing into his eyes.

"You are ready for this," Jasper said, cupping his cheeks. "*'For I know the plans I have for you,' declares the Lord, 'plans to prosper you and not to harm you, plans to give you hope and a future.'* Remember?"

"I remember. Jeremiah, right?"

"Go on out there and wow them."

Confidence warmed Nicky's chest. "It's all for you, you know. The old stuff and the new stuff too."

"I know."

They kissed, and Ramona punched Nicky on the arm. "Showtime, asshole."

Nicky high-fived Sez, who still looked like he might puke, and then the three of them walked on stage, with their new bassist Perry following behind them.

The roar of the crowd rattled deep in his bones, and he lifted his eyes, blinded by the show lights. He smiled and waited for Sez to work the crowd.

Sez messed with the mic and then looked over at Nicky with crazed eyes.

Nicky pulled his own mic closer and spoke into it. "Hey, we're Vespertine."

The crowd went wild and he could barely hear himself go on. "It's been a while since our last show. We lost someone important to us and we know you miss him too."

The crowd screamed. Nicky slung his guitar over his shoulder and placed his fingers on the fretboard to start the first song. "We've continued on, though, and we hope we honor his memory with our new music. And yeah, we've got some of our new stuff for you tonight. Hope you like it." The crowd made his body shake with their yells. He nodded at Ramona, who clicked a count off. "This one's for Jazz," Nicky said, and started to play.

Sez looked like he might choke entirely, but just in time his voice burst in, rough and sincere, taking them through the verses and hitting the chorus at full tilt.

Kiss me,

Kiss me like cloudburst.

Hold me,

Hold me like dreams.

We're soaked to the bone,

And never alone,

In love and safe in our skin.

Nicky sneaked a look toward the side of the stage and grinned to see Jasper there, bouncing on his toes to the rhythm, his eyes glowing like stars.

A year ago, he'd gone home to Little Bay to get a fresh start, and now he was right back on stage again. But everything about it was so different. He'd gotten his fresh start. His world had ended and begun again. The crowd might be screaming for Nico Blue, but in Jasper's arms, he was Nicholas Blumfeld, in love and safe in his skin.

THE END

Letter from Leta

Dear Reader,

Thank you so much for reading *Vespertine*! I hope you enjoyed reading it as much as we enjoyed crafting it.

Be sure to follow me on BookBub or Goodreads to be notified of new releases. And look for me on Facebook for snippets of the day-to-day writing life, or join my Facebook Group for announcements and special giveaways. To see some sources of my inspiration, you can follow my Pinterest boards or Instagram.

If you enjoyed the book, please take a moment to leave a review! Reviews not only help readers determine if a book is for them, but also help a book show up in site searches.

Also, for the audiobook connoisseurs out there, *Vespertine* is available narrated by the wonderfully talented Michael Ferraiuolo. Many of my other books are also in audio, also narrated by John Solo or Michael Ferraiuolo. I hope to eventually add my entire backlist to my audiobook roster over the next few years.

Thank you for being a reader!

Leta

Standalone

COWBOY SEEKS HUSBAND

by Leta Blake & Indra Vaughn

Walker Reed's Louisiana cattle ranch is in debt after costly repairs from hurricane damage. To get the money, his family schemes to make Walker the star of a new bachelor reality series: *Queer Seeks Spouse.* How hard can it be to fake interest in a dozen handsome men for a few weeks in exchange for enough money to solve all of their problems?

Roan Carmichael never got his Masters degree after his mother was diagnosed with cancer. With medical bills piling up, and a costly experimental treatment available, Roan signs on to be a suitor on *Queer Seeks Spouse.* While he hates having to leave his sick mother long enough to win the cash for her treatment, he's willing to do whatever it takes.

Can two men who are just in it for the money fake their way into real and lasting love?

Cowboy Seeks Husband, the latest book by *Vespertine* authors Leta Blake and Indra Vaughn, features a cowboy, a hipster, opposites attract, steamy scenes, and heart tugging moments that will leave you wanting more.

Standalone

ANY GIVEN LIFETIME

by Leta Blake

He'll love him in any lifetime.

Neil isn't a ghost, but he feels like one. Reincarnated with all his memories from his prior life, he spent twenty years trapped in a child's body, wanting nothing more than to grow up and reclaim the love of his life.

As an adult, Neil finds there's more than lost time separating them. Joshua has built a beautiful life since Neil's death, and how exactly is Neil supposed to introduce himself? As Joshua's long-dead lover in a new body? Heartbroken and hopeless, Neil takes refuge in his work, developing microscopic robots called nanites that can produce medical miracles.

When Joshua meets a young scientist working on a medical project, his soul senses something his rational mind can't believe. Has Neil truly come back to him after twenty years? And if the impossible is real, can they be together at long last?

Any Given Lifetime is a stand-alone, slow burn, second chance gay romance by Leta Blake featuring reincarnation and true love. This story includes some angst, some steam, an age gap, and, of course, a happy ending.

Standalone

THE HOUSE ON HANCOCK HILL

by Indra Vaughn

Pastry chef and bakery owner Jason Wood bakes a mean chocolate soufflé, yet his love life keeps falling flat. He'd blame his past if he wasn't trying so hard to avoid it.

When his family's farmhouse burns to the ground, he's summoned to identify a body found in the ashes. Jason returns to Hancock, Michigan, and reunites with a childhood friend, small town vet Henry McCavanaugh.

After fifteen years apart, their rekindled friendship soon develops into much more. But Jason's baggage threatens their blossoming romance, and he leaves town unannounced to escape his feelings—and Henry's feelings for him. He's learned the hard way if something seems too good to be true, it's best to run for the hills.

Jason stress-bakes more confections than he knows what to do with before wondering if he's running in the wrong direction.

Originally published by Dreamspinner Press. Now published by Indra Ink.

Standalone

THE RIVER LEITH

by Leta Blake

Amnesia stole his memories, but it can't erase their love.

Leith is terrified after waking up in a hospital bed to find his most recent memories are three years out of date.

Worse, he can't even remember how he met the beautiful man who visits him most days. Everyone claims Zach is his best friend, but Leith's feelings for Zach aren't friendly.

They're so much more than that.

Zach fills Leith with longing. Attraction. Affection. **Lust**. And those feelings are even scarier than losing his memory, because Leith's always been straight. Hasn't he?

For Zach, being forgotten by his lover is excruciating. Leith's amnesia has stolen everything: their relationship, their happiness, and the man he loves. Suddenly single and alone, Zach knows nothing will ever be okay again.

Desperate to feel better, Zach confesses his grief to the faceless Internet. But his honesty might come back to haunt them both.

The River Leith is a standalone MM romance with amnesia trope, hurt/comfort, bisexual discovery, "first time" gay scenes, a second chance at first love, and a satisfying happy ending.

Gay Romance Newsletter

Leta's newsletter will keep you up to date on her latest releases and news from the world of M/M romance. Join the mailing list today and you're automatically entered into future giveaways.
letablake.com

Leta Blake on Patreon

Become part of Leta Blake's Patreon community in order to access exclusive content, deleted scenes, extras, bonus stories, rewards, prizes, interviews, and more.
www.patreon.com/letablake

Other Books by Leta Blake

Any Given Lifetime
The River Leith
Smoky Mountain Dreams
Angel Undone
The Difference Between
Omega Mine: Search for a Soulmate

The Home for the Holidays Series
Mr. Frosty Pants
Mr. Naughty List

The Training Season Series
Training Season
Training Complex

Heat of Love Series
Slow Heat
Alpha Heat
Slow Birth
Bitter Heat

Stay Lucky Series
Stay Lucky
Stay Sexy

'90s Coming of Age Series
Pictures of You
You Are Not Me

Co-Authored with Indra Vaughn
Vespertine
Cowboy Seeks Husband

Co-Authored with Alice Griffiths
The Wake Up Married serial
Will & Patrick's Endless Honeymoon

Gay Fairy Tales Co-Authored with Keira Andrews
Flight
Levity
Rise

Leta Blake writing as Blake Moreno
Heat for Sale

Leta Blake writing as Halsey Harlow
Bring on Forever

Audiobooks
Leta Blake at Audible

Free Read
Stalking Dreams

Discover more about the author online:
Leta Blake
letablake.com

Other Books by Indra Vaughn

The House on Hancock Hill
Patchwork Paradise

Christmas Books
Dust of Snow
The Winter Spirit

Shadow Mountain Series
Fated
Fragmented

Co-Authored with Leta Blake
Vespertine
Cowboy Seeks Husband

Short Stories
Hooked
Chasing Ghosts
Ties That Bind
Halcyon Hush

Audiobooks
Indra Vaughn at Audible

About the Author

Author of the bestselling book Smoky Mountain Dreams and the fan favorite Training Season, Leta Blake's educational and professional background is in psychology and finance, respectively. However, her passion has always been for writing. She enjoys crafting romance stories and exploring the psyches of made up people. At home in the Southern U.S., Leta works hard at achieving balance between her day job, her writing, and her family.

Printed in Great Britain
by Amazon